Growing Up
in
Lancaster County

4-IN-1 STORY COLLECTION

WANDA &
BRUNSTETTER

BARBOUR
PUBLISHING

ISBN 978-1-61626-255-6

All Pennsylvania Dutch words are taken from the *Revised Pennsylvania German Dictionary* found in Lancaster County, Pennsylvania.

Scripture taken from the HOLY BIBLE, NEW INTERNATIONAL VERSION®. NIV®. Copyright © 1973, 1978, 1984 by International Bible Society. Used by permission of Zondervan. All rights reserved.

This book is a work of fiction. Names, characters, places, and incidents are either products of the author's imagination or used fictitiously. Any similarity to actual people, organizations, and/or events is purely coincidental.

Cover and chapter art illustrations by Richard Hoit.

For more information about Wanda E. Brunstetter, please access the author's website at the following Internet address: www.wandabrunstetter.com.

Published by Barbour Publishing, Inc., P.O. Box 719, Uhrichsville, Ohio 44683, www.barbourbooks.com

Our mission is to publish and distribute inspirational products offering exceptional value and biblical encouragement to the masses.

Printed in the United States of America.
Dickinson Press, Inc., Grand Rapids, MI 49512; May 2011; D10002809

A Happy Heart

Dedication

To the children at Riverside Christian School in Yakima,
Washington. Thanks for letting me share
my life as an author with you.
To Dr. Richard Ehlers and Dr. Ben Jaramillo,
my kind and helpful eye doctors.

Glossary

absatz—stop
ach—oh
aldi—girlfriend
bensel—silly child
blos—bubble
boppli—baby
brieder—brothers
bruder—brother
buwe—boy
daed—dad
danki—thank you
dumm—dumb
ekelhaft—disgusting
fehlerfrie—perfect
felder—fields
fingerneggel—fingernails
gees—goat
geh—go
grank—sick
grossdaadi—grandfather
guder mariye—good morning
gut—good
hund—dog

hungerich—hungry
jah—yes
kapp—cap
kichlin—cookies
kinner—children
lachlich—laughable
lecherich—ridiculous
mamm—mom
mied—tired
mudder—mother
naas—nose
naerfich—nervous
narrish—crazy
nee—no
pescht—pest
retschbeddi—tattletale
schlang aage—snake eyes
schmaert—smart
schnell—quickly
schpassich—odd
schweschder—sister
wunderbaar—wonderful

Bass uff as du net fallscht.
Du kannscht mich net uffhuddle;
    ich bin zu schmaert
Duh net so laut schmatze.

Geb acht, schunscht geht's letz!

Grummel net um mich rum.
Sei so gut.
Was in der welt?
Wie geht's?

Take care you don't fall.
You can't confuse me;
    I'm too smart.
Don't make such a noise
    when you eat.
Watch out, or else things
    will go wrong!
Don't grumble around me.
Please.
What in all the world?
How are you?

Chapter 1

A *Lachlich* [Laughable] Day

This is so much fun!" Ten-year-old Rachel Yoder squealed as her end of the teeter-totter shot into the air.

"My stomach feels like it's in my throat!" Audra Burkholder shouted when her side of the teeter-totter dropped down and then sprang up again.

Rachel waved one hand in the air. "Whe-e-e-e!" she hollered.

"Are you gonna ride that thing all day or does somebody else get a turn before recess is over?"

Rachel looked down. Freckle-faced Orlie Troyer stared at her. Rachel and Orlie had become friends during the year, but Rachel didn't want anyone at school to know she was friends with a boy so she kept it a secret.

"Well?" Orlie asked, tapping his foot. "Can I have a turn on the teeter-totter?"

Rachel squinted at him as her side of the teeter-totter dropped again. "Is that any way to ask for something?"

"Maybe he doesn't know how to say *sei so gut*

[please]." Audra said, wrinkling her nose. "Maybe he doesn't know about manners."

Orlie squatted in the dirt, raised his hands in front of his chest, and said, "Can I please have a turn on the teeter-totter?"

Rachel giggled. "You look like Jacob's dog when he sits up and begs."

Woof! Woof! Orlie bounced up and down.

"Oh, all right, you can have a turn while I get a drink of water." When Rachel climbed off the teeter-totter, she held the handle so Orlie could get on.

"This is sure fun!" Orlie shouted as his end of the teeter-totter rose. A gust of wind whipped his straw hat from his head and spun it away. He tipped his head back and howled with laughter.

Rachel raced to the pump, grabbed a paper cup, and pumped the handle up and down. When the cup was full of water, she took a big drink. Then she pumped until her cup was full again.

Rachel's brother, Jacob, nudged Rachel's arm. "Save some of that for me, would ya?"

Water sloshed out of Rachel's cup and splashed her dress. "Say, watch what you're doing!"

"I figured you might need a bath." Jacob snickered.

She glared at him. "Very funny."

"I thought so, little *bensel* [silly child]." He leaned back and laughed until his face turned red.

"Stop calling me a silly child!" Rachel dipped her

finger into the cup and flicked water at Jacob's shirt. "And there's plenty of this to go around!"

"A little water doesn't bother me," Jacob said with a shrug. "In fact, it feels kind of nice on this warm spring day."

"Puh!" Rachel hurried across the playground, still holding her cup of water. "I'm back," she said as Orlie's side of the teeter-totter shot up. "It's time for you to get off now."

When the teeter-totter came down, Orlie shook his head. "I don't want to; I'm having too much fun."

"I said you could take a turn while I got a drink," Rachel announced. "So now you need to get off."

Orlie grinned but didn't budge.

Rachel glanced at Audra as Orlie's end of the teeter-totter rose and Audra's end dropped. "Can I take your place?"

Audra pushed a strand of dark hair under her *kapp* [cap] and shook her head. "Sorry, Rachel, but I'm having too much fun."

Rachel tapped her foot impatiently. If she'd known this would happen, she wouldn't have gotten off the teeter-totter. She would have waited until recess was over to get a drink.

Suddenly, Orlie leaped off the teeter-totter, sending Audra thudding to the ground.

Audra squealed. "That wasn't nice! You should have warned me that you were getting off!"

"I decided I was thirsty!" Orlie snatched the cup out of Rachel's hand and drank. "Ah. . .that's better."

"Aren't you worried about germs?" Audra asked as she scrambled off the teeter-totter.

"Nope." Orlie took another drink and handed the cup back to Rachel.

"*Eww.*" Audra wrinkled her nose. "That's so *ekelhaft* [disgusting]!"

Rachel pushed the cup at Orlie. "You may as well keep it, 'cause I won't drink from it again."

Orlie shrugged and drank some more.

"Let's play on the swings," Rachel said to Audra. "Okay."

The girls had only been swinging a few minutes when Orlie headed toward them wearing his straw hat. He stopped in front of the swings, swayed back and forth, and fell on the ground. The paper cup flew out of his hand and landed in a clump of weeds. His straw hat flew off his head and landed in the dirt.

Rachel rushed over to Orlie and dropped to her knees. "Orlie's what's wrong? Are you *grank* [sick]?"

He stayed with his eyes closed, unmoving.

Audra gasped. "*Ach* [Oh], do you think he's dead?"

Rachel touched Orlie's arm, but he didn't move. She clasped her hand over her mouth. "Maybe he *is* dead. I'd better get the teacher!"

Rachel raced for the schoolhouse, but she hadn't gone far when someone pushed her. She whirled around. There stood Orlie, wearing his tattered hat and a lopsided grin.

"Ha! Ha! I got you good!" he said, slapping his knee.

"Orlie Troyer, you should be ashamed of yourself, scaring us like that," Audra said in a shaky voice. "We thought you were a goner. *Jah* [Yes], we sure did."

Rachel shook her head. "Not me; I knew he was only pretending to be dead. I was just playing along."

Orlie's lips twitched, his shoulders shook, and he laughed so hard tears streamed down his cheeks. Then he dropped to the ground and rolled in the grass.

Orlie looked so funny that Rachel laughed, too. Soon Audra joined in.

"Now you really do look like Jacob's dog." Rachel pointed at Orlie. "Whenever Buddy has an itch on his back, he rolls in the grass just like you're doing."

Woof! Woof! Orlie sat up and begged.

Rachel giggled. "What a lachlich day!"

When Rachel and Jacob got home from school that afternoon, Rachel still felt like laughing. She'd laughed so much during recess that she couldn't concentrate on her schoolwork the rest of the day. In fact, a couple of times the words in her spelling book had looked a bit blurry. She figured it was because she had tears in her eyes from laughing so much.

"How come you're wearing such a silly grin?" Jacob asked.

"I just feel happy today."

Jacob stared at Rachel a few seconds. Finally, he shrugged and opened the door. "We're home, Mom!"

"Mmm. . .it smells like Mom's been baking today," Rachel said, heading for the kitchen. "I hope she made maple syrup cookies, because they're my favorite."

Jacob tickled Rachel in the ribs. "Every kind of cookie is your favorite, sister."

Rachel giggled and tickled Jacob back.

He snickered. "Stop that. You know how ticklish I am—especially my ribs!"

"Then you shouldn't have started it."

"What's all this silliness about?" Mom asked when they entered the kitchen.

"Rachel's in a lachlich mood today," Jacob said.

Mom removed a tray of cookies from the oven and placed them on the counter. "It's good to be in a laughable mood. When we laugh it makes us have a happy heart," she said, peering over her metal-framed glasses at Rachel.

Rachel nodded and smiled. "I've had a happy heart most of the day."

"Wash your hands and have a seat at the table," Mom said. "Then you and Jacob can have a glass of milk and some of my freshly baked maple syrup cookies."

Rachel patted her stomach. "Yum. . .that sounds *gut* [good] to me."

Rachel and Jacob raced to the sink. They reached

for the bar of soap at the same time, and—*woosh!*—it slipped off the soap dish and landed in a bowl of water sitting in the sink. *Floop!* A spurt of water flew straight up and splashed Rachel's face.

"That soap's sure slippery." She giggled and dried her face on a towel.

"I'll bet it won't be too slippery for me." Jacob plunged his hand into the bowl of water and scooped up the soap. He'd just started to scrub his hands when the soap slipped through his fingers and landed back in the water with a splash.

Rachel chuckled. "I warned you about that, Jacob."

"Will you two please quit fooling around and wash your hands?" Mom said, shaking her head. "I'm going to see if Grandpa's up from his nap."

When Mom left the room, Jacob lunged for the soap, just as Rachel bumped his arm. The soap flew in the air, bounced onto the floor, and slid all the way to the table.

Rachel laughed as Jacob scrambled after the soap, his feet sliding with every step he took.

Smack! Jacob banged into the table, knocking over a carton of milk. "Oh no," he moaned as the milk dribbled onto the floor. He took a step back, and his legs sailed out from under him. He landed on the floor with a thud.

Rachel rushed forward. "Are you all right?"

Jacob grabbed the soap and scrambled to his feet.

"I'm fine—I'm not hurt a bit."

"I'd better get the mop and clean this before Mom comes back." Rachel hurried to the cleaning closet and removed the bucket and mop. She leaned the mop against the counter, set the bucket in the sink, filled it with warm water, and added some detergent.

"This bucket is sure heavy," Rachel said as she struggled to lift it out of the sink. "I'm not sure I can carry it now that it's full of water."

"Here, let me help." Jacob reached around Rachel, put the soap in the soap dish, and grabbed the bucket handle.

"Careful now. You don't want to spill any water."

"Don't worry; I know what I'm doing." Jacob lifted the bucket. *Bang!* It bumped the edge of the sink, sloshing water all over the floor.

"Oh, no," Rachel groaned.

"Look at it this way," Jacob said with a chuckle, "the water's already out of the bucket. Now you only have to mop the floor."

Rachel grabbed the mop and pushed it back and forth. "This isn't getting the water up," she muttered. "There's too much of it on the floor."

"Say, I have an idea." Jacob tossed two dish towels on the floor. He put his left foot on one towel and his right foot on the other; then he starting moving around the room.

"That looks like fun." Rachel grabbed two more

towels, tossed them on the floor, and followed Jacob. "Whe-e-e—this *is* fun! It's almost like skating on a frozen pond!"

"*Was in der welt* [What in all the world]*?*"

Rachel whirled around. Mom stood inside the kitchen door with her arms folded, frowning. "Would someone please tell me what's going on in here?"

"The bar of soap fell on the floor," Rachel explained. "Then Jacob bumped the table and spilled the milk. I was going to mop up the mess, but the bucket of water spilled on the floor." Rachel drew in a quick breath. "We couldn't get the water up with the mop, so we decided to use some towels."

"I'm sure you meant well, but that isn't the way to mop the floor." Mom stepped toward Rachel.

"Don't come in here!" Rachel shouted. "You might slip and fall."

"That's right," Jacob said. "You wouldn't want to break a bone or hurt the *boppli* [baby]."

Mom placed her hands against her bulging stomach. "You're right; I do need to be careful." She pointed to the mop. "One of you needs to hold the head of the mop over the bucket and wring out the water. That will make it easier to mop."

"I'll do it!" Jacob grabbed the mop.

Mom pointed to the sopping wet towels. "Rachel, please get some clean towels to help Jacob mop up the water."

"That's what I was trying to do," Rachel said.

Mom shook her head. "Not with the towels under your feet. That's dangerous. You need to kneel on the floor, mop up the water with the dry towels, and wring them into the sink. You'll also need to wring out the wet ones you and Jacob used under your feet."

Rachel nodded. "Okay, Mom."

Mom watched until Rachel and Jacob had finished mopping up the water. When the floor was dry, she stepped into the kitchen and motioned to the table. "Shall we have cookies and milk now?"

"That sounds good to me." Jacob smacked his lips. "All that hard work made me *hungerich* [hungry]."

Mom went to the refrigerator for another carton of milk. As she placed it on the table, Grandpa entered the room. He motioned to the cookies. "I hope some of those are for me."

"Of course. Sit down and help yourself while I pour some milk," Mom said.

They all sat at the table, and Grandpa smiled at Rachel. "How was your day?"

"It's been a lachlich day." Rachel grinned at Jacob. "Isn't that right?"

He nodded.

"Laughable days are the best kind of days." Grandpa reached for a cookie and dunked it in his milk. "I learned some time ago that even if things aren't going my way, it helps to put on a happy face."

"What are some things that make you feel happy?" Jacob questioned.

Grandpa wiggled his bushy gray eyebrows. "For one thing, I like to tell at least one good joke every day."

Rachel touched Grandpa's arm. "Would you tell us one now?"

"Jah, sure." Grandpa combed his fingers through the ends of his long gray beard. "Let me see now. . ."

"Why don't you tell the one about spinach?" Mom suggested. "You used to tell that joke when I was girl, and it always made me laugh."

"Well, when I was a boy, my *mudder* [mother] used to say, 'Now son, eat your spinach, because it will put color in your cheeks.'" A smile spread across Grandpa's face as he leaned close to Rachel. "You know what I had to say to that?"

She shook her head.

Grandpa gently pinched Rachel's cheeks. "I would say to my mudder, 'Who wants green cheeks?'"

Rachel giggled, Mom chuckled, and Jacob snickered.

"All's well when you laugh and grin," Grandpa said with a wink.

Rachel gave Grandpa a hug. "I'm glad you're my *grossdaadi* [grandfather]. I'm gonna try to make every day a lachlich day."

Chapter 2

Crazy Rooster

When Rachel and Jacob arrived home from school the next day, Rachel was pleased to see that Mom had set fresh fruit cups out for a snack.

Rachel's stomach rumbled as she pointed to the treats. "Mmm. . .those sure look good."

Mom smiled. "Wash your hands and take a seat at the table."

Jacob raced for the kitchen sink, but Rachel hurried to the bathroom. After the trouble she'd had yesterday with the soap and water, she wasn't about to wash her hands at the same sink with Jacob.

When Rachel returned to the kitchen, Jacob was already eating his fruit and drinking a glass of milk. "*Danki* [Thank you], Mom, for fixing us such a nice snack," Rachel said.

"Jah, danki." Jacob smacked his lips, chomped on a hunk of apple, and slurped his milk.

"*Duh net so laut schmatze* [Don't make such a noise

when you eat]," Mom said. "Eat a little quieter." She pulled out a chair and sat beside Rachel. "How was school today?"

"It was good." Rachel plucked a piece of banana from her fruit cup and popped it in her mouth. "Audra and I played on the teeter-totter during recess again. It was lots of fun."

Mom smiled. "It's nice that you and Audra have become such good friends."

Rachel nodded. When Audra had first moved to Lancaster County, she and Rachel hadn't gotten along so well. That was mainly because Rachel had missed her cousin Mary, who'd moved to Indiana. After Rachel realized that Audra was nice and also needed a friend, she and Audra had gotten along quite well.

"Where's Grandpa this afternoon? Is he taking a nap?" Rachel asked.

Mom shook her head. "He and your *daed* [dad] went to town to pick up some supplies for the new greenhouse they hope to build."

"Did Henry go with them?" Jacob asked.

"No, he went to see his *aldi* [girlfriend], Nancy."

Rachel frowned. "I'm disappointed that Grandpa went to town without me. He said I could help him choose some of the plants for the greenhouse."

"I don't think he and your daed are looking for flowers today," Mom said. "I believe they went to get lumber and supplies to build the greenhouse."

Rachel smiled. She felt better knowing Grandpa hadn't left her out of his greenhouse plans. Maybe they could shop for flowers and plants soon.

"When you two are finished with your snack, I have a few chores for you to do," Mom said.

Jacob's forehead wrinkled. "What chores?"

"I'd like you to clean the horses' stalls while Rachel feeds and waters the chickens and checks for eggs." Mom peered at Rachel over the top of her glasses. "I was going to do that earlier, but I went over to Anna Miller's for a visit after you left for school. I stayed longer than I'd planned, so I didn't get to the chicken coop."

Rachel didn't look forward to taking care of the chickens, but she knew better than to argue with Mom. "Can we play after we finish our chores?" she asked.

"Of course." Mom patted Rachel's arm. "The sooner you get the jobs done, the sooner you can play."

Jacob put an orange slice between his lips and bit. A squirt of juice hit Rachel's forehead.

"Hey! Watch what you're doing!" Rachel dashed to the sink, splashed cold water on her face, and patted it dry with a clean towel. "I'll bet you did that on purpose," she said when she returned to the table.

"Did not."

"Did so."

"Did not."

"Did—"

Mom clapped her hands. "If you don't stop

squabbling, you may not play when you're done with your chores."

"Sorry," Rachel and Jacob both mumbled.

Grinning, Jacob looked over at Rachel and said, "I love you, *schweschder* [sister]."

On her way to the chicken coop, Rachel spotted Buddy sleeping on the roof of his doghouse. His nose was tucked between his paws, and his floppy ears covered both eyes. Rachel hadn't liked Buddy when he'd first come to live with them, because she was afraid he would hurt her cat. But Buddy and Cuddles had become friends, just like Rachel and Audra. Now Rachel only had to worry about Buddy giving her sloppy wet kisses. She tried to stay away from Buddy whenever Jacob let him out of his dog run.

Rachel glanced at the barn, where Jacob was cleaning the horses' stalls. A gray and white ball of fur streaked across the lawn and ducked into the barn. Rachel figured Cuddles was probably after a mouse.

Rachel opened the door to the chicken coop. As soon as she stepped inside, she knew she was in for trouble. *Squawk! Squawk! Squawk!* Hector, the biggest, noisiest rooster, flapped his wings and flew around the coop, dropping feathers everywhere.

Rachel didn't know if Hector was carrying on because he was hungry, or if he was just being ornery. As long as he didn't try to peck Rachel or get in her way, she didn't care how crazy he acted.

Rachel opened the lid on the bucket of chicken feed, scooped some out, and poured it into the feeders. Squawking and flapping their wings, all the chickens in the coop swarmed around the feeders, pecking at the food.

While the chickens ate, Rachel took the water dishes outside. Using the hose, she filled them with fresh water and hauled them back to the coop. She'd just set the last one inside when Hector started carrying on again.

Squawk! Squawk! Cock-a-doodle-do! He strutted across the floor with his wings outstretched. When he reached the open door, he flew past Rachel and landed in the yard. With another noisy squawk, Hector headed straight for Buddy's dog run. He stuck his head through a hole in the fence and grabbed food from Buddy's dish.

Rachel dashed across the yard, waving her hands. "Stop that, you *narrish* [crazy] rooster! You have your own food in the coop!"

Hector kept eating. *Chomp! Chomp! Chomp!*

Rachel clapped her hands. "Buddy, wake up! Hector's stealing your food!"

Buddy opened his eyes, stretched, and scratched his ear.

Rachel pointed to the rooster. "Don't you care that he's robbing your food? Chase him away, Buddy!"

With a shake of his furry head, Buddy jumped to his feet and leaped off the doghouse. *Woof! Woof! Woof!* He rammed the fence with his nose.

Hector screeched and jerked away from Buddy's dish, but when he tried to pull his head through the hole in the fence, he got stuck. *Bawk! Bawk! Bawk!*

Grrr. Woof! Woof! Buddy swiped at the rooster's head with his paw.

Bawk! Bawk!

Woof! Woof! Woof!

"What's all the ruckus about?" Jacob shouted as he raced from the barn. "What's wrong with Buddy?"

Rachel pointed to the chicken. "Hector was trying to steal Buddy's food. Then Buddy went after him, and now Hector's head is stuck. Can you do something, Jacob? I'm afraid Buddy might hurt him."

Even though Rachel had wanted Hector to stop eating Buddy's food, she didn't want Buddy to hurt the poor critter.

"Jah, okay. I'll see what I can do." Jacob opened the gate to Buddy's dog run and stepped inside. "Here, Buddy. Come, boy!"

Grrr. Buddy was nose to beak with the rooster and wouldn't budge.

"Bad dog! Come when I call!" Jacob grabbed Buddy's collar and pulled him away from the chicken. "See if you can get the rooster's head out now," he said to Rachel.

Rachel squatted beside Hector and placed her hands around his neck. Slowly, gently, she pulled.

Bawk! Bawk! Hector's head popped free. Looking a bit dazed, he stood there a few seconds, shook his head, and then wobbled across the yard, crowing all the way. *Cock-a-doodle-do!*

"What a narrish chicken," Rachel muttered. "He ought to know better than to stick his beak where it doesn't belong."

Jacob snickered. "Jah, just like some people I know."

Rachel glared at him. "What's that supposed to mean?"

"Oh, nothing." Jacob patted the dog's head, stepped out of the dog run, and closed the gate. "Be good, Buddy. I'll come back to play with you after I finish my chores in the barn."

Buddy plodded back to his doghouse; only this time he crawled inside instead of jumping on top.

"That was a close call for the rooster," Rachel said as she walked beside Jacob.

Jacob shrugged. "That's what the critter gets for trying to steal Buddy's food."

Rachel's brows furrowed. "How would you like it if some big animal came along and tried to eat Buddy?"

"I wouldn't like it," he said.

"When the rooster was acting crazy inside the chicken coop, I was angry with him, and when he went after Buddy's food, it really made me mad." Rachel sighed. "Even so, I didn't want the chicken to get hurt."

"I see what you mean. I'll have to think about what

I'm saying from now on."

"Does that mean you won't tease me anymore?"

"I'm your *bruder* [brother], so I'll probably still tease," Jacob said. "But I'd never do anything on purpose to hurt you."

Rachel smiled and headed for the chicken coop. It was comforting to know Jacob would never hurt her intentionally. She just hoped he would stop teasing her.

"Where are you going?" Jacob called. "Haven't you finished feeding the chickens?"

"Jah, but I forgot to check for eggs."

"I have one more stall to clean, and then I'll take Buddy for a walk." Jacob disappeared into the barn.

Rachel stepped into the coop and picked up the basket Mom kept near the door. Checking under each hen, she found only three eggs. "Guess that's better than none," she said, heading back to the house.

When Rachel entered the kitchen, she was surprised that it was empty. She had figured Mom would have started supper by now. She cleaned the eggs and put them in the refrigerator, then headed to the living room to get the book she'd left there last night.

Rachel found Mom asleep on the sofa, so she picked up the book and tiptoed quietly out of the room.

Outside, Rachel sat on the porch swing and opened the book. She'd only read a few pages when she heard a horrible shriek, followed by *thump-thump-thump!*

"I hope Buddy isn't after Cuddles now," Rachel

moaned. She set the book on the swing and stepped into the yard to investigate.

She scanned the area, but didn't see anything unusual.

Thumpety-thump-thump!

Rachel bent down and peered under the porch. Two beady eyes stared back at her.

Hector wobbled out from under the porch, shaking his head and ruffling his feathers.

Rachel's mouth fell open. The crazy rooster had a yogurt cup stuck on his beak!

"Hold still, Hector." Rachel crept closer to the chicken. "Let me get that off you."

Squawk! Squawk! The rooster hopped onto the porch, shaking his head and flapping his wings.

Rachel felt sorry for the bird, but she still laughed. The critter looked hilarious, dancing around the porch, flipping his head from side to side.

She tried to corner Hector between the swing and the porch railing, but he darted around her and leaped off the porch, leaving red feathers in her hands.

Rachel ran into the yard after the rooster, but every time she came close, he turned another way. With a frustrated sigh, she went to get Jacob.

"Are you done cleaning the horses' stalls?" she asked when she found Jacob sitting on a bale of straw.

He nodded.

"I need your help again."

"What is it this time, Rachel?"

"Hector got his beak stuck in a yogurt cup, and I can't catch him to get it off."

"No problem. I'll capture that crazy rooster."

Rachel followed Jacob out of the barn. They found Hector banging the yogurt cup against the horses' watering trough.

"I'll catch him!" Jacob dashed across the yard, took a flying leap, and landed in the water trough with a splash!

Rachel laughed so hard she could barely breathe, and tears rolled down her cheeks.

"That wasn't funny," Jacob mumbled as he pulled himself out of the trough. He shook his head, splattering water all over Rachel.

Rachel jumped back. "Hey! Watch what you're doing!"

"Since you thought it was so funny to see me wet, I thought I'd share the water with you."

Rachel was about to tell Jacob what she thought, when the rooster wobbled up and stopped at her feet. He tipped his head back and looked at her as if to say, "Would you please get this thing off my beak?"

Rachel grasped the cup with both hands, and— *floop!*—it popped right off!

Hector shook his head and flew up to the fence. Tilting his head back, he let out a garbled *Cocker-doodle-de-do!*

Rachel looked at Jacob, and they both laughed. "I'm glad we live on a farm," she said. "Around here something funny is always going on."

Chapter 3

Disappointments

On Saturday morning a few weeks later, Rachel headed down the driveway to the mailbox. The harsh wind smacked against her body with such force she nearly toppled over. The ties on her kapp whipped around her face. The spring day had started so nicely. She hoped the wind would die down soon so she could do something fun. Maybe later she could jump on the trampoline, play in the barn with Cuddles, or catch some frogs at the creek. Those were always fun things to do.

Rachel opened the mailbox and pulled out a stack of mail. "All right! I got a letter from Mary!" she exclaimed when she saw the envelope on top addressed to her.

Rachel raced up the driveway, eager to read her cousin's words. She sat on the porch step and ripped open the letter. She'd only read the first two words, when—*whoosh!*—a gust of wind tore the letter from her hands, carrying it across the yard, along with some blowing loose straw from the piles stacked near the barn.

Rachel placed the rest of the mail on the small table near the back door and raced after the runaway letter. It zoomed across the grass, flew into the maple tree, and fluttered to the ground.

Rachel lunged for it, and—*whoosh!*—another gust of wind carried the letter away.

"Come back here!" Rachel shouted as she continued the chase. No way was she going to let Mary's letter get away from her!

Huffing and puffing, she dashed after the letter, but it drifted on the wind and whooshed away again. She watched it sail through the air and land in the pasture where Pap's herd of brown and white cows grazed.

The wind settled down, and Rachel climbed over the fence. Her fingers almost touched the letter, when— *snort!*—one of the cows nudged the letter with her nose, and the piece of paper flew against the fence and stuck.

"Ah-ha! I've got you now!" Rachel grabbed the letter, and—*rip!*—it tore right in two!

"Oh no," she groaned. "How can I read Mary's letter now?"

Rachel raced back to the porch, scooped up the mail on the table, and opened the door. "The mail's here," she said when she entered the kitchen.

Mom motioned to the table. "Just put it over there."

"I got a letter from Mary, but the wind took it away. Then one of Pap's cows nudged it with her nose and it stuck to the fence. When I grabbed the paper, it ripped in two!" Rachel frowned and lifted both halves of the letter.

Mom set the broom aside. "Lay the pieces on the table, and we'll tape them together." She got clear tape from the desk, taped the pieces, and handed the letter to Rachel. "Here you go—good as new."

Rachel sat at the table to read Mary's letter. *"Dear Rachel: How are you—"* She squinted as she tried to figure out the next words. They looked blurry. "I wonder why Mary wrote with such tiny letters," she mumbled. "I can't read some of the words."

"Maybe you're having problems reading the letter because it was torn. Would you like me to see if I can read it?" Mom asked.

Rachel nodded and handed her the letter.

Mom pushed her glasses to the bridge of her nose and began to read.

Dear Rachel:

How are you doing? Are you having nice weather there in Pennsylvania? It's nice here in Indiana, and I'm glad it's spring. Last Saturday our family went to the Fun Spot amusement park. We liked it so much! We went on lots of rides and saw some interesting animals. I wish you could have been with us.

"I wish we could go someplace like that," Rachel

interrupted. "All we ever do is stay around here and work."

"That's not true," Mom said. "We've had some fun times with Esther and Rudy whenever they've come here for supper or we've gone over to their house."

Rachel bit her bottom lip. Visiting her big sister was nice, but it wasn't as much fun as going to an amusement park. Maybe she should ask Pap to take them to Hershey Park. She'd heard a lot of fun rides were there.

"Where's Pap?" she asked.

"He's in the barn."

Rachel jumped up and started for the door.

"Where are you going?" Mom called.

"I need to talk to Pap."

"What about Mary's letter? Don't you want to hear what else she said?"

Rachel nodded. "Jah, okay. I guess I can talk to Pap after you're done."

Mom smiled and continued to read.

How's Cuddles doing? My cat, Stripes, is fine, but I think he misses her. Maybe when we come for a visit, we can bring Stripes.

"Does she say when that might be?" Rachel asked.

Mom shook her head. "I'm sure it won't be until after school gets out."

"What else does Mary say?"

"Let's see. . ." Mom's glasses had slipped to the end of her nose, and she pushed them back in place again.

I went to my friend Betty's house yesterday afternoon. We baked chocolate chip cookies and drew some pictures. We both like horses, so that's what we drew. Next week Betty's coming over to my house with her mamm [mom], *and we're going to bake some pies.*

Rachel smiled. At one time she would have been jealous to hear what Mary had done with her new friend. Now that Rachel had Audra as a friend, she didn't mind so much when Mary mentioned Betty in her letters.

"Is there more?" she asked Mom.

"Just a bit," Mom said. "Here's how Mary closes her letter: *'Take care and write back soon. I'm looking forward to seeing you again. Love, Mary.'"*

"Danki for reading the letter to me." Rachel raced for the back door. "I'm going to the barn to see Pap," she called over her shoulder.

Rachel found Pap, Jacob, and Henry grooming the horses. "Can I speak to you a minute?" she asked Pap.

He nodded. "Jah, sure, what did you want to say?"

"I got a letter from Mary today." Rachel gulped

in a quick breath. "She said her folks took her to an amusement park in Indiana."

"That's nice." Pap brushed old Tom's back.

"She said they had fun and went on lots of rides and saw some animals."

"Umm. . .I see."

Rachel moved closer to old Tom and rubbed his soft nose. "Could we hire a driver to take us to Hershey Park some Saturday? I think it would be fun to go on some of the rides there." She looked up at Pap. "Can we go? Can we go there soon?"

Pap shook his head. "You know I'm in the middle of spring planting. We'll have too much farmwork for several months. Besides, your mamm isn't feeling up to such an outing right now."

"Maybe after the baby is born—then can we go to Hershey Park?"

"I don't know, Rachel. We'll have to wait and see."

"Couldn't we go sometime this summer before school starts again?" Rachel persisted.

"If we go at all, it probably won't be this year," Pap said as he combed old Tom's mane. "Since the boppli will be born in July, he or she will be too young to make a trip like that."

"Then when can we go?"

"I don't know, Rachel. We'll have to see."

"I never get to do anything fun," Rachel mumbled as she left the barn. She was halfway to the house when she saw Grandpa heading her way.

"I'm going to town to pick up some supplies for your daed." Grandpa smiled. "Would you like to go along, Rachel?"

She nodded eagerly. "Jah, Grandpa. That sounds like fun. Will you look for plants for the greenhouse, too?"

"Not today. Your daed's real busy with farm chores right now. He won't start on my greenhouse until late May or early June."

"But June's two months away."

"I know." Grandpa smiled and patted Rachel's head. "We must learn to be patient. Good things come to those who wait, you know."

Rachel nodded, trying not to show disappointment. She looked forward to helping in Grandpa's greenhouse, but she wished they didn't have to wait so long.

"Do you still want to ride to town with me?" Grandpa asked.

"Oh jah. It will give us a chance to visit awhile."

"Okay, but you'd better go inside and check with your mamm first," Grandpa said. "While you're doing that, I'll get the horse and buggy ready to go."

Rachel hugged Grandpa and sprinted to the house. She found Mom sitting in front of her sewing machine. "Grandpa's going to town, and he invited me to go along. Is that okay with you?"

"Not today, Rachel," Mom said as she pumped her feet up and down on the treadle to get the machine going.

"If I can't ride to town with Grandpa, can I go to Audra's and play?"

"Sorry, but no."

"How come?"

"Because you—"

"Can I go outside and jump on the trampoline?"

Mom shook her head. "If you hadn't interrupted, I was going to say you may not play until all your chores are done."

"But I finished my chores after breakfast."

"You finished the ones you normally do, but as soon as I finish mending these trousers for Jacob, I want to do some cleaning." Mom looked up and smiled at Rachel. "I'll need your help."

Rachel bit the end of a fingernail. She'd done enough work today. It wasn't fair that Mom expected her to do more. She felt like all she ever did was work.

"Don't bite your *fingerneggel* [fingernails], Rachel," Mom said. "I've told you it's a bad habit. Besides, your fingernails are full of germs."

"Sorry," Rachel mumbled. "I wish I didn't have more chores to do. I was hoping to do something fun today."

"After we finish the cleaning, maybe we can walk to the creek. That sounds like fun, doesn't it?" Mom asked.

Rachel shrugged. If she went to the creek, she could probably wade in the water and look for frogs, but it wouldn't be nearly as much fun as going to town with Grandpa.

Mom pushed away from the sewing machine. "I'm done with my mending now, so while I clean the living room floor and dust, I'd like you to wash the living room windows."

Rachel groaned. Washing windows didn't sound like fun at all!

She'd just entered the utility room to get the window cleaning solution and a clean rag when she heard the back door creak open and Grandpa call, "Rachel, are you ready to go to town? I have the horse and buggy ready to go!"

Rachel stepped out of the utility room and met him with a scowl. "I can't go to town with you, Grandpa. Mom says I have to do some cleaning." Her chin quivered, and she blinked a couple of times to keep her tears from spilling over.

Grandpa pulled Rachel to his side and hugged her. "It's okay. You can go to town with me another time when you're not so busy."

"I'll probably always be busy," she said with a groan. "The older I get, the more chores I have to do."

Grandpa patted the top of her head. "Then make your chores fun."

"How do I do that?"

"Make a game out of what you're doing."

Rachel tilted her head. "Huh?"

"Let me give you an example," Grandpa said. "When I was a *buwe* [boy] and had to wash dishes,

I pretended that the dishes were *kinner* [children], swimming in a pond." A smile stretched across Grandpa's face. "It was fun to make the dishes dive into the pond. It made lots of bubbles, and they splashed in my face."

Rachel giggled as she pictured Grandpa dropping silverware into the soapy water and bubbles breaking on his nose. "Guess I'll have to try that the next time I do the dishes."

"It doesn't just have to be when you're doing the dishes," Grandpa said. "You can pretend all sorts of things while you're doing different chores."

Rachel nodded. "I'll try that on the chores I do today."

Grandpa hugged her again. "Good girl." He turned toward the door. "Well, I'd best be on my way. I'll see you later this afternoon."

Rachel hurried to the living room. She figured if she got the windows cleaned quickly, Mom might let her play.

She held the spray bottle up to the window. *Squirt! Squirt!* She squeezed the lever until the window had plenty of liquid. *Swish! Swish! Swish!* She pretended she was painting a pretty picture as she swiped the rag up, down, and all over the window.

"How's it going?" Mom asked, stepping up to Rachel.

"Fine. I'm almost done with my picture."

Mom eyebrows lifted as she looked at Rachel. "What picture?"

Rachel's cheeks warmed. "Oh, I—uh—pretended I

was painting a picture while I washed the window."

"I see." Mom peered at the window. "Ach, Rachel, look at all the streaks you've left! You'll have to do that window again."

Rachel leaned close to the glass and squinted. "I don't see any streaks."

"Right there." Mom pointed to a spot on the lower half of the window. "Do you see it now?"

Rachel nodded. She saw it, but it looked fuzzy. "Something must be wrong with the window cleaner," she said.

"Here, let me try." Mom took the rag and bottle from Rachel. *Squirt! Squirt! Swish! Swish! Swish!* "There, that's better. You probably weren't rubbing hard enough." She handed the window cleaner and rag back to Rachel.

Rachel leaned close to the window again and looked outside. "I think you must have missed a few spots, because some things in the yard look blurry."

Squirt! Squirt! Swish. . .swish. . .swish—she scrubbed at the window some more.

"You can stop now, Rachel. That window's as clean as it can be."

Rachel leaned close to the window again and stared outside. Everything still looked blurry, but if Mom thought the window was clean enough, she wouldn't say anything more. "Now can I go outside and play?" Rachel asked hopefully.

Mom shook her head. "We still have more cleaning to do."

"Like what?"

"I'd like you to shake the living room rugs while I mop the kitchen floor."

"Is that all you need me to do?"

Mom's glasses had slipped to the end or her nose, and she pushed them back in place. "I believe so; unless I think of something else." She smiled and left the room.

Rachel bent down and grabbed the small braided rug in front of the sofa. She hauled it to the porch. Pretending the porch was a trampoline and she was jumping on it, she gave the rug a few good shakes. Then she draped it over the railing. She went back to the living room to get the rug in front of Grandpa's rocking chair. She gave that a couple of shakes, imagining again that she was bouncing up and down on the trampoline. When her arms grew tired, she draped the rug over the railing and returned to get another rug near the front door.

When Rachel stepped onto the porch again, she gasped. Buddy had one of the rugs in his mouth! *Grr.* He growled and shook it for all he was worth!

"*Absatz* [Stop]! You're a bad *hund* [dog]!" Rachel tugged on the dog's collar, but he didn't let go of the rug.

Grr. . .Grr. . . Buddy continued to shake and growl.

Rachel gritted her teeth and tugged Buddy's collar again. "If you tear a hole in that rug, you'll be in big trouble with Mom!" She thought about the towel Buddy had stolen from the laundry basket and ripped in two. Mom hadn't been happy about that at all!

Grr. . .Grr. . .Shake! Shake! Shake!

Rachel let go of Buddy's collar and cupped her hands around her mouth. "Jacob Yoder, you'd better come get your dog, *schnell* [quickly]!"

No response.

Rachel figured Jacob must still be in the barn helping Pap and Henry groom the horses. She thought about going to get him but was afraid if she left, Buddy would tear the rug.

Suddenly, an idea popped into Rachel's head. She ran down the porch steps, raced to the water spigot, and turned on the hose. Aiming it at the porch, she sprayed Buddy's face.

Buddy let go of the rug and howled. He leaped off the porch, circled around Rachel, jumped up, and— *slurp!*—licked her face.

"Yuk! Get down, you big hairy mutt!" Rachel shot Buddy with another spray of water.

Woof! Woof! Woof! Buddy circled her again, bounded onto the porch, and darted into the house.

"Oh great! I should have shut the door!"

Rachel raced into the house. When she heard Mom scream, "Ach no!" she knew Buddy must be in the kitchen. She ran after him.

"Look what this dog has done!" Mom clucked her

tongue as she pointed to the muddy paw prints on the kitchen floor. "Now I'll have to wash the floor again!"

"I'm sorry, Mom," Rachel panted, "but that flea-bitten hund grabbed one of the rugs and wouldn't let go. He kept growling and shaking the rug." She gulped in a quick breath of air. "So I turned on the hose and sprayed him with water. He let go, but then he ran around the yard, got his feet dirty, and ran into the house before I could stop him."

Buddy circled Mom, barking and chasing his tail. *Woof! Woof! Woof!*

When he made the next pass, Mom bent down and grabbed his collar. "Rachel, take this hund outside and put him in his dog run! Then hang the rug on the clothesline, because I'm sure it got wet from the hose."

"Okay, Mom," Rachel said as she led Buddy out the back door.

Woof! Woof! Woof! Buddy's tail swished the skirt of Rachel's dress.

"You're nothing but trouble," she muttered.

By the time Rachel had put Buddy in his dog run and hung the rug on the line to dry, she was tired. She trudged up the porch steps, wondering what other chores Mom had for her to do. At this rate, they would never get to take that walk, and she would probably have no time for play.

When Rachel entered the house, she peeked into

the kitchen. The floor was clean, but Mom was no longer there. Thinking Mom might have gone to the living room to do more cleaning, Rachel headed in that direction. She found Mom lying on the sofa with her eyes shut.

Rachel tiptoed across the room. "Are you sleeping?" she whispered.

Mom opened her eyes. "Almost."

"What about our walk to the creek?"

Mom released a noisy yawn. "I'd better not today, Rachel. After all that cleaning, I'm really tired. You're free to go outside and play while I take a nap."

Rachel shook her head. "I'm not in the mood now." She trudged up the stairs, stomped into her room, and fell on the bed. "Always trouble somewhere!"

She stretched her arms over her head until they bumped the headboard. "We can't go to Hershey Park; I couldn't go to town with Grandpa; the greenhouse won't be built until June; I had to do chores all afternoon; and now Mom's too tired to walk to the creek. What a disappointing day!"

Chapter 4

Seeing Is Believing

"Did ya see that pretty butterfly?" Orlie asked Rachel when she and Jacob entered the school yard Monday morning.

Rachel looked around. "Where? I don't see a butterfly."

"Over there!" Orlie pointed to a bush across the yard. "Do you see it?"

Rachel grunted. "No, I don't. Are you teasing me, Orlie?"

"Of course not." Orlie's nose twitched when he gave her a crooked grin. "I never tease—you know that."

"Jah, right! You tease a lot, and I'm sure you're teasing about the butterfly."

"No, I'm not." Orlie poked Rachel's arm. "Maybe you can't see the butterfly because your eyes have gone bad. Maybe you should go to the doctor and get your eyes checked."

"I don't need a doctor. I can see just fine!" Rachel's long skirt swished around her legs as she ran through the grass. She was almost to the schoolhouse steps when she heard a squeal. She looked around. She saw Audra cowering in the bushes near the porch.

"What's wrong?" Rachel asked.

Audra's chin trembled. "I—I dropped my backpack." She stood up and pointed to the backpack lying in the bushes. "I–I'm afraid to pick it up b–because there's a spider on it."

Rachel knew Audra was afraid of bugs, but she'd never realized how much until now. The poor girl was actually shivering, and it wasn't the least bit cold.

Rachel stared at Audra's backpack. "I don't see a spider. It must have crawled away."

Audra continued to point. "It's still there. See. . .on the flap."

Rachel squinted. "I don't see a spider. Are you teasing me, Audra?"

"Of course not. Why would I tease about seeing a spider?" Audra's face turned red. "Would you kill it for me, Rachel?"

Rachel shook her head. "Huh-uh. If there is a spider on your backpack, then the little critter has the right to live." She turned toward the porch.

Audra dashed to Rachel and clutched her arm. "Please, don't go. I—I need you to kill that spider!"

"*Du kannscht mich net uffhuddle; ich bin zu schmaert* [You can't confuse me; I'm too smart]," Rachel said.

"I'm not trying to confuse you. There really is a

spider," Audra said in a shaky voice.

Rachel grunted. "If you think so, you'd better kill it yourself, because I'm not going to."

"*Eww. . .*I could never do that! What if it jumped at me?" Audra thrust out her lower lip. "Please, Rachel. If you won't kill the spider, will you at least get it off my backpack?"

With a frustrated grunt, Rachel bent, scooped up the backpack, and gave it a shake. "Is the spider gone now?"

Audra studied the backpack and nodded. "Jah, it's gone. Danki, Rachel."

Rachel plodded up the stairs, shaking her head. She couldn't believe Audra was afraid of a little bitty spider. She couldn't believe she hadn't been able to see it on Audra's backpack either.

What was going on? First the butterfly Orlie said was there but Rachel never saw, and now an invisible spider! Either she was going blind, or Orlie and Audra were in cahoots and had decided to make this "tease Rachel day."

Well, if anyone else saw anything that wasn't really there, Rachel would just play along. No point giving them the satisfaction of thinking they'd pulled a fast one on her!

When the teacher, Elizabeth, dismissed the scholars for recess that morning, Rachel headed straight for the swings. She was the first one there, so she got to choose her favorite swing.

She started by making the swing go side to side, then she swirled around a couple of times until she felt dizzy. Finally—*pump. . .pump. . .push. Pump. . .pump. . . push*—she moved her legs fast and was soon swinging so high she felt like a bird soaring up to the sky. "Whee . . .this is so much fun!"

"Did you see that pretty bird in the tree over there?" Orlie asked when he joined Rachel on the swings.

"What bird?"

"That one—in the maple tree."

Rachel slowed her swing so she could get a better look. She did see the bird, but it looked like a blurry blob.

"Do you see it, Rachel?" Orlie asked.

"Uh—jah, it's real pretty."

Orlie started pumping his legs really fast. "Bet I can swing higher than you can."

"Bet you can't." *Pump. . .pump. . .push. Pump. . . pump. . .push.* Rachel got her swing going as high as she could.

"You'd better watch out, or you'll fly right off and land in the tree with that bird!" Orlie hollered.

Rachel giggled as she flew up. "My swing's higher than yours," she shouted. "I win!"

"You didn't give me a fair chance. I can go higher if I want to."

"No you can't, because recess is over." Rachel started to drag her feet to slow the swing. "See, all the scholars are heading inside."

Orlie groaned. "I'll beat you the next time; just wait and see."

"That's what you think, Orlie Troyer!" Rachel jumped off the swing, dashed across the yard, and—*floop!*—dropped to her knees!

"What happened?" Audra rushed to Rachel and helped her to her feet.

Rachel brushed the dirt from her dress. "I—I guess I must have tripped on something."

"I think it was that." Audra motioned to the hose stretched across the yard. "Didn't you see it?"

Rachel shook her head. "I—I wasn't looking down."

"Are you hurt?"

Rachel inspected her knees. "I'm okay. My knees aren't even bleeding."

"You need to be more careful." Audra patted Rachel's back. "Were you in a hurry to get inside?"

"Jah, I was." Rachel started moving toward the schoolhouse again. She was almost to the porch when she heard a bird twittering from the tree nearby. She tipped her head back and squinted. There was that blurry blob again. She didn't understand why everything looked so fuzzy lately. Could something be wrong with her eyes? Would she need to see a doctor? Oh, she hoped not!

"Are you gonna play ball with us?" Jacob asked Rachel during lunch recess that day.

Rachel shrugged. "I thought I might swing or play on the teeter-totter with Audra."

"Aw, come on, Rachel." Jacob nudged her arm. "You're a good ball player; we need you."

"I'd rather not."

"Please, Rachel. I'd like you to be on my team."

"Oh, okay," Rachel finally agreed. She was pleased that Jacob thought she was good at playing ball. He didn't often say nice things to her.

Rachel followed Jacob to the baseball field. "Play center field," he said.

"Why can't I play second or first base?"

"You're good at catching fly balls, so that's where I want you to go."

"Where are you gonna play?" she asked.

"I'll be the pitcher." Jacob cupped his hands around his mouth. "Orlie, you're on my team, too, so play in left field."

"Let's get the other team out schnell," Orlie said to Rachel. "I can't wait till I'm up to bat, because I plan to bat a home run!"

"You always like to win," Rachel mumbled as she walked to center field.

"What was that?" Orlie called.

"Oh, nothing."

The first few balls never made it past the infield, so

that made two outs. Then came a couple of foul balls. Rachel wondered if any balls would ever come her way, when suddenly—*smack!*—Aaron King hit a ball that sailed right over Jacob's head.

"Catch it, Rachel!" Orlie hollered. "Get that ball!"

Rachel saw a blur of white whiz past her head, but when she reached out to grab it, the ball flew over her glove. She lunged for it and fell on her face. *Oomph!*

"Are you all right, Rachel?" Audra called from first base. "Your *naas* [nose] isn't bleeding, I hope."

Rachel touched her nose and was relieved not to see any blood on her fingers. Last month, when she'd been playing ball, she'd gotten smacked in the nose and ended up with a nasty nosebleed.

"What's the matter with you, Rachel?" Jacob called. "Didn't you see that ball coming?"

"I saw it. I just missed, that's all." Rachel wasn't about to admit that the ball had looked like a blurry snowball whizzing past her head.

Jacob frowned. "Jah, well, you'd better keep a close watch on the ball from now on."

Rachel wrinkled her nose. "Maybe I should have played on the teeter-totter or swings. At least no one would be picking on me."

"Oh, don't be like that," Jacob said. "When our team's up to bat, I'm sure you'll do better."

Maybe Jacob's right, Rachel thought. *I am pretty good at hitting the ball. I might even make a home run.*

That would show Orlie.

Rachel sat on the bench waiting for her turn to bat. Orlie went first and hit a ball that took him to second base. Then Jacob was up, and his ball sailed into right field and brought Orlie home. Lonnie Byler was up next, but he struck out. Then Audra batted, and she struck out, too.

Now it was Rachel's turn. She stepped up to the plate, took her stance, and waited for the ball. It came quickly—*swish!* Rachel swung—and missed.

"Strike one!" David Miller shouted.

"Don't swing unless it's right over the plate," Jacob called to Rachel.

"I won't!"

The pitcher threw the ball again, but the blur of white whizzed right past Rachel.

"Strike two!"

Rachel gripped the bat tighter. The fuzzy white ball came again—*swish!* She swung hard—and missed.

"Strike three—you're out!"

Rachel groaned. So much for getting a home run! So much for showing Orlie how well she could play! He probably thought she was a real loser today.

"What's the matter with you, Rachel?" Jacob grumbled. "You acted like you couldn't even see that ball!"

"I could see it. I just missed, that's all."

Jacob wrinkled his nose. "Jah, well, I'll think twice before I ask you to be on my team again."

"That's fine with me. I'd rather play on the swings anyway!" Rachel dropped the bat and hurried away. She'd never admit it to Jacob, but she was worried. Was it possible that she hadn't seen the ball clearly because something was wrong with her eyes? Oh, she hoped not!

Chapter 5

Blurry Words

Are you coming with me to see Grandpa and Grandma Yoder?" Rachel asked Jacob as they walked home from school the next day.

"I don't think so," Jacob said. "Pap's gonna need my help this afternoon."

"When I saw Grandma at church the other day, she said Grandpa was going fishing today, and she thought it would be nice if she and I baked something." Rachel smiled. "I'll probably bring home some cookies."

"Just be sure you don't mess up the recipe like you did before."

Rachel glared at Jacob. "Why do you always say mean things?"

"I was just stating facts."

Rachel kicked a stone and kept walking. She figured that if she said anything back to Jacob, they'd end up arguing, and she didn't want to arrive at Grandma's in a bad mood. That would ruin their afternoon together.

"Good-bye," Jacob said as they approached the driveway leading to Grandma and Grandpa Yoder's house. "I'll see you at supper."

Rachel turned up the driveway, calling over her shoulder, "Have fun in the *felder* [fields]!"

"Have fun baking *kichlin* [cookies]," Jacob called in return. "Oh, and one more thing: *Geb acht, schunscht geht's letz* [Watch out, or else things will go wrong]!"

Rachel gritted her teeth and hurried along. As she approached Grandma and Grandpa's house, she noticed her three-year-old cousin Gerald sitting on the front porch of his house with a jar of bubbles. Gerald and his parents, Aunt Karen and Uncle Amos, had moved into the house next door to Grandma and Grandpa soon after Mary and her family moved to Indiana.

Rachel decided to visit with Gerald a few minutes. Maybe she could blow some bubbles.

"*Blos* [Bubble]," Gerald said when Rachel took a seat on the step next to him. He lifted the jar of bubbles.

She smiled. "Can I blow some?"

He nodded and handed her the plastic wand.

Rachel dipped it into the jar and waved it around. A stream of colorful bubbles blew into the yard.

Gerald squealed and clapped his hands. "Blos! Blos! *Geh* [Go]!"

Rachel dipped the wand into the jar again. Only this time, instead of waving the wand, she blew on it. More bubbles floated into the yard.

"Blos! Blos!" Gerald hollered. He snatched the wand from Rachel and dipped it into the jar. Holding the wand in front of Rachel's face, he blew. A big bubble formed, but before the wind could catch it, Gerald poked it with his finger, and—*pop!*—it burst in Rachel's face!

"Ach, that stings!" she cried as she rubbed her eyes. Rachel blinked several times, trying to clear her vision. "I should have expected something like this to happen," she mumbled. The last time she'd visited Gerald, she'd given him a horsey ride, and he'd smacked her in the eye.

When the stinging stopped, she handed Gerald the jar of bubbles and stood. "I have to go. Grandma's expecting me, and I don't have any more time to play."

Gerald didn't seem to notice as she walked away. He was too busy blowing more bubbles.

Thump! Thump! Thump! Rachel knocked on Grandma's door.

"Come in," Grandma called.

Rachel entered the house and sniffed the delicious odor of cinnamon and molasses. "Did you bake the cookies without me?" she asked when she stepped into the kitchen and found Grandma sitting at the table reading the newspaper.

Grandma looked up and smiled. "Of course not. I promised that we would bake the cookies together."

Rachel sniffed the air again. "Then why do I smell cinnamon and molasses?"

"That's from the gingerbread I baked earlier today." Grandma pushed the newspaper aside and stood. "Would you like a piece?"

Rachel shook her head. "No thanks. I'll wait until the cookies are done and have some of those."

"All right. Are you ready to begin?" Grandma asked.

Rachel nodded eagerly. "What kind of cookies are we gonna make?"

"How about some maple syrup cookies?" Grandma wiggled her eyebrows. "Those are some of your daed's favorites."

Rachel leaned on the counter. "I didn't know that. No wonder Mom bakes them so often."

Grandma bobbed her head. "I used to make maple syrup cookies at least once a week when your daed was a buwe. I gave your mamm the recipe as soon as they got married."

"I like maple syrup cookies real well, too." Rachel patted her stomach and grinned. "Guess I take after my daed."

"I guess you do." Grandma opened a cupboard door and took down her recipe box. She opened it, pulled out a recipe, and handed it to Rachel. "Why don't you read the recipe and then get out the ingredients while I preheat the oven?"

"I can do that." Rachel placed the card on the counter and opened the cupboard where Grandma kept her baking supplies. As she studied the recipe, the words looked blurry. *I'll bet I still have some of that bubble Gerald popped in my eye,* she thought.

Rachel ran to the bathroom. She opened both eyes wide and splashed water on her face. *That ought to do it.*

She blinked a few times and looked in the mirror. *Hmm. . .my face even looks blurry. I wonder how long it's been since Grandma cleaned this mirror.*

"Rachel, where are you?" Grandma called.

Rachel dried her face on a towel and ran back to the kitchen. "I was in the bathroom, rinsing my eyes."

Grandma's forehead wrinkled. "Is something wrong with your eyes?"

"I was having trouble reading the recipe, and I thought I might have bubble solution in my eyes."

Grandma frowned. "How would you get bubble solution in your eyes?"

"Before I came here, I blew bubbles with Gerald, and he popped one in my face. I think that blurred my vision." Rachel pointed to her eyes. "Even after I rinsed them, my face looked blurry in the bathroom mirror. I wonder if the mirror is dirty, Grandma."

Grandma shook her head. "I cleaned that mirror this morning." She pursed her lips. "Come closer and let me look at your eyes."

Rachel stood in front of Grandma and opened her eyes as widely as she could.

"I don't see anything." Grandma motioned to the recipe card. "Were you having trouble reading the whole recipe, or just a few words?"

"All of it," Rachel admitted. "Could something have gotten spilled on the recipe?"

Grandma ran her fingers over the card. "I don't see or feel anything." She faced Rachel. "Maybe you need a pair of glasses."

Rachel gasped. "Ach, I hope not! I never want to wear glasses!"

"Why not?"

"Because I think they would make me look *schpassich* [odd]. Jacob and the kinner at school might make fun of me if I wore glasses."

Grandma touched the nosepiece on her own glasses. "Do you think I look schpassich?"

"Of course not," Rachel said, shaking her head. "I only meant. . . Well, some of the kinner might think I look odd because I've never worn glasses before."

Grandma touched Rachel's chin. "If I were you, I'd be more concerned about seeing well than worrying about what others might think."

Rachel thought about that a few seconds. "Do you like wearing glasses?" she asked.

Grandma nodded. "I don't mind them at all. Fact is, I've worn glasses since I was a teenager. They've become a part of me now. Sometimes I even fall asleep with them on." She chuckled. "I'll never forget the day, soon after I'd turned sixteen, when I forgot I was wearing my glasses."

"What happened?"

"Some of my friends and I had gone to the lake to swim," Grandma said. "I forgot to take my glasses off before I went in the water and almost lost them."

"Did they float away?"

Grandma shook her head. "They started to sink, but I grabbed them in time."

Hearing how Grandma had nearly lost her glasses in the lake made Rachel hope all the more that she would never have to wear glasses. She pointed to the recipe card. "It might be better if you read the recipe and tell me what ingredients I should get from the cupboard."

Grandma smiled. "Jah, okay."

"Oh, and one more thing," Rachel said.

"What's that?"

"Please don't say anything to Mom or Pap about me not being able to read the recipe card. I don't want to worry them."

Grandma tapped her finger against her chin as she considered this. "I won't say anything for now, but if your vision continues to blur, then you'd better tell your folks right away."

"Okay," Rachel said, nodding.

"Third and fourth graders, I've written your English assignment on the blackboard," Elizabeth said during school the next day. "I want you to look at the sentences and then write down every noun, verb, and adjective you see."

Rachel leaned forward with her elbows on her desk and studied the sentences her teacher had written. If she squinted, she could read some of the words, but most of them looked fuzzy.

She blinked several times, hoping her eyes would focus, but it was no use. She couldn't see well enough to know what the sentences said.

Rachel leaned across the aisle and whispered, "*Psst. . .* Audra. . .can you read those sentences?"

Audra nodded. "Of course I can."

"What do they say?"

Audra's eyebrows pulled together as she stared at Rachel. "Can't you read them?"

"Well, I—"

"No talking, please!" Elizabeth's stern voice caused Rachel to jump.

Rachel raised her hand.

"What is it, Rachel?" Elizabeth asked.

"The words on the board look kind of blurry, and I was asking Audra if she knew what they said."

"Rachel, please come here," Elizabeth said. "We need to talk."

Rachel's cheeks burned with embarrassment when she noticed that everyone in class seemed to be looking at her. She wished she hadn't said anything. She wished she could crawl under her desk and stay there until school was over.

Rachel shuffled to the front of the room.

Elizabeth leaned close to Rachel. "Now what's all this about blurry words on the blackboard?"

"I—I can't tell wh–what all the words say," Rachel stammered as she wiped her sweaty hands on her skirt.

"Have you had trouble seeing other things?" Elizabeth questioned.

Rachel thought about the letter from Mary and the recipe card at Grandma's. She hadn't been able to read either one of those. She remembered the baseball that had looked like a white blur; the spider and the butterfly she hadn't been able to see; and the bird that had looked like a blurry blob. A knot formed in her throat. Maybe something *was* wrong with her eyes. Maybe she *would* end up wearing glasses whether she liked it or not.

"Rachel, did you hear my question?"

"Jah."

"Have you had trouble seeing other things?"

Rachel nodded slowly, and her throat felt so swollen she could hardly swallow.

Elizabeth reached into her desk and withdrew a notebook. She wrote something on the paper and handed it to Rachel. "This is a note for your parents. I'm letting them know that you're having trouble seeing the letters on the blackboard. I've suggested they make an appointment to get your eyes examined."

Thump! Thumpety! Thump! Thump! Rachel's heart hammered in her chest. She'd never had her eyes examined before. Would it hurt? Would the doctor be nice? Would he make her wear glasses? If he did, would the glasses cost a lot of money? So many questions swirled around in her head that she could hardly think.

"I'll move your desk closer to the blackboard so you can see better," Elizabeth said.

As Elizabeth pushed Rachel's desk to the front of the room, Rachel made a decision. She would hide the note from Mom and Pap so she wouldn't have to see the doctor. Even if she had to keep her desk at the front of the room for the rest of the school year, it would be better than wearing glasses!

That night at supper, Rachel stared at her plate of fried chicken, mashed potatoes, and pickled red beets. These were some of her favorite foods, but she didn't feel like eating. She could only think about the note at the bottom of her backpack.

"You're awfully quiet," Grandpa said, touching Rachel's arm.

"She hasn't eaten much supper, either," Henry added.

"Are you feeling grank?" Mom asked, looking at Rachel with concern.

Rachel shifted in her seat, unsure of what to say. "I'm not sick." She took a bite of chicken, but it tasted like cardboard, and she had a hard time swallowing.

"I'll bet she's thinking about that note our teacher gave her today," Jacob said.

Rachel glared at him. If he were sitting closer, she

might have kicked him under the table.

"What note?" asked Pap, looking at Rachel.

Rachel felt as if she had a glob of peanut butter stuck in her throat. She reached for her glass of water and took a drink.

"What note?" Pap asked again.

Rachel set the glass on the table and blew out her breath. "Elizabeth thinks I should have my eyes examined."

Mom stared at Rachel over her glasses. "What makes her think that?"

"Well, uh—the words on the blackboard looked kind of blurry today, and I—uh—couldn't tell what they said."

Pap stared at Rachel so hard her toes curled inside her sneakers. "When were you planning to give us the note?"

Rachel moistened her lips with the tip of her tongue. "Well, I—"

"I'll bet she wasn't going to give you the note," Jacob said. "I'll bet she—"

Mom held up her hand and frowned at Jacob. "You'd best stay out of this, son." She turned to Rachel. "If Elizabeth thinks you should have your eyes examined, I'll call the eye doctor tomorrow and make an appointment." She shook her finger at Rachel. "The next time your teacher gives you a note, I expect you to give it to me right away. Is that clear?"

Rachel nodded as tears pooled in her eyes, making

everything on the table look blurry. "I'm not hungry," she mumbled, struggling not to cry. "May—may I be excused?"

Mom gave a quick nod. "But remember, there will be no dessert if you don't finish your supper."

"I don't care about dessert!" Rachel sucked in a huge sob, pushed back her chair, and raced from the room. "I don't want to wear glasses! I'd rather see blurry words for the rest of my life!"

She dashed up the stairs two at a time. *Thunk!*—she tripped on the last step and dropped to her knees.

Rachel grabbed the railing and pulled herself up as tears coursed down her cheeks. "Trouble, trouble. . . there's always trouble somewhere!"

Chapter 6

Learning the Truth

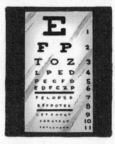

Rachel stared out the window of their driver's van and tried to concentrate on the scenery going by—anything to keep from thinking about where they were going. *Zip! Zip! Zip!* It felt as if a bunch of butterflies were flying around in her stomach.

Mom had made an appointment for Rachel to see the eye doctor today. She'd hired their English neighbor, Susan Johnson, to take them to Lancaster for the appointment. Susan had picked them up as soon as Rachel got home from school. Rachel wished she could be anywhere but here. Even doing chores would be better than getting her eyes examined.

"Don't look so *naerfich* [nervous]." Mom gently squeezed Rachel's arm. "The doctor's just going to look at your eyes."

"And probably make me wear glasses," Rachel mumbled.

"We won't know that until after the examination. Besides, wearing glasses isn't so bad." Mom pushed her glasses onto the bridge of her nose. "Without my glasses I wouldn't be able to see nearly as well. Grandma Yoder wears glasses, too," she added with a smile. "And Grandpa Schrock needs glasses for reading."

"I know that, but no one at school wears glasses. If the doctor says I have to wear them, I'll be the only scholar with glasses." Rachel swallowed hard. "Wearing glasses would make me stick out like a sore thumb!"

"You won't stick out like a sore thumb." Mom patted Rachel's knee. "Even if no one else wears glasses now, it doesn't mean they never will."

Rachel leaned back in her seat and closed her eyes. She tried to imagine how some of her friends would look with glasses. Would they wear the metal-framed kind like Mom, Grandma Yoder, and Grandpa Schrock wore; or would they wear colored plastic frames like she'd seen on other folks? She almost giggled when she pictured Orlie wearing a pair of glasses with thick lenses that made him look like a frog.

Audra's brother, Brian, had a round face, so if he wore glasses, he might look like a pumpkin. Phoebe Byler's nose was thin, and she had small, beady eyes, so if she wore glasses she'd probably look like a bird.

Mom nudged Rachel's arm. "We're here!"

Rachel's eyes popped open. The butterflies in her stomach started zipping again.

Rachel and Mom sat in the doctor's waiting room.

Mom read a magazine. Rachel took deep breaths and tried to relax. It was easy for Mom to say there was nothing to be nervous about; she wasn't the one getting her eyes examined today. She wasn't the one who might get teased if she wore glasses at school, either.

A middle-aged woman with short red hair stepped up to Rachel. "My name is Mrs. Dodge, and I'm the doctor's assistant. Will you please come with me?"

Rachel stood and wiped her sweaty palms on her dress. "Will you come with me?" she asked Mom.

Mom nodded. "Of course."

Rachel and Mom followed Mrs. Dodge into another room. She motioned to a chair that looked similar to the one Rachel sat in the last time she'd gone to the dentist—only this chair had a strange-looking machine in front of it.

Mrs. Dodge asked Rachel several questions: how old she was; had she ever worn glasses; was she having any trouble with her eyes; and had she ever had an eye exam. When she finished her questions, she looked at Rachel and said, "Now look straight ahead at the chart on the wall. Do you see some groups of letters?"

Rachel nodded. "I see them, but some are fuzzy."

"That's okay. Just read the smallest line that you're able to see clearly."

"The top line looks the clearest," Rachel said.

"That's fine. Please read the letters on that line."

"F, E, L, O, P, Z, D."

"Can you read the next line?"

"D. . .No, I think that's an O." Rachel squinted as she concentrated on each letter. "F. . .No, that's an E. Well, maybe it is an F. I—I can't really be sure."

Mrs. Dodge plucked a bottle from the shelf across the room, and moved closer to Rachel. "Hold your head still. I'm going to put some drops in your eyes."

Rachel flinched. "Wh–why do I need drops in my eyes?"

"The drops are to dilate your eyes," Mrs. Dodge explained. "Dilating makes the pupils larger and helps the doctor see the backs of your eyes."

"Why does he need to look at the backs of my eyes?" Rachel wanted to know.

"To see if there's any swelling or disease."

Rachel didn't think her eyes were swollen, and she hoped they had no disease. "W–will the eyedrops hurt?" she asked shakily.

"They might sting a little, but the stinging sensation won't last long."

Mom took hold of Rachel's hand. "It's okay. Just relax."

Rachel drew in a deep breath, leaned her head against the back of the chair, and tried not to blink.

Squirt. Squirt. "There now; you did just fine," Mrs. Dodge said. "The doctor will be in to see you soon." She handed Rachel a tissue and scurried out of the room.

Rachel dabbed at her watery eyes. "What's this for, Mom?" she asked, pointing to the big machine in front of her.

Mom sat in a chair near the door. "When the doctor comes in, he'll have you look at the eye chart again, only this time you'll be looking through the large lenses attached to the machine. He'll also look at your eyes with a bright light."

"Will the bright light hurt?"

"No Rachel." Mom smiled. "Now please sit back and relax."

Rachel closed her eyes and sighed, wishing the doctor would hurry. The longer she waited, the more nervous she became. She opened her eyes and fiddled with the strings on her kapp, knowing Mom would scold her if she bit a fingernail.

Finally, the door squeaked open. A tall man wearing metal-framed glasses entered the room. "Hello, Rachel. I'm Dr. Ben. I understand you're having some trouble with your eyes."

"Well, uh—some things look a little blurry lately, but I hope I won't need to wear glasses."

He touched the earpiece of his glasses then rubbed his chin. "Do you have something against glasses?"

She swallowed a couple of times. "Not really. I just think I'm too young to wear them."

Dr. Ben winked at Mom. Then he sat on the stool near the front of the strange-looking machine. "Now let's take a look at your eyes so I can see what's going on."

"W—will it hurt?"

"No Rachel, I'm just going to examine your eyes."

The doctor shined a bright light into Rachel's eyes. It didn't hurt, but it was hard to keep her eyes open.

Then Dr. Ben positioned the machine in front of Rachel's face. "Now lean forward so your forehead is resting against the machine and your chin is on the chin rest."

Rachel did as he asked. The exam included a lot more than she'd expected, but so far it had been easy enough.

"Do you see the eye chart through the lenses, Rachel?"

"Yes."

"I'll adjust the lenses," Dr. Ben said. "I want you to let me know if you can see the letters any better." *Click! Click!*

"Oh, yes, they're much clearer now," she said as the letters came into focus.

Click! Click! The doctor made a few more adjustments. "Is this better?"

"I—I think the first one was better."

"How about this?" He changed the lenses a few more times, always asking Rachel which one was better. Finally, he pulled the machine away from her face.

"We're all done." He looked over at Mom and said, "Rachel's eyes have a slight astigmatism."

"Astigmatism," Rachel repeated. "What's that?"

"It's when the front surface of the eye is shaped like an egg," Dr. Ben explained.

Rachel frowned. She had no idea her eye looked like an egg.

"When a person has astigmatism, it can affect vision and distort shapes so letters and numbers that look similar are often confused." Dr. Ben looked over at Mom again. "Rachel is also farsighted in one eye and nearsighted in the other."

"What does farsighted and nearsighted mean?" Rachel asked.

"Farsighted is an eye condition that makes it hard for you to see things that are close. Nearsighted means you have a hard time seeing things that are far away."

Tears pricked the backs of Rachel's eyes as the doctor's words sank in. Something *was* wrong with her eyes, and she *would* have to wear glasses. She'd probably never be able to see well without them.

Dr. Ben patted Rachel's shoulder. "Once you get your glasses, you'll be able to see everything much better." He wrote something on a small notepad and handed it to Mom. "Here's the prescription for Rachel's new glasses."

Mom nodded. "Thank you, Dr. Ben."

Rachel swallowed. She wanted to see better, but she didn't want glasses!

Dr. Ben motioned to the door. "You can go next door to the optical department and give them the prescription for Rachel's glasses. Then she can pick out a nice pair of frames."

The butterflies in Rachel's stomach started zipping around again. The tears she'd been holding back flooded her eyes, making her vision even blurrier. "Are—are you sure I have to get glasses?"

He nodded. "But if you wear them all the time for the next few years, maybe your eyes will get stronger and you won't have to wear them at all."

Hope welled in Rachel's chest. "Really?"

He nodded and handed her a pair of cardboard glasses with dark lenses. "The dilation will last for several hours, and your eyes will be sensitive to light, so put these on before you go outside."

Rachel grimaced. She couldn't get out of it; she would have to wear glasses. She just hoped it wouldn't be forever.

"Do you want plastic frames or metal frames?" Mom asked when she and Rachel entered the optical shop.

Rachel shrugged.

"Let's look at some plastic frames. I think those will look good on you." Mom led Rachel to the wall where rows of glasses with plastic frames hung. Rachel could hardly tell how they looked because her eyes were blurrier than normal from the dilation.

"What do you think of these?" Mom asked, lifting a pair of glasses. "They're a nice of shade of blue, and they'll match your pretty eyes. What do you think, Rachel?"

"I—I guess they'll be all right." Rachel swallowed a couple of times and drew in a deep breath. She didn't want to cry right here in the optical shop.

A short man with thinning brown hair stepped up to them. "May I help you?"

Mom handed him the prescription Dr. Ben had given her. "My daughter needs new glasses, and we think this pair would look nice."

Rachel just stared at the floor.

"Let's go over to the table so I can get some measurements and see how the glasses look on your face," the man said.

Rachel flopped into a chair in front of the table. She didn't care what color the glasses were or how well they looked on her face. She wished she could turn back the hands of time—back to when she could see everything clearly and didn't need glasses.

Later that afternoon, Rachel sat on the porch swing thinking about her eye examination and about the frames Mom had picked for her.

In just one week I'll have my new glasses, she thought. *I hope I'll like them. I hope no one at school will make fun of me.*

Rachel thought about what Mom had said about the frames. *I'll bet Mom was only trying to make me feel better when she said the new glasses would match my eyes.* She pushed the swing back and forth and tried to relax.

Bzzz. . .bzzz. Rachel recognized the sound. Even though she only saw a little blur, she knew a bee was buzzing near her head.

Bzzz...bzzz...bzzz. She didn't want to get stung, so she swatted at the bee.

"Ouch!" Rachel bumped her elbow on the back of the swing, and a tingling pain shot up her arm.

Bzzz...bzzz. The pesky bee continued to buzz around her head.

Rachel jumped up, raced for the door, and stumbled over one of Mom's flowerpots. "Trouble, trouble, trouble," she muttered.

The back door swung open. "Oh Rachel, I was just coming to get you," Mom said. "Supper's almost ready, and the table needs to be set."

Rachel hurried into the kitchen and slammed the door. At least she was away from that buzzing bee!

Mom motioned to the refrigerator. "After you put the dishes and silverware on the table, you can set out the iced tea. And could you also get the sour cream? It's in a plastic bowl in the refrigerator."

"Okay, Mom."

"Oh, and when you're done with that, please fill the sugar bowl. The sugar is in the cupboard."

Rachel opened the silverware drawer and took out the knives, forks, and spoons. As she placed them on the table, she thought about making a game of it but wasn't in the mood. When she finished setting the table, she went to the refrigerator and took out the iced tea and the container of sour cream. Then she filled the sugar bowl and had just set it on the table when Pap,

Henry, Jacob, and Grandpa entered the kitchen.

"Mmm. . .something smells mighty good." Grandpa combed his beard with his fingers and sniffed the air.

"I'll bet Mom made meatloaf tonight," Henry said. "I'd recognize that *wunderbaar* [wonderful] smell anywhere."

"You're right, Henry," Mom said, smiling. "I made your favorite supper."

Rachel frowned. It didn't seem fair that Mom had fixed Henry's favorite dish. Rachel was the one who'd had a rough day. Mom should have fixed her favorite meal—fried chicken, potato salad, biscuits with jam, and pickled beets.

"Supper's on the table," Mom said. "So, let's sit down."

Henry grinned and patted his stomach. "And we'll eat till we're full!"

"After we pray, of course," Pap said, nodding.

Everyone took seats at the table, and all heads bowed for prayer.

"Dear Lord," Rachel silently prayed, *"I don't like the idea of wearing glasses, but I did like Dr. Ben; he seemed real nice. When I get my new glasses next week, help me get used to wearing them. . . . And please don't let anyone at school make fun of me."*

When Pap cleared his throat, Rachel opened her eyes and sipped her water.

Henry cut his baked potato in half and put a pat of butter in the center. "Would you pass me the sour cream, Rachel?"

Rachel handed the bowl to Henry. He spooned some onto his potato, took a big bite, and puckered his lips. "This isn't sour cream; it's whipping cream!" He frowned at Rachel. "Did you set the table?"

She nodded, and her cheeks burned with embarrassment. She'd obviously made a mistake.

"Why'd you put out whipping cream instead of sour cream?" Henry asked. "What were you thinking?"

"I—I didn't do it on purpose. My eyes are still dilated, and everything looks real blurry."

Henry scraped the whipping cream off his baked potato, stomped to the refrigerator, took out another plastic bowl, and tromped back. "Now this is sour cream," he said, spooning some onto his potato.

Rachel's head started hurting. She rubbed her forehead with her fingertips.

"Would someone please pass the sugar?" Grandpa asked. "I like my iced tea a little sweeter."

Mom handed him the sugar bowl.

"Danki." Grandpa put two teaspoons of sugar in his glass of iced tea, stirred it, and took a drink. His lips puckered, his nose twitched, and his eyebrows pulled together. "What happened to this iced tea? It tastes salty."

Mom picked up the sugar bowl, spooned a little onto her plate, and took a bite. She looked at Rachel. "When I asked you to fill the sugar bowl, I meant with sugar, not salt."

Rachel's face grew hotter as she slumped in her

chair. "The writing on the bag looked blurry. It—it must have been salt, and I thought it was sugar."

Grandpa reached over and patted Rachel's arm. "It's okay. Everything will be better once you get your new glasses. Then things won't look blurry anymore."

Rachel blinked against the tears stinging her eyes. She hoped Grandpa was right. She needed to believe things would soon be better.

After the supper dishes were done, Rachel asked Mom if she could go to the barn to play with Cuddles.

"I guess it would be all right," Mom said. "But don't stay out there too long. It'll be bedtime soon."

"Okay, Mom." Rachel scurried out the back door.

She dashed across the yard, eased the barn door open, and peeked inside. The familiar smells comforted her—grain, hay, dust, and even the strong animal odors.

Rachel spotted Cuddles sleeping on a bale of hay. She hurried to pick up the cat. Cuddles purred and nestled against Rachel's chest.

"I have to wear glasses, Cuddles," Rachel complained. "I'm going to get them next week, and I'm not happy about it." Her shoulders rose and fell as she struggled not to cry.

Meow. Cuddles opened one eye and looked up at Rachel as if to say, "I'm sorry you're unhappy. I'm still your friend."

Rachel sat with the cat in her lap, surrounded by

a restful silence. Even as a kitten, Cuddles had often offered Rachel comfort.

Rachel yawned, stretched, and wiggled her bare toes, as a silent prayer floated through her mind. *Dear God, Danki for Cuddles.*

Chapter 7

Four Eyes

Rachel stared out the window of Susan Johnson's van. She and Mom were on their way to pick up her new glasses, and butterflies zipped around in her stomach again.

What if the glasses didn't help her see better? What if she didn't like how she looked in them? What if Jacob and the kids at school made fun of her?

Rachel was about to chomp off the end of a nail, when Mom reached for her hand. "No nail biting, Rachel."

"Sorry, Mom, but I'm feeling naerfich." Rachel touched her stomach. "It feels like butterflies are fluttering around in here."

"Are you nervous about getting your glasses?"

Rachel nodded.

"Don't be nervous. Why, once you get your glasses and can see things better, you'll be happy as a lamb."

"I hope so." Rachel tapped her foot and squirmed.

Mom squeezed Rachel's fingers. "Try to think of

something else so you won't feel naerfich. Think of something pleasant—something you enjoy."

Rachel let her head fall against the seat and closed her eyes. She thought about her cuddly cat. She thought about their old horse, Tom, and how he seemed glad to see her whenever she visited him in the pasture or barn. She thought about her cousin Mary and all the fun things they used to do. She thought about the coming summer and how she looked forward to spending time with Audra. She hoped Audra could come over to her house and jump on the trampoline. Maybe she could go over to Audra's and skateboard in the barn. She thought about wading in the creek behind their house and picnics at the pond down the road. She could do so many fun things in the summer.

"We're here," Mom said, nudging Rachel's arm.

Rachel's eyes snapped open. The dreaded moment had arrived: Time to get her glasses.

When they entered the optical shop, the man who'd waited on Rachel the week before asked her to sit in front of a table. He brought out the pair of glasses with light blue frames that Mom had chosen for Rachel. He smiled and slipped them on Rachel's face, checking to be sure they fit on the bridge of her nose and behind her ears.

"Can you see better now?" he asked, handing her a small chart with some words on it.

Rachel blinked as she stared at the chart. She could hardly believe it! The letters were so clear and bright, they seemed to jump right off the page!

"Can you see the words clearly?" he asked.

She nodded.

"Would you like to see how you look in your new glasses?"

"Yes."

He handed her a small mirror.

Rachel gasped at her reflection. She hardly recognized the girl looking back at her! She turned to Mom and asked, "What do you think?"

Mom smiled. "I think your new glasses look very nice. In fact, I think you look quite grown up."

"Really?"

"Jah."

Rachel grinned at her reflection. Maybe the glasses did make her look older. They sure helped her see better. Maybe wearing glasses wouldn't be so bad after all.

When they left the optical shop, Rachel couldn't stop grinning. Everything outside looked so crisp and clear. The sun looked brighter; the sky looked bluer; the trees looked greener. She stared at the clouds and studied the different shapes. She hadn't even realized how many things she hadn't been able to see well before. Looking through her new glasses was like seeing the world in a brand-new light. She was sure she'd be able to see the blackboard and the words in her schoolbooks better, too.

"Can we stop by Esther and Rudy's on the way home?" Rachel asked Mom as they climbed into Susan's van. "I'd like to show them my new glasses."

"I suppose we could stop for a few minutes if Susan has the time," Mom said.

"I have plenty of time, and I'd be happy to take you to Esther and Rudy's," Susan called over her shoulder.

"Danki, we appreciate that." Mom smiled at Rachel. "Rudy might be working in the fields today, but I'm sure Esther will enjoy seeing your new glasses."

When Susan's van pulled in front of Esther and Rudy's house, Rachel spotted Esther sitting in a chair on her front porch. Rachel hurried up the sidewalk ahead of Mom and Susan.

Esther smiled when Rachel stepped onto the porch. "Look at you, little schweschder. You have new glasses!"

Rachel nodded. "Do you like them?"

"Jah, very much. They're a pretty color, and they make you look so grown up."

"That's what Mom said, too."

Esther hugged Rachel. "Can you see better now?"

"Oh, jah. Everything looks so bright and clear. No more blurry vision for me," Rachel said, shaking her head.

"I'm glad."

"*Wie geht's* [How are you], Esther?" Mom asked as she and Susan stepped onto the porch.

Esther smiled and touched her stomach. "Other than a little morning sickness, I'm doing quite well."

"That's good to hear." Mom patted her own stomach. "I'm not having bouts of morning sickness at all anymore. I'm sure it will be over for you soon, too."

"I hope so, because I don't want to feel sick to my stomach the whole time I'm waiting for my baby to be born."

Mom shook her head. "I'm sure you won't."

Esther smiled at Susan. "Thank you for bringing Rachel by so she could show me her new glasses."

Susan smiled and touched her own plastic-framed glasses. "I saw how excited Rachel was when she came out of the optical shop. I felt the same way when I got my first pair of glasses."

"How old were you when you got glasses?" Rachel asked.

"I was twelve years old."

Rachel's heart felt like it had sunk all the way to her toes. *If Susan began wearing glasses when she was a girl, and she's still wearing them now, does that mean I'll be wearing glasses when I become a woman?* she wondered. *Maybe Dr. Ben only told me I might not always have to wear them to make me feel better. Maybe I'll have to wear glasses the rest of my life.*

"I made fresh lemonade. Would you care for some?" Esther asked.

"That sounds good," Mom said.

Susan and Rachel nodded.

"I'll go inside and bring it out," Esther said.

"Do you need help?" Mom asked.

"That's all right; I can manage." Esther went into the house and returned a few minutes later with a pitcher of lemonade and four paper cups.

"Umm. . .this is refreshing." Susan smiled. "Thank you, Esther."

"You're welcome." Esther moved over to the porch swing and was about to sit, when Rudy rushed out of the barn, hollering and waving his hands. "Come back here, you silly *gees* [goat]!"

Ma-a-a! Ma-a-a! The goat leaped over the laundry basket under Esther's clothesline and darted across the lawn. Rudy's feet slipped on the grass, and he nearly fell, but righted himself and continued the chase.

Rachel thought Rudy might need some help, so she hopped off the porch and raced after the goat.

The frisky critter zipped under Rudy's legs, circled twice around Rachel, and headed back toward the laundry basket. Rachel lunged for the goat, but it slipped through her hands, and she fell on her knees. "Ach, stupid *gees*!" she shouted.

Ma-a-a-a! The goat backed up and stood there, as if taunting her.

Rachel clambered to her feet and lunged again, but the goat darted toward Rudy.

Ma-a-a! Ma-a-a! Ma-a-a!

Rudy sprinted to the left. Rachel scuttled to the right. Mom, Esther, and Susan stood on the porch cheering them on. Suddenly, the goat scampered to Rachel and stopped.

She squinted. For some reason the goat looked blurry. She blinked a couple of times and reached up to touch her glasses. They were gone!

Rachel gasped. "My glasses! Where are my glasses?"

"Be careful!" Mom shouted. "Your glasses are on the ground behind you!"

Rachel turned, and—*wham!*—she was knocked to the ground.

"*Dumm* [dumb] gees," she muttered, realizing the goat had butted her.

Rudy grabbed the goat. "Are you all right, Rachel?"

"I—I'm okay." She scooped up her glasses and scrambled to her feet.

"I'm real sorry," Rudy said. "That mischievous goat never misses an opportunity to butt someone."

Mom left the porch and rushed across the lawn. "Ach, I hope your glasses aren't broken!"

"I—I think they're okay." Rachel handed them to Mom.

Mom studied the glasses and smiled. "Thankfully, they're fine." She gave them back to Rachel. "Maybe I can rig up an elastic strap that connects to the earpiece and fits around the back of your head so you won't lose your glasses when you're outside playing."

Rachel wrinkled her nose. She didn't like the sound of that. Even if the children at school didn't make fun of her glasses, someone—probably Jacob—would surely tease her if she wore a strange strap around the back of her head. "No Mom, please!" she said. "I'll be careful not to let my glasses fall off my face."

"We can talk about this later," Mom said. "We need to get home so I can start supper."

Rachel nodded. After that wild goat chase, she was more than ready to go home.

When Susan pulled up to the house, Rachel thanked her, climbed out, and hurried inside while Mom paid for the ride. Rachel could hardly wait to show her new glasses to everyone in the family. She hoped they liked them as much as Mom and Esther did.

She spotted Grandpa in the rocking chair in the living room. His eyes were closed, and she wondered if he was asleep.

When she stepped into the room, he opened his eyes and greeted her with a smile. He leaned forward so fast the rocker almost tipped him out. "Your glasses look real nice, Rachel. Can you see better now?"

She nodded. "When I'm wearing them, nothing looks blurry."

"That's good to hear. It's not fun to have blurry vision."

"You only wear glasses for reading, right?"

Grandpa nodded. "Have for a good many years."

"The eye doctor said if I wear my glasses for a couple of years, I might not have to wear them all the time." Rachel frowned. "I'm worried that he might have said that just to make me feel better, though. What if I have to wear them for the rest of my life?"

"That wouldn't be so bad," he said. "Your mamm's worn glasses for a good many years, and she's never complained."

Rachel glanced at Mom, who'd just stepped into the living room.

"Sorry we're late," Mom said. "We stopped by Esther's so she could see Rachel's glasses, and then Rachel and Rudy got involved in a wild goat chase."

Grandpa chuckled. "I've chased plenty of goats in my day, I'll tell you. Always left me feeling plenty *mied* [tired]."

Rachel nodded. "I was feeling meid after our goat chase, too."

"That's how it usually is after a good goat chase." Grandpa tugged his earlobe. "I remember one day when I was boy, my daed's old billy goat stole my hat and chewed off the brim. So I took out after him and we ran around the yard so many times we made a path in the grass."

Mom clucked her tongue. "Ach, how you exaggerate, Dad."

"I'm not exaggerating." Grandpa shook his head. "That story really happened, just the way I told it."

"Did you ever catch the goat?" Rachel asked.

"Sure did. I caught him out behind the barn when he was trying to get through the fence." Grandpa pulled his other earlobe. "Silly goat ended up getting his head caught instead."

Rachel snickered. It was nice to know she wasn't the only one who'd ever had trouble with a goat.

Just then, the back door squeaked open, and Pap entered the room.

"Hi, Pap. Do you notice anything new about me?" Rachel asked, stepping up to him.

He studied her a few seconds and smiled. "Are you wearing a new dress?"

She shook her head.

He glanced down at her feet. "New shoes?"

"*Nee* [No]. They're the same shoes I had on this morning."

"Hmm. . ." Pap stroked his beard then rubbed the bridge of his nose. "Now I wonder what could be new with my Rachel today?"

Mom poked Pap's arm and rolled her eyes. "Your daughter got her new glasses this afternoon, Levi."

Pap leaned closer to Rachel, studied her for a few seconds, and grinned. "Well, well. . .so you did. Those glasses are nice, Rachel. Jah, very nice indeed."

"What's very nice?" Henry asked when he entered the room.

"Your sister's new glasses." Pap motioned to Rachel.

"Come see what you think."

Henry moved over to Rachel. "I see you picked out some blue ones to match your eyes."

She nodded. "Do you think they look all right?"

"They look more than all right. They look *fehlerfrie* [perfect] for you."

Rachel smiled. "Danki, Henry."

Jacob stepped into the room. "I'm finished with my chores. How soon till supper?"

"It'll be a while," Mom said. "Rachel and I were at the optical shop, and then we stopped by Esther and Rudy's to show them her new glasses."

Jacob squinted at Rachel.

"What do you think?" she asked.

"I didn't realize your glasses would be so thick." Jacob's lips turned up at the corners. "Ha! Now you have four eyes instead of two!"

"What?" Rachel's chin trembled, and her eyes filled with tears.

Mom frowned at Jacob. "Apologize to your sister for saying such a mean thing."

"Your mamm's right," Pap put in. "That remark was uncalled for and not even true."

"Sorry, Rachel," Jacob mumbled.

Rachel didn't reply. She raced to the bathroom and looked in the mirror. *Do I really look like I have four eyes? If I do, I don't see how I can go to school tomorrow. I'll have to come up with a good reason to stay home.*

Chapter 8

Jacob's Promise

Bam! Bam! Bam! "Mom wants you downstairs for breakfast!" Jacob called as he banged on Rachel's bedroom door. "If we don't eat now, we'll be late for school!"

Rachel pulled the covers over her head.

"Schnell, Rachel! Schnell!"

"Okay, okay. I'll be there soon." Rachel climbed out of bed and hurried to get dressed. She still hadn't come up with a good reason to stay home from school today, but she hoped she could think of something during breakfast.

Or maybe, she thought as she slipped into her shoes, *I won't wear my glasses at school.*

Rachel left her glasses lying on her dresser, hurried from her room, and rushed downstairs.

"*Guder mariye* [Good morning]," Mom said when Rachel entered the kitchen. "We're ready to eat, so have a seat at the table."

Rachel pulled out the chair beside Grandpa and sat down.

Pap looked at Rachel and frowned. "Where are your glasses?"

"I—I left them in my room."

Mom placed a bowl of oatmeal in front of Rachel. "Be sure you get them right after breakfast."

Rachel fiddled with the edge of her napkin. "Maybe I—uh—shouldn't wear them today."

"Why not?" Pap asked. "You're supposed to wear them all the time, right?"

"Jah, but—" Rachel could barely speak around the lump in her throat. She took a drink of milk. "What if the kinner laugh at me the way Jacob did last night? What if someone calls me 'four eyes'?"

"I'm sure no one at school will tease you about your glasses," Mom said, sitting on the other side of Rachel. "Elizabeth would never allow such a thing." She looked at Jacob and frowned. "You'd better not tease your sister about wearing glasses again."

"Okay, Mom," Jacob said with a nod.

"What if someone teases me during recess when Elizabeth's not there to hear?" Rachel asked.

"Then you should find the teacher and tell her what was said," Henry spoke up.

"If I do that, the kinner will call me a *retschbeddi* [tattletale]."

Jacob looked at Rachel and wrinkled his nose. "That's because you *are* a retschbeddi."

"Am not."

"Are so."

"Am not."

"Are so."

"Am—"

"That will be enough!" Pap said loudly. "Now bow your heads for silent prayer, and be sure when you pray that you make things right with God for arguing with each other this morning."

As Rachel headed to school wearing her glasses, she noticed the colorful flowers along the way. She wished she had time to stop and pick a few.

She looked at the fluffy clouds floating lazily overhead. It would be nice to lie in the grass and study the shapes of the clouds.

When they came to a tree where some birds were singing, Rachel stopped and listened to their melody.

Jacob nudged her arm. "Hurry up, slowpoke. You're gonna make us late to school if you don't keep walking."

"I am walking."

"No you're not. You've been looking at the sky and stopping every few minutes to smell the flowers."

"I haven't been smelling the flowers; I've only looked at them."

"Whatever you say, little bensel."

Rachel frowned. "Mom said you weren't supposed to tease me."

"I wasn't teasing." Jacob kicked a pebble with the toe

of his boot. "You *are* a little bensel."

"I am not a silly child, and you'd better stop calling me that!"

"I will, when you stop acting like one." Jacob walked faster. "See you at school!"

When Rachel arrived at the schoolhouse, the bell was already ringing. She hurried inside and put her lunch pail on the shelf.

"I see you got new glasses," Orlie said. "They sure make you look different."

"Different in a good way?" she asked hopefully.

Orlie shrugged and grinned. "I think they make you look like you've got four eyes." He looked at Audra's brother, Brian, and said, "Don't you think Rachel looks like she has four eyes?"

Brian stared at Rachel a few seconds; then he looked back at Orlie. "I think her glasses look like *schlang aage* [snake eyes]."

Rachel clenched her fingers. "Have you two been talking to Jacob?"

Orlie shook his head. "Huh-uh."

Audra put her lunch pail on the shelf beside Rachel's. "Don't listen to Orlie and Brian. They just like to tease." She patted Rachel's arm. "I think your glasses are nice. They make you look grown up and real *schmaert* [smart]."

"Do you really think they make me look smart?"

Audra nodded. "Sure do."

Brian nudged Audra's arm. "That's *lecherich* [ridiculous]. Glasses don't make a person look smart. They just tell the world you can't see."

"I'm sure Rachel can see real well now that she's got glasses," Audra said. "Isn't that true, Rachel?"

Rachel nodded. She was glad Audra had stuck up for her, but after the comments Brian, Orlie, and Jacob had made, she didn't feel smart or grown up. She felt ugly in her glasses. Maybe she shouldn't wear them at school anymore. Maybe she should only wear them at home.

After lunch, Rachel went outside for recess. She spotted Jacob and some other boys sitting on one end of the fence. Orlie was there, too, only he stood on the other end of the fence—his left foot on one railing—his right foot on the railing above.

"*Bass uff as du net fallscht* [Take care you don't fall]," Rachel told him.

He grinned. "Don't worry; I won't."

"I thought I wouldn't fall from the tree when I tried to rescue Cuddles," she said, "but remember what happened?"

He nodded. "You broke your arm."

"That's right, and if you fall, you might break something, too."

"Ah, you worry too much. I know what I'm doing."

Orlie wrinkled his freckled nose. "And just because you're wearing glasses that make you look scholarly doesn't mean you're smarter than me."

Rachel shook her head—one quick shake, and then another. "I don't think I'm smarter; I'm just saying you could get hurt if you're not careful."

His lips twitched with a smile, and he puffed out his chest. "Want to see me stand on one leg?"

"No."

"Well, here I go!" Orlie pulled his left leg up so he stood with both legs on the top railing. Then, holding his arms straight out to keep his balance, he lifted his right leg.

Rachel's heart thumped in her chest as Orlie wobbled. She glanced over to see if Jacob saw what Orlie had done, but he was talking to Brian and didn't seem to notice.

"Orlie, please come down from there," she pleaded.

"Aw, quit worrying; I'm doin' fine." He switched to the other leg, and—*whoosh!*—tumbled right to the ground.

Rachel's heart pounded. She rushed forward and dropped beside Orlie. "Are you okay?"

Orlie stared at her, his mouth opening and closing like a fish out of water.

The boys who'd been sitting on the fence hopped down and crowded around Orlie.

"Are you hurt?"

"Did you break anything?"

"Should we get the teacher?"

Everyone spoke at once.

Orlie grunted and pulled himself to a sitting position. "I—I'm okay. Just had the wind knocked out of me."

Rachel clucked her tongue, the way Mom often did, and shook her finger at Orlie. "I told you standing on the fence was a bad idea. You're lucky you weren't hurt. You'd better not do that again."

Orlie stood and brushed the dirt from his trousers. "You're not my mamm, Rachel. You have no right to be tellin' me what to do." *Aaa-choo!* He sneezed.

"When you do foolish things, someone needs to tell you about it." Rachel looked at Jacob. "Standing on the fence with one leg is dumm, isn't it?"

Jacob shrugged. "If Orlie wants to stand on the fence with one leg or two, that's up to him." He pointed at Rachel. "You, little bensel, should mind your own business!"

Hot tears pushed against Rachel's eyelids, and she gritted her teeth. Why couldn't Jacob stick up for her—especially when he should know she was right?

Rachel whirled around and walked away. Maybe swinging would make her feel better.

"Where ya goin'?" Orlie called after her.

Rachel kept walking.

"She's probably going to look for some flowers to smell." Jacob snickered. "Now that she's got new glasses, she can see what she's smelling!" He tipped his head back and howled with laughter.

The other boys joined right in. "Ha! Ha! Ha!"

"Say, Rachel," Brian hollered, "how's it feel to have four eyes? Do those glasses make you see double?"

Rachel covered her ears to block out their teasing and ran as fast as she could. She didn't want to swing now, so she headed for the schoolhouse.

"Four eyes!"

"Snake eyes!"

"Little bensel!"

The boys scampered past Rachel and raced up the schoolhouse stairs, laughing all the way.

Audra caught up to Rachel and slipped her arm around Rachel's waist. "You should tell the teacher on them. It's not right the way they tease."

Rachel sniffed and swiped at the tears running down her cheeks. "If I tell, they'll call me a retschbeddi and tease me even more."

"Maybe I should tell the teacher then," Audra said.

Rachel shook her head. "Please don't. I'll think of some way to deal with this."

On the way to school the following morning, Rachel made a decision. She decided to take off her glasses before she got to school and put them back on before she got home.

She stopped near the schoolhouse driveway,

removed her glasses, and put them inside the small case she'd put in her backpack.

Jacob frowned at Rachel. "What are you doing?"

"What's it look like?"

"It looks like you're not planning to wear your glasses today."

She nodded. "That's right."

"Why?"

"Because I don't like being called 'four eyes', 'snake eyes', and 'little bensel'."

"Okay, I won't tease you anymore," Jacob said.

"That won't keep Brian and Orlie from teasing." She started walking again. "I've thought it through, and I've decided not to wear my glasses at school."

"But if you're not wearing your glasses, then how will you see?"

Rachel shrugged. "I'll get by. I got by before, and I'll do it again."

"Don't be lecherich, Rachel. You have to wear your glasses."

"No, I don't."

"Jah, you do. Mom and Pap would be very upset if they knew you weren't wearing your glasses."

Rachel grabbed Jacob's arm. "Promise you won't say anything?"

He shook his head. "I can't promise that. It would be wrong to lie, and you know it."

"I'm not saying you should lie. Just don't tell them

I'm not wearing my glasses."

Jacob folded his arms and tapped his foot. "Hmm. . . I don't know, Rachel."

"If you keep quiet, I'll do one of your chores for a whole week."

His eyebrows shot up. "Really?"

She nodded. "Just name a chore—any chore at all, and I'll do it."

"Okay. You can feed and water Buddy."

Rachel wrinkled her nose. "You know what will happen if I go anywhere near that mangy dog of yours."

"Okay, forget I mentioned it. I'll just tell Mom and Pap you put your glasses in your backpack and didn't wear them at school today."

"If you do that you'll be a retschbeddi."

He shrugged. "So, I'll be a tattletale. At least I'll be telling something they should know."

Rachel rubbed her chin as she thought. If she continued to wear her glasses at school, Orlie and Brian would make fun of her. If she didn't wear them and Jacob told Mom and Pap, she'd be in big trouble.

"Oh, all right," she finally agreed. "I'll feed and water Buddy for one week."

As Rachel sat behind her school desk that morning, her stomach knotted. Not only had she promised to feed and water Jacob's flea-bitten mutt, but now that she wasn't wearing her glasses, she couldn't see the writing on the blackboard or read her schoolbooks well.

"*Psst...* Audra," Rachel whispered as she leaned across the aisle. "What do the words on the blackboard say?"

"You'd know what they said if you were wearing your glasses." Audra wrinkled her nose. "Why aren't you wearing them?"

Rachel started to respond, but Elizabeth stepped up to her desk. "What's all the talking about, Rachel?"

"She was asking me what's written on the blackboard," Audra said.

Elizabeth looked at Rachel curiously. "Why aren't you wearing your glasses?"

Rachel bit her lip as she tried to think of how to answer her teacher's question.

Elizabeth tapped her foot. "I'm waiting, Rachel."

"Well, I—uh—don't have my glasses with me today."

"Why not?"

Rachel swallowed. She knew it was wrong to lie but was afraid to tell the truth. If she told Elizabeth that her glasses were in her backpack, Elizabeth would ask why. Then she'd have to tattle on the boys who had made fun of her.

Elizabeth touched Rachel's shoulder. "Why didn't you bring your glasses with you today?"

"I—uh—forgot them."

"I see. Well, since you're having a problem seeing the blackboard, I'm going to move your desk close to the front of the room like I did before you got glasses."

Elizabeth pushed Rachel's desk to the front row.

Rachel followed with her head down. She heard a few snickers from some of the boys and ground her teeth. If she had to sit up front every day, all the scholars would watch her. On the other hand, if she admitted that she'd lied about leaving her glasses at home, she'd be in trouble with Elizabeth and be embarrassed in front of the class.

Rachel bit the end of a fingernail. *Why do I always have so much trouble?*

Chapter 9

Plenty of Trouble

When Rachel headed to school the next day, she stopped near the schoolhouse driveway, took off her glasses, and put them in her backpack.

"I forgot to ask. . .how'd it go when you fed Buddy last night?" Jacob asked.

"It went fine. He was so hungry he headed straight for his food." Rachel smiled. "I was surprised he didn't lick me, not even once."

"That's good, I guess." Jacob leaned close to Rachel. "So how long do you plan to keep taking your glasses off before you get to school?"

She shrugged.

"You're not gonna do well with your schoolwork if you can't see."

"I can see. Some things are blurry, that's all."

"Jah, well, Mom and Pap paid good money for those glasses, and you should be wearing them to school."

Rachel yanked the zipper closed on her backpack.

"I might wear them to school if I knew certain people wouldn't say mean things!"

"Want me to have a talk with Orlie and Brian?"

She shook her head. "They'd probably think I was a retschbeddi who had to ask her older bruder to speak for her."

"Then speak to them yourself. Wouldn't that be better than not being able to see clearly and lying about forgetting to bring your glasses to school?"

Rachel thought about that a few seconds. She didn't feel good about lying, but she didn't feel good about being made fun of, either. Would it help if she tried talking to Orlie and Brian? If she could get them to stop teasing, she'd be able to wear her glasses at school again.

She glanced across the playground and saw Orlie near the swings, talking to Brian. *Maybe I will try talking to them,* she decided. "I'll be right back," she said to Jacob.

"Where are you going?" he asked.

"I'm going to have a little talk with Orlie and Brian."

"Want me to come with you?"

"No thanks. I think I should do this on my own."

"Okay, suit yourself."

Rachel hurried off. By the time she got to the swings, only Orlie was there. Brian was on the teeter-totter with Audra.

"Hey, Rachel," Orlie said, "I see you're not wearing your other set of eyes today. You sure look funny in those glasses."

Rachel shook her finger. "You should be ashamed of yourself for saying such mean things to me. I used to think you were my friend, but not anymore."

A smile flickered across Orlie's face. "Aw, come on, Rachel, don't take everything so personally." He brushed past her as the school bell rang. "See you inside, four eyes."

Rachel grimaced. She'd probably never be able to wear her glasses to school without being teased. She stomped toward the schoolhouse. *I'll probably be feeding and watering Jacob's dog until I graduate from school!*

"Where are your glasses?" Elizabeth asked when Rachel sat at her desk.

"I—I forgot them again." Each lie Rachel told seemed to cause another lie, and even though she knew it was wrong, she couldn't seem to stop.

"You'll have to sit close to the blackboard then," Elizabeth said. "And if you keep forgetting your glasses, I'll have to send a note home to your parents asking that they remind you to wear them to school."

Rachel gulped. She couldn't let that happen. She'd have to think of something to keep Mom and Pap from finding out she hadn't worn her glasses to school for two days, and she'd have to think of it soon!

"Good morning, boys and girls," Elizabeth said after she'd tapped the bell on her desk."

"Good morning, Elizabeth," the scholars replied.

Elizabeth opened her Bible and read a verse of scripture, but Rachel didn't even hear the words. All she could think about was how miserable she felt, and wondered what to do about her glasses.

When it was time to do her schoolwork, Rachel had to lean close to her book to read. Even then, some words were blurry, and her eyes watered from staring so hard. She was tempted to turn around and ask Phoebe to tell her what some of the words were, but if she did that and Elizabeth saw her, she'd be in trouble again.

Hee-hee. Rachel heard snickering to her right, and she glanced that way. Brian grinned at her as he made circles with his fingers and then held them in front of his eyes like he was wearing glasses.

Rachel swallowed hard and looked away. She was going to cry if she wasn't careful.

Brian snickered again, but Rachel refused to look at him.

On the way home from school that day, Rachel waited until they were a safe distance from the schoolhouse. Then she opened her backpack, took out her glasses, and put them on her face. It was a relief to be able to see things clearly again. She wished she felt free to wear her glasses at school.

"What are you going to do when we get home?" Jacob asked.

She shrugged. "I don't know."

"Don't forget about feeding and watering Buddy."

"I won't forget." She groaned. "But I wish I could."

Jacob poked her arm. "Aw, you'll get used to it after a while. You might even think it's kind of fun."

Rachel glared at him. "I'll never get used to that mutt's smelly breath or his slimy tongue slurping my face. He's nothing but a big hairy mutt!"

Jacob chuckled and sprinted for home.

When Rachel entered their yard, she spotted Grandpa in the garden. He called her over to him. "Let's go see what Grandpa wants," Rachel said when she caught up to Jacob.

"You go ahead," he said. "I'm going to change into my work clothes and help Pap and Henry in the fields."

"Okay. See you at supper." Rachel sprinted across the yard to the garden.

"How was your day, Rachel?" Grandpa asked. A smudge of dirt decorated his cheek, and if Rachel hadn't felt so sad, she might have laughed.

"My day was all right."

"Just all right?"

She nodded slowly.

"Well, how would you like to help me plant some seeds?"

"Are they vegetable seeds or flower seeds?"

"They're flower seeds, and when the flowers get big enough, I hope to sell some of them in my greenhouse." Grandpa's blue eyes twinkled like fireflies on a hot summer evening, and his bushy gray eyebrows jiggled. "Even though the building's not up yet, I need to prepare and stock up on things."

"I guess that's a good idea," Rachel said.

"So, would you like to help me?"

"Jah, okay. I'll plant some seeds."

"You should run into the house and change out of your school clothes first," Grandpa said.

She nodded. "I'll do that right now."

Rachel scurried into the house. She stopped in the kitchen long enough to tell Mom hello, then rushed upstairs to change out of her school dress. When she came down a few minutes later, she saw a plate of peanut butter cookies on the table.

"Jacob had a few cookies before he went out to the fields," Mom said. "Would you like to sit at the table and have something to eat?"

She shook her head. "I don't have time. I'm going to help Grandpa plant some flower seeds."

"Why don't you take a few cookies for you and Grandpa?" Mom suggested.

"That's a good idea. Grandpa might be hungry." Rachel plucked four cookies off the plate, wrapped them in a napkin, and scooted out the door. Her bare feet tingled as she skipped across the lawn. Maybe this wasn't such a bad day after all.

"Are you hungry? Mom sent some cookies for us," Rachel said when she joined Grandpa in the garden.

"That sounds good. I've been working hard, and the hurrier I go the behinder I seem to get. Maybe a little break and some tasty cookies will fuel my fire."

Rachel smiled. Grandpa Schrock always said such funny things. She remembered him saying that he liked to tell one joke every day.

Rachel opened the napkin, gave Grandpa two cookies, and ate the other two. "If you're tired, why don't you sit on the porch and rest?" she suggested.

"That's not a bad idea," he said. "After I show you what to do, I might sit a few minutes and rest my back."

"Is your back hurting today?"

"Not really, but it gets a little stiff if I try to do too much."

"Then you'd better sit." Rachel patted Grandpa's hand. "Once you show me what to do, I'm sure I can manage."

"I'm sure you can, too." Grandpa smiled. "Are you getting used to your glasses, Rachel?"

"Uh—jah, I guess so."

"I'll bet you're doing better in school now that you can see things more clearly."

Rachel swallowed. *What would Grandpa think if he knew I've been taking my glasses off at school? He'd probably lecture me and tell Mom and Pap.*

"It'll sure be exciting when we have a greenhouse," Rachel said.

Grandpa nodded. "I love working with flowers. Every

day in my new greenhouse will be exciting for me."

"I hope I'll be able to help out."

"When you're not doing other things, I'd appreciate the help." He handed her a packet of seeds. "Are you ready to plant?"

"Jah, sure."

Grandpa explained which seeds Rachel should plant and where he wanted them planted. "I'll give you one packet now, and when you finish that, if you still want to help, you can have more."

"Okay, Grandpa."

"Guess I'll head to the porch now and stretch out on a lawn chair for a little while." Grandpa turned to go but stubbed his bare toe on a rock and yelped.

"Are you okay?" Rachel asked, rushing forward.

"It smarts a bit, but I'll be all right." A smile spread across Grandpa's face. "Do you know what a big toe is best used for?" he asked.

She shook her head.

"It's a way to locate sharp objects in the dark," he said with a deep chuckle. "I've always been good at stubbing my toe whenever I get out of bed at night."

Rachel snickered. What a fun-loving grandpa she had. She wished she could feel this happy all the time.

Grandpa patted the top of Rachel's head. "I'm off to rest now. Let me know when you need more seeds."

"Okay."

When Grandpa walked away, Rachel took the tip

of her shovel and made a long, shallow rut in the dirt. Then she opened the packet of sunflower seeds and was about to drop some into the dirt, when—*floop!*— Cuddles leaped into the air and hit her hand, scattering seeds everywhere.

"Ach Cuddles, now look what you've done! I'll never get all these seeds picked up!" Rachel glanced at the house to see if Grandpa had seen what happened, but he didn't move. She figured he'd fallen asleep.

Ribet! Ribet! Rachel spotted a frog leaping through the garden. Since she couldn't do much with the seeds Grandpa had given her, she thought it might be fun to try and catch the frog.

She crawled slowly along, and when the frog stopped beneath one of the rhubarb plants, Rachel reached out her hand.

Meow! Cuddles leaped through the air and pounced in the dirt near the frog.

The frog jumped. *Ribet! Ribet!*

Cuddles jumped. *Meow! Meow!*

Back and forth across the garden they dashed, kicking up the dirt and scattering the sunflower seeds Rachel had spilled. She didn't know whether to laugh or cry.

Ribet! Ribet! The frog hopped out of the garden and leaped away.

Cuddles chased it.

Rachel grunted and brushed the dirt from her dress.

Then she hurried across the lawn. When she stepped onto the porch, she saw that Grandpa's eyes were closed. She didn't know whether she should wake him or not.

Suddenly, Grandpa's eyes snapped open. "What's wrong, Rachel?" he asked. "You're clenching your teeth so hard your cheeks are twitching."

"I had some problems with the seeds," she said.

He yawned and stretched his arms over his head. "What kind of problems?"

"Cuddles was fooling around in the garden and landed on my hand." Rachel frowned. "Then she chased after a frog, and now the seeds are scattered everywhere."

Grandpa reached into his pocket and took out another packet of seeds. "I guess we'll have to start all over again."

"What about the scattered seeds?"

Grandpa squeezed Rachel's shoulder. "Some of the seeds will make a nice meal for the birds that come into our yard, and the rest will probably come up wherever they choose."

Rachel smiled as she followed Grandpa to the garden. She was glad she had such a nice grandfather. He hadn't even yelled or given her a lecture for spilling the seeds.

After Rachel finished helping Grandpa plant two rows of seeds, she went to do her most dreaded chore— feeding and watering Jacob's smelly mutt.

She found the dog food in the barn and scooped some into an empty coffee can. When she got to the dog run, she set the can of food on the ground and struggled to open the squeaky, stubborn gate.

I wish Pap would oil this, Rachel thought. *But if I ask him about it, he'll probably want to know what I was doing in Buddy's dog run. Then I'll have to explain that I was giving food and water to Buddy, and Pap will ask why.* Rachel gritted her teeth. *No, it's best not to say anything about the stubborn gate. After my week of caring for Buddy is over, feeding and watering that unruly hund will be Jacob's worry.*

With another push on the gate, Rachel entered the dog run. She was about to pour food into Buddy's dish when he bounded up to her wagging his tail. *Woof! Woof! Slurp! Slurp!* He licked her face with his long, pink tongue.

"Get down, you hairy beast!" Rachel pushed Buddy with her knee.

Woof! Woof! Buddy swiped his tongue across her arm.

"Leave me alone! It's time for your supper!" Rachel poured the food into his dish and quickly stepped aside.

Buddy stuck his nose in the dish. *Chomp! Chomp! Chomp!*

Rachel hurried out of the dog run and raced across the yard to get the hose. When she returned to fill Buddy's water dish, he jumped up and knocked the hose out of her hands. A stream of water shot straight up and squirted Rachel's face!

"Now look what you've done, you—you dumm hund!" Rachel sputtered. "Thanks to you, my face is wet!"

Woof! Woof! Buddy darted out of the dog run and tore across the yard.

Rachel chased him. "Come back here, you beast!"

"What's Buddy doing out of his dog run?" Jacob asked as he came around the side of the barn.

"He got out after he knocked the hose out of my hand." Rachel sniffed. "Thanks to that mutt, my face is wet!"

"Don't cry, Rachel," Jacob said with a grin. "You're already wet enough."

She grunted. "You'd better teach that hund some manners, or I'm not going to feed and water him anymore!"

"If you back out of our agreement, I'll tell Mom and Pap that you haven't worn your glasses at school for two days," Jacob threatened.

"You wouldn't."

"Jah, I would."

Rachel squeezed her hands into a ball. "You do and I'll tell that you teased me about my glasses, even after you said you wouldn't."

Jacob shrugged. "Go ahead. I'll bet you'll be in a lot more trouble for not wearing your glasses at school than I will for teasing you."

Rachel sighed. "All right, you win." She started for

the house but turned back around. "What are you doing here anyway, Jacob? I thought you were supposed to be out in the field helping Pap and Henry."

"I was, but Pap needed something from the barn. I'll put Buddy back in his pen first, though."

"Good luck with that." Rachel handed Jacob the empty coffee can and hurried away.

As she stepped onto the porch, the steps creaked beneath her feet; then she heard a bird whistling joyously from a nearby tree. Rachel tilted her head to get a good look at the bird. "At least somebody's happy today," she muttered.

She opened the door and was greeted with a wonderful aroma coming from the kitchen.

"What are you cooking?" Rachel asked Mom.

Mom turned from the stove and smiled. "Come take a look."

Rachel peered into the kettle sitting on the stove. Chunks of vegetables, slivers of meat, and floating spices made her mouth water. She loved Mom's tasty stews. "Mmm. . .I can't wait for supper."

Mom turned down the stove and shuffled across the room. "Your hair and face are wet, Rachel," she said, lowering herself into a chair. "What did you do, take a drink from the hose?"

Rachel's thoughts tumbled around in her head like a windmill going full speed as she searched for the right words. "I—uh—got shot in the face with the hose when

I was giving Jacob's dog some water."

Mom raised her eyebrows. "Caring for Buddy is supposed to be Jacob's job. Why were you doing it?"

Rachel shifted from one foot to the other. "I—uh—was doing Jacob a favor." The lie stuck in her throat like a glob of gooey peanut butter, only it didn't taste good.

Mom tapped her fingers on the edge of the table. "Did Jacob do a favor for you?"

Rachel shook her head.

"So you just gave Buddy some water to be nice?"

"Uh—jah."

Mom smiled. "That was kind of you. It shows that you're maturing."

Rachel swallowed so hard she nearly choked. "I'm going to the bathroom to wash my hands. When I come back, I'll set the table."

"Danki, Rachel. Take your time."

With the lie she'd told Mom still burning in her throat, Rachel dashed from the room.

Chapter 10

Vanished

When Rachel fed and watered Buddy the next day, things went much better. He licked her hand when she poured food in his dish, but then he ate and left her alone.

"Good dog," Rachel said. She hurried out of the dog run and closed the gate.

Rachel raced back to the barn and put the empty can in the bag of dog food. She'd just turned around when she heard a faint *meow*. Cuddles was curled up on a bale of hay, licking her paws.

Rachel sat on the hay and placed the cat in her lap. "Did you have a hard day today, Cuddles?"

Cuddles nuzzled Rachel's hand with her little pink nose.

"My day wasn't easy, either," Rachel said. "I lied to my teacher and said I forgot to wear my glasses again."

Purrr. . .Purrr. Cuddles kneaded her paws against Rachel's chest.

"Yesterday Elizabeth said if I forgot my glasses again

she would give me a note to take home." Rachel leaned against the wall behind her. "But I think Elizabeth forgot about the note because she never mentioned it again. She has been making me sit near the front of the room though."

Cuddles lifted her head and opened one eye. *Meow!*

Rachel stroked the cat's ear and closed her eyes. *What can I do about the problem with my glasses?* she wondered. *If I lost my glasses, I wouldn't have to wear them at all, and I wouldn't have to keep telling Elizabeth I left them at home.*

Rachel placed Cuddles on the bale of hay. She glanced around the barn, wondering where she might safely put her glasses. She spotted a small box on a shelf near the door and went to look at it.

The box was empty, so she took off her glasses and placed them inside. Then she slipped the box under her arm and climbed the ladder to the hayloft.

Let's see. . .where's a good place to hide this box?

Rachel noticed several bales of hay stacked against the wall, so she wedged the box between them.

Screech. It sounded like someone had come into the barn. "Who's there?" Rachel called.

No response.

She listened. "Jacob, is that you?"

No answer—just a snorting sound coming from the stall where Pap kept his buggy horse.

Rachel scurried down the ladder and raced out of the barn.

When Rachel entered the kitchen, she found Mom in front of the sink, humming as she peeled potatoes. "Is it time to start supper?" Rachel asked.

"I've started the potatoes, so you can set the table." Mom turned from the sink. "Ach, Rachel, why aren't you wearing your glasses?"

"Well, I—uh—don't know where they are." Another lie slid off Rachel's tongue as easily as she and Jacob slid down the hay chute in their barn. One lie seemed to lead to another. . .and another. . .and another.

Mom's eyebrows shot up. "You lost your glasses?"

Rachel nodded and stared at the floor.

"You were wearing them when you got home from school, right?"

"Jah."

"Where'd you put them?"

"I—I don't know."

"Think about it, Rachel. Did you take them off to wash your face after school?"

Rachel shook her head. "I haven't washed my face since this morning."

"Where have you been since you got home? Let's retrace your steps."

Rachel's heart pounded. She hated lying to Mom, but if she told the truth now, she'd be in big trouble—and she'd be forced to wear her glasses at school.

"Where have you been?" Mom asked again.

"I—uh—took a walk to the garden, and then I

went to—" Rachel halted her words. She'd almost told Mom that she'd fed and watered Buddy again. If she let that slip, Mom would ask why she was doing Jacob's chore for the second day in a row, and she might get suspicious.

Mom started for the door. "Let's go outside and look for them. Maybe they fell off your face when you were in the garden. Or they could be somewhere on the lawn."

With shoulders slumped, Rachel followed Mom out the door.

When they reached the garden, Mom walked between the rows while Rachel stood to one side.

"What are you looking for, Miriam?" Grandpa asked when he joined them in the garden.

"Rachel's glasses," Mom said. "They seem to have vanished."

"Is that so?" Grandpa looked over at Rachel. "You were wearing your glasses when you came home from school; isn't that right?"

"Jah."

"Where have you been since you got here?" he asked.

Rachel kicked at a clump of grass. "I'm—uh—not sure."

"She said she came out here to the garden, but I don't see her glasses anywhere," Mom said.

Grandpa scratched his bearded cheek. "Did you go to your room to change your clothes after school?"

Rachel nodded.

"Maybe you left your glasses there."

"I don't think so." Every lie Rachel told burned in her throat like a lump of hot coal. She figured the best thing to do was go out to the barn, get her glasses, and say that she'd found them. "I—uh—think I know where I left them," she mumbled.

"Where would that be?" asked Mom.

"In the barn. I went there to pet Cuddles," Rachel said. "I'll go and see."

"I was going to walk out to the fields to see if your daed's done for the day," Grandpa said. "Maybe I should go to the barn and help you look for your glasses instead."

Rachel shook her head. "That's okay. I'm sure I can find them."

"All right then. I'm off to the fields." Grandpa headed in that direction.

"I'm going back in the house to finish peeling potatoes," Mom said. "If you don't find your glasses in the barn, let me know, and we'll get your daed and *brieder* [brothers] to help us look as soon as they come in from the fields."

"Okay." Rachel raced into the barn, scampered up the ladder to the hayloft, and dropped to her knees in front of the bales of hay. She slipped her hands into the place where she'd hidden the box and gasped. It was gone!

She searched again, looking between every bale

of hay. A chill rippled through her body. No box! No glasses! She knew she had no choice but to go back to the house and tell Mom that she'd hidden her glasses in the hayloft and now they were gone. A sudden thought shook her all the way to her toes. Someone must have found the box and taken it! But who?

With tears burning her eyes and legs trembling like a newborn colt, Rachel climbed down the ladder. She'd just stepped out of the barn when she spotted her schoolteacher's horse and buggy at the hitching rail.

It's almost suppertime. I wonder what Elizabeth's doing here?

Rachel hurried into the house and found Elizabeth in the kitchen, talking to Mom.

Mom frowned at Rachel. "Elizabeth has given me distressing news. She said you haven't worn your glasses at school for the last few days."

Thump! Thumpety! Thump! Thump! Rachel's heart hammered as she stared at the floor.

"Is it true, Rachel?" Mom asked.

"Jah."

"But you were wearing your glasses before you left for school every day this week. You never mentioned losing them until this afternoon."

Rachel shifted from one foot to the other as tears welled in her eyes. The lies she'd told had only made things worse. She wished she could take them all back.

"Rachel, answer me, please."

"I—I took off my glasses before I got to school, and I—I put them in my backpack," Rachel said in a quavering voice.

"But you told me you'd forgotten your glasses at home," Elizabeth said.

"I—I'm sorry I lied." *Sniff! Sniff!* Rachel wiped the tears rolling down her cheeks.

"I don't understand. Why did you lie about leaving your glasses at home?" Mom asked.

"Some of the boys at school made fun of my glasses, and I—I felt ugly wearing them." Rachel's voice broke on a sob. "So I—I decided not to w—wear them at school anymore."

"What?" Mom's mouth fell open, and her glasses slipped to the end of her nose.

"Why didn't you tell me about the teasing?" Elizabeth asked.

"I was afraid they'd call me a retschbeddi and tease me more."

"At times it's necessary to tell on someone, and this was one of those times." Elizabeth placed her hand on Rachel's shoulder. "Your glasses don't make you look ugly, and you shouldn't worry about what others think or say. It's important that you wear your glasses so you can see well enough to do your schoolwork."

"Elizabeth is right," Mom agreed. "You should have told her and us about the teasing, and you shouldn't have lied about losing your glasses."

Rachel nodded. "I know, and I'm truly sorry."

Mom touched the tip of Rachel's nose. "Where are your glasses now? Are they really lost, or did you put them in your backpack again?"

Rachel swallowed around the lump in her throat. "I—I put them in a box I found in the barn, and I hid them in the hayloft."

"Then you'd better get them, schnell," Mom said.

"I went there a few minutes ago," Rachel said tearfully, "but the box was gone." She drew in a shaky breath. "Now my glasses really *have* vanished."

Mom's forehead wrinkled. "You truly don't know where they are?"

Rachel shook her head. "I'm afraid I might never see my glasses again."

Just then the back door opened and Jacob stepped into the kitchen. "What's going on? I saw Elizabeth's horse and buggy outside."

"Your teacher came by to tell me that Rachel hasn't been wearing her glasses at school." Mom stared at Jacob. "Did you know that Rachel had been putting her glasses in her backpack before she got to school?"

Jacob nodded, and his face turned red.

"Why didn't you tell Elizabeth or us what was going on?"

"Well, I—"

Elizabeth cleared her throat. "I think I'd better head for home and let you work things out with your kinner."

122

"Jah, of course." Mom followed Elizabeth to the door. When she returned to the kitchen, she turned to Jacob and said, "I'd like to know why you kept quiet about Rachel not wearing her glasses at school."

"I made him promise not to," Rachel spoke up.

"Did you now?" Mom gave Jacob a curious stare. "What did Rachel promise to do in order for you to keep quiet?"

The color in Jacob's cheeks deepened. "She said she'd feed and water Buddy for a whole week."

Tap! Tap! Tap! Mom's foot thumped against the kitchen floor. "I'm disappointed in both of you." She slowly shook her head. "Now Rachel's glasses are missing, and if they're not found, we'll have to buy her a new pair." *Tap! Tap! Tap!* "That's money we don't have to spare right now."

"Rachel's glasses aren't lost," Jacob said. "I know where they are."

Rachel's mouth fell open and she gasped. "You do?"

He nodded. "I was in one of the horse's stalls when you hid your glasses in the hayloft. After you left the barn, I went up there and found the box. I hid it in my room."

"I thought I heard someone in the barn." Rachel glared at Jacob. "Why'd you take my glasses?"

"To teach you a lesson."

"What a mean thing to do, Jacob Yoder!" Rachel's chin trembled. "What were you trying to do—get me in trouble?"

"You're the one who didn't want to wear your glasses."

"That's true, but—"

Mom stepped between them. "No more quarreling! You both did wrong things, and you shall both be punished." She pointed to the stairs. "Jacob, go up to your room and get Rachel's glasses!"

"All right, Mom." Jacob hurried out of the room and sprinted up the stairs.

Mom turned to Rachel. "From now on you are to wear your glasses at school and at home. Is that clear?"

Rachel nodded as tears dribbled down her cheeks. "I will, Mom. Even if the kinner at school tease me, I promise I'll wear my glasses."

Chapter 11

Happy Medicine

I wish I could have stayed home today," Rachel mumbled as she and Jacob walked to school the next day. She picked up a twig and sent it flying. "And I wish I didn't have to wear glasses!"

Jacob pulled the strings on Rachel's kapp. "*Grummel net um mich rum* [Don't grumble around me]."

Rachel pushed his hand away. "I have good reason to grumble."

"Why?"

"You ought to know, Jacob. I have to wear my glasses to school, and when I get there, I'll have to put up with Orlie and Brian calling me names." Rachel kicked at a pebble. "If that's not bad enough, I have double chores to do for two whole weeks, and I can't go anywhere or do anything fun—all because we lied to Mom and Pap."

Jacob shook his head. "Not *we*, Rachel. It was *you* who lied. All I did was promise not to tell Mom and

Pap you weren't wearing your glasses at school."

Rachel ground her teeth together. "Humph! You forced me to feed and water your dumm hund!"

"I didn't force you to take care of Buddy. You said you'd do it if I kept quiet about the glasses." He poked her arm. "And don't forget, I have double chores, too. I'll be working late in the fields tonight, so I was wondering if you would feed Buddy for me."

"You're kidding, right?"

He shook his head.

"After all that mutt did to me the other day, you expect me to go back in his pen?" Rachel shook her head so hard the ties on her kapp flipped up in her face.

"No, I'm never feeding your hund again!"

He grunted. "Fine then! Be that way, little bensel!"

Rachel kicked another rock so hard it hurt her toe. She was tired of Jacob calling her a silly child, and she was worried about how things would go today at school.

When Rachel entered the school yard, she spotted Orlie on the porch. She wished he would move. She didn't want to be around him.

Rachel waited near the swings until the school bell rang. When Orlie went inside, she hurried up the stairs and into the schoolhouse. She halted when she saw Orlie standing near the shelf where their lunch pails were kept.

"I see you remembered to wear your glasses," Orlie said.

She brushed past him and put her lunch pail on the shelf.

Orlie followed. "Aren't you talking to me? Did you lose your voice on the way to school? Should we send out a search party to look for it?"

Rachel ground her teeth together, determined to ignore him.

"What's the matter, four eyes? Why are you wearing such a big old frown?"

"Leave me alone. I have nothing to say to you, Orlie Troyer!" Rachel whirled around and hurried to her desk.

Ding! Ding! Ding! Elizabeth rang the bell on her desk. "Good morning, boys and girls."

"Good morning, Elizabeth," Rachel said with the others in her class.

Elizabeth opened her Bible. "I'll be reading from Ephesians 4:32: 'Be kind and compassionate to one another, forgiving each other, just as in Christ God forgave you.'"

Elizabeth closed the Bible and looked at the class. "Before we recite the Lord's Prayer, there's something I'd like to say." She leaned forward with her elbows on the desk. "Poking fun at someone and making rude remarks is wrong. I won't tolerate anyone in this class making fun of another person for any reason at all. Do you understand?"

All heads bobbed up and down, and Rachel breathed a sigh of relief. She hoped none of the scholars would say mean things to her anymore.

During recess that afternoon, Rachel sat on a swing while most of the others played baseball.

"Hey, Rachel, aren't you going to join us?" Jacob called from the ball field.

Rachel shook her head. She was afraid if she played ball, her glasses might fall off. She remembered Mom saying she could make a special strap to hold the glasses in place, but Rachel had talked Mom out of it.

Orlie walked by Rachel and snickered.

"What's so funny?" she asked.

He held up four fingers and pointed to his eyes.

Rachel turned her head and looked the other way. Should she say something to their teacher or ignore Orlie's teasing?

She pumped her legs faster. *I'll ignore him. Jah, that would be the best thing to do.*

Rachel stayed on the swing until the ball game was over. When she headed to the schoolhouse, Brian sauntered up to her and made circles with his fingers and placed them around his eyes like he was looking through a pair of glasses.

Rachel looked away. She would ignore him just as she'd done with Orlie.

*Hisss. . .hisss. . .*Brian smirked at Rachel but didn't say a word. He headed for the schoolhouse, hissing like a snake all the way.

Audra grabbed her brother's arm. "Stop teasing Rachel! If you don't, I'm going to tell the teacher!"

"If you do, I'll tell Mom and Dad you're a retschbeddi."

"I don't care if you do tell them I'm a tattletale. You either stop teasing Rachel, or I'm going to tell Elizabeth!"

"Whatever," Brian mumbled as he walked away.

Audra hugged Rachel. "I'm sorry my bruder is such a *pescht* [pest]."

Rachel swallowed around the lump in her throat and struggled not to cry. "My life's been miserable ever since I got glasses. I wish I could see better without them."

"Try not to be so sad. If you ignore the boys, they'll get tired of teasing you." Audra patted Rachel's back. "Things will get better soon—you'll see."

Rachel kicked at a clump of grass. "I wish I *could* see."

Audra gave Rachel a strange look.

"I wish I could see without my glasses."

"Just be glad someone invented glasses. Millions of people in the world wouldn't be able to see well if it weren't for their glasses."

"I guess you're right," Rachel said. "Even so, I wish I wasn't one of the millions who need glasses."

When Rachel got home from school, Mom had a list of chores waiting for her. One of them was taking the dry towels off the line.

"I wish I didn't have so many chores all the time," Rachel grumbled as she lugged the wicker basket to the clothesline.

Plunk! Plunk! Plunk! She pulled the pins from the towels and dropped everything into the basket.

Rachel glanced across the yard and saw Cuddles running out of the barn. Tears trickled down Rachel's cheeks, and she reached up to wipe them away. *I wish I could play with Cuddles instead of doing chores. I wish I wasn't me.*

Rachel picked up the basket and turned toward the house. She'd only taken a few steps, when—*Honk! Honk!*—their mean old goose charged across the lawn. Rachel remembered the last time the goose had pecked the backs of her legs. She didn't want that to happen again, so she ran for all she was worth!

By the time Rachel reached the back porch, she was huffing and puffing so much she could barely catch her breath.

Thump! Thump! Thump! She hurried up the steps and turned to see if the goose had followed. *Honk! Honk!* The goose flapped her wings, stuck out her long neck, and pecked at the porch.

Rachel set the basket down and fluttered her hands. "Shoo! Shoo! Go away you ornery goose!"

Clip-clop! Clip-clop! A horse and buggy rolled into the yard. The horse whinnied and pawed the ground. The goose honked and waddled away.

"Good riddance," Rachel muttered.

"Hello, Rachel!" Esther called as she climbed down from the buggy. "Is Mom home?"

Rachel nodded. "She's in the house writing a letter to Aunt Irma."

Esther smiled as she stepped onto the porch. "I need to do some letter writing of my own." She patted her stomach. "But with the boppli coming this fall, I've been busy sewing baby clothes and painting the baby's room. So I haven't had the time to write any letters."

"Speaking of letters. . .I got one from Mary a few weeks ago."

"That's nice. What did Mary say?"

"She said they'd gone to the Fun Spot amusement park." Rachel groaned. "I asked Pap if he'd take us to Hershey Park sometime, but he said he was too busy, and that Mom wasn't up to such an outing right now."

"I don't expect she would be." Esther patted the top of Rachel's head. "Maybe after our baby brother or sister is born, Pap will take the whole family to Hershey Park."

Rachel folded her arms and frowned. "I doubt it. Once the boppli comes, Pap will probably think of some other reason we can't go."

Esther put her thumb under Rachel's chin and tipped her head up so Rachel was looking right at her. "Now what's that sour expression all about? You look like you've been sucking on a bunch of bitter grapes."

Rachel pointed to her glasses. "Ever since I got these, I've had nothing but trouble!"

"What kind of trouble?"

"Boys at school say mean things to me." Rachel sniffed. "Orlie called me 'four eyes,' and Brian said my glasses make me look like a snake."

Esther hugged Rachel. "I'm sure the boys were only teasing. That's what most boys like to do, you know." She laughed, but Rachel didn't think it was one bit funny.

She nudged the wicker basket with her toe and grunted. "I hid my glasses and lied about it to Mom. Now I've got double chores to do for two whole weeks!"

"I'm sorry to hear you lied, Rachel." Esther frowned. "I hope you realize that it was the wrong thing to do."

Rachel nodded as a familiar lump lodged in her throat.

"Mom and Pap love you very much, but it's their job as good parents to punish their children when they do something wrong, especially when it goes against God's teachings."

Rachel nodded again, as tears flooded her eyes.

Esther patted Rachel's shoulder. "Now put on a happy face, do what's right, and things are bound to get better."

Rachel stared at the basket of towels. "I don't see how I can put on a happy face when I have so many chores."

"You have many reasons to smile. I have a bookmark at home that lists 101 reasons to smile." Esther chuckled. "Of course, I can't remember all of them, but here are a few: last day of school, a warm summer day, a beautiful sunset, fresh-cut flowers, and an unexpected hug." She pulled Rachel to her side and hugged her again. "Maybe what you need is a good dose of happy medicine."

Rachel tilted her head. "Happy medicine?"

"Come with me, and I'll show you." Esther took Rachel's hand and led her down the steps. When she came to a patch of dirt, she squatted down and picked up a twig. Then she drew a heart in the dirt, and added a smiley face. "Make up your mind to be happy, learn to find pleasure in simple things, and whenever you're feeling sad and grumpy, quote this verse from Proverbs 17:22: " 'A cheerful heart is good medicine, but a crushed spirit dries up the bones.' "

Rachel nodded. "I see what you mean. I'll do my best to have a cheerful heart and put on a happy face."

Chapter 12

A Day of Surprises

Rachel couldn't believe today was the last day of school, but here she was, walking to school carrying Cuddles in a cat carrier.

She glanced at Buddy, plodding along on his leash beside Jacob, grunting and kicking up dust with his big furry paws. *What a goofy dog,* she thought.

Elizabeth had told the scholars they could bring their pets today. Since Rachel knew some dogs might not get along well with her cat, she'd put Cuddles in the carrier to protect her. She would only take the cat out of the carrier if someone wanted to pet or hold her.

"I hope you're planning to keep Buddy tied up," Rachel said, looking at Jacob. "If you don't, he'll probably jump up and lick everyone's face."

Jacob shook his head. "I don't think so. My hund saves all his kisses for you."

"Very funny!"

Jacob snickered. "Come on, Rachel; don't be so

grouchy. You know you like Buddy. He's a good dog."

She shrugged. "He's okay, and I'm glad he and Cuddles have become friends. I just wish he didn't jump up and lick my face all the time."

"Buddy wouldn't do it if he didn't think you were his friend."

Woof! Woof! Buddy wagged his tail and looked at Rachel with big brown eyes.

She patted his head. "I do like you, Buddy. I just don't like your—"

Slurp! Slurp! Buddy licked Rachel's hand with his sloppy pink tongue.

Rachel pulled her hand back. "See what I get for trying to be nice?"

Jacob slapped his knee and chuckled.

Rachel gritted her teeth. She didn't think Buddy's slimy wet kisses were the least bit funny!

"Let's play a game of baseball," Orlie said during afternoon recess. He smiled at Rachel. "Would you like to be on the same team as me and Jacob?"

Rachel shook her head. "I'd rather not play."

"Why not?"

She pointed to her glasses. "I don't want to lose these. They might fall off my face and get broken."

"Oh, come on, Rachel, I'm sure your glasses won't fall," Orlie said. "I'd like you to be on our team."

"Why don't you take your glasses off and leave them

on the picnic table?" Audra suggested. "Can you see well enough to play without them?"

Rachel thought about the last time she'd played ball, before she'd gotten her glasses. She'd had trouble seeing the ball when it was thrown to her, and she'd struck out. "I can see some things without my glasses, but not nearly as well as I can with my glasses on," she said. "You go ahead and play without me."

Audra shook her head. "If you're not going to play, neither am I. I'll sit on the sidelines and watch with you."

Rachel didn't want Audra to sit out of the game because of her, but she didn't want to play ball with her glasses on, either.

Audra remained at Rachel's side.

"Okay, I'll play!" Rachel removed her glasses and placed them on the picnic table. She turned to Orlie and said, "You'd better not complain if I don't play well enough."

He grinned. "I won't complain; I promise."

Rachel took her place in center field. The first person up to bat was Aaron King, and he hit a ball that went right into the catcher's mitt.

"You're out!" shouted Orlie. "Two more outs and our team's up to bat."

The game continued, and even though Rachel couldn't see very well without her glasses, she had fun playing ball. By the time the game was over, she'd caught a couple of balls and had even made a home run.

She smiled. Even more surprising than how well she played was that no one had made fun of her for wearing glasses. Maybe the boys had decided to quit teasing and leave her alone.

"Can I hold your cat?" Phoebe asked Rachel.

Rachel nodded. "Jah, sure, but let me get my glasses first." She headed across the playground, but when she got to the picnic table, she halted. Her glasses were gone!

She looked around frantically. They weren't on any of the picnic tables.

"Has anyone seen my glasses?" Rachel shouted.

"Not me," said Orlie.

"Me neither," several others said.

Rachel fiddled with the ties on her kapp, fighting the temptation to bite off a fingernail. "They couldn't have just disappeared," she said. "Someone must have them."

"I'll help you look," Audra offered.

"Danki."

"Maybe someone picked up your glasses and took them into the schoolhouse," Audra said. "Should we go see?"

Rachel nodded.

They were almost to the schoolhouse porch, when Buddy ambled up to Rachel, wagging his tail. *Woof! Woof!*

Rachel's mouth fell open; she could hardly believe her eyes. Her glasses were perched in the middle of Buddy's long nose!

Brian and Jacob looked at each other and laughed. Rachel figured they must have put the glasses on the dog.

Woof! Woof! Buddy pranced in circles.

Now everyone laughed—even Rachel. She had to admit, Jacob's dog looked pretty funny. Even so, she was worried that her glasses might fall off Buddy's nose and get stepped on, so she plucked them off his big hairy nose.

Woof! Woof! Woof! Buddy slurped Rachel's hand.

"Stop that!" She pulled her hand away and put the glasses on her face.

"See, what did I tell you? Buddy likes you, Rachel." Jacob snickered. "He likes you so much he wanted to borrow your glasses."

Rachel shook her head. "I'll bet you're the one who put my glasses on Buddy. You probably did it to irritate me."

"I only did it to make everyone laugh," Jacob said.

"It was kind of funny," Rachel admitted. "But don't do it again, because I don't want my glasses ruined."

"Ah, Buddy wouldn't hurt your glasses."

"If they'd fallen off his nose, he could have stepped on them."

"Well, they didn't fall off, so don't get so worked up about it."

"I'm not worked up."

"Jah, you are."

"Am not."

Phoebe nudged Rachel's arm. "What about Cuddles? Can I hold her now?"

"Jah, sure." Rachel hurried to Cuddles' cage and was shocked to find the door hanging wide open. She peeked inside and gasped. Cuddles was gone!

"Who took my cat?" she shrieked. "Someone had better not be playing a trick on me!"

"What's all the yelling about?" Elizabeth asked as she came out of the schoolhouse.

"Someone opened the door to Cuddles' carrier, and now she's gone!" Rachel's voice shook and she bit her lip to keep from sobbing.

"Did any of you open the door to Rachel's cat carrier?" Elizabeth asked.

Everyone shook their heads.

"Has anyone seen the cat?"

"Not me," said Orlie.

"Me neither," Brian put in. "She probably got out while we were playing ball. I'll bet she's long gone."

Tears sprang to Rachel's eyes as she thought about the last time her cat had disappeared. The day Pap's barn burned down, he said he thought all the animals had gotten out of the barn in time. Rachel was worried Cuddles might have been killed in the fire. She'd been relieved to discover that the cat had gone back to the Millers' place where she'd been born.

But this time it might be different, Rachel thought as she looked around helplessly. *This time Cuddles might have gotten lost for good.* She shivered. *I shouldn't have brought Cuddles to school today. I might never see her again.*

Jacob touched Rachel's arm. "Don't look so sad. It'll be okay."

"Jah, don't be sad," Orlie agreed. "I'll bet Cuddles went home. She'll probably be waiting for you when you get there."

Rachel's heart pounded with sudden hope. "D–do you really think so?"

He nodded.

"I agree with Orlie," said Jacob. "Cuddles is a schmaert cat. I'm sure she'll find her way home."

As Rachel walked home from school with Jacob and Buddy, she glanced at Cuddles's empty cat carrier, and a lump formed in her throat. What if Cuddles never came home? What if Rachel never saw her sweet cat again?

"Here Cuddles," she called. "Come, kitty, kitty."

"I don't know why you're calling her." Jacob shook his head. "Like Orlie and I said earlier, the cat probably went home."

"What if she didn't? What if—"

"Don't be such a worrier," Jacob said. "As Grandma Yoder always says, 'Worry is nothing more than thinking about something you don't want to happen.'"

Rachel blinked against the tears stinging her eyes. "I don't want anything bad to happen to Cuddles."

"Then quit worrying and pray that she's okay."

Rachel nodded. She'd been so worried and upset over Cuddles's disappearance that she'd forgotten to pray. *Dear God,* she prayed silently, *please keep my cat safe and bring her back to me.*

When Jacob and Rachel entered their yard, Rachel made a dash for the house. Cuddles wasn't on the porch.

Rachel dropped the cat carrier and her backpack on the table by the door and raced into the house. "Is Cuddles here?" she asked when she entered the kitchen and found Mom at the table with a glass of iced tea.

Mom shook her head. "I haven't seen Cuddles since you took her to school this morning."

Thump! Thump! Thump! Rachel's heart beat so hard she thought it might burst open. "Cuddles got out of her carrier, and now she's missing!"

"She could be in the barn," Mom said.

"I'll go check." Rachel raced out of the house.

"Are you here, Cuddles?" she called when she entered the barn.

"Here kitty, kitty!" Rachel listened carefully.

Only the soft nicker of the horses in their stalls.

Rachel sank to a bale of hay, letting her head fall forward into her hands. This day couldn't get much worse!

Please, God, she prayed through her sniffling sobs. *Please bring Cuddles home to me.*

That evening as Rachel set the table for supper, she kept thinking about her cat. The other day she'd decided to be more cheerful, but now she just wanted to cry.

Rachel had just placed the last dish on the table when Jacob entered the house with a gloomy look.

"What's wrong?" Mom asked. "You look upset."

Jacob nodded. "I am upset. I let Buddy wander around the yard while I went to the barn to get his food, but when I came back, he was gone." He slowly shook his head. "I called and called, but Buddy didn't come. I even tried blowing the silent whistle I bought to train him, but that didn't work either." His chin quivered as if he was on the verge of tears. "Now my dog and Rachel's cat are both missing."

"I hope Buddy didn't go out on the road," Mom said. "With all the cars going by this time of night, he might have—" Her voice trailed off as she looked out the window. "Well, well. . .what do you know?"

"What is it?" Rachel asked.

Mom motioned to the window. "You'd better come see this, too, Jacob."

Rachel and Jacob scurried over to the window.

"It's Buddy!" Jacob hollered. "He's carrying Cuddles by the scruff of her neck!"

Rachel dashed out the door. "Cuddles! Are you okay?"

Buddy ambled up the steps and set Cuddles on the porch.

Cuddles looked up at Rachel. *Meow!*

Rachel scooped the cat into her arms. This had sure been a day of surprises! "Oh Cuddles," she said, nuzzling the cat's head with her nose, "I'm so glad to see you!"

Woof! Woof! Woof! Buddy looked up at Rachel as if to say, *Aren't you happy to see me, too?*

Rachel patted Buddy's head. "I don't know where you found Cuddles, but thank you for rescuing her."

Woof! Woof! Buddy wagged his tail and licked Rachel's hand.

This time Rachel didn't mind being slurped by Jacob's hairy mutt. She gave Buddy's head another pat. "Good dog!"

Jacob and Mom came out on the porch, and Jacob dropped to his knees. He wrapped his arms around Buddy's neck. *Slurp! Slurp! Slurp!* Buddy licked Jacob's nose, his chin, his cheeks, and even his ears.

"Knock it off, Buddy," Jacob said with a grunt. "That's way too many kisses."

Rachel giggled. At least she wasn't the only one getting Buddy's wet, sloppy kisses.

"I wonder where Buddy found Cuddles," Mom said, reaching out to pet the cat.

Rachel shrugged. "I don't know, and I don't care. I'm just glad she's safe and home where she belongs."

Jacob stood and faced Rachel. "This is the second time my dog has rescued your cat, you know."

Rachel nodded. "Buddy and Cuddles have been

friends ever since the day Cuddles fell in the creek and
Buddy jumped in after her."

Buddy flopped onto the porch with a grunt. Cuddles
leaped from Rachel's arms and curled in front of
Buddy. She stuck out her little pink tongue and—*Slurp!
Slurp!*—licked the end of Buddy's nose. Then she licked
his ears, his head, and even his paws. *Slurp! Slurp! Slurp!*
She kept on licking.

"Ha! Ha! Ha!" Rachel laughed and laughed. When
she finally quit laughing, she looked up at Mom and
smiled. "Esther was right when she said it's important
to have a happy heart. Right after supper, I'm going to
paint a happy face on one of my rocks to remind me
that even when things don't go my way, I should smile
and put on a happy face."

Recipe for Grandma Yoder's
Maple Syrup Cookies

1 teaspoon baking soda
1 tablespoon milk
1 egg
½ cup plus 2 tablespoons shortening
1 cup maple syrup
3 cups flour
3 teaspoons baking powder
½ teaspoon salt
1 teaspoon vanilla
1 (8 ounce) package semisweet chocolate chips

Preheat oven to 350°. In a small cup, dissolve baking soda in milk and set aside. Cream egg, shortening, and syrup. Add flour, baking powder, salt, vanilla, and baking soda mixture; blend well. Stir in chocolate chips. Drop by teaspoons onto greased cookie sheet and bake 12–15 minutes.

Just Plain Foolishness

Dedication

To Ella Schrock. Thanks for letting me tour your wonderful greenhouse. To the children and teachers at the Pine Creek Amish schoolhouse in Goshen, Indiana. I enjoyed meeting you and introducing you to my Grandma Yoder puppet. And to Elvera Kienbaum. Thanks for sharing your wonderful strawberry story with me.

Glossary

ach—oh
aebeer—strawberry
aebier—strawberries
alt—old
bensel—silly child
boppli—baby
bopplin—babies
brieder—brothers
bruder—brother
busslin—kittens
buwe—boy
daed—dad
danki—thanks
dechder—daughters
dumm—dumb
gans—goose
grossdaadi—grandfather
gut—good
hund—dog
jah—yes

kapp—cap
kinner—children
kumme—come
maedel—girl
mamm—mom
maus—mouse
meis—mice
naerfich—nervous
schee—pretty
schissel—bowl
schliffer—splinter
schmaert—smart
schnell—quickly
schtinkich—stuffy
schwach—feeble
schweschder—sister
sei so gut—please
shillgrott—turtle
windel—diaper
wunderbaar—wonderful

Bisht du an schlaufa? — Are you sleeping?
Des kann ich finne. — I can find it.
Die Rachel is die ganz zeit am grumble. — Rachel is grumbling all the time.
Dummel dich net! — Take your time! Don't hurry!
Geb's mir! — Give it to me!
Grummel net um mich rum. — Don't grumble around me.
Guder mariye. — Good morning.
Gut nacht. — Good night.
Hallich gebottsdaag. — Happy birthday.
Hoscht du schunn geese? — Have you already eaten?

Ich hei–ah die bells an ringa.	Morning bells are ringing.
Letscht nacht hab ich	I had an earache
ohreweh ghat.	last night.
Schweschder Hannah	Sister Hannah
She dich, eich, wider!	See you later!
Was in der welt?	What in all the world?
Wie geht's?	How are you?

Chapter 1

Grandpa's Greenhouse

*B*ang! Bang! Bang!

Rachel Yoder stepped onto the back porch and shielded her eyes from the glare of the morning sun. She was excited to see Grandpa Schrock's new greenhouse going up on the front of Pap's property. More than a dozen men from their Amish community had come to help.

Pap, Henry, and other men kept busy pounding nails into the wood framing, while Rudy and another group of men sawed the lumber. Rachel's brother Jacob and several other boys carried lumber and other supplies to the men. Grandpa helped wherever he could and supervised everything.

"I wish I could help build Grandpa's greenhouse," Rachel said when Mom stepped onto the porch with a jug of water and a stack of paper cups. "It looks like the men are having so much fun."

Mom nodded, and her glasses slipped to the end of

her nose. Rachel was glad her own blue plastic-framed glasses stayed in place. But that was probably because the bridge of her nose wasn't as thin as Mom's nose.

"I'm sure the men enjoy what they're doing, but it's a lot of hard work," Mom said, pushing her glasses back in place. "That's why we need to keep taking snacks and cold drinks to them."

She handed Rachel the jug of water and paper cups. "Would you please take these out to the workers? They must be thirsty by now."

Rachel groaned. "Do I have to carry water? I'd rather help build the greenhouse."

"That's just plain foolishness, Rachel. Hammering nails and sawing wood is men's work." Mom nudged Rachel's arm. "Now hurry and take this water to the workers."

Gripping the handle of the water jug in one hand, and holding the package of paper cups under her arm, Rachel stepped off the porch.

Her bare feet tingled as she trudged through the cool grass. When she reached the graveled driveway, she walked carefully so she wouldn't step on any sharp rocks. Halfway there, she met Jacob.

"How are things going with Grandpa's greenhouse?" she asked.

"Real well. I'll bet we'll have it up before the day's out." He motioned to the entrance of the building being framed with wood. The rest of the greenhouse would be built with plastic pipe and covered with heavy plastic.

Rachel sighed. "I wish I could help build the greenhouse. It's not fair that you get to have all the fun."

Jacob grunted and wiped a trickle of sweat running down his forehead. "*Jah* [Yes], right. Helping build the greenhouse is not all fun and games, sister. It's hard work—men's work!"

She snickered. "What would you know about men's work? You're not a man."

Jacob puffed out his chest and lifted his chin. "I'll be thirteen years old in a few months. Before long I'll graduate from school and start helping Pap on the farm full-time—just two more years."

"I'll turn eleven before you turn thirteen," Rachel said. "In case you've forgotten, my birthday's only a few weeks away."

Jacob shrugged. "You're still two years younger than me. That means I'm a lot smarter than you are."

"No, it doesn't."

"Jah, it does."

Rachel shook her head. "Grandpa thinks I'm *schmaert* [smart]. If he didn't, he wouldn't have said I could help him in the greenhouse after it's built."

Jacob snorted. "That doesn't mean you're schmaert. It just means you'll be busy in the greenhouse. Maybe that will help you stay out of trouble for a change."

"What's that supposed to mean?"

"Trouble seems to follow wherever you go. Always

trouble somewhere. Isn't that what you say?"

Rachel shrugged. "I guess that's true, but I'm hoping I'll have less trouble and more fun after Grandpa's greenhouse is open for business."

"We'll see about that." Jacob motioned to the lumber pile on the other side of the driveway. "I'd better get more wood for the men who are building."

"Can I carry some wood?" Rachel asked.

Jacob shook his head. "If you want to help, stick with what you're doing and see that everyone gets plenty of water."

Rachel frowned. "What's so helpful about hauling water?"

"It helps the thirsty men," Jacob called as he sprinted up the driveway.

When Rachel arrived at the worksite, she set the water and paper cups on the piece of plywood being used as a table.

"I brought you some water," Rachel said when she spotted Grandpa near the entrance of his greenhouse.

He smiled. "*Danki* [Thanks]. I could use a cool drink about now."

"How's everything going?" she asked after he'd helped himself to a cup of water.

"Real well. I think we should have my greenhouse finished by the end of the day."

"Sure wish I could help build it," Rachel said. "It would be a lot more fun than hauling water or helping

Mom make sandwiches and lemonade."

Grandpa raised his bushy gray eyebrows high. "Sorry, Rachel, but building the greenhouse is hard work—too hard for a young girl like you." He patted Rachel's back. "You'll get to help me inside the greenhouse once it's open for business."

"How soon will that be?" she asked.

"Probably in a week or two. I need time to get everything set up."

"Will it be open before Mom has her *boppli* [baby]?"

"Probably so," he said with a nod. "Unless the baby decides to appear early."

Rachel thrust out her bottom lip. "I hope it doesn't come early."

Grandpa tipped his head. "You're not anxious to see your little *bruder* [brother] or *schweschder* [sister]?"

"I—I guess so, but I'm more anxious to help in your greenhouse. If Mom doesn't keep me too busy with chores, that is." Rachel frowned. "I'm afraid once the boppli comes I'll have more chores to do than ever."

Grandpa tweaked Rachel's nose. "I'm sure you'll have some free time to help me."

Pap stepped up to the table and greeted Rachel with a smile. "I see you brought us some water." He poured some into a paper cup and drank. "Ah. . . now that sure hits the spot! Danki, Rachel."

"You're welcome." Rachel decided to stay and watch the workers awhile. Suddenly, the ladder Uncle Amos stood on wobbled, and his hammer dropped to the ground with a thud.

Rachel rushed forward and reached for it. *Smack!*— she bumped heads with her oldest brother, Henry, who'd also reached for the hammer.

"Ouch!" Rachel and Henry said at the same time.

"Are you two okay?" Grandpa asked with a look of concern.

"I'm fine. It's just a little bump," Rachel said.

Henry nodded. "I'm okay, too." He looked at Rachel. "You shouldn't have tried to pick up that hammer."

"I was only trying to help." She rubbed her forehead.

"I was going to get it." Henry shook his head. "You shouldn't even be near the worksite, Rachel. Don't you realize this is men's work?"

Rachel clamped her teeth together. *The men and boys get to have all the fun,* she thought. *I wish I'd been a boy!*

Pap touched Rachel's shoulder. "Maybe you should go see if your *mamm* [mom] has something for you to do."

"That's right." Grandpa smiled at Rachel. "We'll see you at noon, when it's time for lunch."

With head down and shoulders slumped, Rachel headed up the driveway. *Oomph!*—she ran right into someone, spilling a can of nails all over the ground.

She looked up. Orlie Troyer, her friend from school, stared at her.

"Are you okay?" he asked.

She nodded. "I–I'm fine. I'll help you pick up the nails."

"Don't bother; I can manage." Orlie scooped up a handful of nails and tossed them back in the can. "What are you doing out here by the worksite, Rachel?"

"I took water to the men."

"Well, you'd better get back to the house before you get hurt. Working on the greenhouse is men's work."

"What would you know about that? You're not a man!" Before Orlie could respond, Rachel hurried away.

When she came to the pile of lumber, she paused. Some pieces didn't look so big. She figured she could probably carry a few of them to the worksite. Maybe then everyone would see that she could help with the greenhouse, too—even if she wasn't a man.

Rachel bent and picked up a piece of wood. "Ouch! Ouch!"

Tears filled her eyes as pain shot through her thumb. She let the wood fall to the ground and stared at her hand. An ugly splinter was stuck in her thumb!

Jacob rushed to her. "What are you yelling about, Rachel?"

She held out her hand. "I've got a nasty *schliffer* [splinter] in my thumb."

"How'd you do that?"

"I picked up a piece of wood to take to the worksite." Rachel's chin trembled as she struggled not to cry. She didn't want Jacob to call her a boppli. "I didn't know there'd be splinters in the lumber."

"It's wood, little *bensel* [silly child]. It's bound to

have splinters." Jacob clicked his tongue the way Mom often did. "You can help best by going to the house and helping Mom get our lunch ready."

"I will—after she takes the schliffer out of my finger." Sniffling and blinking, Rachel hurried to the house.

Rachel found her sister, Esther, as well as Mom, Grandma Yoder, and several other women, scurrying around the kitchen, making sandwiches.

Mom motioned to the refrigerator. "Good, you're just in time to help us with—" She stared at Rachel. "Have you been crying?"

Rachel nodded. "I—I had some trouble outside."

"What kind of trouble?" Esther asked.

"First I bumped heads with Henry when I was trying to pick up a hammer. Then I ran into Orlie and knocked a can of nails out of his hand." Rachel sniffed a couple of times. "Then I was going to carry some wood over to the worksite, but I ended up with this!" Rachel held up her throbbing thumb.

"*Ach* [Oh], that's a nasty-looking schliffer," Mom said, clicking her tongue. "I'd better get that out for you."

Sniff! Sniff! "It's gonna hurt, isn't it?"

"Taking it out might hurt a little, but it will hurt much worse if the splinter stays in your thumb," Mom said.

Grandma nodded. "And if you don't take it out, it could get infected."

"Sit down and I'll take care of it." Mom went to the

cupboard and returned with bandages, antiseptic, a pair of tweezers, and a needle from her sewing basket.

Rachel sank into a chair and closed her eyes. She hoped it wouldn't hurt too badly. She hoped she wouldn't start sobbing.

Esther held Rachel's hand and spoke soothing words while Mom dug out the splinter. "It's okay, Rachel. The schliffer will be out soon."

Rachel kept her eyes shut and struggled not to cry as Mom poked at the splinter with the needle.

"Got it!" Mom dabbed Rachel's thumb with some antiseptic and covered it with a bandage. "Does that feel better?"

Rachel opened her eyes. "It still hurts a little, but not as much as it did before."

Grandma patted Rachel's shoulder. "You're a brave little girl."

Rachel liked hearing that she was brave, but she didn't like being called a little girl. She figured it was best not to tell that to Grandma, though.

"It's sure a warm day." Mom fanned herself with the corner of her apron.

"It is a bit *schtinkich* [stuffy] in here," Esther agreed.

"Why don't you two sit and rest awhile?" Grandma suggested. "Rachel and I can finish making the sandwiches. Isn't that right, Rachel?"

Rachel nodded. At least Grandma thought she was grown up enough to help with lunch. She glanced out the kitchen window and spotted Jacob and Orlie hauling more wood to the worksite. They walked slowly down the driveway. Rachel figured they were probably hot and tired.

I guess it is hard work. It might be more fun for me to watch the men build the greenhouse than try to help with it. Rachel smiled as she thought, *I can hardly wait to help Grandpa after the greenhouse is open for business!*

Chapter 2

A Trip to Town

The sun cast an orange tint into Rachel's room as she scrambled out of bed on Monday. Since school was out for the summer, Grandpa had promised to take Rachel to town with him. He was going to buy some things he needed for his new greenhouse. Rachel looked forward to spending the day with Grandpa.

Rachel raced to the closet, put on a clean dress, and rushed out the door. When she got to the bottom of the stairs, she stopped and sniffed. The sweet smell of cinnamon coming from the kitchen made her stomach rumble.

I'll bet Mom baked cinnamon rolls. Rachel smacked her lips in anticipation.

When she entered the kitchen, she was surprised to see just one bowl and a small plate on the table. Mom was the only one in the room.

"*Hoscht du schunn geese* [Have you already eaten]?" she asked when Mom turned from the sink, where she was washing dishes.

Mom nodded. "I ate with your *daed* [dad] and *brieder* [brothers] before they went to work in the fields."

"What about Grandpa?" Rachel asked. "Has he eaten, too?"

"Jah. He's in the barn getting his horse and buggy ready to go to town."

Rachel sighed. "I was afraid he might have left without me."

Mom pointed to the table. "You'd better hurry and eat your cereal and cinnamon roll."

Rachel scurried to the refrigerator and took out a carton of milk. She poured some into her bowl then returned to the refrigerator and grabbed a pitcher of apple juice.

The juice sloshed in the pitcher as she bounded back across the room.

"*Dummel dich net* [Take your time, don't hurry]!" Mom said, shaking her head. "You have plenty of time. If you spill juice, it'll make a sticky mess, and I just scrubbed the floor."

"Sorry, Mom. I want to eat quickly so I can go to town with Grandpa." Rachel poured a glass of juice and put the pitcher back in the refrigerator.

"That's fine, but wash your breakfast dishes before you go."

"I will." Rachel sat at the table and bowed her head for silent prayer. *Dear God, Danki for this day I get to spend with Grandpa. Bless this food to my body. Amen.*

"I'll leave the dishwater in the sink for you to use, and then I'm going outside to hang a few clothes on the line," Mom said when Rachel finished her prayer. "If I see your *grossdaadi* [grandfather], I'll tell him you're eating breakfast and will be out soon."

"Okay, Mom."

Rachel quickly ate her cinnamon roll. Then she drank the apple juice. "Mmm. . ." She smacked her lips. "This is so *gut* [good]. I think I'll have some more." She hurried to the refrigerator and poured another glass.

When she started back, she nearly dropped her glass. Cuddles sat on the table, lapping milk from Rachel's bowl of cereal!

Rachel clapped her hands, and the cat leaped off the table. "Shame on you, Cuddles! You know you're not supposed to be up there!"

Meow! Cuddles looked at Rachel as if to say, "I was hungry."

"Oh, all right." Rachel put the cereal on the floor beside the cat. "It's full of germs now anyway, so you may as well eat it!"

Lap. . .lap. . .lap. Cuddles slurped the milk with her little pink tongue. *Crunch. . .crunch. . .crunch.* She ate the rest of the cereal.

"What is that cat doing eating from your *schissel* [bowl]?" Mom hollered when she entered the kitchen.

Rachel gulped. "I–I'm sorry, Mom," she stammered.

"I went to the refrigerator to get more juice, and when I turned around, Cuddles was on the table, eating my cereal."

"And just how did your cereal bowl get on the floor?" Mom asked.

"I—uh—figured since Cuddles had already eaten out of my bowl and it was full of germs, I may as well let her eat the rest of it."

Mom frowned. "You know how I feel about animals eating from our dishes." She pointed to Cuddles. "Take her outside right now!"

Rachel picked up the cat and set her on the porch. "Now you be good," she said as Cuddles curled into a ball and began to purr.

"I'll wash my dishes now," Rachel said when she returned to the kitchen. She set the bowl, plate, and glass in the sink and plunged her hands into the soapy water.

"Cuddles probably got in when I went to hang my clothes on the line, so I know it wasn't your fault she was on the table." Mom peered at Rachel over the top of her glasses. "But I'd better never see that cat eating out of your dish again! If I do, you'll wash all the dishes after every meal for a whole week. Is that clear?"

"Jah, Mom," Rachel nodded. "I'll make sure it doesn't happen again."

A little later, as Rachel and Grandpa headed for town, the buggy hit a pothole in the road, nearly knocking

Rachel out of her seat.

"Sorry about that," Grandpa said. "I didn't realize there was a rut, or I would have avoided it."

Rachel looked at him and smiled. "It's okay, Grandpa. I'm enjoying the ride."

He grinned and patted her knee. "I like your positive attitude today, Rachel. It's always good to look on the bright side of things."

"Sometimes, when things don't go so well, it's hard for me to see the bright side," Rachel admitted.

Grandpa nodded. "That's when we need to remember Psalm 32:11: 'Rejoice in the Lord and be glad.' We should try to rejoice no matter what happens—even in the middle of our troubles."

Rachel smiled and relaxed against the seat. She enjoyed listening to the steady *clip-clop, clip-clop* of the horse's hooves and watching all the cars zip past in the opposite lane. She dreamed about riding in a convertible some day, but she wondered if that dream would ever come true. She was sure it would be exciting to travel fast with the top of the car down and the wind in her face.

Beep! Beep! A horn honked as a car whipped around them.

A muscle on Grandpa's face quivered as he gripped the reins and guided the horse closer to the side of the road. "There's way too much traffic today," he mumbled. "I wish I'd picked a different day to go to town. Maybe we should have stayed home."

"You're not going back, I hope." Rachel had looked forward to spending the day with Grandpa. She'd be disappointed if he decided to go home.

Grandpa shook his head. "Don't worry. I won't go home until my errands are done. Fast cars just make me *naerfich* [nervous], and I don't like all this traffic."

Rachel didn't mind the traffic, and she thought fast cars were exciting. She decided not to mention that, though. She didn't want to say anything that might spoil her day with Grandpa, so she decided to change the subject.

"Did you know my birthday's coming soon?" she asked.

"I think I may have heard something about that. Remind me now—how old will you be?"

"Eleven."

"Hmm. . ." Grandpa's lips twitched. "You've gotten so tall, I thought maybe you'd skipped a few years and had become a teenager."

Rachel giggled. "Are you teasing me?"

He nodded and chuckled. "You know me. . . . I do like to tease now and then."

She smiled. "That's one of the things I like about you, Grandpa. You're always so much fun to be with."

"I enjoy being with you, too." Grandpa looked at her and winked. "So what do you hope to get for your birthday?"

"I'd really like a trip to Hershey Park." Rachel

sighed. "But I'm sure that won't happen."

"What makes you think so?"

"Because when I asked Pap about going, he said he was too busy, and that Mom wasn't up to making the trip." She slowly shook her head. "I'll probably never go to Hershey Park, or anyplace else where there are fun rides."

"Never say never," Grandpa said. "Sometimes the things we want happen when we least expect them."

Hope rose inside Rachel. Maybe Mom and Pap would surprise her with a trip to Hershey Park for her birthday. Maybe Grandpa knew about it and was keeping it a secret.

"I don't know about you, but I'm getting hungry," Grandpa said when they had purchased flower pots, potting soil, gardening gloves, and packets of seeds. These were all things he would either use or sell in his greenhouse.

Rachel patted her stomach. "I'm hungry, too."

"I'll let you choose where we'll have our lunch," Grandpa said.

Rachel smiled. "I'd like to eat at the Bird-in-Hand Family Restaurant. They have real tasty food there."

"I like eating there, too," Grandpa said as he guided the horse and buggy onto the road.

When they entered the restaurant, Rachel's stomach rumbled and her nose twitched. The delicious aromas coming from the kitchen made her even hungrier.

The hostess showed them to a table. Then a waitress asked what they would like to drink.

"I'll have a glass of iced tea," Grandpa said. "How about you, Rachel?"

"I'd like a glass of milk."

"Do you know what you'd like to eat?" the waitress asked.

"I think I'll have the buffet." Grandpa smiled at Rachel. "Does that sound good to you?"

"That suits me fine." She licked her lips. "There are always lots of good things on the buffet, and they even have pickled beets on the salad bar!"

Grandpa chuckled. "You take after your mamm, Rachel. She's always liked pickled beets."

"Help yourself when you're ready," the waitress said. "I'll have your beverages at the table when you get back."

Rachel pushed her chair aside and scurried to the salad bar. She didn't care much for lettuce, but she liked some of the other vegetables there. So she loaded her plate and made sure she got plenty of pickled beets.

A girl with blond hair in a ponytail stepped up to Rachel and studied her a few seconds. "Is your name Rachel Yoder?"

"Yes," Rachel said.

"I thought so. We met at the farmers' market last summer." The girl tilted her head. "You look different than the last time I saw you. I don't think you wore glasses then."

"I got my glasses about a month ago." Rachel smiled at the girl. "Your name's Sherry, isn't it?"

"That's right."

"You had a cute dog with you. I remember we took it for a walk."

"Yes, we did. You should see how much Bundles has grown since then."

"My cat, Cuddles, has grown a lot, too—especially around the middle. I think it's because she eats so much," Rachel said.

"What are you doing here?" Sherry asked. "Are you going to the farmers' market?"

Rachel shook her head. "I came with my grandpa so he could buy some things for his new greenhouse."

"That sounds interesting."

"Yes, and I'm going to help him there when I'm not busy with other things," Rachel said. "What are you doing here?"

Sherry motioned to a woman sitting at a table across the room. "I came with my mother. We went shopping for a new quilt to put in our guest room."

"My mother made a quilt for my sister when she got married," Rachel said. "She used the Lone Star pattern."

"Will you help in your grandpa's greenhouse all summer?" Sherry asked. "Or will your family take a vacation?"

Rachel shook her head. "My mom's due to have a baby soon, so we won't go on vacation. How about you?"

"We may visit my aunt and uncle in California. My brother's planning to take me to Hershey Park sometime this summer, too."

Rachel couldn't help but feel envious. Hearing that Sherry was going to Hershey Park made her wish all the more that she could go there.

"It was nice to see you, Rachel." Sherry turned away from the salad bar. "Maybe I'll see you sometime later this summer."

Rachel smiled. "That would be nice."

When Sherry walked away, Rachel finished filling her plate and took it to the table where Grandpa waited. Despite longing for things she might never get to do, she was excited about the things they'd bought for Grandpa's greenhouse. And she was excited about helping him there. At least that was something to look forward to.

Chapter 3

Trouble by the Road

"The hurrier I go, the behinder I get," Grandpa mumbled as he hurried toward his greenhouse the following morning.

"I wish I could help you today," Rachel called from the garden, where she and Jacob were picking strawberries.

"Maybe you can help me later," Grandpa called as he kept walking.

Rachel dropped two berries into the basket by her knees. "I don't think there's much chance of that. When I'm done here, I'll have to spend the rest of the day selling these *aebier* [strawberries] from our roadside stand," she said as Grandpa disappeared.

"*Grummel net um mich rum* [Don't grumble around me]." Jacob tossed a berry, and it splattered on Rachel's arm.

"Stop! I'll end up with berry juice all over my dress!" Rachel grabbed a berry and threw it at Jacob. She laughed when it hit his nose.

"You'd better quit fooling around! You'll be in trouble if Mom sees you're playing."

"What about you?" Rachel frowned. "You threw an *aebeer* [strawberry] at me first."

"You didn't have to throw one back, little bensel."

"Stop calling me a silly child!" Rachel's fingers itched to pitch another berry at Jacob, but she heard the screen door open and saw Mom step onto the porch.

Plunk! Plunk! Plunk! Rachel dropped one strawberry after another into the basket. When Mom disappeared around the side of the house, Rachel popped a juicy berry into her mouth and giggled. "Mmm. . .this tastes *wunderbaar* [wonderful]."

"You'll never get enough berries picked to sell if you keep eating 'em," Jacob said, shaking his head.

"I only ate one." Rachel glared at Jacob. "And quit telling me what to do. You're not my boss."

"Someone has to tell you what to do when you're fooling around."

"I'm not fooling around." Rachel lifted her basket. "I have just as many berries as you do."

"Whatever you say, little bensel." Jacob snickered and moved to the next row.

That was fine with Rachel; she'd rather not work too close to her teasing brother.

She leaned over, plucked off another berry, and was about to put it in her basket, when—*Peck! Peck!*—their mean old goose nipped the back of Rachel's legs.

"Yeow!" Rachel dropped the berry and whirled around.

Honk! Honk! Honk! The goose flapped her wings and grabbed a berry in her beak.

Before Rachel could react, Jacob waved his hands and hollered, "Get away from here you stupid *gans* [goose]!"

The goose bobbed her head up and down, sounded another loud *Honk!* and waddled away.

Rachel sighed with relief. "Danki, Jacob. I thought that goose was gonna get me."

"I think she was after the strawberries and just wanted to get you out of her way," Jacob said. "She likes to sneak to the garden and help herself when no one's looking."

Rachel's hand trembled as she picked up the berry. "That gans is nothing but trouble. I wish Pap would get rid of her!"

"If she keeps getting into trouble, maybe he will." Jacob grabbed his box of berries. "I've filled eight boxes now, so I think I'll take 'em out to the stand. Are you ready to join me, or did you want to pick more?"

"I have eight boxes, too, so I'm gonna stop picking," Rachel said. "But before I come to the stand, I think I'll go inside and get some of my painted rocks to sell."

"I don't think anyone will want a *dumm* [dumb] old rock, but if you want to try selling some, then suit yourself." Jacob gathered all the berries and put them in the wheelbarrow. "I'll see you at the stand!" He wheeled the boxes of berries down the driveway toward the roadside stand Pap had built.

Rachel hurried into the house, raced up the stairs, and opened her dresser drawer, where she kept several painted rocks. She found an empty box in her closet and put three ladybug rocks inside, along with two rocks she'd painted to look like turtles. She grunted when she picked up the box. The rocks sure made it heavy!

Huffing and puffing, Rachel stumbled down the stairs. When she stepped onto the back porch, she noticed Mom sitting in a chair, shelling peas.

"What are you doing, Rachel?" Mom asked. "I thought you and Jacob were in the garden picking aebier."

Rachel's arms hurt, so she set the box of rocks on the small table by the door. "We were. Jacob took the strawberries out to the stand while I came to get some painted rocks to sell."

"That's a good idea, Rachel. I hope you sell them." Mom smiled. "I'll let you know when lunch is ready, and then you and Jacob can take turns coming up to the house to eat."

"Can't we eat lunch at the stand? I don't want to leave my rocks with Jacob. He might give them away."

Mom shook her head. "I don't think Jacob would do something like that, but if you'd like to eat at the stand, I'll bring lunch to you when it's ready."

"Danki." Rachel picked up the box and trudged down the stairs, panting as she made her way down the driveway.

"This is sure heavy," she said, placing the box on one end of the stand.

Jacob rolled his eyes. "I still think selling rocks is a dumm idea. I'll bet no one will even look at them."

"I bet they will."

"Bet they won't."

Rachel bit her lip. There was no point arguing about it. Jacob would see that he was wrong when she sold her first painted rock.

"Have you had any customers?" Rachel asked as she set the rocks on the other side of the strawberries.

He shook his head. "Only a couple of cars have passed, and no buggies at all."

Rachel shielded her eyes from the sun's glare. "It's still early. I'm sure someone will stop soon."

"I hope so, because it's already hot and muggy, and I don't want to sit out here all day and sweat."

"Now who's grumbling?" Rachel nudged Jacob's arm with her elbow. "Huh?"

"I'm not grumbling, just stating facts." He wiped the sweat on his forehead with his shirtsleeve. "If it's this hot so early in the day, I can only imagine how it'll feel this afternoon."

Rachel sat on the folding chair beside Jacob. She glanced at the other side of the driveway, where Grandpa's greenhouse had been built. No cars or buggies were there either. "It looks like we're not the only ones who don't have customers," she said. "Grandpa's greenhouse looks deserted."

Jacob nodded. "Everyone must either be at home, working, or shopping in town."

Rachel leaned on the wooden counter. "If you could be doing anything else right now, what would it be?"

"I'd be sitting on a big rock at the creek with my bare feet dangling in the water." Jacob looked over at Rachel. "What would you be doing?"

"The creek sounds nice, but I'd probably be in the greenhouse helping Grandpa." She sat up straight. "No, wait. I'd be on one of those wild rides at Hershey Park."

Jacob grunted. "I'd enjoy that, too, but it doesn't look like we'll go anywhere this summer. Not with so much work in the fields and the boppli coming soon."

Rachel sighed. "I wonder if I'll ever get to do anything fun."

Before Jacob could respond, Audra rode up on her scooter. It reminded Rachel of her skateboard. Unlike English scooters that sometimes had engines, Audra's *Amish scooter was similar to a skateboard with handles.*

"Wie geht's [How are you]?" Audra asked, smiling at Rachel.

"Okay. How about you?"

"I'm doing good." Audra stepped down from the scooter and leaned on the counter. "I came to see if you could play."

"I can't today. Jacob and I have to sit here and try to sell these *aebier*." Rachel motioned to the box of berries sitting closest to her. "Would you like to buy some?"

"Sorry, but I don't have any money with me." Audra looked up at the yard. "Can't you leave the stand for a while? I was hoping we could jump on your trampoline."

"I wish I could, but I'll be in trouble with Mom if I don't try to sell these berries."

"Should I come back later this afternoon?" Audra asked. "Maybe you'll be free to play then."

Rachel shook her head. "If the berries sell, I'll help Grandpa in his new greenhouse this afternoon. If they don't sell, I'll probably be stuck here in the hot sun for the rest of the day."

"Die Rachel is die ganz zeit am grumble [Rachel is grumbling all the time]," Jacob said to Audra.

Rachel nudged him. "That's not true. Besides, you grumbled about how hot it is. Remember?"

"Jah, but I don't grumble all the time. You always grumble about something."

"Do not."

"Do so."

"Do not."

"Do so."

"I'd better go," Audra said. *"She dich, eich, wider* [See you later]!" She waved at Rachel and glided away.

Rachel looked over at Jacob. "I wonder why Audra

doesn't have to work today. It doesn't seem fair, does it?"

"You're grumbling again."

"Am not. I'm just stating facts."

"Oh good, I think a customer's coming." Jacob motioned to a car coming down the road. But instead of stopping, it sped up and passed the stand. A small rock from the road hurled through the air. It hit the front of the stand, putting a hole through the letter *S* in the STRAWBERRIES FOR SALE sign Jacob had painted and nailed to the stand.

"That's great!" Jacob mumbled. "Now our sign says, 'TRAWBERRIES FOR SALE." He looked at Rachel and shook his head. "Who's ever heard of trawberries, and who's gonna stop at a stand selling some weird kind of berry?"

Rachel poked Jacob. "I guess you think you're funny, huh?"

Jacob laughed. "Jah, I'm the man selling strawberries with a great sense of humor."

Rachel grunted. "You're not a man!"

"I will be soon."

A car pulled into the driveway, and a bald, middle-aged man got out of the car. He walked to the stand and pointed at the strawberries. "How much are you asking?"

"One dollar a box," Rachel said.

"I'll take two boxes." The man motioned to Grandpa's greenhouse. "I'm going to look at some plants. Would you please put the strawberries on the front seat of my car while I'm gone?" He hurried away before Rachel could respond.

"That was rude," Jacob said. "He didn't even pay for the berries."

"Maybe he'll pay for them when he's done at the greenhouse." Rachel picked up two boxes of berries and took them to the man's car. She opened the door on the driver's side and placed them on the seat. Then she closed the door and raced back to the stand.

"I'm thirsty," Jacob said. "I think I'll run up to the house and get something cold to drink."

"That sounds good. Could you get something for me, too?"

"Jah, sure." Jacob scurried up the driveway.

The man finally returned to his car, but instead of coming to the stand to pay for the berries, he jumped into his car and started to drive away.

Suddenly, he slammed on the brakes and climbed out of the car. He stomped to the stand and shook his finger at Rachel. "Did you put those berries on the front seat of my car?"

"Yes," she admitted.

"Just look what you've done!" He whirled around.

Rachel gasped. Bright red berry juice covered the man's tan-colored pants!

"I—I only set them there because you told me to," she said in a shaky voice.

"I did tell you to put them on the seat, but I didn't think you'd put them where I would sit on them!" A muscle of the side of the man's neck quivered, and his pale eyebrows pulled together.

"I–I'm sorry. I thought you'd come back to the stand to pay for the strawberries, and I was gonna tell you then that the berries were in the front seat of your car." She drew in a quick breath. "But you didn't come back."

"Oh, you're right, I should have paid for the berries, and I did tell you to put them in my front seat. So I guess it's more my fault than yours." The man reached into his pants pocket and handed Rachel four dollars. "The berries in my car are too smashed to eat, but here's enough money for two more boxes, plus the ones I sat on."

Rachel shook her head. "You don't have to pay for the ones that are ruined."

He placed the money on the counter and picked up two boxes of berries. "I'll pay for all four boxes. Maybe my wife can make jelly out of the squished ones."

Rachel smiled. "Thank you."

"You're welcome." The man hurried back to his car and drove away just as a horse and buggy pulled in. It was Rachel's aunt Karen and her little boy, Gerald.

"Wie geht's?" Aunt Karen asked, walking to the stand.

"I'm doing okay," Rachel said. "How about you?"

"Gerald and I are well." Aunt Karen patted Gerald's

head. "We were on our way home from town and noticed you, so I decided to stop and see what you have for sale."

"Jacob and I are selling strawberries." Rachel motioned to her painted rocks. "And these."

"Those are nice. Did you paint them yourself?" Aunt Karen asked.

Rachel nodded. "Painting rocks is a hobby of mine."

Gerald eyed a turtle rock; then he tugged his mother's skirt and said, "*Shillgrott* [Turtle]. *Geb's mir* [Give it to me]*!*"

Aunt Karen shook her head. "That's no way to ask for something. You must say *sei so gut* [please]."

Gerald looked at his mother with pleading eyes. "Sei so gut?"

Aunt Karen squeezed his shoulder. "Jah, you may have the turtle." She opened her purse. "How much are the rocks, Rachel?"

"I'm asking a dollar for them, but since Gerald's my cousin, he can have one for free," Rachel said.

Aunt Karen shook her head. "You worked hard to paint these nice rocks, and I will pay."

"Danki," Rachel said as she took the dollar Aunt Karen handed her. "Would you like a box of strawberries, too?"

"I have a big strawberry patch in my garden, so I really don't need any more." Aunt Karen smiled. "Your berries are nice and plump, so I'm sure you'll sell them in no time."

"I hope so, because I don't want to spend the whole day out here in the hot sun."

"It is quite warm," Aunt Karen agreed. She handed Gerald his turtle rock. "We'd best be on our way home now. Tell your mamm I said hello."

"I will," Rachel called as Aunt Karen and Gerald walked away.

Their buggy had just pulled out of the driveway when Jacob returned.

"I brought some of Pap's cold root beer," he said, handing Rachel a mug.

Rachel smiled. "Danki. It looks good."

Jacob took a big drink from his mug. "This sure hits the spot." He ran his tongue across his upper lip, where some foamy root beer had gathered.

Rachel laughed and sipped from her mug. "You're right; this does hit the spot! Pap makes the best root beer!"

Jacob glanced at the strawberries. "Looks like you sold two more boxes of berries while I was gone."

"Jah." Rachel told Jacob how the man had bought two more boxes of berries after he'd sat on the ones she'd put in his car. "I really felt bad about the man's pants," she added.

"That was a dumb thing to do, Rachel."

"The man said it was as much his fault because he told me to put the berries on the front seat."

Jacob shrugged. "I guess it was partly his fault then."

"Then Aunt Karen and Gerald came by." Rachel pointed to the spot where the painted turtle rock had been sitting. "She bought one of my rocks for Gerald."

"Really?"

"Jah. I told you I'd sell some rocks today."

"Puh!" Jacob flapped his hand like he was swatting a fly. "You've only sold one, and to a member of our family. I'd be more impressed if you'd sold the whole lot of them to a stranger."

Rachel frowned. "You don't have to be so mean."

"I wasn't being mean; I was just stating facts." He gulped more root beer. "Selling a rock to a relative doesn't count."

"Jah, it does."

"Does not."

"Does too, and I think you ought to stop—"

Woof! Woof! Jacob's dog, Buddy, bounded up to the stand and licked Rachel's arm with his big pink tongue.

"Get away from me!" Rachel pushed Buddy down. "Your breath is awful!"

Thunk!—Buddy's tail hit a berry box, knocking it to the ground.

"Oh, no," Rachel moaned. "Now the berries are dirty!" She bent over and was about to pick them up, when— *thunk!*—Buddy whacked another box with his tail.

Rachel glared at Jacob. "Look what your hairy mutt's done! He's always causing trouble! Why's he out of his dog run?"

Jacob shrugged. "I don't know, but I'll put him back right away." He reached for Buddy's collar, but the dog put his paws in Rachel's lap and licked her face.

"Yuck! Go away, you hairy beast!"

Buddy grunted and flopped down on the berries he'd knocked to the ground.

Rachel groaned. "Trouble. . .trouble. . .Buddy's always causing trouble!" She pointed at Jacob. "You'd better pick some more berries!"

Jacob frowned. "Why me?"

"Because your *hund* [dog] knocked over the berries and squished them with his big hairy body. So you should be the one to pick more berries!"

"Oh, okay. It'll be better than sitting here listening to you grumble." Jacob scooped up the berry boxes and led Buddy up the driveway, mumbling, "Stupid hund!"

Rachel leaned on the counter and closed her eyes. She hoped the whole summer wouldn't be full of trouble.

Chapter 4

Camping Surprise

When Rachel stepped onto the porch the next morning, she spotted Cuddles lying on her back, playing with a piece of string.

"You're getting fat! You must be eating too many mice." Rachel scratched the cat's bulging belly. "Maybe I should cut back on your food."

Meow! Cuddles looked up at Rachel as if to say, "You'd better not!"

Rachel continued to rub the cat's belly. "Oh, don't worry; I promise I won't let you starve."

Cuddles closed her eyes and purred.

Rachel closed her eyes, too. It felt good to sit on the porch in a patch of warm sun. She wished she could stay here and pet Cuddles all day, but she had chores to do.

"I'm going to the chicken coop to feed the chickens. When I get back, I'll give you some food," Rachel said, giving the cat's stomach one final rub.

When Rachel entered the chicken coop, she was

relieved that the big red rooster wasn't there. She figured he must be outside hunting for bugs, taking a dirt bath, or chasing the smaller roosters around the yard. Usually when Rachel went into the coop and the big rooster was there, he caused trouble. Maybe she would have an easier time feeding the chickens today.

Rachel opened a can of chicken feed and poured some into the dishes. *Bawk! Bawk! Bawk!* A dozen red hens crowded around the dish, pecking at each other and gobbling up the food.

"There's plenty for everyone, so don't be in such a hurry," Rachel scolded. "If you eat too much, you'll get fat like Cuddles."

Bawk! Bawk! The chickens continued to peck one another, eating as if this was their last meal.

Rachel took the watering dishes outside to fill.

"Rachel, check for eggs while you're in the coop," Mom called from the back porch.

Rachel cupped her hands around her mouth. "I will, Mom!"

Rachel rinsed the watering dishes and filled them with fresh water; then she carried them back to the coop. While the hens continued to eat and drink, she checked for eggs.

When she returned to the house, she found Mom in the kitchen, frying bacon.

"I got six eggs," Rachel said.

"That's good." Mom turned from the stove and

smiled. "Would you please wash them and put them in the refrigerator?"

Rachel went to the sink and turned on the water. "I still need to feed Cuddles, but I'm not gonna give her as much food as normal."

"Why not?" Mom asked.

"She's getting fat. She looks like she's eaten too many *meis* [mice]. I think she needs to go on a diet."

Mom clicked her tongue. "Cuddles doesn't need to lose weight, Rachel. She's in a family way."

Rachel's mouth dropped open. "Cuddles is going to have *busslin* [kittens]?"

"That's right. I thought you knew."

Rachel shook her head. "I thought she'd been eating too much."

"No, she's going to have a batch of kittens. I'm guessing it will be soon."

"Oh, that's wunderbaar!" Rachel was so excited, she felt like doing a little dance. "I hope she has a whole bunch of busslin!"

Mom held up her hand. "Now don't get too excited. No matter how many kittens she has, you can't keep them. You'll need to find each of them a good home."

"Can't I keep just one?"

"Well, maybe. We'll have to wait and see." Mom turned back to the stove. "Oh, and Rachel, you'd better find a box in the barn and fill it with shredded newspaper. That way, Cuddles will have a nice, safe place to have her kittens." She pointed to the stack of newspapers inside the woodbox. "You can use some of those. We don't want Cuddles to have her babies in some strange place we don't know about."

"I'll fix it right after breakfast." Rachel could hardly wait until the kittens were born!

For the next several days, Rachel closely watched Cuddles. She'd taken her into the barn and shown her the box she'd prepared. Cuddles didn't show much interest in the box. She just slept on the porch while her stomach grew bigger.

"I saw Audra's mamm at the grocery store yesterday," Mom said to Rachel during breakfast on Thursday morning. "She said Audra would like you to spend Friday night with her."

"At her house?" Rachel asked.

Mom nodded.

"Couldn't Audra come over here? I don't want to leave Cuddles."

"Why not?"

Rachel reached for a piece of toast and slathered it with creamy peanut butter. "What if she has her *bopplin* [babies] while I'm gone? I should be here for that."

Jacob, who sat beside Rachel, grunted and nudged her arm. "The cat doesn't need you. She'll do just fine on her own."

"I understand why Rachel would want to be with

Cuddles," Grandpa said. "I remember when I was a boy and my dog was expecting pups." He had a faraway look in his eyes. "I made sure I was there when Cindy's pups were born."

Mom patted Rachel's hand. "If it's all right with Audra's mamm, Audra can spend the night here."

"Oh good. Can I walk over there after breakfast and ask her?" Rachel asked.

"Jah, but not until all your chores are done," Pap said.

Rachel nodded.

"This is so exciting!" Audra said as she and Rachel entered the tent Pap set up for them in the backyard on Friday evening. "It's just like going camping; only we're not in the woods."

Rachel nodded. "It should be lots of fun."

Rachel was about to crawl into her sleeping bag when Audra hollered, "Wait! You'd better not get in!"

"Look! There's a big lump in there!"

Rachel studied her sleeping bag. Something was at the bottom of it! "Maybe it's a *maus* [mouse]," she said.

Audra covered her mouth and squealed. "Ach, I hope not! I don't like mice!"

"If it is a maus, I'd better let it out." Rachel unzipped the sleeping bag and pulled it open. *Was in der welt* [What in all the world]?" She slowly shook her head.

"Wh–what is it?" Audra's voice trembled as she darted for the tent door.

"Look, it's Cuddles. She had her busslin inside my sleeping bag!"

Audra crept back in and peered inside the sleeping bag. "You're right!" Her eyes widened. "How many kittens do you think she has?"

Rachel studied the kittens. "I think I see six, but it's hard to tell for sure." She touched Audra's arm. "Aren't they tiny?"

Audra nodded. "Are you gonna leave them in the sleeping bag?"

"I don't know. I think I'd better get Pap." Rachel jumped up. "He'll know what to do!"

Rachel and Audra scurried out of the tent. "Pap, come quick!" Rachel shouted as they ran into the house.

Pap, who was sitting beside Mom on the living room sofa, looked up from the newspaper he was reading and frowned. "What are you yelling about, Rachel? I thought you and Audra had gone to bed."

"Cuddles had her busslin inside my sleeping bag!" Rachel dashed to the sofa. "Should I move them to the barn, Pap? Or leave them in the bag?"

"I'll see about moving them tomorrow," Pap said. "For tonight, I think it's best that you and Audra sleep in your nice clean bed and let Cuddles alone with her kittens."

"But what about our campout?" Rachel was glad the kittens had been born, but she was disappointed that she and Audra couldn't sleep in the tent. "Audra and I were going to pretend we were camping in the woods. It was gonna be lots of fun."

"You can have your backyard campout some other time," Mom said. "Since your cat chose your sleeping bag to have her kittens in, you won't be able to sleep in it until it's been washed."

"Okay, Mom." Rachel grabbed Audra's hand. "Let's go to my room. We can pretend we're camping there."

Audra followed Rachel up the stairs. "I don't see how we can pretend we're camping when we have no tent," she said when they entered Rachel's room.

Rachel pointed to her bed. "We can sleep under there."

Audra frowned. "You want to sleep on the floor under your bed?"

Rachel nodded. "One time, before my cousin Mary moved to Indiana, she and I slept under my bed because a bat got into the room and we were scared."

Audra shivered. "I hope no bat gets in your room tonight. I'd really be scared!"

Rachel shook her head. "That won't happen, because the window's closed." She grabbed a quilt and two pillows, shoved them under the bed, and crawled in behind them. "Are you coming?" she called to Audra.

Audra finally crawled in beside Rachel.

Rachel pulled the quilt around them and laid her head on a pillow.

"I didn't get as good a look at the busslin as I wanted

to," Audra said, "but they looked like cute little things. Didn't you think so?"

"Jah, but I think all baby animals are cute." Rachel looked over at Audra. "Would you like to have a kitten when they're old enough to leave their mamm?"

"That would be nice. I'll have to ask my folks first, though." Audra yawned. "I'm awful sleepy all of a sudden. *Gut nacht* [Good night], Rachel."

"Gut nacht, Audra." Rachel closed her eyes. Soon she was fast asleep, dreaming of campfires, toasted marshmallows, and cuddly kittens.

When Rachel awoke the following day, she forgot where she was, and—*whack!*—she bumped her head on the bed when she tried to sit up. "Ouch, that hurt!" Then she remembered that she and Audra had pretended they were camping last night and slept under her bed.

Rachel glanced at Audra. "Wake up sleepyhead," she said, poking Audra's arm.

Audra yawned and stretched her arms across the floor. "What time is it?"

"I don't know, but there's a ray of sun streaming through a hole in my window shade," Rachel said. "Don't sit up straight or you might bump your head like I did."

"I'll be careful. Now let's hurry and get dressed so we can go see the kittens," Audra said as the girls crawled out from under the bed.

"That's a good idea." Rachel rubbed her lower back. "That floor was sure hard. I think we should have slept in the bed instead of under it."

Audra nodded. "My back feels sore, too."

"I'm sure we'll feel better when we move around," Rachel said. "At least that's what Grandpa always says after he's been sitting awhile."

Audra laughed. "When my daed comes home after working at the blacksmith shop all day, he says he feels better after he lies down."

"Pap says that after he's worked in the fields, too." Rachel went to her closet and took out a clean dress. "If Mom hasn't started breakfast yet, we can go outside and check on the kittens right away."

"I still can't believe Cuddles had her busslin inside your sleeping bag," Audra said.

"I guess she was looking for a place that was nice and soft." Rachel grabbed Audra's hand. "Let's hurry downstairs, *schnell* [quickly]!"

When they entered the kitchen, Rachel was glad to see that Mom wasn't there. If she had been, she would have expected Rachel to help with breakfast.

Rachel opened the back door and stepped onto the porch. Audra followed. They entered the tent, and Rachel pulled her sleeping bag open. She was surprised to see that it was empty.

Audra frowned. "What happened to Cuddles and her kittens?"

"I don't know. She might have moved them, or maybe Pap took them to the barn."

"Let's go see!"

The girls raced across the yard and into the barn. Pap and Henry were there, feeding the horses.

"Cuddles and her busslin aren't in my sleeping bag!" Rachel said as she stepped up to Pap. "Do you know where they are?"

He motioned to the wooden box Rachel had made for Cuddles. "I put them in there."

Rachel and Audra dashed across the room and skidded to a stop in front of the box.

"Oh, just look at them! There's six busslin, just like I thought." Rachel grinned at Audra. "Aren't they the cutest little things you've ever seen?"

"They sure are." Audra pointed to a gray and white one that looked just like Cuddles. "If my mamm says it's all right, I'd like to have that one when it's big enough."

Rachel nodded. "If you get to have one of Cuddles' kittens, whenever we get together to play, our cats can play, too."

"My birthday's in six weeks," Audra said. "Do you think the kitten will be ready to leave Cuddles by then?"

"I'm sure it will, and it would make a great birthday present." Rachel squeezed Audra's arm. "Speaking of birthdays, my birthday's next Friday, and Pap said he might take our family out for supper that night. Maybe he'll let you go along."

"I'd like that very much," Audra said with a nod.

"I'll be right back!" Rachel raced over to Pap. "Can Audra go with us when we eat out for my birthday?"

Pap smiled. "I don't see why not. Of course, she'll have to get her parents' permission."

"All right!" Rachel clapped her hands, spun around in a circle, and raced back to Audra. "Pap said you can join us!"

Audra smiled. "Would you like anything special for your birthday?"

"You don't have to bring me a present," Rachel said.

"I want to." Audra hugged Rachel. "You're my best friend, and best friends always give each other something for their birthday."

"I'm sure I'll like whatever you give me." Rachel could hardly wait until Friday!

Chapter 5

A Birthday Surprise

When Rachel woke on Friday morning, one week later, she threw back the covers, leaped out of bed, and quickly dressed. Today was her eleventh birthday! She could hardly wait to see what surprises waited for her downstairs!

When Rachel entered the kitchen there was no sign of Mom. None of the usual good smells came from the kitchen, either. That was strange.

She glanced around. No birthday presents waited on the counter or the table. That wasn't a good sign.

She looked at the clock above the refrigerator. It was 7:00 a.m. Surely Mom must be up by now.

Rachel hurried to her parents' bedroom and nearly bumped into Grandpa as he stepped out of his room. "I'm glad to see you're up, Rachel," he said. "Your mamm asked me to give you a message."

"What?"

"She's in labor, and your daed hired a driver to take

them to the hospital." Grandpa squeezed Rachel's shoulder. "Soon you'll be a big sister. Isn't that exciting?"

Rachel's mouth dropped open. "Mom's having the boppli today?"

Grandpa nodded. "It seems so."

"B–but she can't have it today." Rachel's lip quivered. "Today's my birthday. Pap's supposed to take us out for supper tonight. Audra's planning to go with us."

"Babies don't wait, Rachel, and your mamm certainly won't go anywhere this evening. We'll have to celebrate your birthday some other night. Oh, and I ordered a birthday present for you, but it hasn't come in yet." Grandpa hugged Rachel. "*Hallich gebottsdaag* [Happy birthday], Rachel. What a great birthday present you'll get! Your baby schweschder or bruder."

Rachel swallowed around the lump that had formed in her throat. She wasn't sure she wanted a baby sister or brother. And she sure didn't want the baby to be born on her birthday!

"I'm going out to the phone shed to check the answering machine," Grandpa said. "When your daed calls to tell us the boppli's been born, we'll go to the hospital to meet the new baby." He patted Rachel's head. "Would you like that?"

She nodded slowly. "I—I guess so."

"While I'm in the phone shed, would you like me to phone the Burkholders and let Audra know we won't go to supper tonight?"

"I—I guess she does need to know." The lump in Rachel's throat tightened. What a disappointing day!

"I haven't had breakfast yet, and neither has Jacob or Henry," Grandpa said. "Would you fix us all something to eat?"

"Okay, Grandpa." Rachel trudged off to the kitchen. She would fix breakfast for Grandpa and her brothers, but she didn't think she'd be able to eat. Her birthday was ruined, and the only surprise was that Mom was at the hospital having a baby.

"Why don't you eat your oatmeal?" Jacob asked Rachel as they sat at the table with Grandpa and Henry.

Rachel shrugged. "I'm not hungry."

"You'd better eat or you won't have the strength to do your chores," Henry said.

Grandpa looked at Rachel and raised his eyebrows. "Your bruder's right; you do need to eat."

"Maybe I'll have a piece of toast," she mumbled.

"Have you checked the answering machine?" Jacob asked Grandpa.

He nodded. "I went to the phone shed right before breakfast, but there wasn't a message from your daed yet. I'll check again after we eat."

Jacob nudged Rachel. "How come my oatmeal doesn't have any raisins? Mom always fixes it with raisins."

Rachel glared at him. "You should be glad I fixed your breakfast at all—especially since today's my birthday!"

"Oh, that's right," Henry said. "Hallich gebottsdaag, Rachel."

"Jah, happy birthday," Jacob mumbled, oatmeal filling his mouth.

Rachel frowned. Was that all she would get—a mumbled happy birthday? *I wonder how Jacob would like it if today was his birthday and no one cared.*

She pushed away from the table, biting her bottom lip so she wouldn't cry. "I'll get you some raisins!"

"Danki," Jacob said.

Rachel opened the cupboard where Mom kept her baking supplies. She didn't see any raisins. She opened another cupboard. Still no raisins.

"Can't you find the box of raisins?" Jacob called over his shoulder.

"Des kann ich finne [I can find it]," Rachel said.

"Are you sure? Do you need me to help look for it?"

"Just stay where you are! I don't need your help!"

Grandpa turned and looked sternly at Rachel. "You don't have to be so snappish. Jacob was only offering to help."

"Sorry," Rachel mumbled as she choked back tears. It didn't seem fair that Grandpa was taking Jacob's side. Nothing about today seemed fair!

Rachel rummaged through a couple more cupboards and finally found the raisins next to a box of crackers. Someone must have put them there by mistake.

She plunked the box of raisins in front of Jacob. "Here you go!"

"Don't need 'em now." Jacob pointed to his empty bowl. "I finished my oatmeal."

Rachel clamped her teeth together. She knew if she told Jacob what she thought she'd get a lecture from Grandpa. She put the box of raisins back in the cupboard. Then she sat at the table and forced herself to eat a piece of toast.

When everyone had finished their breakfast and the men had gone outside, Rachel cleared the table and washed the dishes. She'd just dried the last dish when Grandpa stepped into the kitchen wearing a huge smile.

"Your daed called," he said.

"What'd he say? Has Mom had the boppli?"

He nodded. "They won't come home from the hospital until tomorrow, so we'll go over there today and meet your little sister."

Rachel dropped the dish towel. "A baby girl?"

"Jah. I guess we'll find out what they've named her when we get to the hospital."

Rachel drew in a deep breath. She hadn't even thought about the baby needing a name. She wondered what name Mom and Pap would call her little sister. She wondered what the baby looked like. She wondered what it would be like having a baby in the house.

Rachel stared at the scenery as she sat in the back of Harold Johnson's van. She and Grandpa were on their way to the hospital. Jacob and Henry had stayed home because they had so much work to do. Esther and Rudy had gone to the farmers' market in Ephrata, so they didn't even know the baby had arrived. They were supposed to be back in time to join Rachel's family for her birthday supper and didn't know it had been canceled.

Zip! Zip! Zip! Rachel placed her hand on her stomach. She felt like a zillion butterflies were zipping around in there. She was anxious to meet her baby sister, but she was also nervous. She hadn't felt this anxious since the day she'd gone to the eye doctor and found out she had to wear glasses.

"We're here," Harold announced. "Do you know how long you'll be?" he asked Grandpa.

"No more than an hour, I'm sure," Grandpa replied. "We don't want to tire my daughter and her wee one."

"That should work out fine," Harold said. "I have a few errands to run, but I'll be back in plenty of time to pick you up."

"Thank you." Grandpa opened the door for Rachel, and she stepped out of the van.

"Are you as excited as I am?" he asked as they entered the hospital.

"Jah." Her voice squeaked, and she swallowed a couple of times. She was really more nervous than excited.

"Your daed said your mamm's room is number 322, so we'll have to ride the elevator to the third floor."

When they stepped into the elevator, the butterflies in Rachel's stomach started zipping around again. What if she didn't like the baby? What if Mom and Pap liked the baby more than they liked her? Rachel had been the baby in their family for eleven years. Now she was not the youngest child anymore.

As they headed toward Mom's room, Rachel's heart hammered.

"Here we are," Grandpa said. "Room 322!" He pushed the door open, but Rachel hesitated. "Go on in," he said. "I'm right behind you."

Rachel entered the room and saw Mom lying in a bed. She held a baby in her arms. Pap sat beside the bed wearing a huge smile.

"Wie geht's?" Grandpa asked Mom.

"I'm a little tired, but doing fine."

Rachel stood to one side, unsure of what to say or do.

Mom smiled and motioned to Rachel. "*Kumme* [Come]. Kumme see your little schweschder."

Rachel moved to the bed and peered at the baby in Mom's arms. She had blond hair, the same color as Rachel's, and her little nose was turned up, the same as Jacob's.

"What do you think of our little Hannah?" Pap asked. "Isn't she a *schee* [pretty] boppli?"

Rachel nodded. She had to admit, Hannah was kind of pretty. "Why did you name her Hannah?" she asked.

"Because it was my mamm's name," Mom said. She

looked at Grandpa and smiled. "We thought you might like having a granddaughter with the same name as Mama."

"Hannah's a very nice name; I'm glad you chose it." Tears welled in Grandpa's eyes. "Daughter, you do have a very schee boppli," he said, taking Mom's hand. "I only wish your mamm was here to meet her namesake."

Mom nodded and reached under her glasses to wipe away her own tears. "I wish that, too, but I'm grateful Mama's in heaven. I'm also happy you'll get to know our little Hannah." She smiled at Rachel again. "Where's Henry and Jacob? I want them to meet their baby sister, too."

"They're still working," Grandpa said. "They said to tell you that they're excited about the boppli and will see her when you bring her home tomorrow."

Mom nodded. "There's a lot of work to be done on the farm, and with Levi here at the hospital, it's good that our boys are such hard workers."

Pap nodded. "I called Rudy and Esther and left a message after the boppli was born, so I expect they'll be here soon."

Rachel shook her head. "They were planning to go to the farmers' market in Ephrata today, remember?"

"Oh, that's right." Pap stroked the baby's head. "I guess they'll have to meet Hannah when we take her home tomorrow."

Mom motioned to the empty chair on the other

side of her bed. "Rachel, would you like to sit down and hold your baby sister?"

Rachel swallowed hard. "I–I'm not sure I should."

"Why not?" asked Pap.

"She might cry or wet her *windel* [diaper]."

"She's sound asleep, so I'm sure she won't cry. And I just changed her before you got here, so you shouldn't have to worry about that either," Mom said.

"Oh, okay." Rachel took a seat, and Pap placed the baby in her arms. Weren't Mom and Pap going to say anything about Rachel's birthday? Didn't they care that she'd missed her birthday dinner because of Hannah being born?

Pap placed his hand on Rachel's shoulder. "Since Hannah chose today to be born, the two of you will always share the same birthday," he said.

Rachel was glad Pap hadn't forgotten, but did he have to mention that she and Hannah would share the same birthday? And he still hadn't said a word about them not going to supper tonight, or even mentioned whether he and Mom had bought Rachel a present.

"Did you hear what I said about you and Hannah sharing a birthday?" Pap asked, nudging Rachel's arm.

Rachel nodded. She couldn't tell Mom or Pap that she didn't like the idea of sharing a birthday with Hannah.

As Mom took a nap and Pap and Grandpa talked about crops, Rachel thought about her birthday.

Wait! She suddenly thought. Henry and Jacob stayed home. *Maybe they're not working in the fields. Maybe they're planning something special for my birthday!*

Last year they had surprised her with a skateboard. Maybe they were making something for her. Or maybe Esther and Rudy had returned from the farmers' market and were helping them make a special dinner at home. The more Rachel thought about it, the more sure she became that the rest of her family was preparing to surprise her.

Awhile later, Rachel eagerly climbed into Harold Johnson's van. She barely noticed the other cars on the road or the scenery whizzing by. She was too busy wondering what her brothers might have planned.

"I'm glad to see you looking happier than you were earlier," Grandpa said to her as they rode along. "I thought you would enjoy seeing the boppli."

"Jah," Rachel said absently.

Finally, Harold's van pulled up to Rachel's house. While Grandpa paid Harold, Rachel dashed into the house, expecting to smell Esther's tasty dinner. "Hello! We're home!" she called as she banged the door behind her.

Silence answered her call. No pleasant aromas of her favorite dinner greeted her. She looked around the empty house.

"Well, Rachel," Grandpa said as he came through the door. "Your brothers will be in from the fields soon.

They'll be hungry and tired. I guess it's up to you to find something for us all to eat." Grandpa walked into his room and closed his door.

Rachel bit her lip as she walked into the kitchen. Tears stung her eyes as she realized that none of her birthday dreams were going to come true. She sighed and opened the refrigerator door to figure out what to make for dinner. *Looks like the boppli will bring even more trouble into my life!*

Chapter 6

Trouble in the Greenhouse

The next morning, as Rachel had begun to wash the breakfast dishes, she saw Harold Johnson's van pull into the yard. "Harold's here," she said to Pap, who was sitting at the table drinking a second cup of coffee.

Pap jumped up and looked out the window. "I hired him to take me to Lancaster this morning."

"Does that mean you won't work today?" Rachel asked.

"That's right. I'm going to the hospital to see your mamm and sister. Henry and Jacob will work alone in the fields again today, but I'll help them tomorrow."

"Are Mom and the boppli coming home today?" Rachel asked.

"Jah, but probably not until later this afternoon."

"Then why are you leaving so early?"

"Because Harold has a dental appointment and several errands to run in Lancaster. So he's taking me to the hospital this morning. Hopefully, by the time he's done with everything, your mamm and Hannah will be ready to come home." Pap grabbed his straw hat from the wall peg near the door. "I'm heading out now, Rachel. Have a good day."

"Can I go?" she asked.

He shook his head. "No. Someone needs to be here to fix lunch for Grandpa, Henry, and Jacob, and I'm afraid that has to be you."

Rachel frowned. "Can't they fix their own lunches?"

"I'm sure they could, but since Grandpa will be busy in his greenhouse all day and your brothers are working, it makes sense that you fix lunch for everyone."

"But I wanted to help Grandpa today," Rachel whined. "He said I could help him this summer, and I haven't been there very much at all."

"You can go to the greenhouse after doing the breakfast dishes. I also want you to make sure the house is clean before we get home. Your mamm will feel good to see a clean house when she returns." Pap smiled and headed out the door.

Rachel dropped her sponge into the soapy water. Several bubbles floated up and hit the ceiling. "Work, work, work. All I ever do is work," she grumbled. "I wish I could spend the day at the creek or helping Grandpa. Summer's half over and I haven't done anything fun. I didn't even have fun on my birthday!"

Rachel sloshed the sponge against a dirty plate as she continued to grumble. "After I finish these dishes, I'll clean the house quickly so I can go to the greenhouse. That will be a lot more fun than doing dishes or cleaning house!"

Rachel's bare toes tingled as she raced through the grass toward Grandpa's greenhouse that afternoon. She loved going barefoot during summer months. She especially liked dangling her feet in the cool creek, but she probably wouldn't have time for that today. When she finished helping Grandpa, she'd have to start supper and then clean more dishes.

When Rachel entered the greenhouse, she found Grandpa sitting behind the counter. His eyes were closed, his head leaned against the wall, and his mouth hung slightly open. She figured he would soon start snoring. That wouldn't be good if a customer showed up.

"Are you napping?" Rachel asked, touching Grandpa's shoulder.

Grandpa's eyes popped open. "Uh, no—I was just resting my eyes."

Rachel snickered. "Mom says that sometimes when I find her on the sofa with her eyes closed."

"Like father, like daughter." Grandpa yawned and stretched his arms. "I am kind of tired this morning."

"Didn't you sleep well last night?"

He touched his left ear. "*Letscht nacht hab ich ohreweh ghat* [I had an earache last night]."

"I'm sorry to hear you had an earache. Does it feel better today?"

Grandpa nodded. "Jah, but my muscles ache from tossing and turning all night. Guess I'm just getting *alt* [old] and *schwach* [feeble]."

Rachel shook her head. "You're not so old, Grandpa, and I don't think you're feeble, either. You get around pretty well."

"Sure feels like I'm alt and schwach sometimes— especially when I have to deal with aches and pains." Grandpa pushed back his chair and stood. "I think I'll go to the house and take some aspirin. Would you keep an eye on things while I'm gone?"

"I can do that. Do you want me to do anything special while you're gone?"

"Would you water the plants?"

Rachel smiled. "I'd be glad to." Even though Rachel didn't enjoy doing chores in the house, she didn't mind working in the greenhouse at all.

"All right then; I'll be back soon," Grandpa said.

"Take your time. I can manage fine," Rachel called as Grandpa left the greenhouse.

Rachel drew in a deep breath, enjoying the fragrance of the flowers and plants growing on one side of the greenhouse. Several vases filled with cut flowers smelled equally nice.

Someday, when I'm grown up, I'd like to own a greenhouse just like this, Rachel thought as she grabbed the watering can and turned on the faucet. *I think tending flowers and plants would be a whole lot more fun than getting married and taking care of babies.*

Rachel began watering the plants closest to her. The door opened, and Audra entered the greenhouse, carrying a small paper sack.

"Hi, Rachel." Audra smiled. "I went up to the house looking for you, but your grossdaadi said you were out here."

Rachel nodded. "I'm watering plants for him while he takes aspirin for his achy muscles."

"He said I should tell you that he'll be a few more minutes because he has to go to the phone shed to make a few calls."

Rachel shrugged. "No problem. I'm getting along fine."

"Jah, I can see." Audra held out the paper sack. "Since we couldn't go out to celebrate your birthday last night, I wanted to come by and give you your present. Hallich gebottsdaag, Rachel."

Rachel smiled as she set the watering can down and took the sack. At least someone had given her a birthday gift. She set the sack on the counter and opened it. Inside was a book about a cat named Sam, along with a gray cloth mouse.

"The book's for you," Audra said. "And I thought Cuddles would like the mouse 'cause it's filled with catnip."

"Danki," said Rachel. "I'm sure we'll both enjoy our treats."

Audra leaned on the edge of the counter. "I heard your mamm had a baby girl yesterday."

Rachel nodded. "Hannah is coming home from the hospital sometime today."

"I'll bet you're real excited."

Rachel moistened her lips. "Well, I—"

"If I had a baby sister, I'd be excited," Audra said.

Rachel motioned to the plants she'd been watering. "Being here in the greenhouse—that's what excites me!"

"I guess it would since you like flowers so much." Audra moved toward the door. "I'd better go. My mamm needs help cleaning the house, and I told her I wouldn't be gone long."

"Okay. Danki for coming—and for the gifts." Rachel followed Audra across the room. "If we ever go for supper to celebrate my birthday, I'll let you know."

"Okay. See you later, Rachel."

Audra scurried out the door, and Rachel picked up the watering can. She'd only watered a few plants when she heard a commotion outside.

Woof! Woof!

Meow! Meow!

Woof! Woof! Woof!

Meow!

Thinking Cuddles and Buddy must be playing in the yard, Rachel set the watering can down and opened the door. "What's going on out here?" she hollered when Cuddles zipped past the greenhouse. "Why aren't you in the barn with your busslin, Cuddles?"

The cat turned and darted into the greenhouse.

Woof! Woof! Their neighbor's collie dog, Chester, bounded in behind the cat. Well, at least it wasn't Buddy causing trouble this time.

Cuddles jumped onto the table where some new plants had been set, and Chester swatted at her tail with his paw. *Woof! Woof! Woof!*

Meow! Cuddles leaped off the table and jumped into a hanging basket full of petunias. The basket swung back and forth. Chester barked, and Cuddles laid her ears back and hissed.

Rachel knew she wouldn't be able to get Cuddles out of the petunia basket until Chester was gone, so she grabbed the collie's collar and led him toward the door.

Woof! Chester jerked free and raced to the back of the greenhouse with his tail swishing.

"Come back here, you crazy mutt!" Rachel hollered. "You'll knock something over if you're not careful!"

Rachel had no sooner said the words when— *thunk!*—Chester smacked a pot of pansies with his tail and it toppled to the floor. The pot broke and dirt went everywhere!

"Oh, no! Now look what you've done!" Rachel groaned. "You're a cute dog, but you're as rowdy as Jacob's hund!"

Rachel lunged for Chester, but he darted away. Round and round the greenhouse they went, Chester barking, Cuddles meowing, and Rachel shouting.

Thunk! Crash! Chester knocked another pot of pansies to the floor.

"You're in big trouble now!" Rachel dashed to a faucet with a hose connected and turned on the water. She pointed the hose at Chester and shot water in his face.

Woof! Woof! Woof! Chester zipped out the open door.

Rachel slammed the door behind him and drew in a deep breath. She needed to calm down. She needed to check on Cuddles.

After turning off the water, she hurried to the hanging plants and looked up. There was no sign of her cat in the petunia basket!

"Cuddles, where are you? Come here, kitty, kitty!"

No response. Not even a faint meow.

"You can come out of hiding now, Cuddles. That mean old dog is gone. Go back to the barn and take care of your kittens. They're probably hungry." Rachel walked up and down the rows of plants, calling for Cuddles. She was about to check behind the counter when her wild-eyed cat leaped over a tray of vegetable plants sitting on the floor.

"No! No! You'll wreck the—"

Meow! Cuddles leaped into the air and—*floop!*—landed on top of a struggling cherry tomato plant, squishing it!

Rachel gasped. "If Grandpa sees the mess you and

Chester made, he'll be upset. I'd better get this cleaned up before he comes back."

Just then, the door swung open. Cuddles darted outside, right between Grandpa's legs. "I'm back!" Grandpa said as he entered the building. "How's everything going?"

Before Rachel could tell Grandpa what had happened, his bushy eyebrows rose high and he pointed at the broken pots and dirt all over the floor. "What in all the world happened, Rachel?"

"I—uh—heard a commotion in the yard, and when I opened the door, Cuddles ran into the greenhouse. Then the neighbor's collie darted in after her." Rachel drew in a quick breath and pointed to the plants Chester had knocked over. "He was worse than Buddy. I had a terrible time getting him outside." She pointed to the tomato plant. "When I did get Chester out, Cuddles jumped on this and smashed it."

The wrinkles in Grandpa's forehead deepened, and his cheek muscle quivered. "I'm very disappointed, Rachel. I thought I could depend on you to take care of things while I was gone. I didn't think I'd come back and find a mess like this!"

"I–I'm sorry. I didn't expect the dog to run in here and make a mess." She grabbed the broom leaning against the wall. "I'll clean everything up, and I'll work extra hours in the greenhouse until I've made enough money to replace the ones that were ruined."

Grandpa leaned against the workbench and folded his arms as Rachel swept up the dirt. She could almost feel him watching her. He probably thought she didn't know how to clean the mess. Did he think she couldn't do anything right?

A few minutes later, Grandpa touched Rachel's shoulder. "I'm sorry for snapping at you. This was obviously an accident. It wasn't your fault." He took the broom from her. "Let me finish sweeping while you look for your cat."

Rachel hugged him. "Danki, Grandpa."

He patted her head. "I was young once, too, you know. And I never liked being scolded for something that wasn't my fault."

Rachel smiled. She was glad she had such an understanding grandpa. She looked forward to spending more time with him in the greenhouse this summer. And she hoped no cats or dogs ever got into the greenhouse again!

Chapter 7

Hannah Comes Home

Later that afternoon, Rachel sat at the kitchen table thinking about what she might cook for supper. Her mind began to wander. She thought about Cuddles and how she wished she could keep all six of her kittens. She knew Mom would never agree, though. If she were lucky, she might be allowed to keep one kitten.

She thought about all the work she'd done and wished she could run to the creek. She'd be happy for just a few minutes—long enough to slip her feet in the water and get cooled off. It was so hot and muggy; Rachel felt she deserved a break.

Rachel was about to go to the greenhouse and ask Grandpa if she could go to the creek for a while, when she heard a horse whinny. She rushed to the window and saw Esther's horse and buggy coming up the driveway.

When Rachel stepped onto the back porch, Esther smiled and waved.

"Wie geht's?" Rachel called as she ran out to Esther's buggy.

"I'm doing well. How are things with you?"

Rachel shrugged. "Okay, I guess."

"Just okay?"

"Jah."

"You look droopy. Do you feel all right?"

"I'm not sick—just tired from working so hard."

"What have you been doing?" Esther asked.

"I fixed breakfast and lunch, did the dishes, picked up the house, and helped Grandpa in the greenhouse." Rachel sighed. "Now it's time for me to start supper. If I can think of something good to fix, that is."

"It does sound as if you've had a busy day," Esther said as she unhitched her horse from the buggy.

Rachel motioned to the house. "If you came to see Mom, she's not here. She had her boppli yesterday."

"I know about the baby. When we got back from the farmers' market our answering machine had a message saying that Mom had a baby girl named Hannah." Esther smiled. "Is Mom coming home soon?"

Rachel shrugged. "Pap went to the hospital after breakfast, but they're not here yet. You can come back later if you want."

"No need for that; I'm planning to stay. In fact, I came to make supper for the family. Rudy will join us when he's finished working." Esther reached into the buggy and pulled out a cardboard box. "I also came by to give you a birthday present."

"Oh, what is it?"

Esther set the box on the ground. "Why don't you open it and see?"

Rachel knelt down, opened the flaps on the box, and gasped when she saw what was inside. It was a shiny new skateboard, just like the one she'd put in layaway at Kauffman's store last summer!

Rachel's eyes filled with tears as she looked at Esther. "I never expected to get another skateboard—especially not one so new and nice. Danki, Esther."

"You're welcome. I knew you gave Audra your skateboard after you accidentally broke hers, so I thought you'd like to have a new one." Esther bent and hugged Rachel. "I'm sorry for not getting the gift to you on time, but I want to wish you a happy birthday now, little sister."

"It's okay," Rachel said. "With Hannah being born on my birthday, I think everyone in the family forgot about me. I wish Hannah had been born on a different day."

"Women don't get to choose the day or time their babies will be born," Esther said. "I'm sure you were disappointed that you didn't get to have supper out, but I don't want you to think everyone forgot about you."

"I know you didn't, or else you wouldn't have given me the skateboard."

"That's right, and I'm sure Mom and Pap will give you something besides a baby sister when she gets home from the hospital and is settled in." Esther reached into the buggy again and pulled out a paper sack. "In the meantime, I brought everything we'll need for supper. So if you can carry this sack and your skateboard, would you take it to the house while I put my horse away?"

Rachel nodded. "I can manage both. When you come inside, I'll help you make supper."

"Wouldn't you like to try your new skateboard?"

"Maybe later. The only good place I have to skateboard is in the barn, and it's too stuffy in there right now." Rachel blew out her breath so hard the ties on her *kapp* [cap] floated up. "With all this hot weather, I feel like a wet noodle."

Esther chuckled. "Then why don't you go to the creek and cool off?"

"What about supper?"

"I can manage on my own." Esther squeezed Rachel's shoulder. "I'll ring the dinner bell when I need you to come and set the table. How's that sound?"

"It sounds real good. Danki." Rachel smiled at Esther. "See you later then."

Rachel took the sack of groceries to the kitchen and rushed to the barn to put away her new skateboard.

"Where are you going, pretty bird?" she sang as she sprinted for the creek. "Where are you going, pretty bird? I am going to my tree, I am going to my tree, I am going to my tree, sweet Rose."

After getting such a nice birthday gift from

Esther, Rachel felt better about life. When Esther had suggested she go to the creek, she felt loved and appreciated. Maybe things weren't as bad as she thought. Maybe when Pap brought Mom and the baby home from the hospital, they would have a birthday present for her to open.

Rachel sat on a big rock by the creek. She dangled her bare feet in the cool water and wiggled her toes. After working so hard all day, she was glad to sit and relax. She felt even better to know she didn't have to fix supper this evening.

She leaned her head back and watched puffy clouds float lazily across the sky. It was so peaceful and quiet by the creek. The only sound was the steady gurgling of the water rolling over the rocks. Her eyes felt heavy, and she let them close. If she sat here long, she could easily fall asleep.

"Yahoo! This will sure feel good!"

Rachel's eyes snapped open to see Jacob barrel into the creek. Sloshing through the water, he kicked and splashed, sending water all over Rachel's dress.

"Cut that out!" she shouted. "You're getting me all wet!"

"If you don't want to be wet, then you shouldn't be here at the creek!" Jacob splashed more water in her direction and laughed.

Rachel jumped up and, using her foot, splashed him

right back. "How do you like that, Jacob Yoder?"

"I like it just fine. The cool water feels good on a hot day like this!" Jacob played in the creek, laughing and making ripples of water go in all directions. Then he dropped to his knees, leaned over, and dunked his head under the water. When he came up, he shook his head like a dog, showering Rachel with even more water. She had to admit it felt pretty good, and it gave her some relief from the sticky summer day.

"Maybe we should go to the house and put on our swimsuits," she said. "Then we can get as wet as we like."

"Good idea. Last one to the house has to feed Buddy his supper tonight!"

"No way!" Rachel shook her head. "I'm not feeding your mutt ever again, so I won't race you to the house after all!"

Jacob shrugged. "Suit yourself." He dashed away, and Rachel sprinted behind him. She was halfway there when—*ding! ding! ding!*—the dinner bell rang.

"That must be Esther," Rachel said. "She's at the house fixing supper and said she'd ring the bell when she needed me to set the table."

"Does that mean you're not going swimming?" Jacob asked.

"Probably not, and if supper's almost ready, you won't be going swimming either." Rachel hurried past Jacob and ran to the house. "Ha! Ha! I won the race!" she shouted as Jacob stomped up the steps behind her.

"So what? It doesn't matter who won the race, because I was planning to feed Buddy anyway!"

When Rachel entered the kitchen, she encountered a wonderful aroma. "Mmm. . .what are you cooking?" she asked, stepping to the stove where Esther stirred something in a large kettle.

Esther smiled at Rachel. "Chicken and dumplings. There's also a tossed green salad and some pickled beets in the refrigerator."

Rachel licked her lips. She knew Jacob liked chicken and dumplings, and she loved pickled beets, so they would both enjoy this meal!

"Do you need me to do anything besides setting the table?" she asked Esther.

"You can peel some carrots when you're done if you like."

"Okay."

Rachel had just finished setting the table when she heard a vehicle rumble into the yard. She rushed to the window to see Pap help Mom out of Harold's van. Mom held the baby in her arms.

Esther opened the back door and rushed outside. Rachel was right behind her.

"Welcome home!" Esther said when Mom and Pap stepped onto the porch. "I got your message about the boppli. How are you feeling, Mom?"

"I'm pretty tired but doing okay." Mom glanced at Rachel. "How are things here at the house? Did you manage okay while I was gone?"

"Things are fine," Rachel said. "Esther came over to fix supper, and I just set the table."

Pap smiled at Mom. "Aren't we fortunate to have two thoughtful *dechder* [daughters]?"

Mom nodded.

"Speaking of your daughters," Esther said, pointing to herself, "your oldest daughter is eager to hold her new baby sister."

"Why don't we all go into the living room?" Pap suggested. "Then you can get to know our sweet little Hannah."

Esther smiled. "That suits me just fine!"

Rachel followed Mom, Esther, and Pap into the living room. Esther sat in the rocking chair, and Mom placed the baby in Esther's lap. Then she sat on the sofa, and Rachel sat beside her.

Pap moved toward the door. "I think I'll walk to the fields and let the boys know we're home. I'd also like to see how they've managed in my absence." He turned around and looked at Rachel. "Where's your grossdaadi?"

"Grandpa's still at the greenhouse," Rachel replied. "I'm sure he'll be coming in soon for supper, though."

"I expect you're right about that." Pap bent over and gave the baby a peck on the cheek; then he hurried out the door.

As Esther rocked the baby with a dreamy look on

her face, she sang a lullaby. Then she looked at Mom and smiled. "You are so blessed to have such a sweet little boppli."

Mom nodded as tears welled in her eyes. "You'll feel the same blessing in a few months, after your boppli is born."

"Jah, I'm sure I will." Esther looked at Rachel. "There's a gift for the boppli in the paper sack I brought with the supper items. It's sitting on the kitchen counter. Would you get it for me?"

"Okay." As Rachel walked past the rocking chair, she glanced at her baby sister. Hannah's eyes were closed, and her little chest rose up and down as she breathed. She looked so peaceful nestled in Esther's arms. Rachel wondered if she had been that tiny and cute when she was a baby. If so, no one had ever mentioned it to her. Eleven whole years had passed since she'd been born; maybe they'd forgotten what she had been like when she was that little.

"Oh Rachel, one more thing," Esther called.

"What's that?"

"While you're in the kitchen, would you check on the chicken and dumplings?"

"Sure, no problem."

When Rachel entered the kitchen, she lifted the lid on the kettle and sniffed. "Yum. . .this sure smells good." Her stomach rumbled. "I can hardly wait until supper!"

Rachel found the gift and took it to the living room. "Here you go," she said, handing it to Mom.

Mom tore the wrapping off and removed a pair of pink baby booties and a matching cap. "These are so nice. Did you knit them, Esther?"

Esther nodded. "I made a blue set, too. . .in case you had a *buwe* [boy]."

"Maybe you'll have a buwe," Mom said. "Then he can wear the other set."

Esther sighed and nestled Hannah against her shoulder. "I think Rudy wants a buwe, and I hope he won't be disappointed if it's a *maedel* [girl]."

"Why would he be disappointed if you had a girl?" Rachel questioned.

"I think he'd like a boy to carry on his name and to help him on the farm," Esther said.

Rachel folded her arms. "Well, I hope you have a maedel. We don't need any more buwe in this family."

Mom clicked her tongue. "We shall all love your boppli whether it's a buwe or a maedel."

Esther kissed the top of Hannah's head. "That's right, and we'll love this little one, too, because she's a real sweetie."

Mom nodded. "I feel so blessed to have a new baby daughter. I'm pleased that our two little ones will only be a few months apart." She smiled at Esther. "They can grow up together, and hopefully they'll become good friends."

"That's what I hope for, too," Esther said.

A pang of jealousy stabbed Rachel's heart. Did Mom and Esther care more about Hannah and Esther's baby than about her? When Esther's baby was born, would Rachel be ignored even more than she was now?

"I guess I'll go cut up those carrots now," Rachel mumbled as she shuffled toward the kitchen.

Esther started singing to the baby again.

Tears rolled down Rachel's cheeks as she entered the kitchen. She felt so forgotten. Mom hadn't even told her happy birthday last night or today either. Mom and Esther could only talk about babies! Rachel probably wouldn't get a birthday present from Mom and Pap this year at all!

If I ever do get married and have any bopplin, Rachel thought, *I'll make sure their birthdays are always special! I'll make sure they get a nice gift every year, too.*

Chapter 8

Nothing but Trouble

*W*aaa! *Waaa! Waaa!*

Rachel covered her ears with her pillow and moaned. Her baby sister might be cute and cuddly, but she sure did cry a lot. In the three weeks since Mom had brought Hannah home from the hospital, every night Rachel was awakened by the baby's cries. How was she supposed to do her chores when she couldn't get a good night's sleep?

She wondered if Hannah's crying bothered anyone else. If so, they hadn't said anything. In fact, the only thing Mom and Pap said about Hannah was how cute she was, and how blessed they felt to have a baby in the house again. Even Grandpa, Henry, and Jacob made over Hannah with silly baby sounds.

Waaa! Waaa! The irritating cries from Mom and Pap's bedroom continued to float up the stairs. Rachel pushed the pillow tighter against her ears, hoping to drown out the sound. It was no use. Hannah's cries seemed to be getting louder.

With an exasperated sigh, Rachel pulled her sheet aside and crawled out of bed. She plodded over to the window and lifted the shade, squinting at the rising sun.

I guess if the sun's up, I may as well be, too, she decided. *Audra's birthday is just a few weeks away. Maybe I can paint a rock for her before I help Mom with breakfast.*

Rachel frowned. They still hadn't gone out for her birthday supper, and she'd almost given up on the idea. She'd asked Pap several times, but he always said they would do it later—as soon as Mom felt stronger, and when he and the brothers weren't so busy.

Maybe Mom would never feel up to going out for supper. Maybe she'd be tired for a long time, the way their neighbor, Anna Miller, was after her last baby was born.

Pushing her troubling thoughts aside, Rachel gathered up her painting supplies, picked out a nicely shaped rock, and headed downstairs. She'd just set everything on the kitchen table when Mom stepped into the room.

"*Guder mariye* [Good morning], Rachel," Mom said. "I'm surprised to see you up so early."

Rachel yawned. "I couldn't sleep. The baby woke me with all that crying."

"She was hungry." Mom smiled. "She's been fed and had her windel changed, so she's sleeping peacefully again."

"That figures," Rachel mumbled.

"What?"

"Oh nothing."

Mom motioned to the table. "I'm going to start breakfast, so you'll need to put your paints away and set the table."

Rachel frowned. "Since it's so early, I figured I'd have plenty of time to paint a rock for Audra's birthday before you started breakfast."

"I thought you planned to give Audra one of Cuddles's kittens."

"I do, but I want to give her a painted animal rock before she and her family leave for Sarasota."

"Oh, I didn't realize they were going to Florida," Mom said.

Rachel nodded. "Her grandparents live there, and they invited Audra's family to celebrate Audra's birthday with them."

"Oh, I see."

Rachel motioned to the rock sitting on the table. "Since the kittens aren't quite old enough to leave their mamm, I wanted to give Audra something for her birthday before she leaves."

"That makes sense," Mom said with a nod, "but you'll have to paint some other time. Your daed wants to get an early start in the fields this morning before it becomes too hot. So we'll need to eat an early breakfast."

Rachel sighed. "Okay, Mom."

"Speaking of birthdays," Mom said, "I've been meaning to give you the gift your daed picked up for your birthday when he was in town the other day. We're late with your gift this year because of Hannah being born on your birthday."

Anticipation welled in Rachel's chest. "Where is it?" she asked excitedly.

Mom pointed to the cupboard where she kept her sewing supplies. "It's in there."

Rachel stared at the cupboard. She hoped it wasn't another sewing kit like the one Mom had given her last year. Rachel didn't like to sew much, and she certainly didn't need two sewing kits!

"Go ahead and get it," Mom said. "It's in a cardboard box on the bottom shelf."

Rachel opened the cupboard door and took out the box. She set it on the table and opened the lid. A blue-eyed, blond-haired baby doll dressed in Amish clothes stared back at her. Rachel took it out of the box and faced Mom. "You bought me a baby doll for my birthday?"

Mom smiled. "Actually, your daed got the doll, but that's what I told him to get."

"Why? I already have the faceless doll Audra gave me, and you know I hardly ever play with it."

Mom's cheeks turned pink. "Well, I—I thought, with you having a baby sister now, you might like to play with the doll and pretend to feed it whenever I'm feeding Hannah."

Rachel swallowed around the lump in her throat. *It figures that my gift would have something to do with Hannah.* "Maybe I'll set the doll on my dresser," she said. "Then when Hannah's old enough, I'll let her play with it."

Wrinkles formed in Mom's forehead. "Don't you like the doll?"

Rachel bit her lower lip as she tried to think of something to say that wouldn't be a lie or hurt Mom's feelings. "The doll's nice," she said, "but I'm getting too big to play with dolls. So if you don't mind, I'll just set it on my dresser."

Mom shook her head. "I don't mind, but—"

"I'll put these paints away now." Rachel scooped up the bottles of paint, put them in the box, and forced a smile. "Danki for the birthday present, Mom."

Before Mom could reply, Rachel scurried out the back door and set the box of paints on the little table on the porch. She was afraid that if she stayed in the kitchen one minute longer, she would burst into tears. Mom still saw her as a little girl who played with dolls. Mom was so busy with the baby that she couldn't even see that Rachel was growing up and might want something more exciting for her birthday than a baby doll.

"I guess things will never be the same around here now that Hannah's living with us," Rachel mumbled. "I guess no one will think much about me ever again."

Rachel had just finished drying the breakfast dishes
when Mom said, "I'm going to the cellar to wash some
clothes. When I'm done, I'd like you to hang them on
the line while I feed the boppli."

Rachel sighed. More work. Maybe she could get
out her paints while Mom washed clothes. She could
probably finish painting the rock before it was time to
hang the laundry on the line.

"One more thing," Mom said as she started for the
door.

"What's that?" Rachel asked.

"While I'm washing the clothes, I'd like you to
watch Hannah."

Rachel frowned. "I thought she was sleeping."

Mom nodded. "She is—in her cradle in the living
room. Of course she might not stay asleep."

"What should I do if she wakes up and starts crying?"

"Give her the pacifier."

"Oh, okay."

Mom left the kitchen, and Rachel picked up another
dish to dry. She figured that if Hannah woke up while
she was painting, it wouldn't take much time to put the
pacifier in her mouth. Then she could get right back to
work on the rock.

Rachel soon had all her paints laid out on the table.

She picked up her brush, dipped it into the black paint, and was getting ready to paint the body of the ladybug, when—*Waaa! Waaa!*—the baby's shrill cry almost caused her to jump out of her seat.

"Oh, great!" Rachel set the rock aside and hurried into the living room. The pacifier wasn't in the cradle with Hannah, and she didn't see it on the table by the sofa, either. Maybe Mom had left it in the bedroom.

Rachel ran into her parents' room and looked around. She didn't see the pacifier anywhere.

Waaa! Waaa! Waaa! Baby Hannah's cries grew louder.

Rachel dashed from the room and down the cellar stairs. She found Mom bent over their gas-operated washing machine with a pair of trousers in her hand.

"What are you doing down here, Rachel?" Mom asked. "Can't you hear the boppli crying?"

"I hear her all right." Rachel frowned. "I can't make her stop crying because the pacifier's gone."

"I'm sure it's in her cradle."

"I didn't see it."

Mom's glasses had slipped to the end of her nose, and she pushed them back in place. "You'd better look again."

"Okay." Rachel tromped back up the stairs. At this rate she would never get Audra's ladybug rock painted!

When Rachel entered the living room, the baby's cries grew louder, and her little face had turned bright red.

Rachel covered her ears. She wished Mom wasn't washing clothes. She wished the baby would stop crying. She wished she could find that pacifier!

Waaa! Waaa! Hannah's face turned redder.

Rachel put her fingers to her lips. "Shh. . . . Please go back to sleep."

Hannah continued to wail.

Maybe a song will help, Rachel thought. She leaned close to the cradle and began to sing. "*Bisht du an schlaufa; bish du an schlaufa? Schweschder Hannah, Schweschder Hanna? Ich hei-ah die bells an ringa. Ich hei-ah die bells an ringa.* [Are you sleeping; are you sleeping? Sister Hannah, Sister Hannah? Morning bells are ringing. Morning bells are ringing.] Ding-dong-ding! Ding-dong-ding!"

Hannah stopped crying for a few seconds; then she scrunched up her nose and let loose with a shrill *Waaaaa!*

Rachel rocked the cradle back and forth. Hannah cried. Rachel made silly faces. Hannah cried more.

In desperation, Rachel reached into the cradle and picked up Hannah. To her surprise, there was the pacifier—right where the baby had been lying!

Rachel placed Hannah back in the cradle and put the pacifier in her mouth.

Hannah's lips moved in and out as she sucked on the pacifier. Rachel sighed with relief.

She hurried back to the kitchen, dipped her brush

into the paint, and had finished half of the ladybug's body when—*Waaa! Waaa!*—Hannah began to wail.

Rachel groaned. "No! No! Not again! Is there no end to my troubles?"

She set the rock down and returned to the living room. Hannah's face had turned red again, and she waved her little hands. The pacifier had fallen out of her mouth; this time it was beside her.

Rachel put the pacifier in Hannah's mouth; then she headed back to the kitchen. She'd just sat down when the baby started howling again.

"I give up!" Rachel marched to the living room, picked up the baby, and sat in the rocking chair. She remembered how Hannah had fallen asleep when Esther had rocked her. She hoped that might work now.

Squeak. . .squeak. . .squeak. The old chair protested as she rocked back and forth. Soon Hannah's cries turned to soft snores, and Rachel knew Hannah had finally fallen asleep.

She was getting ready to put the baby back in her cradle when Mom stepped into the room. "I'm glad to see you holding the boppli," she said, smiling at Rachel. "You haven't held her much since we brought her home."

"She kept crying, and nothing helped. So I decided to try rocking her." Rachel nodded at the cradle. "I was just getting ready to put her back to bed."

"The clothes are washed and the basket's sitting

by the clothesline," Mom said, taking the baby from Rachel. "I feel tired, so I think I'll rest a bit while you hang the clothes out to dry."

"Okay. When that's done I'm going back to the kitchen to finish painting Audra's ladybug rock."

Mom shook her head. "You'll have to find another place to do that, Rachel. After I catch my breath, I need to cut out some material to make a few dresses for Hannah. I need the table for that."

Rachel fought the urge to bite her fingernail. Everything seemed to revolve around her baby sister these days, and nobody cared about her.

As she started across the room, Mom called, "Why don't you take your paints outside? After you hang the laundry, you can use the little table on the porch to paint Audra's rock."

"I guess I could do that." Rachel went to the kitchen, gathered her painting supplies, and carried them to the porch. Then she dashed across the yard, reached into the basket for a towel, and hung it on the line.

As she took out another towel, she spotted Jacob's dog lying on the porch with his nose tucked between his paws. She figured Buddy was asleep, but just in case, she would hurry to get the towels hung on the line. The last thing she needed was for him to grab a towel and tear it to shreds, as he'd done one other time.

When the towels were all hung, Rachel stepped

onto the porch and opened a jar of black paint. At last, she could paint Audra's rock.

"What are you up to?" Grandpa asked when he stepped out the back door.

"I'm painting a ladybug rock for Audra," Rachel said. "Her birthday's coming, and I want her to have it before she leaves for Florida."

"I'll bet it'll be hot in Florida this time of the year," Grandpa said as he sat on the porch swing.

Rachel dabbed her sweaty forehead with the corner of her apron. "It's hot here, too."

He nodded. "Jah, hot and plenty humid."

"Why aren't you working in your greenhouse?" Rachel asked.

"I haven't had much business this morning, so I decided to close it and come to the house for a nap."

"Didn't you sleep well last night?"

He shook his head. "Hannah's crying kept me awake, and since she's crying right now, I decided to see if I could catch a few winks on the porch."

"Well, don't let me stop you," Rachel said. "I'll quietly paint Audra's rock, and I promise not to make any noise."

"I appreciate that." Grandpa leaned his head against the back of the swing and closed his eyes. Soon he began to snore softly.

Buddy got up and plodded across the porch. He stood by the swing and nudged Grandpa's hand with his nose. Grandpa didn't budge. Rachel figured he must be really tired.

Grandpa's snores grew louder. Buddy tilted his head and whined.

"Be quiet, Buddy," Rachel said. "If you wake Grandpa, I'll put you back in your dog run where you belong."

Buddy plodded over to Rachel, and—*slurp! slurp!*—licked her face.

"Stop that, you hairy mutt!" Rachel pushed the dog aside and dipped her brush into the paint.

Oomph! Buddy bumped into the table, knocking the jar of paint over and spilling some onto the porch.

"Now look what you've done!" Rachel shook her finger at Buddy. "You're nothing but trouble!"

She dashed into the yard and grabbed the hose. Then she squirted the paint with water.

Woof! Woof! Buddy bumped Rachel's hand with his big nose. Water shot out of the hose and hit Grandpa right in the face!

"Yeow!" Grandpa jumped off the swing. "What are you doing, child?" He pointed his finger at Rachel. "Why'd you squirt me with the hose?"

"I–I'm sorry, Grandpa. I—I didn't do it on purpose." Rachel ran into the yard, turned off the hose, and stepped onto the porch. "I was trying to wash off the paint Buddy made me spill on the porch, and then the mangy critter bumped my arm and the hose got you."

Grandpa wiped his face with his shirtsleeve and motioned to the greenhouse. "Looks like I've got a customer, so I guess it's a good thing I woke up. I just didn't expect such a cold awakening." He started down the steps but turned back around. "You'd better put Buddy in his dog run. I don't want him coming out to the greenhouse and bothering my customer."

"I'll see to it right away."

Grandpa was halfway across the yard when Rachel called, "Do you need my help in the greenhouse?"

He shook his head. "No thanks. I can manage this afternoon."

Disappointed, Rachel reached for Buddy's collar, but he dashed across the porch, slid into one of Mom's flower pots, and darted into the yard.

Rachel ran after him, waving her hands. "Come back here, you troublesome dog!"

Woof! Woof! Woof! Buddy ran in circles then took off toward the barn.

Rachel dashed after him, slipped on a pile of hay inside the barn, and landed on her knees. "Trouble. . . trouble. . .trouble," she mumbled. "I'm so sick of all this trouble!"

Buddy screeched to a halt, pranced up to Rachel, and—*slurp!*—licked her nose.

She grabbed his collar. "You're coming with me, you hairy, bad-breathed brute."

Slurp! Slurp! The dog gave Rachel's nose a couple

more swipes with his big wet tongue.

Holding tightly to Buddy's collar, Rachel led him across the yard. When they reached his dog run, she opened the gate and ushered him in. "You're nothing but trouble," she muttered as she slammed the gate. "But at least you won't cause me any more trouble today!"

Chapter 9

A Thrilling Ride

A trickle of sweat rolled down Rachel's forehead and nearly ran into her eyes. With the corner of her apron, she wiped it from her forehead. Pap, Henry, and Jacob were in the fields this morning; Grandpa was working in his greenhouse; and Mom had taken the baby to the doctor's for a checkup. Rachel had been left at home to clean her room. She'd already made her bed, swept the floor, and washed the windows. Now she sat on the floor going through some old things she'd found in her dresser drawer.

"I wish I didn't have so many chores to do. It's not fair that I never get to do anything fun. I wish I could help Grandpa in the greenhouse today," Rachel grumbled as she tossed two broken pencils into the trash can.

Tears stung her eyes, and she removed her glasses to wipe her face. When she put the glasses back on, she noticed a smudge on the lens. "Oh great; now I can barely see!" She took off her glasses and placed them on the dresser, then went to the window and looked out. Everything in the yard looked blurry without her glasses, reminding Rachel that she needed to wear them all the time.

When she'd first gotten the glasses, she hadn't liked them at all—especially when boys at school had called her "four eyes." Eventually the boys quit their teasing, and Rachel had gotten used to wearing her glasses. She'd also realized that wearing glasses didn't make her look ugly or stupid. In fact, Audra said glasses made Rachel look smart.

Rachel put the glasses back on and continued to stare out the window. Even with the smudge she could see Cuddles and her little ones frolicking in the grass. The kittens were getting so big. By the time Audra and her family got back from Sarasota, the kittens should be old enough to leave their mother. Then she could give Audra the one she'd picked out.

Rachel thought about how excited Audra had been when she'd given her the ladybug rock the night before. She'd told Rachel that she and her family would leave on the bus for Sarasota this morning. She said she'd take the painted rock as a reminder that she had a friend waiting to greet her when she returned home.

"At least someone still likes me," Rachel mumbled as she moved away from the window and sat on the floor. "I used to feel like part of the family until Hannah came. Now, unless someone needs me for something, I'm ignored. I bet they love Hannah more than they do me. I bet they wouldn't even know if I was gone."

Tears streamed down Rachel's face, and her nose started to run. "I'm only good for work, work, work. I should run away from home!" She choked on a sob. "If I went away and never came back, that would show them!" *Sniff! Sniff!* "But where would I go? If I went over to Grandma Yoder's or Aunt Karen's, they'd send me right home. I can't go to Audra's house because she's in Florida."

She turned away from the window. "Orlie's folks wouldn't let me stay there either, but I could walk over to Orlie's and show him my new skateboard. I shouldn't have to stay in this hot, stuffy house and do nothing but work!"

Rachel put the drawer back in the dresser, slipped on her sneakers, put on her kapp, and hurried from the room.

When she got downstairs, she cleaned her glasses at the kitchen sink and dried them with a clean dish towel. She figured she would be back from Orlie's before Mom got home, but just in case, she wrote a note saying where she'd gone and left it on the table. Then she went to the barn, got her skateboard, and headed toward Orlie's house.

As Rachel walked along, she was tempted to ride her skateboard, but then she remembered that Mom had warned her not to ride it near the road. So she carried the skateboard under one arm and walked in the tall grass near the shoulder of the road.

As Rachel trudged along, she thought about last summer, and how she and her family had gone on a picnic the day school let out. They'd had so much fun—until she'd fallen into the pond and had gotten her clothes wet and muddy. They'd also had several barbecues last summer, eaten a few meals at restaurants, played in the creek, gone to the farmers' market, and made several batches of delicious homemade ice cream.

This summer it seemed that Rachel had done nothing but work. Even being in Grandpa's greenhouse involved work, although she did enjoy that more than any other work. Rachel wondered if she would have any real fun before it was time to return to school.

She kicked a stone with her sneaker and grunted. It would be hard to go back to school and listen to the other scholars tell about the family trips and the other fun things they'd done. All Rachel would have to talk about was her new baby sister and how she was expected to do more work now that Hannah lived with them.

Beep! Beep!

Rachel whirled around as a blue convertible pulled onto the shoulder of the road. She recognized the blond-haired English girl in the passenger's seat. It was Sherry. A teenage boy sat in the driver's seat, but Rachel had never met him.

"Hi, Rachel," Sherry called. "Where are you going with that neat-looking skateboard?"

"I'm heading to my friend Orlie's house to show him what my sister gave me for my birthday," Rachel replied.

"It looks nice," Sherry said. "Have you tried it out yet?"

Rachel shook her head. "Where are you going? Are you headed to the farmers' market?"

"Nope. We're on our way to Hershey Park," the boy said.

Rachel felt envious. "I've always wanted to visit Hershey Park," she said, staring at the ground.

"Would your folks let you go with us?" Sherry asked. "We could drive you home so you could ask."

Rachel looked up. *Thump! Thump! Thump!* Her heart hammered in her chest like a woodpecker tapping on the trunk of a tree. She would really like to spend the day at Hershey Park, and she'd give almost anything to take a ride in a convertible.

She moistened her lips with her tongue as she thought. "My mom's not at home right now, and my dad and brothers are in the fields, so there's really no one to ask."

Rachel thought about Grandpa. She knew he was working in his greenhouse. She also knew she should ask him before she went anywhere with Sherry and

Dave. But since she'd left a note on the table saying she was going to Orlie's, she didn't think her family would worry if they came into the house and found her gone. Besides, she probably wouldn't even be missed—unless someone wanted a chore done.

Rachel smiled at Sherry. "I'd be happy to go to Hershey Park with you."

"Great!" Sherry motioned to the teenage boy beside her. "This is my brother, Dave. He's almost eighteen, and he's a really good driver."

Rachel smiled. "It's nice to meet you."

"Same here." Dave pointed to the back seat. "Climb in and buckle up. Then we'll be on our way!"

Rachel climbed in, put her skateboard on the floor, buckled her seat belt, and removed her glasses so they wouldn't fall off during the ride, which she was sure would be fast and exciting. She could hardly believe the very thing she'd dreamed about for such a long time was coming true. Not only was she going to Hershey Park, but she was about to take a ride in a shiny blue convertible!

Dave pulled the car onto the road and turned on the radio.

Rachel gasped as a gust of wind hit her in the face. It seemed like they were going awfully fast—much faster than their horse and buggy could go! Much faster than she imagined a convertible would go either.

The ties on Rachel's kapp whipped around her face,

and suddenly—*whoosh!*—the kapp lifted right off her head and sailed away with the wind. "Stop! My kapp blew off!" Rachel shouted.

Dave kept driving. Between the noise of the wind and the blaring radio, she knew he probably hadn't heard what she'd said.

Rachel tapped him on the shoulder.

"What do you want?"

"My kapp blew off. We need to stop so I can get it!"

Dave shook his head. "There's no way I'm stopping for your kapp. Besides, some car's probably run over it by now."

Rachel swallowed hard. When she returned home without her kapp, how would she explain things to Mom? She knew she'd be in trouble if she said she'd taken a ride in Dave's car without anyone's permission, but she also knew it was wrong to lie. If she got home before Mom, maybe she wouldn't have to say anything about where she'd been. But what reason would she give for not wearing her kapp?

I'll deal with it later, Rachel decided.

"I'm sorry about your kapp," Sherry called over her shoulder. "Do you have another one at home?"

"I do, but—" Rachel's voice was drowned out when Dave turned up the radio. She leaned back in her seat, realizing she could do nothing about her kapp. *I may as well relax and enjoy the ride,* she decided.

As they approached the freeway, the car sped up.

Rachel thought it was exciting to go so fast, but it was also frightening. She wasn't used to traveling this fast. And that loud music put her nerves on edge. It was worse than Hannah's crying!

By the time they pulled into the parking lot at Hershey Park, Rachel felt so jittery she couldn't catch her breath. She slipped her glasses on and looked around. Cars and people were everywhere!

"We'll ride the tram to the park," Dave said. "It'll be quicker than walking."

Rachel's heart beat faster as they sat near the back of the tram. She had finally ridden in a convertible, and soon she'd go on some exciting rides inside Hershey Park. What a fun day this was turning out to be!

The man driving the tram explained that Hershey Park opened in 1907 as a place for the employees of the Hershey Chocolate Factory to picnic and have fun. He said it offered sixty attractions, including ten different roller coasters.

As they approached the park, their driver pointed to a large building. "That's Hershey's Chocolate World," he said. "You can take a free ride inside the building that will show you how candy is made, and you'll learn a lot of interesting information about the cocoa beans harvested in the jungles of Brazil."

Dave grinned at Rachel. "If we have time, we might take a tour of Chocolate World, but I think we'll probably stay busy going on all the rides inside Hershey

Park. Besides, we can buy candy at the concession stands in the park."

The mention of candy made Rachel's mouth water.

When the tram stopped in front of the main gate, Rachel, Sherry, and Dave stepped out. "Now we need to purchase tickets." Dave looked at Rachel. "I hope you brought plenty of money along, because there's lots of good food in the park, not to mention all the souvenirs."

Rachel's mouth felt so dry she could barely swallow. She hadn't even thought about needing money. Tears welled in her eyes. It didn't look like she'd visit Hershey Park after all. It looked like she'd stay right here while Dave and Sherry had all the fun.

Chapter 10

An Exciting Day

W hat's wrong? You look like you're gonna cry."
Sherry touched Rachel's arm. "I thought you'd be happy
to be at Hershey Park."

"I—I didn't bring my purse, so I have no money."
Rachel choked back tears. "I guess I won't be able to see
Hershey Park after all."

"It's okay," Sherry said. "Dave has plenty of money.
I'm sure he'll pay for all of us."

"Oh, no, that wouldn't be right. I couldn't accept—"

"It's no big deal," Dave said. "I'll be glad to pay
your way in." He winked at Rachel. "And when you get
hungry, I'll even buy you some lunch."

Rachel smiled. "Thank you."

"You're welcome."

When they entered the park, Rachel couldn't believe
her eyes. She'd never seen so many people in one
place—not even at the farmers' market!

Rachel's stomach rumbled as they passed a stand

selling hot dogs, and her mouth watered when she spotted a young girl eating pink cotton candy. Her nose twitched as they approached stands selling hamburgers, french fries, peanuts, and popcorn. All the delicious smells made her feel hungry.

As they walked on, colorful balloons caught Rachel's attention. Then she saw stuffed animals in all sizes, wild looking hats, and shiny trinkets being given as prizes for games won on the midway.

"Never mind those things," Dave said, leading the way toward the rides. "We've got more important things to do."

Rachel heard laughter and shrill screams coming from the whirly-looking ride ahead. Being at Hershey Park was better than anything she could have imagined!

"Let's go on some rides before we eat." Sherry tugged on Rachel's arm. "If we eat first, we might get sick when we ride all those wild roller coasters."

Wild roller coasters? Rachel's stomach flip-flopped. If riding a roller coaster might make her sick, she wasn't sure she wanted to ride one.

"Maybe we should go on that!" Rachel pointed to a ride called the Lady Bug.

"No way!" Sherry wrinkled her nose. "That's a baby ride, Rachel."

"How about the Bizzy Bees or Frog Hopper?" Rachel pointed to one ride and then the other.

"You've got to be kidding!" Dave snorted. "We didn't

come here to go on kiddy rides!"

Rachel motioned to the carousel. "Can we go on that?"

"I guess so," Sherry said with a nod. "I always enjoy riding the carousel."

"Not me!" Dave shook his head. "I'm getting in line for the Sooper Dooper Looper roller coaster ride!"

"You go ahead," Sherry said. "Rachel and I will ride the carousel, and then we might ride on the Dry Gulch Railroad. After that we'll meet you in front of the Ferris wheel."

Dave shrugged. "Sounds good to me. See you soon."

Rachel's excitement mounted as she stepped onto the carousel. She climbed on a shiny black horse and took the reins in her hands.

Sherry climbed onto a brown and white horse beside Rachel.

The music started, and the carousel went round and round—slowly at first—then faster. Rachel giggled as her horse moved up and down in time to the music. "This is so much fun!" she shouted.

Sherry nodded. "Just wait until we go on the Ferris wheel!"

Rachel couldn't imagine that the Ferris wheel could be any better than this, but she was eager to try it.

When the carousel ride was over, the girls rode the train, modeled after an old steam-powered railroad. Rachel had never been on a train before, but she knew some Amish people who had ridden across the country by train.

"Are you still having fun?" Sherry asked when they stepped off the train.

Rachel nodded. "Oh yes! This is exciting!"

"I hope you don't get in trouble when you get home," Sherry said.

Rachel gulped. She wished Sherry hadn't brought that up. *If Mom gets home before I do and reads my note, she'll think I went to Orlie's house. Maybe I won't have to tell her I went to Hershey Park.*

Sherry nudged Rachel's arm. "Did you hear what I said?"

Rachel nodded. "I'm having too much fun to worry about what will happen when I get home. I don't want anything to ruin this exciting day."

"All right then, let's get over to the Ferris wheel and meet Dave!"

Rachel followed Sherry. Her excitement mounted with each step. She wondered if riding the Ferris wheel would be anything like swinging on one of the swings in the school yard.

Dave was there waiting when Rachel and Sherry arrived at the Ferris wheel. "How was the roller coaster?" Sherry asked.

Dave grinned, and his eyes sparkled. "It was awesome!"

"We had fun on the carousel and train ride," Rachel said.

Dave grunted. "I can only imagine."

Sherry tugged her brother's shirtsleeve. "Are you ready to go on the Ferris wheel?"

Dave shook his head. "You two go ahead. I'll stay here and watch."

"Are you afraid of heights?" Rachel asked.

"Of course not. I just rode the Sooper Dooper Looper, and that's taller than the Ferris wheel."

"Then why don't you want to ride with us?"

"Because the Ferris wheel is boring."

"No, it's not!" Sherry grabbed Rachel's hand. "Come on, Rachel. We don't need him to have fun."

As Rachel and Sherry sat down, the man running the Ferris wheel said, "Have you been on this ride before?"

Sherry nodded, but Rachel shook her head. "This is my first time at Hershey Park."

"Then you're in for a treat!" He snapped the bar across their laps. "This Ferris wheel goes nearly a hundred feet in the air, and it's sure to give you a thrill."

Rachel had never been afraid of heights until she'd fallen from a tree and broken her arm. So she was a little nervous about riding the Ferris wheel, but she wouldn't tell Sherry that, because she was also sure it would be fun.

As each car in the Ferris wheel filled with people, Rachel and Sherry's car went higher and higher. Finally, they were at the very top.

When Rachel looked down, she felt dizzy. The people below looked like ants. This was a lot higher than being in a tree or in the hayloft.

The Ferris wheel turned around and around, bringing them close to the ground then back up again. "This is so much fun!" Sherry shouted. "What an exciting day!"

Rachel nodded. "If I never get to visit another amusement park, I'll remember this day for the rest of my life!"

When the Ferris wheel stopped and the girls stepped off, Rachel's legs felt like two sticks of rubber. "Can we sit awhile?" she asked as they stepped up to Dave.

He shook his head. "I want to go on the Wild Mouse next."

"What's the Wild Mouse?" Rachel wanted to know.

Dave pointed straight ahead. "It's a wooden roller coaster with a lot of quick turns and drops that make your stomach do flip-flops."

Rachel's heart pounded. "M–maybe I should stay here and watch."

"Oh, no, Rachel, you have to go on the Wild Mouse with us," Sherry insisted. "It'll be so much fun; you'll see!"

"Oh, all right," Rachel finally agreed.

"Looks like there's quite a lineup," Dave said. "We may have to stand in line awhile."

Sherry groaned. "I hope the wait's not too long, because I'm getting hungry."

Dave reached into his pocket and took out a pack of gum. "Here's something to tide you over until lunch."

He handed a stick of gum to Sherry and one to Rachel.

"Thank you." Rachel popped the gum into her mouth and chewed.

Sherry wrinkled her nose. "Chewing gum won't take my hunger away."

Dave poked her. "Maybe not, but it'll keep your mouth busy so you can't complain."

She glared at him. "Very funny!"

"Make sure you spit the gum out before we get on the roller coaster," Dave said. "You might swallow it on one of those dips."

"Don't worry about me." Sherry returned the stick of gum. "Here you go, Dave. I'm not going to chew this!"

Dave shrugged and put the gum back in his pocket. "Suit yourself, picky little sister."

"I'm not picky!"

"Yeah, you are!"

Rachel bit back a smile. It seemed that she and Jacob weren't the only siblings who didn't always get along.

As they waited in line, Sherry continued to complain about being hungry. Rachel was too busy watching people and listening to the screams coming from the Wild Mouse to think about her empty stomach.

Finally, it was their turn to ride the roller coaster. Sherry and Rachel sat together, and Dave sat behind them with a young boy.

"Hang on tight and get ready to scream," Sherry hollered in Rachel's ear as the coaster moved forward.

"This will probably be the most exciting part of your day!"

As the Wild Mouse climbed higher and higher, Rachel hung on to the bar in front of her until her knuckles turned white. Suddenly, the roller coaster made a sharp turn, and down. . .down they went!

Rachel's stomach seemed to fly up, and her breath caught in her throat. When she opened her mouth to scream—*gulp!*—her gum slid down her throat! She'd forgotten to spit it out.

She swallowed a couple more times. Then she clung tighter to the bar and screamed as the roller coaster dipped up and down and rocked side to side. No wonder they called it the Wild Mouse!

When the coaster stopped, Rachel's legs shook so much she could barely stand.

"That was sure fun! Let's get in line and go again!" Sherry shouted.

Dave looked at Sherry as if he didn't believe her. "I thought you were hungry."

"I was, but my hunger's gone, and I want to ride again." Sherry looked at Rachel. "What about you? Wouldn't you like to ride the Wild Mouse one more time?"

Rachel shook her head. "I've had enough of wild rides for now. But if you two want to go again, I'll wait here for you."

"The line's gotten even longer, so it might be some

time before we get on," Sherry said.

Dave handed Rachel a few dollars. "Why don't you get something to eat? If you'd like to look around a bit, that's okay, too." He glanced at his watch. "It's eleven thirty now, so make sure you're back here by twelve thirty. If our ride's over before then, we may decide to go on something else, but we'll meet you here, and then we'll have lunch."

"Okay, thank you." Rachel headed for the nearest stand selling cotton candy. She bought some and was about to sit on a bench when—*thunk!*—a teenage boy bumped her arm, and the cotton candy went right in her face!

"Sorry," he mumbled as he dashed away.

Rachel licked her lips to get the cotton candy off, but she could feel it on her cheeks and her nose. She ate the rest of the cotton candy and went to find a restroom.

After she'd washed the mess off her face, she looked for a drinking fountain. She bent over, took a drink, and let the cool water roll around on her tongue before she swallowed again.

An elderly couple walked by, and Rachel asked them, "Excuse me, but do you know what time it is?"

"Ten minutes to twelve," the man answered.

"Thanks." Rachel walked until she came to a sign pointing to Zoo America, which she realized was another part of the park. She remembered her cousin

Mary saying in one of her letters that she'd visited a zoo in northern Indiana. It sounded like a lot of fun, and Rachel had been envious. Now she could visit a zoo, too.

Rachel followed the signs pointing to the zoo, but when she got to the entrance, she saw there was an admission fee. Since she'd spent the money Dave had given her on cotton candy, she couldn't go inside.

As Rachel walked away, she spotted a young boy eating a soft pretzel. *That pretzel sure looks good,* she thought. *I wish I had some money to buy one.*

She wandered on, her mouth watering as she watched people eating ice cream, popcorn, and caramel apples. Oh, how she wished she could buy something to eat.

She stopped to watch teenagers try to pop some balloons with darts. When she moved on, she heard music and spotted a strolling guitar player and a man playing a drum.

Someone dressed in a candy bar costume asked if Rachel would like her picture taken. She shook her head and hurried on.

Next, she went into a gift shop where they sold T-shirts with the word HERSHEY written on the front. There were also a bunch of key chains and several shelves full of souvenirs.

I wonder what Jacob would say if he knew where I was, she wondered. *I'll bet he'd be jealous.*

Rachel could hardly wait to write Mary and tell her about the exciting time at Hershey Park! She was sure she would always remember this day.

Her stomach rumbled noisily. She stopped and asked another lady what time it was.

The woman looked at her watch. "It's twelve fifteen."

"Okay, thanks." Rachel decided to head back to the Wild Mouse roller coaster, figuring Sherry and Dave would be off the ride by now and were probably waiting for her. But when Rachel reached the Wild Mouse, she couldn't find Sherry or Dave. She wondered if they'd gone on another ride.

She nibbled on a fingernail. *Should I wait here or walk around some more?*

The sun beat on Rachel's head, and she wiped her sweaty forehead with the back of her hand. It had turned into such a sticky day! Maybe another drink of water would help.

Rachel spotted a drinking fountain and was almost there when she noticed some money on the ground.

She looked around, wondering who had dropped it, but the people walking by didn't seem to notice.

Rachel bent and snatched it up. Her mouth dropped open when she saw that it was a twenty-dollar bill! *With this much money, I could buy something to eat,* she thought. *And since I don't know who dropped the money, I guess it's okay to keep it.*

She hurried to the nearest refreshment stand and

bought a hot dog. She took a big bite. "Mmm. . . this tastes wunderbaar."

She still had plenty of money, so when she finished the hot dog, she decided to play a few games of ring toss. She did quite well and had soon won a stuffed bear. Excited, she kept playing until she'd won a souvenir T-shirt and a matching hat.

Finally, the money was gone, so Rachel headed back to the Wild Mouse. She was disappointed to see that Dave and Sherry still weren't there.

She walked up to a teenage girl waiting in line and said, "Do you know what time it is?"

The girl looked at her watch. "One o'clock."

Rachel's heart started to pound. It was thirty minutes past the time she was supposed to meet Sherry and Dave! Could they have left the park and gone home without her?

Chapter 11

Lost

Stay calm. Don't panic, Rachel told herself. *Sherry and Dave wouldn't have left without me. They must be here someplace. Oh, I hope they're still here.*

Rachel sat on a bench and placed the things she'd won beside her. She drew in a couple of shaky breaths. Dave had told her to meet them by the Wild Mouse roller coaster at twelve thirty. If he and Sherry had arrived at that time and had seen that she wasn't there, what might they have done?

Think, Rachel, think. Maybe they went looking for me. Maybe I should look for them. She rubbed her forehead and tried to relax. *But where? Hershey Park is so big. I might spend all day looking and never find them!*

An elderly woman sat beside Rachel. "It's sure warm today," she said, fanning her face with her hands.

Rachel nodded.

The woman frowned. "If I'd known it was going to be this hot, I wouldn't have come here with my son and his family. I would have stayed home where it's air conditioned."

Rachel swallowed around the lump in her throat. "If I'd known I was going to lose my friends, I wouldn't have come here either."

The woman raised her eyebrows. "Are you lost?"

Rachel shrugged. "I–I'm not really lost, but I was supposed to meet my friends here, and I don't know where they are."

The woman squeezed Rachel's arm. "Why don't we go to the Lost and Found booth? Maybe your friends are waiting there."

Hope welled in Rachel's chest. "Do you think so?"

"There's only one way to find out. Let's go see." The woman took Rachel's hand, and they walked through the crowd until they came to a booth marked LOST AND FOUND.

"This young girl has lost her friends," the woman said to the man who sat behind the counter. "Has anyone been here looking for her?"

The man studied Rachel and shook his head. "No one I know of has asked about anyone who looks like you. What's your name?"

"Rachel Yoder."

"Sorry, but no one's come by asking for anyone by that name." The man motioned to a bench. "Why don't you have a seat, and I'll call your friends' names over the loudspeaker. If they're in the park, they should hear my message."

"O—okay." Rachel sat down and placed the things she'd won in her lap.

"What are your friends' names?" he asked.

"The girl's name is Sherry, and her brother is Dave."

"What's their last name?"

Rachel's forehead wrinkled as she tried to remember. She thought Sherry had mentioned her last name when they'd met at the farmers' market last summer, but she couldn't think of what it was. "I—uh—can't remember," she mumbled.

The man frowned, and he looked at Rachel as if he didn't quite believe her. "You don't know your friends' last name?"

She shook her head.

He shrugged and picked up the speakerphone. "Attention: Sherry and Dave. Would you please report to the Lost and Found to pick up your friend Rachel?" The man's voice boomed out over the speakers, and Rachel felt a surge of hope. If Sherry and Dave were still in the park, they were bound to hear their names being called and come to get her.

The elderly woman looked at her watch. "I'd like to wait with you, Rachel, but I'm supposed to meet my son and his family at Chocolate World in ten minutes."

"That's okay," Rachel said. "I'll be all right by myself."

"I'll keep an eye on Rachel until her friends arrive," the man behind the counter said.

The woman smiled and patted Rachel's shoulder.

"You'll be found soon."

Rachel wished she felt as sure about things. She looked at the woman and forced a smile. "Thanks for helping me."

"You're welcome." The woman smiled and hurried away.

Rachel watched more people walk past. She hoped and prayed Sherry and Dave would come for her soon. She was getting ready to ask the man if he would call Sherry and Dave's names again when a young woman approached the building, pushing a baby stroller. Seeing the baby made Rachel think of Hannah, and a lump formed in her throat. Even though she didn't like being awakened at night when Hannah cried, and even though she felt ignored since the baby came home from the hospital, she missed her family and was worried that she might never see them again.

"My name's Sherry," the woman with the baby said to the man behind the counter. "Were you calling me over the loud speaker? I have a friend whose name is Rachel, but I don't think she's at Hershey Park today."

The man motioned to Rachel. "Do you know that little girl? She seems lost."

The woman looked over at Rachel then back at the man and shook her head. "Sorry, but I've never seen her." She looked at Rachel with sympathy. "I'm sure someone will come for you though."

"I—I hope so."

The woman smiled at Rachel and walked away, pushing the baby stroller.

Rachel fidgeted on the bench as more people walked by, but still no Sherry and Dave. "Can you call my friends' names again?" she asked the man behind the counter.

He nodded and picked up the speakerphone. He'd just started to speak when a middle-aged man stepped up to the booth. "My name's Dave," he said. "Were you calling me?"

The attendant motioned to Rachel. "Do you know this young girl?"

The man shook his head. "Sorry, I don't."

"Then I guess you're not the Dave we're looking for."

Rachel's heart felt as if it had sunk all the way to her toes. Probably hundreds of people named Sherry and Dave were at Hershey Park. She could spend the rest of the day sitting here while the wrong Sherry and Dave came to see if their names had been called. The Sherry and Dave she knew might never show up.

Feeling more anxious by the minute, Rachel glanced around. She couldn't stay here. She had to find Sherry and Dave. She had to get home to her family!

When the man behind the counter was busy talking to someone else, Rachel scooped up the things she'd won, jumped off the bench, and ran as fast as she could. She ran all the way to the front gate of the park and waited for the tram to take her to the parking lot. She would go back to the spot where Dave had parked his car and wait for Dave and Sherry beside his car.

When Rachel stepped off the tram, she headed for the spot where Dave had parked the car. Dave's car wasn't where he'd left it! At least she thought this was where he'd parked his convertible.

"They must have left without me!" she wailed. "They didn't hear their names because they're on their way home!"

Feeling as though the strength had drained from her legs, Rachel dropped the stuffed bear and other things to the ground and fell to her knees beside them. She clutched the bear to her chest. She sobbed until she could hardly breathe. She'd made a complete mess of things by getting into Dave's car and coming to Hershey Park. If only she hadn't been so foolish to think she needed a ride in a convertible. If she could turn back time she would have stayed home and spent the whole day cleaning. It would have been better than being alone in a strange place with a bunch of people she didn't know.

Once Rachel's sobs tapered to sniffling hiccups, she picked up her things and found a bench to sit on. Then she bowed her head and closed her eyes. *Dear Jesus, I'm all alone, and I need Your help. I miss my family—even my baby sister who cries too much.*

A song the scholars often sang at Rachel's school, about walking with Jesus whether we're walking in sunlight or shadows, popped into her head. *I might be lost,* Rachel continued to pray, *but I know You're here with me, Jesus. Please help me find some way to get home.*

She opened her eyes and saw an Amish family walking across the parking lot. A sense of hope welled in her soul. Maybe they lived in Lancaster County. Maybe they could help her get home!

Leaving the things she had won on the bench, Rachel dashed across the parking lot. Before she reached the Amish people, a group of teenagers got off the tram, blocking her view. By the time the crowd dispersed, the Amish family had gone.

Tears stung Rachel's eyes. *Will I ever see home again, or will I be stuck in this parking lot for the rest of my life?*

Chapter 12

Unexpected Surprise

A hopeless feeling swept over Rachel as she returned to the bench. She had prayed and asked God to help her. She knew Jesus hadn't left her. Yet she hadn't found Sherry and Dave, and she didn't know if she ever would. Should she go back to the Lost and Found booth, stay here, or what?

Tears welled in her eyes, and she leaned forward, resting her head on her knees. *Please help me, Lord. Show me what to do.*

Tap. . .tap. . .tap. Someone tapped Rachel's shoulder. Her eyes snapped open, and she sat up. There stood Sherry and Dave!

Rachel jumped to her feet and threw her arms around Sherry. "I'm so glad to see you! I—I was afraid you'd gone back to Lancaster without me."

"Well, we should have!" Dave shook his finger at Rachel. "We heard our names being called over the loud speaker and went to the Lost and Found to get you, but when we got there you were gone."

"I—I waited a long time." Rachel's chin trembled and she sniffed. "When you didn't come, I decided to take the tram to the parking lot and wait for you by your car." She sucked in her breath. "Only your car wasn't there, and I was sure you'd gone home without me."

Dave scowled at her. "Leaving the park was a dumb idea! You should have stayed at the Lost and Found booth! What if we'd given up looking for you and had left you here?"

Tears streamed down Rachel's cheeks, and she wiped them with the back of her hand.

"You're lucky we decided to come out here looking for you!"

Sherry glared at her brother. "Stop shouting at Rachel! Can't you see how upset she is?" She gently patted Rachel's back, the way Mom often did. "Don't cry, Rachel. We're here now. Everything's okay."

"Are—are we going home?" Rachel asked.

Dave nodded. "I promised our folks we'd be back by supper, so we'd better leave now or we'll be late."

Rachel breathed a sigh of relief when she crawled into the backseat of Dave's convertible a few minutes later. God had answered her prayers. She was on her way home—going back to the family she loved. She had been foolish to want a ride in a convertible so much that she'd taken off without getting permission or letting anyone in the family know where she was going. Rachel knew she would be punished for her disobedience, but she also knew that what she'd done was wrong, so she deserved to be punished.

"Why didn't you wait for us in front of the Wild Mouse roller coaster?" Dave asked, looking over his shoulder at Rachel.

"I waited a long time there, too, but you never came." Rachel's throat felt raw and scratchy from crying so much, and she had a hard time swallowing. "Then a lady came along, and when I told her I couldn't find you, she took me to the Lost and Found."

"That's where you should have stayed," Dave said as he pulled out of the parking lot.

Sherry bumped his arm. "She panicked, Dave. Don't you realize how scared she was? Wouldn't you have been scared if you'd been in her situation?"

"Yeah, I guess so—at least when I was Rachel's age I would have been scared. I'm sorry for yelling," Dave called over his shoulder. "I was just worried because you'd run off."

"I—I'm sorry, too." Rachel blinked several times as more tears threatened to spill over. "I wish I'd never gone with you to Hershey Park."

"Didn't you have any fun today?" Sherry asked.

Rachel looked at the stuffed bear and other things she'd won, lying on the seat beside her. "I did have fun. . . until I couldn't find you and Dave."

"I'm sorry that happened," Sherry said. "We

shouldn't have left you alone."

"That's all behind us now," Dave said. "Let's just relax and enjoy the ride home."

Rachel leaned against the seat and closed her eyes as the cool breeze blew against her face. In a while she would be home where she belonged.

Rachel had just drifted off when—*thump, thumpety, thump!*—the car shuddered and bumped along. Rachel knew something must be wrong.

Dave steered the car to the shoulder of the road. He got out, went to the passenger's side, and kicked the front tire. "That's just great! We'll be late getting home now for sure!"

Rachel sat up straight. "Wh–what's wrong?"

"I've got a flat tire!"

"Can it be fixed?"

"I can't fix the tire, but I do have a spare." Dave reached into his pants pocket and pulled out a cell phone.

"What are you doing?" Sherry asked.

"I'm calling Mom and Dad to let them know we're going to be late."

"That's a good idea," Sherry said.

Rachel thought about asking Dave if she could call her folks, but she changed her mind. It could be several hours, and maybe not until tomorrow, before someone in the family checked the answering machine in their phone shed.

When Dave hung up the phone, he went to the trunk of the car and got another tire. "You two will have to get out of the car while I change the tire."

"Can we help?" Sherry asked as she and Rachel scrambled out.

Dave shook his head. "Just stand back from the car and stay as far away from the road as you can. There's a lot of traffic, and I don't want either of you getting hit."

Sherry and Rachel did as Dave said. While they watched him change the flat tire, Rachel couldn't resist the urge to nibble a fingernail. It was getting late, and she knew Mom was probably home from town by now. She most likely would have read the note Rachel had left on the table and would think she was still at Orlie's. When it was time to start supper and Rachel still wasn't home, Pap would probably go over to the Troyers' house to get her.

Rachel bit the end of two more fingernails. *Only I won't be there, and Orlie will tell Pap that I never went there.* Tears stung the backs of her eyes. *Will they be worried and think something bad happened? Will they search for me or call the sheriff?*

"Are you worried?" Sherry asked. "Sometimes I bite my nails when I'm worried about something."

Rachel studied her hands. Her fingernails didn't look very nice when she chewed them. "I know I shouldn't bite my nails," she said. "Mom tells me that whenever she catches me doing it, but I only bite my nails when I'm feeling nervous."

"Are you nervous right now?"

Rachel nodded.

Sherry draped her arm across Rachel's shoulders. "Don't be nervous. Dave will be finished with the tire soon, and then we'll be on our way home."

"I'm gonna be in big trouble when my folks find out where I went." A tear slipped out of Rachel's eye and dribbled onto her cheek. "My brother calls me a little bensel, and I guess he's right."

"What's a bensel?" Sherry asked.

"A silly child." A few more tears fell, and Rachel wiped them with the back of her hand. "I'll never go anywhere again without my parents' permission."

"It's as much my fault as it is yours," Sherry said. "I shouldn't have invited you to go unless your folks were home and said it was all right."

Rachel shook her head. "It's not your fault."

"Yes, it is."

"No, I—"

"The tire's fixed!" Dave opened the car door. "So if you two will quit jabbering, we'll get back on the road."

Sherry wrinkled her nose. "You don't have to be so mean."

"Sorry," he mumbled, "but I'm feeling stressed right now."

Rachel could understand that. She felt stressed, too. But then she remembered what Grandpa had said about rejoicing in every circumstance—even in the midst of troubles, and she smiled. At least they would soon be home.

When Dave pulled his convertible into Rachel's driveway, her heart beat faster. He'd just turned off the engine when Mom and Grandpa rushed out of the house. Pap, Henry, and Jacob stepped out of the barn.

"Rachel, where have you been?" Pap shouted as Rachel, Sherry, and Dave got out of the car. "I just returned from Orlie's, and he said you hadn't been to his house all day." He motioned to the phone shed. "I was about to phone the sheriff."

"Jah, and because of you taking off, we can't go to supper tonight," Jacob said, scowling at Rachel.

"You—you were going out to supper?" she asked.

Pap nodded. "We planned to take you out for a belated birthday supper, but now that will have to wait."

Rachel's eyes filled with tears. "I—I did something I shouldn't have done, and I'm so sorry."

"What did you do?" Mom asked, slipping her arm around Rachel's waist.

"I went to Hershey Park."

"Hershey Park?" Mom and Pap said at the same time.

Rachel nodded; then she motioned to Sherry and Dave. "This is Sherry and her brother, Dave. I met Sherry at the farmers' market last summer, and I saw her again when Grandpa and I went to the Bird-in-

Hand restaurant a few weeks ago." Rachel gulped in a quick breath. "When I was heading to Orlie's to show him my new skateboard, Dave and Sherry drove by and stopped to say hello. Then they said—"

"We said we were going to Hershey Park, and I invited Rachel to join us," Sherry said.

Mom looked at Rachel and scowled. "And you agreed to go without getting our permission?"

Rachel nodded slowly. "I—I thought no one would miss me." She sniffed. "I thought no one cared about me anymore."

Henry shook his head. "That's just plain foolishness, Rachel. How could you even think such a thing?"

"Ever since Hannah came home from the hospital, everyone has made over her and ignored me—unless they wanted me to do some chore." *Sniff! Sniff!*

"It's true, we have made over the baby, and you have been asked to do more chores." Mom pulled Rachel to her side. "But it's not because we love Hannah more." She shook her head. "We love all our *kinner* [children] the same, and when there's work to be done, we're all expected to pitch in and help."

"That's right," Pap agreed. He moved closer to Rachel. "If you felt no one cared about you, you could have said something so we could make things right instead of running off to Hershey Park."

Rachel nodded. "I know what I did was wrong, and I promise I'll never do anything like that again."

"I should hope not." Pap squeezed Rachel's shoulder. "We were very worried when we didn't know where you were. We were afraid something bad had happened to you."

"That's right," Jacob agreed. "Pap paced the barn floor after we got back from Orlie's."

"And your mamm was pacing inside the house," Grandpa said.

Mom nodded. "Jah, pacing and praying."

"While I was at Hershey Park, I got separated from Sherry and Dave for a while," Rachel said. "I was praying then, too."

Grandpa patted Rachel's head. "And God brought you safely home to your family."

"Speaking of home," Dave spoke up, "Sherry and I need to go now. I don't want our folks to worry."

Rachel moved over to Sherry and hugged her. "Come by sometime and visit if you can."

Sherry nodded. "I'd like that. Maybe you can come to our place and visit me, too. We live in a big white house just down the road from the Plain and Fancy farm."

Rachel looked at Mom.

Mom shook her head. "I'm sorry, Rachel, but you won't be going anywhere except to church for the next several weeks. You'll not be allowed to have any company for a while either."

Rachel didn't argue.

Sherry climbed into the car beside Dave. "Oh,

Rachel, don't forget your skateboard and the stuffed animal and other things you won."

"I'll get my skateboard, but I don't want the other things," Rachel said. "Why don't you keep them?"

"Are you sure?"

Rachel nodded as Sherry handed her the skateboard. "I'm very sure."

"Thanks, Rachel." Sherry smiled as Dave started the car. "See you soon!"

Rachel turned and started for the house. "Is Hannah awake?" she asked Mom. "I'd like to hold her."

"She's sleeping right now, but you can hold her after supper," Mom said.

"And after you've washed and dried the dishes," Pap added.

Rachel nodded. She was so glad to be home she'd be willing to do any chore without complaint. Anything but feed and water Jacob's hairy mutt, that is.

"Before we go inside, I have something to give you," Grandpa said.

"What is it?" Rachel asked.

"It's a late birthday present. Remember when I told you a few weeks ago that I'd ordered something for your birthday but it hadn't arrived yet?"

She nodded. "I'd forgotten about it."

"Well, come with me, and I'll show you what I ordered." Grandpa led Rachel to his greenhouse. When he and Rachel stepped inside, he pointed to a box wrapped in white tissue paper. "Go ahead, Rachel. Open your gift."

Rachel tore the wrapping away from the box and opened it. When she lifted a wooden sign out of the box, her mouth dropped open. "Grandpa, this says GRANDPA AND RACHEL'S GREENHOUSE."

Grandpa nodded. "That's right, Rachel."

"But I—I don't understand."

He patted her back. "Someday, when I retire, this greenhouse will be yours."

Tears welled in Rachel's eyes, and she hugged Grandpa. "Danki, Grandpa. This is the best birthday present I've ever had; and being back home with my family makes it even more special."

As Rachel and Grandpa walked back to the house, she thought about the rest of summer. Even though she might not be able to go anywhere for several weeks, she would enjoy every day right here at home. And that was exactly where she belonged!

Jumping to Conclusions

Dedication

To the students and teachers of the Walnut Valley School near Walnut Creek, Ohio. Getting to meet you was great!

Glossary

abastz—stop
ach—oh
an lauerer—eavesdropper
appeditlich—delicious
baremlich—terrible
bensel—silly child
blos—bubble
boppli—baby
bopplin—babies
brieder—brothers
bruder—brother
bussli—kitten
buwe—boy
daed—dad
danki—thanks
dumm—dumb
gaul—horse
grank—sick
grossdaadi—grandfather
grossmudder—grandmother
gut—good
heiraat—marriage
hund—dog
iem—bee
jah—yes
kapp—cap
katze—cats

kinner—children
kinskinner—grandchildren
kumme—come
lecherich—ridiculous
maedel—girl
mamm—mom
missverschtand—
    misunderstanding
munn—moon
naas—nose
naerfich—nervous
pescht—pest
peschte—pests
retschbeddi—tattletale
schmaert—smart
schnarixer—snorer
schnuppich—snoopy
schtann—stars
schteche—sting
schweschder—sister
umgerennt—upset
verhuddelt—mixed-up
wasser—water
windel—diaper
wunderbaar—wonderful
zoll—inches

Bass uff, as du net fallscht!   Take care you don't fall!
Guder mariye.   Good morning.
Ich kann sell net geh!   I cannot tolerate that!
Mir hen die zeit verbappelt.   We talked away the time.
Raus mitt!   Out with it!

She dich, eich, wider!　　　　See you later!
Was in der welt?　　　　　　What in all the world?
Wie geht's?　　　　　　　　How are you?

Chapter 1
Good News

I'm going out to get the mail!" Rachel Yoder called to her mother as she raced out the back door.

"Oh no, you don't!" Rachel's brother Jacob shouted as he dashed out the door behind her. "Getting the mail is Buddy's job!"

Rachel screeched to a halt and whirled around to face Jacob. "Since when is it Buddy's job to get the mail?"

"Since I started training him to open the mailbox." Jacob grinned at Rachel, and the skin around his blue eyes crinkled. "Today I'm gonna teach him how to take the mail from the box and then bring it to the house and put it on the kitchen table."

Rachel snickered and waved her hand. "Like that'll ever happen. That big, hairy *hund* [dog] of yours isn't *schmaert* [smart] enough to get the mail."

"*Jah* [Yes], he is. Buddy's the smartest dog I've ever owned," Jacob insisted.

"That's because he's the *only* dog you've ever owned."

Rachel blinked her eyes several times. "Buddy's nothing but trouble!"

"Is not."

"Is too."

"Is not." Jacob pointed at Rachel. "You're the one who's trouble!"

Rachel frowned and shook her head. "I am not trouble!"

"Jah, you are."

"Am not."

"Are so."

"Am not. Buddy's the troublemaker, and he's not schmaert enough to get the mail!"

"He is so schmaert enough, and I'm gonna prove it to you right now!" Jacob dashed across the yard and yanked open the door to Buddy's dog run.

Woof! Woof! Buddy leaped off the roof of his doghouse, where he liked to sleep, and dashed out of the dog run. Then he raced to Rachel, put both paws on her chest, and—*slurp!*—licked her face.

"Yuck!" Rachel pushed Buddy down and swiped her hand across her face. "Stay away from me, you big, hairy beast! I don't want any of your slimy kisses!" She wrinkled her nose. "Besides, you have bad breath!"

Jacob chuckled and slapped his knee. "He's just letting you know how much he likes you. You should realize that by now."

"Humph!" Rachel folded her arms and glared at

Jacob. "The only thing I realize is that Buddy's a big *pescht* [pest], and I don't enjoy his sloppy, stinky kisses!"

Jacob thumped Rachel's back. "You'll get used to them some day!" He clapped his hands and gave an ear-piercing whistle. "Come on, Buddy. Let's go get the mail!"

Buddy tore off down the driveway, barking all the way, and sending gravel flying in several directions.

Jacob sprinted behind the dog, yelling, "Go, Buddy! Go!"

Rachel followed. She was curious about how Buddy could get the mail.

When they reached the mailbox by the side of the road, Jacob grabbed the handle and yanked it open with a thunk! He waited a few seconds; then he closed it again. He did this several times. After the fifth time, he pointed to the mailbox handle and said, "Open it, Buddy. Open the mailbox!"

Woof! Woof! Buddy wagged his tail and stared at the mailbox as if to say, *What are you talking about?*

Jacob opened and closed the mailbox door several more times; then he said, "Open it, Buddy! Open the mailbox now!"

Much to Rachel's surprise, Buddy grabbed the handle on the mailbox in his teeth, pulled, and— *thunk!*—the door popped open.

Woof! Woof! Buddy wagged his tail and stared at the mailbox as if to say, *Look what I did!*

Rachel rushed forward to grab the stack of letters. Jacob stepped in front of her. "How's Buddy gonna learn to get the mail if you do it for him?"

Rachel rolled her eyes. "Buddy might be schmaert enough to open the mailbox, but he's not schmaert enough to take the mail out."

"Sure he is. Just stand back and watch."

"Whatever." Rachel stepped aside, even though she was sure Buddy would not take the mail out of the box.

Jacob pointed to the mail inside the box. "Get it, Buddy! Get the mail out of the box!"

Buddy tilted his head and whined.

Rachel shook her head. "He doesn't have a clue what you're talking about."

"Okay, then, I'll try it another way." Jacob reached into the mailbox, picked up one of the letters, opened Buddy's mouth, and put the letter between the dog's teeth. "You're a good hund!" He patted Buddy's head.

Buddy whimpered and nuzzled Jacob's hand with his big nose.

Rachel reached into the mailbox and snatched the rest of the mail. "I knew he wasn't schmaert enough to get the mail by himself."

"Hey!" Jacob frowned. "How am I supposed to train Buddy to get the mail if you take it first?"

"I don't care if Buddy learns how to get the mail. I just want to take the mail to the house, and—" Rachel stared at the letter in her hand. It was addressed to her.

It was from her cousin Mary!

Mary was not only her cousin but had also been her best friend. Rachel had been very sad when Mary's family moved to Indiana.

"Yippee! I've got a letter from Mary! I've got a letter from Mary!" Rachel shrieked as she waved the letter in the air. "I'm going to the house to read Mary's letter. You and your *schmaert* dog can bring the rest of the mail whenever you're ready."

Rachel started to turn around, but Buddy dropped the letter in his mouth, leaped into the air, and snatched Mary's letter out of her hand!

"Give that back, you big, hairy mutt!" Rachel lunged for the letter.

Woof! Woof! Buddy took off on a run.

Rachel raced after him.

The dog zipped up the driveway then turned and zipped back again. Rachel ran behind him, waving her hands and shouting, "*Abastz* [Stop]! You're a bad dog!"

Jacob doubled over with laughter as Rachel chased the dog. She'd just started down the driveway again when she spotted their friend Orlie Troyer walking up the driveway.

"Catch that *dumm* [dumb] hund!" she shouted to Orlie. "Don't let him get away!"

Orlie cupped his hands around his mouth. "What?" he called.

"I said—"

Woomph! Buddy plowed into Orlie, knocking him to the ground. The letter flew out of Buddy's mouth.

Yip! Yip! Buddy tore across the field on the side of their property, yapping all the way.

"Bad dog!" Rachel shouted.

Jacob dashed after Buddy, waving his hands. "Come back here, Buddy! Come back here right now!"

Rachel ran down the driveway and dropped to her knees beside Orlie. "Are you all right? Buddy didn't hurt you, I hope."

Orlie shook his head. "Just knocked the wind out of me, that's all." He clambered to his feet and brushed the dirt from his trousers. "I think Buddy was excited to see me."

"Maybe so, but I think the real reason Buddy plowed into you was because he stole a letter from me and was trying to get away." Rachel snatched the letter Buddy had dropped. "It's from my cousin Mary in Indiana."

"How'd the hund get your letter?" Orlie asked.

Rachel groaned. "Jacob was trying to teach Buddy to get the mail."

"Guess he needs to teach him to come when he's called." Orlie chuckled as he pointed across the field. "Jacob's going to be tired by the time he catches Buddy."

"You mean *if* he catches the hairy hund." Rachel lifted Mary's letter. "I'm going to the house to read my mail. Do you want to come along?"

Orlie grinned. "Jah, sure. I'd like to hear what Mary

has to say, too."

Rachel wasn't sure she wanted Orlie to read Mary's letter, but she didn't want to be rude, so she smiled and said, "Let's go sit down, and I'll read Mary's letter out loud."

When they were settled on the back porch steps, Rachel tore open the letter and began to read.

Dear Rachel

I have some very good news. I'll be coming back to Pennsylvania in a few weeks for—

Woof! Woof! Woof! Buddy darted onto the porch, swiped his sloppy wet tongue across Rachel's face, and then leaped into Orlie's lap.

Jacob, red-faced and sweating, dropped onto the step below them. "That crazy mutt can sure run fast. I'm all worn out!"

Rachel grunted. "You should get rid of him. He's nothing but trouble."

"No way! Buddy's a nice hund." Jacob rubbed Buddy's ears.

Orlie patted the top of Buddy's head. "I'd never have given him to you if it hadn't been for my *mamm's* [mom's] allergies. I'm glad you were able to take Buddy."

Jacob nodded. "I'm glad Buddy came to live with us. He's been a good friend to me."

Orlie's head bobbed up and down. "He was a good

friend to me, too, and he's also a good watchdog."

"You two can sit here all day talking about that dumm hund if you like, but I'm going inside to tell Mom about Mary's letter." Rachel jumped up and raced into the house, banging the screen door behind her. "I got a letter from Mary!" she hollered as she dashed into the kitchen.

Mom was sitting at the table drinking a cup of tea. She looked up and smiled. "That's nice. What'd she say?"

"She's coming to Pennsylvania!"

"When?"

"I don't know. Thanks to Jacob's dumm hund, I didn't get a chance to finish reading Mary's letter." Rachel dropped into a chair and placed the letter on the table. "I'll finish reading it now though. Would you like me to read it out loud?"

"Jah, why don't you?" Mom's metal-framed glasses slipped to the end of her nose, and she pushed them back in place.

Rachel touched the nosepiece of her own plastic-framed glasses. Then she began to read.

Dear Rachel,
I have some very good news. I'll be coming back to Pennsylvania in a few weeks for a visit. I'll be with our neighbor, Carolyn, who's coming there to see her daughter who's expecting a baby. Mama will call soon to let you know when I'll arrive.

Love, Mary.

Rachel looked at Mom and smiled. "Isn't that the best news?"

Mom patted Rachel's arm. "It certainly is. I know how much you've missed Mary. It will be nice for you girls to be together again."

Rachel wiggled in her chair. "I can hardly wait to see Mary again!"

Mom smiled and stood up. "I'd better check on your baby sister. She should be waking from her nap soon. Then she'll need to be diapered and fed."

Mom hurried from the room, and Rachel picked up Mary's letter to read it again.

Clip-clop. Clip-clop.

Pap's new horse pulled their gray, box-shaped buggy down the road the following morning. Rachel and her family were headed to church. It would be held at Howard and Anna Miller's house today.

Rachel enjoyed going to church every other Sunday with her family and friends, and this morning she was even more eager to attend. She wanted to tell her friend Audra Burkholder about her letter from Mary.

When they approached the Millers' barn, Rachel spotted Audra and Orlie across the yard by the swing. As soon as Pap stopped the horse, she hopped out of the buggy and sprinted across the yard.

"*Wie geht's* [How are you]?" Rachel asked Audra.

"Okay," Audra mumbled; then she quickly looked away.

Rachel looked at Orlie and smiled, but he hurried away. Rachel figured he was going to join some of the boys.

"Guess what?" Rachel asked, nudging Audra's arm.

Audra shrugged.

"I got a letter from—"

"Church is about to begin. We need to get inside." Audra hurried toward the buggy shed, where several wooden benches had been set up for the members of their Amish community to sit on during the three-hour church service.

I guess I'll have to wait until church is over to tell Audra about Mary's letter, Rachel thought. She followed behind the others to the shed, her shoulders slumped and her head dropped in disappointment.

Whoomp! Rachel bumped into Sadie Stoltzfus, a widow. "Oops! I'm sorry," she said.

Sadie turned and scowled at Rachel. "You should watch where you're going. Can't you see that there are people in front of you?" Her false teeth clacked when she spoke.

"I—I was looking at the ground and didn't see you."

Sadie blinked her pale green eyes and shook her finger. "Well, you should pay more attention. Hasn't your mamm ever told you to hold your head up when you walk?"

Rachel nodded.

"Then you should listen." Sadie's teeth clacked a little louder, and she shook her finger again. "I'm glad all my *kinskinner* [grandchildren] are grown. I have no patience with little *kinner* [children] anymore."

Rachel thought it was obvious that Sadie didn't care much for children. "I'm sorry I bumped into you," she said. Then she hurried into the building.

When Rachel looked at the women's side of the room, she spotted Audra sitting between Phoebe Byler and Karen Fisher. Rachel was disappointed again. She usually sat by Audra. Maybe they could sit together during the noon meal.

Rachel slipped onto a bench beside Rebekah Mast.

As the group began to sing the first song, Rachel looked at Audra and smiled.

Audra stared straight ahead.

Every few minutes Rachel looked at Audra, but Audra never glanced Rachel's way.

Maybe Audra's afraid she'll get in trouble for fooling around in church, Rachel thought. *That's probably why she won't look at me.*

Rachel heard someone clear her throat loudly. She glanced over her shoulder. Sadie Stoltzfus was frowning at Rachel. Rachel turned back around. She was glad she wasn't one of Sadie's kinskinner.

Harvey Fisher, one of the ministers, began giving his sermon, so Rachel sat up straight and listened.

"He who guards his mouth and his tongue keeps himself from calamity," Harvey quoted from Proverbs 21:23.

Rachel was good at spelling, and she knew that another word for *calamity* was *trouble*. *I have lots of trouble*, she thought. *Trouble seems to find me wherever I go.*

She looked at Audra, but Audra still kept her gaze straight ahead. Rachel frowned. Was trouble brewing with Audra?

When church was over and the noon meal had been served, Rachel looked for Audra. She stopped in her tracks when she saw Audra sitting at a table between Phoebe and Karen.

Is Audra trying to avoid me? Is she mad at me for something? Rachel wondered. *Are those her new best friends?*

Rachel felt like crying. She waited until Audra had finished her lunch; then she stepped up to her and said, "Should we go out to the Millers' barn and play?"

Audra shook her head. "I'm not in the mood."

"Then let's go swing."

"Nope." Audra hurried toward the creek.

Rachel looked after her in dismay. What would she do if Audra didn't want to be her friend anymore? First, she'd lost Mary. Had she lost Audra now, too? Who would she play with? Who would she tell her secrets to? Who would be that special friend to laugh with her?

Tears trickled down Rachel's face. She quickly wiped them away. It wouldn't do for Orlie or anyone to see her cry.

"Well, if she doesn't want to be my friend, that's okay!" she said out loud. As soon as she spoke, she remembered the scripture from the morning. *"He who guards his mouth and his tongue keeps himself from calamity."*

Maybe I shouldn't say such things, Rachel thought. In fact, a little something inside Rachel nudged her to go after Audra. She'd try to talk to Audra one more time before she gave up on their friendship.

At the creek, she found Audra sitting on a rock with her arms folded, staring at the water.

Rachel knelt in the grass beside Audra and touched her arm. "I wanted to tell you that—"

Ribbet! Ribbet! A little tree frog jumped out of the grass and landed on Audra's shoulder.

"Eeeek!" Audra leaped to her feet and hopped up and down. "Get the frog, Rachel! Get the frog off me!"

Rachel plucked the frog from Audra's shoulder and dropped it in the water.

Tears rolled down Audra's flushed cheeks.

Rachel patted her back. "It's okay. Don't cry. The frog's gone now."

Audra pulled away. "I–I'm fine." *Sniff! Sniff!*

"It was just a little tree frog," Rachel said. "It wouldn't hurt you. There's no reason for you to cry."

Audra swiped at the tears running down her cheeks. "I'm not just crying because of the frog."

"Why are you crying?"

"I'm not your best friend anymore."

Rachel tilted her head. "Who says you're not my best friend?"

"Orlie."

Rachel frowned. "Why would Orlie say that?"

"He said you got a letter from your cousin." Audra sniffed a couple more times. "Orlie said Mary's moving back to Pennsylvania, and that she's your best friend."

Rachel could hardly believe Orlie had said those things. Was he trying to cause trouble? Was he mad because she'd called Buddy a dumm hund?

"That's not true," Rachel said. "Mary isn't moving back here. She's only coming for a visit. Orlie didn't even hear all of Mary's letter."

"Really?"

Rachel nodded. "Mary and I used to be best friends, but you're my best friend now." She hugged Audra. "I'm excited for you to meet Mary, and for her to meet you, too."

Audra smiled. "I guess Orlie must have jumped to conclusions."

"What's that mean?" Rachel asked.

"'Jumping to conclusions' is an expression I heard from my mamm," Audra said. "When someone jumps to conclusions, it means they've made a decision without getting all the facts."

Rachel hugged Audra again. "I think Orlie jumped to conclusions as high as that frog jumped."

The girls laughed. Rachel felt so good to be friends with Audra. She didn't dare tell Audra about jumping to her own conclusions.

"As soon as Mary gets here, I'll invite you over to play," Rachel promised.

Audra smiled. "*Danki* [Thanks], Rachel. I'll look forward to that."

Chapter 2

Out of Patience

Rachel hurried to finish the breakfast dishes so she could help Grandpa in the greenhouse. She enjoyed spending time with Grandpa. She also liked being around the plants and flowers.

"Would you hold your baby sister while I go to the garden and pull weeds?" Mom asked Rachel.

"How long do I have to hold her?"

"Until she burps."

Rachel's excitement about going to the greenhouse melted like a brick of ice in the hot sun. "*Ach* [Oh] Mom, you know how long Hannah takes to burp." She motioned to the window. "I promised Grandpa I'd help him in the greenhouse this morning."

Mom draped a piece of cloth over Rachel's shoulder and handed her the baby. "Just keep patting her back. I'm sure she'll burp soon; then you can put her down for a nap and go to the greenhouse."

"All right, Mom." Rachel headed for the living

room, patting Hannah's back as she went.

Hannah nuzzled Rachel's neck with her soft, warm nose, but she didn't burp.

Rachel continued to pat Hannah's back. "Hurry up, Hannah. I need to get out to the greenhouse."

"Goo-goo. Gaa-gaa." Hannah drooled on Rachel's neck.

"Yuck!" Rachel used the cloth Mom had draped over her shoulder to wipe the drool away. "You're a cute *boppli* [baby], but you can sure cause trouble sometimes."

"Gaa-gaa," was Hannah's response.

Rachel sat on the sofa and placed Hannah facedown across her knees.

Squeak! Squeak! Rachel reached behind her to find one of Hannah's squeaky toys. She tossed it across the room.

Hannah whimpered.

Rachel patted Hannah's back.

Hannah started to howl.

Rachel sat Hannah up and rubbed her back.

Hannah stopped crying, but still no burp.

"Just when I thought I could have a little time to help Grandpa, I'm stuck with a baby who won't burp," Rachel grumbled.

Is this going to take all day? Rachel thought about turning Hannah upside down to see if that would make her burp, but she'd be in big trouble if Mom caught her.

She placed Hannah on her knee and bounced her up and down.

Hannah giggled, but still no burp. She didn't look sleepy, either.

Hic! Hic! Hic!

"Oh great," Rachel moaned. "Now you've got the hiccups." She placed Hannah in her cradle, hurried into the kitchen, and filled a baby bottle with water.

When Rachel returned to the living room, Hannah was crying between hiccups.

Rachel picked up the baby, sat on the sofa, and gave Hannah some water.

Hannah spit the water out and hiccuped again.

Rachel gritted her teeth.

Waaa! Waaa! Hannah's face turned bright red.

Rachel put the baby over her shoulder and patted her back.

Blurp! Hannah spit up on Rachel's shoulder.

"Ewww!" Rachel wrinkled her nose. She placed Hannah in her cradle, scampered to her room, and changed into a clean dress.

When Rachel returned to the living room, Hannah was crying again. She picked up Hannah and took a seat in the rocking chair. Mom often put the baby to sleep by humming and rocking her. Rachel hoped it would work for her, too.

Hmm. . .hmm. . .hmm. . . Rachel hummed while she rocked back and forth.

Hannah continued to fuss and squirm.

"Please go to sleep," Rachel begged. "You should be

sleepy by now, Hannah."

Waaa! Waaa! Hannah's face turned even redder, and she waved her chubby little hands in the air.

Just then, Rachel felt something damp on her knee. "That's just great," she said with a moan. "Your diaper must be full, and it leaked on my dress."

Rachel placed Hannah in the cradle and quickly changed the wet diaper. It was not her favorite thing to do!

Hannah finally quit crying and fell asleep. Rachel sighed with relief. Then she hurried upstairs to change her dress so she could go to the greenhouse.

As Rachel skipped across the grass toward Grandpa's greenhouse, she felt like she was floating on a cloud. She still couldn't believe Grandpa had put her name under his on the wooden sign outside the greenhouse. She felt good to know that he wanted her help and almost thought of her as his partner.

Rachel shivered as a cool wind blew several leaves across the yard. Summer was nearly over, and soon school would start again. Usually Rachel looked forward to this time of year, but now things were different. Going back to school would mean less free time to help Grandpa in the greenhouse. Rachel would also have homework every evening.

I won't think about that now, Rachel decided. *I'll just enjoy every day I'm able to work with Grandpa.*

A musty, damp odor met Rachel when she opened the door to the greenhouse. She figured Grandpa must have recently watered the plants.

Rachel looked around but didn't see Grandpa. She decided he was in his office or at the back of the greenhouse where he kept supplies. Sure enough, she found Grandpa pruning a large green plant with pointed leaves.

"I'm sorry for being late, Grandpa." Rachel frowned as she thought about what she'd been through in the last hour. "Mom asked me to burp the boppli, and I had all kinds of trouble."

"That's all right," Grandpa said without looking up.

"What kind of plant are you working on?" Rachel asked.

"This is an ivy plant. It pulls toxins from the air, which helps us breathe better." Grandpa motioned to another plant across the room. "That's a spider plant. It does the same thing."

"I didn't realize plants could clean the air," Rachel said. "Guess I have a lot to learn about greenhouse things."

"You'll learn more as time goes on. It's taken me a whole lifetime to learn what I know." Grandpa's bushy gray eyebrows drew together when he looked at Rachel. "Why are you dressed like that?"

"Like what?"

He motioned to her dress. "It's on backwards."

Rachel touched the neck of her dress and grimaced.

"I had to change my dress because Hannah wet on me. I guess I wasn't paying attention. I'd better run back to the house and change it around before someone comes into the greenhouse and sees me wearing my dress backwards."

Grandpa chuckled. "We sure couldn't have that, could we? If someone saw you wearing your dress backwards they might think I hired a *verhuddelt* [mixed-up] girl to work in my greenhouse."

Rachel blushed. "Do you really think I'm verhuddelt?"

Grandpa hugged her. "Of course not. I just think you get in too big of a hurry sometimes instead of being patient."

Rachel nodded. "I get frustrated when I have to wait for things."

"One of my favorite Bible verses is Psalm 40:1: 'I waited patiently for the Lord.' You should think about that whenever you feel impatient." Grandpa squeezed Rachel's shoulder. "Now run into the house and turn your dress around; then hurry back here so we can play with some plants."

"I'll be back as quick as I can." She hugged Grandpa and scurried out the door.

When Rachel entered the house, she was relieved to see that Hannah was still asleep, and Mom was taking a nap on the sofa. She didn't want Mom to see her dress.

Rachel scrambled up the steps. "The hurrier I

go, the behinder I get," she mumbled. It was one of Grandpa's favorite sayings.

She zipped into her room, slipped off her dress, and put it back on the right way. Then she scurried out of the room, dashed down the stairs, and raced out the back door.

She'd just stepped off the porch when she spotted her English friend Sherry coming up the driveway. Sherry had her fluffy little dog, Bundles, on a leash.

"Hi, Rachel." Sherry waved. "I came over to see if you could play."

"I can't today. I'm supposed to help my grandpa in his greenhouse," Rachel said as she hurried to meet Sherry.

"Oh, that's right." Sherry pointed to the greenhouse. "I still haven't seen it inside. Can I look at it now?"

"I'd be happy to show you around." Rachel pointed at the dog. "Bundles will have to stay outside, though. Grandpa doesn't allow animals in the greenhouse. Whenever they've gotten in by mistake, there's been trouble."

"Okay." Sherry tied Bundles's leash to a fence post.

Bundles plopped on the ground and closed her eyes.

At least she's not the kind of dog who barks a lot, jumps up, and licks you, Rachel thought. Sherry's sweet little dog was nothing like Jacob's troublesome mutt.

Sherry pointed to the sign above the greenhouse door. "I didn't know you owned this place, too."

Rachel shook her head. "Grandpa's the legal owner. I help him here whenever I can, so he included my name on the sign."

"Maybe you'll own it someday—after your grandpa's too old to work anymore."

"I hope that won't be for a long time." Rachel opened the door. She didn't see any sign of Grandpa and figured he was probably in the back room repotting or pruning plants.

"This place is great! There are so many pretty plants and flowers, and it smells good," Sherry said. "My mom's birthday's in a few weeks. Maybe I'll buy a plant for her."

Rachel nodded. "I'm sure she'd like that."

Zzzz. . .zzzz. . .

Sherry tipped her head. "What's that weird noise?"

Rachel listened to the low rumble coming from the back room. "I think it's my grandpa snoring. He must have fallen asleep. He's quite a *schnarixer* [snorer]."

"What's a schnarixer?" Sherry asked.

"It means 'snorer,'" Rachel explained.

Sherry snickered. "My dad's a schnarixer, too."

Rachel chuckled. "My brother's dog sometimes snores. When he does, he sounds like a freight train."

Woof! Woof!

Rachel glanced out the window. "It looks like something's upset your dog; she's barking and tugging on her leash."

Sherry flipped her blond ponytail. "Guess I'd better get out there and see what's riled Bundles."

Rachel followed Sherry out the door. She saw Snowball, one of Cuddles's kittens, prancing around with her tail lifted, just out of Bundles's reach.

"Come here, you silly *bussli* [kitten]." Rachel was about to pick Snowball up when the kitten leaped into the air and landed on Bundles's head.

Woof! Woof! Bundles shook her head, tossing Snowball into a clump of bushes.

Meow!

Rachel gasped. "Snowball! Oh, you poor little thing. Are you hurt?"

She couldn't see the kitten. She only heard a pitiful *Meow!* coming from inside the bushes.

"She probably won't come out as long as your dog's here," Rachel told Sherry.

Sherry nodded. "I'd better head for home."

"What about the plant for your mother?"

"I'll come back another day and pick one out." Sherry scooped up her dog. "I'm sorry for all the trouble, Rachel."

"It's okay. Snowball shouldn't have been teasing Bundles." Rachel glanced at the bushes. "I wish she'd come out, though."

"I'm sure she will once we're gone." Sherry squeezed Rachel's arm. "I'll come over to get the plant soon, and I'll leave Bundles at home."

As Sherry hurried away, Rachel leaned into the bushes and called, "Here Snowball. It's safe to come out now."

No response. Not even a meow.

Rachel pulled the bushes apart and spotted a fluffy white tail. "Come here, you silly bussli."

Snowball swished her tail and went deeper into the bushes.

Rachel stuck her hand inside the bush. She felt around until she touched a soft furry paw.

"Yeow!" Snowball scratched Rachel's hand with her sharp little claws and flew out of the bushes.

Rachel turned to chase after the kitten, but her sleeve caught on the bush. *Rip!* A hunk of material tore loose.

"Trouble, trouble, trouble!" Back to the house Rachel stomped, grumbling and mumbling all the way.

She zipped up the stairs, raced into her room, and flopped onto the bed. This had not been a good morning! Now she really was out of patience!

Chapter 3
Eavesdropping

When Rachel returned to the greenhouse, she was surprised to see Grandpa standing on his head in one corner of the greenhouse.

"*Was in der welt* [What in all the world] are you doing?" she asked, bending down to see Grandpa's face.

"My brain felt foggy," Grandpa said. "I'm letting the blood run to my head so I can think better."

Rachel stared at Grandpa and slowly shook her head. She could hardly believe a man his age was strong enough to stand on his head.

"I've been doing this since I was a *buwe* [boy]," Grandpa said. "I could stand on my head longer than any of my *brieder* [brothers]." He lowered his feet to the floor and slowly stood.

Rachel wondered how many other things Grandpa could do that she didn't know about.

"You sure took a long time turning your dress around," Grandpa said. He studied Rachel. "Say, that's not the same dress you were wearing earlier. Your backwards dress was blue, and this one's green."

"This is the second time I've changed my dress," Rachel said. "Well, really the third time, since the baby wet on my other dress. Oh, and I had another dress before that—until Hannah spit up on it."

Grandpa frowned. "I don't remember you going up to the house more than once."

Rachel told him that her friend Sherry had come over. "I showed her the greenhouse. And we heard you snore," she added.

Grandpa puckered his lips and tugged his long beard. "Was I really snoring?"

"Jah."

"Guess I must have fallen asleep at my desk." Grandpa chuckled. "Your grandma never got used to my snoring. She told our kinner, 'When he snores, he keeps me awake.'"

A look of sadness spread over Grandpa's face, but he quickly covered it with a smile.

Rachel knew Grandpa must still miss Grandma, who had gone to heaven several years earlier. "Since my room's upstairs and yours is downstairs, your snoring never keeps me awake," Rachel said, hoping to change the subject. "I sure can't say that about baby Hannah. She keeps me awake when she cries at night."

Grandpa nodded. "I know what you mean. I finally bought myself a pair of earplugs."

"Maybe I should get some, too." Rachel frowned. "But if I had earplugs, I might not hear my alarm clock ring when school starts next month."

Grandpa tweaked the end of Rachel's nose. "That wouldn't be good, now, would it?"

She shook her head. "Guess I'll have to put up with Hannah's crying until she grows out of it."

"At the rate the boppli's growing, she'll soon sleep all night."

Grandpa pointed to some potted plants on a nearby shelf. "I watered a few of those plants earlier, but I have some office work to do, so why don't you water the plants over there?" He pointed to some plants on the other side of the room.

"Okay." Rachel hurried to the sink, filled the watering can, and headed to a tray of purple and white petunias. She'd just started back across the room for more water when the greenhouse door swung open.

"*Guder mariye* [Good morning]," their neighbor Anna Miller said when she stepped inside.

"Guder mariye," Rachel said with a smile.

"Is your grandpa here?" Anna asked.

Rachel motioned to the small room Grandpa used as his office. "He's at his desk, but you can go in if you like."

"Danki." Anna headed for the office, and Rachel scurried to the sink. As she carried the watering can back across the room, she noticed a praying mantis sitting on the shelf between two pots of pansies.

Rachel watched as it devoured a fly, one limb at a time. Rachel didn't care much for dirty flies, but she almost felt sorry for this one because it had no chance to get away.

"It's sure. . . A worm. . ."

"Jah, that's right. . . . It's kind of. . ."

Rachel listened to Grandpa's and Anna's voices. She figured Grandpa must have spotted a worm someplace, which was strange, since he had no plants in his office.

"It wouldn't be so bad. . .Wasn't full of humility. . ."

Rachel set the watering can down. She eased closer to the office door to better hear what they were saying.

"I can't really blame her. . ."

"I know what you mean. . ."

Rachel put her ear against the door. She wished they would talk a little louder.

Suddenly the door swung open, knocking Rachel to the floor.

"Ach Grandpa, you scared me!" She scrambled to her feet.

Grandpa stepped toward Rachel. "Are you all right?"

"I–I'm fine. It just knocked the wind out of me when you opened the door."

Grandpa frowned. "Why were you by the door? I thought you were watering plants."

Rachel's face warmed with embarrassment. "I—I was, but I heard you and Anna talking about a worm, and—" She glanced over her shoulder. "Is there a worm in your office, Grandpa?"

He shook his head. "Of course not. I don't know where you got such a notion. I never said anything about a worm."

"He said it's a *warm* day. Maybe that's what you heard," Anna said, entering the main part of the greenhouse. "And I said, 'It wouldn't be so bad if it wasn't for the humidity.' "

"I thought you said 'humility,' " Rachel said.

Anna shook her head. "No. Never said a word about humility."

Rachel stared at the floor. She felt foolish.

Grandpa frowned. "I think you'd better get back to work and stop eavesdropping, Rachel."

"Okay." Rachel shuffled back to finish watering the plants.

As Grandpa and Anna continued their conversation, Rachel tried not to listen. It was hard, though, because she was sure they were talking about interesting things.

"I think an African violet would be a perfect plant for her," Grandpa said.

Perfect plant for who? Rachel wanted to ask, but she knew Grandpa wouldn't appreciate her listening to his conversation again.

"Jah, I'm sure she'll like the plant, and I think. . ." Anna's voice trailed off as she moved to the other side of the room.

Rachel wished she could follow, but she had more plants to water.

"That's right; it's not good to be alone. I'm sure you must miss. . ."

Rachel tipped her head and strained to hear the rest of what Anna was saying.

"Marriage is. . ." Anna moved even farther away, and then her voice sounded like a whisper.

Rachel gritted her teeth. She couldn't hear any of Anna's words now.

She raced to the sink, filled the watering can with more water, and started watering plants closer to where Grandpa and Anna stood.

"Thanks for stopping by, Anna," Grandpa said. "When you see Sadie Stoltzfus, tell her I'll be over later today. I need to ask her that question."

Rachel's ears perked up. Why would Grandpa go to see the widow Stoltzfus, who didn't like kids and clacked her false teeth?

Anna paused and smiled at Grandpa. "A fall wedding will be nice, don't you think?"

He nodded, and Anna hurried out the door.

Rachel stood like a statue in front of the flowers, her mouth hanging open. This couldn't happen! No, it just couldn't!

Grandpa nudged Rachel's arm. "What are you doing? Catching flies?"

"Huh?"

"Your mouth's hanging open. I wondered if you were trying to catch a few flies."

Rachel clamped her mouth shut. Her hand shook so badly that some water sloshed out of the watering can and landed on her bare foot.

Grandpa snickered. "Now what are you doing—giving yourself a bath?"

Rachel tried to swallow around the lump in her throat. She couldn't tell Grandpa what had upset her. If she said what she'd heard, he would know she'd been listening to his and Anna's conversation.

"I—uh—guess I wasn't watching what I was doing," she mumbled.

He patted her arm. "If you're done watering, I'd like you to put the watering can away and help me repot some plants that have grown too big for their containers."

Rachel nodded. "I will. . .just as soon as I wipe up the water I spilled."

As Rachel hurried to get a clean rag, she made a decision. She would have to find a way to keep Grandpa from marrying Sadie Stoltzfus!

By the time Rachel had watered all the plants and helped Grandpa repot several, it was time to go to the house and help Mom make lunch.

Rachel had just started across the yard when she spotted Jacob coming around the side of the barn.

"I'm so glad you're here," she said breathlessly. "I need to talk to you."

Jacob eyed her with a curious expression. "What about?"

"Grandpa's on the verge of making the biggest mistake of his life. He's not thinking straight. He needs our help to. . ."

Jacob held up his hand. "Slow down, Rachel. You're talking way too fast."

She shook her head. "No, I'm not. You're listening too slow."

He glared at her. "I'm not listening too slow."

Any other time Rachel might have argued, but right now she needed his help more than she needed to prove she was right.

"Grandpa's planning to take a plant over to Sadie Stoltzfus this afternoon," she said.

"How do you know?"

"I heard him tell Anna Miller."

"So what if he's taking a plant to Sadie? She lives several miles away. It's probably hard for her to hitch the horse to the buggy and travel to Grandpa's greenhouse," Jacob said.

Rachel lowered her voice. "He's not just taking Sadie a plant. He's getting married again."

Jacob raised his eyebrows. "Who's he going to marry?"

Rachel groaned. "Aren't you listening? I'm talking about the Widow Stoltzfus! When he takes her the

African violet, Grandpa's going to ask her to marry him."

Jacob's eyes widened. "Are you sure?"

"Of course I'm sure. I was in the greenhouse when Anna and Grandpa were talking about Sadie Stoltzfus. They talked about a wedding in the fall and about Grandpa needing a wife." Rachel drew in a quick breath. "He said he's going to see Sadie later today, to take her a plant and ask her a question."

Jacob slowly shook his head. "You're an *an lauerer* [eavesdropper], Rachel. You should quit nosing around and mind your own business."

Rachel stomped her foot. "If we don't do something to stop it, we'll end up with a new teeth-clacking *grossmudder* [grandmother] who doesn't like kinner!"

"This is none of our business, Rachel. If Grandpa wants to marry her, that's his decision. You need to keep your nose out of Grandpa's business and spend your time doing something else." He poked her arm. "Maybe you should get busy and clean your room so it'll be ready when Cousin Mary gets here."

"I've been getting ready for Mary, but she won't be here for a week or so." Rachel pursed her lips. "Right now we need to concentrate on—"

"Listening to other people's conversations can lead to trouble," Jacob interrupted. "Besides, you don't even know if you heard correctly."

Rachel knew all about trouble. It seemed to follow her everywhere.

She squinted her eyes at Jacob and said, "If I did hear correctly, then we need to do something to stop it!"

Jacob shook his head. "That wouldn't be right. If Grandpa wants to marry again, you should be happy for him."

Tears welled in Rachel's eyes. "I—I can't be happy about this. If Grandpa marries Sadie, he'll move out of our house, and she'll—"

"How do you know Sadie won't move in with us?"

Rachel gasped. "Do you really think she might do that?"

Jacob shrugged. "All I know is whatever Grandpa does, it's his business, not ours." He walked toward the house. "I don't know about you, but I'm hungry. I'm going inside to eat lunch!"

Rachel sighed. She'd hoped she could count on Jacob, but he'd been no help at all! If anything was going to be done to keep Grandpa from marrying Sadie Stoltzfus, she'd have to do it alone!

Chapter 4
Busybody

Rachel, why aren't you eating your lunch?" Mom asked, nodding at the half-eaten peanut butter and jelly sandwich on Rachel's plate. "Aren't you hungry this afternoon?"

Rachel shrugged. "I have a lot on my mind."

Jacob snickered. "She's probably thinking up some kind of trouble to get into."

Rachel glared at Jacob. "Am not."

"I'll bet you are, little *bensel* [silly child]."

"Oh, quit your jabbering. I'm not a silly child!"

"Jah, you are."

Pap loudly cleared his throat. "That'll be enough, Jacob! Leave your *schweschder* [sister] alone and finish eating your lunch so we can get back to the fields."

"That's right," Rachel's older brother Henry said. "We have a lot of work to do out there yet today."

Jacob grabbed his sandwich and took a big bite.

Rachel did the same. She knew if she didn't finish her lunch, Mom probably wouldn't let her go back to the greenhouse. She needed to go out there so she could talk Grandpa out of going to see Sadie! She had to make him realize that Sadie wasn't the right woman for him to marry.

Rachel wondered if she should say something to her folks about Grandpa marrying Sadie Stoltzfus.

I'd better not, she decided. *If Grandpa hasn't told them, he might not like it if I blab.*

Rachel crumpled her napkin into a tight little ball. *I wonder why Grandpa told Anna Miller about his plans. I don't think he would have said anything to Anna if he didn't want Mom and Pap to know.*

Rachel knew that Anna was one of Mom's best friends. The next time Anna saw Mom, she was bound to say something about Grandpa getting married. Maybe it would be best to let Anna tell. Then Rachel wouldn't get into trouble for listening to Grandpa and Anna's conversation. When Mom heard the news from Anna, she might convince Grandpa that he was doing the wrong thing by marrying Sadie. After all, Grandpa was Mom's dad, and she probably wouldn't like the idea of him getting married again—especially not to a cranky old woman!

"Sure hope we get the rest of the hay cut today," Pap said before picking up his glass to take a drink.

Henry nodded. "If we can keep my little *bruder* [brother] working this afternoon, we should be able to get it done."

Jacob frowned at Henry. "I always work hard; you know I do!"

Henry thumped Jacob's back. "Jah, most of the time."

"You'd better all work hard this afternoon," Grandpa said, "because some rain is heading our way." He pulled his fingers through the ends of his beard and nodded. "Maybe tonight, maybe tomorrow, but I know it's coming."

"How do you know?" Jacob asked.

Grandpa rubbed his hands over his arms. "I feel it in my bones. They always ache a bit when rain is coming."

"It's true," said Mom. "Even when I was a *maedel* [girl] my *daed* [dad] could forecast the weather by the way he felt in his bones." She frowned. "If we're going to have rain, I hope it holds off until I weed my garden."

"If you need help with that, let me know," Grandpa said with a smile. "When I'm not busy with customers in the greenhouse, I'd be happy to help pull a few weeds."

"I'd appreciate that," Mom said. "It's been hard to keep up with the weeds this summer. They've been growing too fast. Of course," she added, "Hannah's growing nearly as fast. She can no longer wear the outfit I brought her home from the hospital in."

Pap chuckled. "You're right, Miriam. Why, it won't be long until our little girl will be all grown up and running around this place causing all kinds of trouble."

"Just like Rachel. Always trouble somewhere, right,

Rachel?" Jacob jabbed Rachel's arm just as she was about to drink her milk.

Whoosh! Milk sloshed out of Rachel's glass, trickled down her chin, and splashed onto the front of her dress.

Rachel opened her balled-up napkin and blotted her dress; then she frowned at Jacob and said, "You did that on purpose, didn't you?"

He shook his head. "Did not. How was I to know you were going to pick up your glass?"

"You shouldn't have poked your sister's arm," Pap scolded. "You should keep your hands to yourself. Now tell Rachel you're sorry."

"Sorry," Jacob mumbled.

Rachel didn't think Jacob looked one bit sorry, but she figured Pap would scold her if she didn't accept Jacob's apology. Without looking at Jacob, she said, "You're forgiven."

"Nothing's more beautiful than watching a woman do her work," Grandpa said as he and Rachel repotted a large split-leafed plant in his greenhouse that afternoon.

Rachel smiled. It made her feel good to be called a woman, even though she still had several more birthdays before she'd really be one. At least Grandpa didn't think of her as a little girl anymore.

That was more than she could say for Jacob. Every chance he got he reminded her that she was two years younger than he was. His constant teasing made her feel like a little girl. She hoped he would stop calling her a little bensel. It would be embarrassing if he still called her that when she was a grown woman.

Rachel glanced over at Grandpa. Since he hadn't said a word about going to see Sadie Stoltzfus, she hoped he'd changed his mind. Maybe he'd had time to think things through and realized that Sadie wouldn't be a good wife for him.

"Are you getting excited about Mary coming to visit?" Grandpa asked, smiling at Rachel.

Rachel nodded. "Oh jah. I'm very excited!"

"I imagine you two will have lots to talk about—lots of catching up to do."

"You're right about that." Rachel grinned. "I can hardly wait to show her the bussli Mom let me keep from Cuddles's litter of kittens."

"I'm sure the two of you will have lots of fun." Grandpa pulled the sack of potting soil closer to them, scooped out some dirt, and poured it into the empty pot. "Are you looking forward to going back to school next month?"

Rachel dug her shovel into the sack and added some dirt to the pot. "I guess so, but I'll miss working here every day."

"You can work after school and on Saturdays," he reminded her.

"I know, but it won't be the same."

"Sure it will. You just won't be working here as

many hours as you are now." Grandpa placed the plant in the pot and patted the soil around it. "I think we're about done with this. Would you clean up the dirt we've spilled?"

Rachel was pleased that Grandpa had said "we" instead of blaming her for spilling the dirt. Jacob would have blamed her for it if they'd repotted the plant together.

"Jah, sure, I can clean up the dirt." Rachel headed to get the broom and dustpan from the back room.

When Rachel returned, she was surprised to see Grandpa wearing his straw hat.

"I'm going to Sadie Stoltzfus's place with an African violet plant," he said.

Rachel's heart beat faster. She had to think of something to keep Grandpa from going. She couldn't let him propose marriage to Sadie!

"Say, Grandpa," she said, tugging on his shirtsleeve, "I'll take the plant to Sadie! That way you'll be here in case any customers come."

"It's a long walk to Sadie's, Rachel." He smiled and squeezed her arm. "Besides, I think you can handle waiting on customers."

Rachel's mouth went dry. "Ach no! I wouldn't be comfortable here alone for that long."

"I won't be gone long, Rachel. What I have to say to Sadie will only take a few minutes."

Rachel thought for a minute. Was Grandpa going

to ask Sadie to marry him and then come right back home? She remembered the evening Rudy had asked Esther to marry him. He'd taken her out for a buggy ride, and they'd been gone a long time. Maybe older folks didn't need such a long time to ask someone to marry them.

"Say, Grandpa," Rachel quickly said, "before you go, could you answer a question for me?"

He nodded. "Make it fast, though. I need to get going."

Rachel pointed to a purple African violet on the shelf across the room. "How come the leaves on that plant are pointing straight up and not out like the others?"

"Because that African violet needs more light." Grandpa handed Rachel the small shovel he'd been holding and headed across the room. "Danki for mentioning it."

He took the plant from the shelf and placed it closer to the window. "You have a good eye for things. I'm glad you're helping me in the greenhouse."

Rachel smiled. She liked to be appreciated for the good things she did. Sometimes she felt as if her family saw only the wrong things she did.

"Guess I'd better head on over to Sadie's now." Grandpa moved toward the door.

Rachel jumped in front of him. "Wait! I have another question."

Grandpa lifted one edge of his straw hat and scratched his forehead. "What is it, Rachel?"

"I've noticed that some African violets have pretty flowers and others don't. Is there a reason why some of them don't have any blooms?"

He nodded. "A plant might not flower for several reasons."

"Like what?"

"It might need more light, a warmer temperature, or a bit more humidity. A special plant food for African violets often helps, too," he said.

"What kind of plant food?" Rachel leaned against the door and gazed at Grandpa. If she could get him talking about plants, he might forget about going to Sadie's.

Grandpa opened a cupboard door and removed a small box. "This is the plant food I'm talking about. It has special nutrients that help a plant produce nice, healthy flowers."

"Hmm. . . That's interesting." Rachel pointed to a miniature rosebush. "Will the same kind of plant food work for that?"

Grandpa shook his head. "African violet food is only for African violet plants." He removed another box from the cupboard. "This plant food is made for roses."

"A person sure needs to know a lot in order to run a greenhouse," Rachel said. "I wonder if I'll ever know as much as you do."

"If you keep helping me out, you'll learn real fast." Grandpa stepped around Rachel and opened the door. "I'm off to see Sadie now. *She dich, eich, wider* [See you later]*!*" He stepped outside.

Rachel slumped against the wall with a groan. "I'm doomed."

A few seconds later, the greenhouse door opened, and Grandpa stepped back inside. "I forgot the African violet, and I need my umbrella because it's beginning to rain." He hurried across the room and was about to pick up a lacy-leafed pink and white African violet when Rachel rushed forward and grabbed his arm.

"Grandpa, I—"

Thunk! Her hand bumped the pot. The African violet crashed to the floor, crushing the plant and spilling dirt everywhere!

Rachel gasped.

Grandpa moaned.

Both of them stared at the floor.

"I'm sorry, Grandpa," Rachel said. "I didn't mean to bump your arm and make such a mess."

"It's not the mess that upsets me, Rachel." Grandpa slowly shook his head. "This is the last African violet I have with lacy pink and white edges. Since that's the kind Sadie wants, I'll have to go empty-handed and explain what happened."

Rachel jumped to her feet. "You're going anyway. . . even without the plant?"

He nodded.

"Can't you propose to Sadie some other time? When you get another lacy-leafed pink African violet?"

Grandpa's bushy eyebrows rose. "Propose what, Rachel?"

"*Heiraat* [marriage]."

He rubbed his forehead. "You think I'm going over to Sadie's to propose marriage to her?"

Rachel nodded as her eyes filled with tears. "I don't want you to marry Sadie, Grandpa. She doesn't like kinner, and she clicks her teeth when she talks."

"Ha-ha! Ho-ho!" Grandpa laughed so hard his face turned bright red and tears rolled down his wrinkled cheeks.

Rachel frowned. She didn't think what she'd said was funny.

When Grandpa finally stopped laughing, he wiped his eyes, walked to Rachel, and bent down to look her right in the eye. "Where in the world did you get the idea that I was planning to marry Sadie Stoltzfus?"

Rachel didn't know what she should say. Grandpa might be mad if she told him the truth.

Grandpa nudged Rachel's arm. "*Raus mitt* [Out with it]!"

Rachel blushed as she explained how she'd heard him and Anna talking. She said, "When you said you were going to take a plant over to Sadie and that you needed to ask her a question, I figured you were going to ask her to marry you."

Grandpa frowned. "You shouldn't have eavesdropped, Rachel. That makes you a busybody, you know."

"I—I didn't mean to listen in. I was worried when I thought you'd decided to marry Sadie," Rachel said. "It was just a big *missverschtand* [misunderstanding], and I'm glad I heard wrong." She was glad she hadn't said anything about Grandpa getting married to anyone but Jacob. She'd have to let him know right away that it was a mistake.

"You're right about it being a misunderstanding, Rachel." Grandpa shook his head. "For your information, Anna and I were talking about her nephew getting married. We also discussed Sadie because she'd told Anna that she wanted a lacy-edged pink African violet to give to her sister as a birthday present."

"But I heard you say it wasn't good to be alone, and that you missed Grandma."

"I do still miss your grandma, but you are mistaken about everything else. Anna mentioned that Sadie lived alone and didn't get out much because she couldn't control the horse and buggy. That's why I said I'd take the African violet to her."

Grandpa's forehead wrinkled. "You should never listen to other people's conversations, and you shouldn't assume anything."

"I'm sorry," Rachel mumbled.

"Sorry is good, but you need to learn a lesson from your mistake." Grandpa snapped his fingers and pointed to the floor. "I'll take a different plant to Sadie and explain that the one I'd chosen fell on the floor. While I'm gone, you clean up that mess. Then you can sweep the rest of the rooms."

Rachel nodded and dropped to her knees. It was never fun to be punished, but at least one thing was good: She didn't have to worry about Grandpa marrying Sadie Stoltzfus! She couldn't wait to tell Jacob the good news.

Chapter 5

Tittle-tattle

One week later, Rachel poked her head into the kitchen and spotted Mom sitting at the table, reading the newspaper and drinking a glass of iced tea.

"I was hoping I'd find you here," Rachel said. "I need to ask you about the message you found on our answering machine in the phone shed this morning."

Mom looked up and smiled. "What message? There were several."

"The one from Aunt Irma, about Mary."

"Oh, that." Mom smiled and winked at Rachel. "What do you want to know about Aunt Irma's message that I haven't already told you?"

Rachel pulled out a chair and sat down. "If Mary arrives when her mamm said, then she should be here sometime tomorrow, right?"

Mom nodded. "I imagine you're pretty excited."

"I am, but I'm also kind of *naerfich* [nervous]." Rachel touched her stomach. "It feels like a bunch of butterflies are zipping around in here."

"Why would you be nervous about Mary coming?" Mom asked.

"What if she doesn't recognize me with my glasses? What if she doesn't like me anymore? What if. . ."

"You're getting yourself all worked up for nothing. You don't look that different with glasses, and I'm sure Mary still likes you. After all, you and Mary have been good friends since you were *bopplin* [babies]." Mom patted Rachel's arm. "Once Mary gets here, I'm sure you'll see that you've worried for nothing."

Rachel nodded. "I hope so."

"Since Grandpa closed the greenhouse today to go fishing, why don't you go visit one of your friends?" Mom suggested. "It might help get your mind off those butterflies in your stomach and keep you from thinking about things that aren't likely to happen."

"I guess I could go to Audra's and see how she's getting along with the kitten I gave her as a birthday present," Rachel said. "I could take Snowball with me, and our kittens could play together."

Mom nodded. "I think that's a *gut* [good] idea. Why don't you get your kitten and head to Audra's right now?"

"Okay, I'll be home in time to help with supper." Rachel raced out the door.

Rachel stepped onto the back porch of Audra's house, holding her squirming kitten against her chest. "Is anyone home?" she called, peering through the screen door.

No response.

Tap! Tap! Rachel rapped on the door.

Several seconds later she heard a faint, "I'm coming."

Audra's mother, Naomi, came to the door. Her cheeks were red, and a wisp of hair from under her *kapp* [cap] was stuck to her sweaty forehead.

"Oh, it's you, Rachel. I hope you haven't been waiting long." Naomi pushed her hair back in place. "I was in the basement getting some fruit jars."

Rachel shook her head. "I haven't been here long. Is Audra at home? I brought my kitten over so we could play."

"Audra and Brian went out to skateboard awhile ago." Naomi pointed to the big red barn. "They're probably getting on each other's nerves, so I'm sure Audra will be happy to see you."

Rachel smiled. "I'll head to the barn then." She scampered down the porch steps. She was glad to know she wasn't the only one who had trouble with her brother.

When Rachel entered the barn, the sweet smell of hay tickled her nose. She saw Brian riding a skateboard on one side of the barn where a wooden ramp had been built, while Audra sat on a bale of hay, frowning.

"Wie geht's?" asked Rachel as she took a seat beside her friend.

Audra shrugged. "I'd be better if my bruder would give me a turn on my skateboard."

"Doesn't Brian have his own skateboard?" Rachel asked.

"He did, but he lost it." Audra tapped her foot. "At least that's what he says. I wouldn't be surprised if he's just saying that so he can ride the one you gave me. It's a lot faster than his."

Rachel held up her kitten. "I brought Snowball along. Why don't we play with our kittens until Brian gets tired of skateboarding?"

"That's a good idea." Audra glanced around. "Of course I have to find Fluffy first."

"Since Snowball is Fluffy's schweschder, I'll bet Snowball can find her." Rachel placed her kitten on the floor. "Go get her, Snowball! Find Fluffy!"

Audra snickered. "Do you really think that just because they're sisters Snowball can find Fluffy?"

Rachel nodded. "Of course. You know everyone in your family, don't you?"

"Jah, but that's different. We're people and—"

"Look!" Rachel pointed across the room. "Snowball's already found Fluffy, and they're rubbing noses."

Audra smiled. "Say, I have an idea. Why don't we go in the house and make bubble solution? Then we can make lots of bubbles and let our kittens chase them."

"That sounds like fun," Rachel agreed. "Do you have an extra bubble wand for me to use?"

"Of course." Audra grabbed Rachel's hand. "Let's go!"

As Rachel and Audra sat on the back porch blowing bubbles, Snowball and Fluffy zipped across the lawn and leaped into the air, trying to pop the colorful bubbles with their paws.

"This is so much fun! I'm glad you came over," Audra said.

"Me, too." Rachel dipped her wand into the bubble solution and blew. A huge bubble formed, and she blew again, making a second bubble, then a third.

Audra's eyes widened. "How'd you do that?"

"Grandpa taught me. We blow bubbles together whenever we can." Rachel waved her wand in the air, and it blew the triple bubble into the yard. "It just takes a little practice, that's all."

Audra dipped her wand into the bubble solution. She blew and made one bubble, but when she blew again, the first bubble popped. "I think I'd better stick to making one bubble for now."

Rachel set her wand aside and leaned back on her elbows. "Tomorrow will be a big day at our house."

"Why?"

"My cousin Mary's supposed to arrive."

"Oh, that's right; I forgot she was coming to see you soon." Audra set her bubble wand down. "I hope you don't forget about me while your cousin's visiting."

Rachel shook her head. "I told you before that you

don't have to worry about losing me as your friend. I still hope you can come over while Mary's there. The three of us can do something fun together."

"Can we jump on your trampoline?"

"Maybe. We can also play at the creek or in the barn."

"I think I'd enjoy jumping on the trampoline most."

"We'll see what Mary wants to do." Rachel noticed that Fluffy and Snowball were lying in the grass, so she stuck the bubble wand in the solution again. "Guess we'd better make some more bubbles for our busslin to chase, because I think they're getting bored."

Audra glanced at the barn. "We may as well, because it doesn't look like Brian will quit skateboarding anytime soon."

"Maybe you should go in and insist that he give it to you," Rachel said. "After all, it's *your* skateboard."

Audra shook her head. "If I did that, he'd keep the skateboard even longer just to make me mad."

Rachel clicked her tongue, the way Mom often did when she was trying to make a point. "Brothers can sure be *peschte* [pests]."

"I agree." Audra blew another bubble and sent it sailing across the yard. "My bruder is the worst pescht of all!" She wrinkled her nose. "There's something else I can tell you about Brian."

"What's that?"

Audra leaned closer to Rachel and whispered, "He sometimes wets the bed."

Rachel gasped. "That's *baremlich* [terrible]!" She was glad no one in her family wet the bed. That would be so embarrassing!

When Rachel arrived home that afternoon, she raced into the house. "Mom, I'm back!"

Mom stepped out of the kitchen, holding a squirming, fussy baby. "Did you have a good time at Audra's?" she asked, raising her voice above Hannah's cries.

Rachel nodded. "But we never got to use Audra's skateboard because Brian hogged it the whole time I was there."

Mom placed Hannah against her shoulder and patted her back. Rachel was glad when the baby stopped crying.

"Did Audra tell her mamm that Brian wouldn't share?" Mom asked, sitting at the table.

Rachel shook her head. "Audra knew if she did that, then Brian would call her a *retschbeddi* [tattletale]."

"Sometimes it's necessary to tell on someone for their misdeeds," Mom said.

Rachel flopped into the chair beside Mom. "If I had a bruder like Brian, I'd probably tell on him all of the time." She leaned closer to Mom. "Do you know what Audra told me?"

"Rachel, I don't think—"

"She said Brian sometimes wets the bed." Rachel wrinkled her nose. "Isn't that awful, Mom? Aren't you glad none of your kinner wets the bed?" She pointed to Hannah. "Except for the boppli, of course."

Mom slowly shook her head. "Rachel, you're being a tittle-tattle."

"What's a tittle-tattle?" Rachel asked.

"It's someone who likes to gossip. It seems to me that you like talking about other people and their problems. Bed-wetting is something Brian will outgrow, and you shouldn't make fun of him." Mom tapped Rachel's arm. "Especially since you've wet the bed yourself."

Rachel's face felt hot. "I don't wet the bed!"

"Not anymore, but you did until you turned five."

"I—I don't remember doing that."

"Well, it's true, and no one in our family made fun of you or told anyone else about it." Mom tapped Rachel's arm again. "You need to be careful not to gossip to anyone about Brian's problem, because someone might make fun of him if you do."

"I won't say a word," Rachel said.

Chapter 6

The Big Day

When Rachel awoke the following morning, she felt like singing at the top of her lungs: "Mary's coming today, and I just can't wait!"

Rachel leaped out of bed, rushed to the window, and lifted the shade. No sign of any car or van in the driveway. Mom had said last night that Mary and her neighbor would probably spend the night at a hotel between Indiana and Pennsylvania. Most likely they wouldn't get here until later today. Even so, Rachel wanted to be ready for Mary's arrival, so she hurried to get dressed and raced down the stairs.

She was almost to the bathroom when the door swung open and Pap stepped out.

"I'm surprised to see you up so early." He tapped the top of Rachel's head. "Did you get up at the crack of dawn to help me do my chores?"

Rachel shook her head and bounced up and down on her toes. "Mary's coming today. I wanted to be sure everything's ready."

"Oh, that's right. Today's the big day." Pap patted Rachel's head again. "It'll probably be several hours before Mary arrives, so calm down and try to relax."

Rachel touched her stomach. It felt like hundreds of butterflies were zipping around again. "I'll try to relax, but it won't be easy."

"If you need something to keep your mind busy, why don't you get breakfast started?" Pap suggested.

Rachel glanced down the hall at her parents' bedroom door. "Isn't Mom getting up?"

"She was up with the boppli several times last night, so I told her to stay in bed awhile longer." Pap motioned to the kitchen. "If you're hungry, you can start breakfast now."

Rachel shook her head. "You know I don't cook well."

"Then why don't you come to the barn and help me?" he suggested.

"What about Jacob and Henry? Aren't they helping?"

"They're in the milking shed, milking the cows."

"Okay," Rachel said with a nod. "As soon as I'm done in the bathroom I'll come to the barn."

When Rachel entered the barn a short time later, she was greeted by the gentle nicker of the horses in their stalls. She spotted Pap across the room, lifting a bale of hay into a large wheelbarrow.

"I'm here, Pap," she called. "What do you need me to do?"

"Why don't you get the hose and give the horses some water while I feed them?"

"Sure, I can do that." Rachel raced to the water faucet and turned on the hose. She was getting ready to haul it to one of the horse's stalls when Pap hollered, *"Bass uff, as du net fallscht* [Take care you don't fall]*!* That floor can get slippery when hay mixes with water."

"I'll be care—" *Whoosh!* Rachel's foot hit a wet spot, and down she went!

"Always trouble somewhere," Rachel grumbled as she scrambled to her feet.

Pap raced across the room. "Are you okay? Did you hurt yourself?"

"I'm okay, but my dress got a little wet."

"Next time put the hose in the trough first and then turn on the water. You should have known better than to do something like that," Pap scolded.

Rachel's face heated up. "I was going to fill the horse's trough, but I slipped on the water coming from the hose. I figured I could save time if I turned on the hose first."

"Saving time isn't always the best way to do something," Pap said.

Rachel nodded; then she hurried into the nearest horse's stall and filled the trough with water. When it was full, she pulled the hose into the next stall. While she watered the horses, she and Pap chatted.

When Rachel was done, she left the hose in one of

the troughs, ran back to the faucet, turned off the water, and put the hose away.

"I think I'll go to the house and see if Mom's up," Rachel told Pap.

He nodded. "That's fine. I'll be in shortly."

Before Rachel left the barn, she stopped to pet Cuddles and Snowball, who were sleeping in a pile of hay.

Cuddles purred. Snowball batted Rachel's hand.

"Abastz!" Rachel scolded. "Stop scratching me!"

Meow! Snowball looked at Rachel as if to say, *I'm sorry*.

Rachel stroked the cats until they went back to sleep; then she hurried out of the barn.

Rachel found Mom in the kitchen, stirring a pot of oatmeal. The sweet smell of cinnamon and butter made Rachel's stomach rumble.

Grandpa sat in a chair near the stove, holding Hannah and humming as he stroked her blond hair.

Mom's glasses had fallen to the middle of her nose, and she pushed them back in place as she looked at Rachel. "Where have you been? When I called you to help with breakfast, you weren't in your room."

"I helped Pap with the animals," Rachel said. "I put water in the horses' troughs."

Grandpa pointed to Rachel's dress. "Looks like you watered yourself some, too."

"I fell, but I didn't get hurt, and only a little of my dress got wet." Rachel didn't explain that she'd been dragging the hose across the floor with the water running. She figured she would get a lecture if she mentioned that. "Should I set the table?"

Mom nodded. "When you finish, you can step onto the porch and ring the dinner bell so the menfolk will know breakfast is ready."

"Okay." Rachel hummed as she placed the silverware on the table; then she raced out the door and rang the bell. *Ding! Ding! Ding!*

"Someone's in a good mood this morning," Grandpa said when Rachel returned.

"Mary's coming today. I can hardly wait to see her!" Rachel grinned. "I've got so much to say to Mary!"

"She'll be here for a whole week," Mom said. "You'll have plenty of time to visit."

Pap, Henry, and Jacob entered the kitchen.

"Is breakfast ready?" Jacob asked as he hung his straw hat on a wall peg near the door. "Milkin' cows is hard work, and I'm hungry as a mule!"

"You're not the only one who worked hard this morning." Pap winked at Rachel. "Rachel helped me care for the horses, and *mir hen die zeit verbappelt* [we talked away the time]."

Jacob rolled his eyes. "I can imagine. Rachel's such a blabbermouth; I'll bet she talked your head off."

Rachel glared at Jacob. "I did not. I only talked a little while I watered the horses."

"Don't let Jacob ruffle your feathers." Henry nudged

Jacob's arm. "He just likes to see if he can rile you, Rachel."

Rachel shrugged. "No one can rile me this morning."

Jacob tickled Rachel under her chin. "You don't think so? I'll bet I can find a way to rile you."

She pushed his hand away. "You do and I'll rile you right back."

"That'll be enough," Mom said as she placed the pot of oatmeal on the table. She took the baby from Grandpa. "Since Hannah's fallen asleep, I'll put her in the cradle, and then we can eat."

When breakfast was over and the dishes were done, Rachel went outside and sat on the porch swing. *Squeak. . .squeak. . .squeak. . .* She pushed her feet against the porch floor to move the swing faster.

"Aren't you coming to the greenhouse this morning?" Grandpa asked when he stepped onto the porch.

Rachel shook her head. "I need to wait for Mary."

"You can wait for her in the greenhouse as well as you can out here," Grandpa said. "Since you don't know what time she'll arrive, you may as well do something constructive while you wait."

Rachel sighed. She knew Grandpa was right, but it would be hard to do anything when she could only think about when Mary might arrive.

"Well, what do you say?" Grandpa grabbed the armrest of the swing, and it slowed. "Are you coming to the greenhouse with me?"

"I guess so." Rachel hopped off the swing and was about to step off the porch when a van pulled into the yard. It stopped near the house, and a young Amish girl stepped out.

"Mary!" Rachel raced to hug her cousin.

"It's good to see you," Mary said. "I think you've grown a few *zoll* [inches] since I moved."

"You've grown taller, too," Rachel said.

Mary stared at Rachel with a strange expression. "Wow, you sure look different with your new glasses."

Rachel touched the frame of her glasses. "Do—do you think I look weird?"

Mary shook her head. "Of course not. I think you look grown-up."

Rachel sighed with relief. She guessed she'd been worried for nothing.

She grabbed Mary's hands, and the girls twirled in a circle until Rachel felt dizzy. Then she drew in a deep breath. "We're gonna have so much fun while you're here! I have so much to show you and tell you!"

Rachel gulped in another breath. "There's Cuddles's kitten, Snowball; Grandpa's new greenhouse; my baby sister, Hannah; and—"

Woof! Woof! Buddy bounded up to them with a bone in his mouth. *Crackle! Crackle! Crunch! Crunch!* He dropped the bone on the ground and—*slurp!*—licked Rachel's hand.

Rachel pushed him away. "Do you remember this

big, hairy mutt of Jacob's?"

Mary giggled and patted Buddy's head. "Jah, and he's still a friendly hund."

Rachel groaned. "Sometimes he's too friendly, and he likes to give big, sloppy, wet kisses!"

Mary patted Buddy's head again. "I like him. He is a nice hund."

"You wouldn't like him if he gave you sloppy kisses all the time!" Rachel grabbed Mary's hand. "Come with me to the barn, and I'll show you Cuddles's kitten."

Mary looked at the van. "I need to get my suitcase."

"I'll take care of that," Grandpa said. "I'd like to meet your neighbor and thank her for bringing you here."

Mary opened the van door and introduced Rachel and Grandpa to Carolyn Freeburg. Then Grandpa invited Carolyn to the house to meet Mom.

"Maybe we should go with them," Mary said.

"Not till I've shown you the kitten." Rachel nudged Mary's arm, but Mary didn't move.

"I think I should go inside first and say hi to your mamm." Mary darted away before Rachel could respond.

Rachel followed slowly, kicking every pebble she could find. Didn't Mary even care about seeing Cuddles's cute kitten?

By the time Rachel entered the kitchen, Mary was already there. She sat in a chair beside Mom, wearing a satisfied smile and holding Hannah.

"Your little sister's sure cute," Mary said, looking at Rachel. "Makes me wish my mamm would have another boppli."

Rachel shrugged. "Hannah is cute, but she cries a lot."

"Only when she's hungry or needs her *windel* [diaper] changed." Mom stroked the top of Hannah's head.

Grandpa and Carolyn stepped into the room. "Miriam, this is Mary's neighbor, Carolyn Freeburg," he said to Mom.

Mom shook Carolyn's hand. "It's nice to meet you. If you'll have a seat at the table, I'll fix us all some refreshments."

Carolyn smiled. "That's kind of you, Miriam, but please don't go to any trouble on my account."

"It's no trouble at all," Mom said. "I was planning to give the girls some lemonade and ginger cookies. This will give us all the chance to sit and visit."

Rachel sighed. If they took time to eat cookies, she and Mary would never get to the barn.

"A glass of lemonade does sound good," Carolyn said. "It's turning into a warm, sticky day." She smiled at Mom. "Can I do anything to help?"

"No, no, just have a seat. My daughter will help me get the refreshments." Mom looked at Rachel and said, "Would you please get out the lemonade and paper cups while I put some cookies on a plate?"

Rachel left her seat to do as Mom asked, while Carolyn and Grandpa sat at the table.

When the cookies and lemonade were handed
out, Rachel and Mom sat down. Mom asked Carolyn
questions about Indiana. Mary continued to play with
the baby while Grandpa leaned back in his chair and
closed his eyes. Rachel fought the urge to chew on her
fingernails. She wanted to show Mary so much, and
here they were wasting time at the table!

Finally, Carolyn stood. "I'd best be on my way now.
I'm anxious to see my daughter and her baby boy." She
patted Mary's shoulder. "Have a good time. I'll be back
next week to pick you up."

Mary nodded. "I'll be ready to go when you get here."

Grandpa opened his eyes, yawned, and stood.
"Guess I'd better head to my greenhouse and get to
work." He patted Rachel's head. "Since Mary's here, I
don't expect you to help me today, but you can show her
around the greenhouse if you like."

Rachel nodded. "I will after we go to the barn to see
Cuddles and Snowball."

"All right. I'll see you two later." Grandpa pulled his
straw hat onto his head and went out the door.

"You'll have to give the boppli to my mamm so we
can go to the barn," Rachel told Mary.

Mary frowned. "Can't we stay here longer? Hannah's
so sweet and cuddly. I like holding her."

"You can hold the boppli later." Rachel started
across the room but turned back around. "Are you
coming, Mary?"

"Jah, okay." Mary handed the baby to Mom; then she followed Rachel out the door.

Rachel took Mary's hand, and they skipped across the yard.

When they entered the barn, Rachel called, "Here, Cuddles! Here, Snowball! Come out, wherever you are!"

No response. Not even a meow.

"Where are those silly cats?" Rachel ran around the barn, calling the cats and searching the obvious places. She still found no sign of Cuddles or Snowball.

Finally, Rachel turned to Mary and said, "They must be outside. I guess we can look for them after I show you the greenhouse."

"That's fine. I'm anxious to see it," Mary said eagerly.

When they stepped inside the greenhouse a few minutes later, Mary's eyes widened. "Oh, how beautiful! I've never seen so many flowers and plants in one place!"

"Haven't you ever visited a greenhouse?" Grandpa asked.

Mary shook her head. "If you're not too busy, can you show me around?"

Grandpa grinned and tugged his beard. "Since I have no customers right now, I'd be happy to give you a tour of the place."

Rachel gritted her teeth. First Mary wanted to visit with Mom. Then she wanted to hold Hannah. Now she wanted Grandpa to show her around the greenhouse. Who had Mary come to visit, anyway?

For the next half hour, Mary followed Grandpa around the greenhouse, asking questions and exclaiming how exciting it must be to work there.

Rachel stood to one side, nibbling on a fingernail and trying to be patient. At this rate, she and Mary would never have any fun together. The big day had turned into a disappointing day!

Chapter 7

Wishful Thinking

"Let's go look for Cuddles and Snowball now," Rachel said after Grandpa had shown Mary every part of the greenhouse.

"Where do you think they might be?" Mary asked.

Rachel shrugged. "Knowing Cuddles, they could be almost anywhere."

"I thought about bringing Stripes," Mary said. "But Mom thought he'd be too much trouble. Besides, now that Cuddles has a kitten of her own, she probably would have ignored my cat."

"Why do you think that?" Rachel asked.

"Cuddles has her kitten to play with now."

Rachel shook her head. "Cuddles usually hides from Snowball, because that lively little kitten can be a real pescht!"

"Does Cuddles ever get jealous when you give Snowball too much attention?" Mary asked as they headed for the creek.

Rachel nodded. "I think she does sometimes, and I can't blame her. I was jealous of Hannah when she was first born and got so much attention. That's one reason I went to Hershey Park with Sherry and her brother and didn't get Mom and Pap's permission."

Mary's eyebrows shot up. "You went to Hershey Park without asking your folks?"

"Jah."

As they walked along the path, Rachel told Mary how she'd gone to Hershey Park with her English friend Sherry and her brother, Dave. "When I wandered off and couldn't find them, I got really scared." Rachel shivered as she remembered the fear she'd felt that day. "I didn't know if I'd ever see any of my family again."

"How did you get home?" Mary asked.

"Sherry and Dave found me in the parking lot." Rachel swallowed hard, remembering how glad she'd felt when they'd gotten home.

"I'll bet your folks were really upset because you ran off without telling them," Mary said.

Rachel nodded. "I wasn't allowed to go anywhere except church for several weeks because of what I did."

Mary squeezed Rachel's hand. "If you ever visit me in Indiana, maybe we can go to the Fun Spot Amusement Park."

"That sounds great." Rachel felt good to know that Mary wanted her to come for a visit. Maybe things were okay between the two of them after all. Maybe Mary wanted to be with Rachel as much as Rachel wanted to be with her.

"I don't see any sign of the cats here," Mary said as they approached the creek. "But since it's such a hot day, why don't we go wading so we can get cooled off?"

"That's a good idea!" Rachel flopped onto the grass, yanked off her sneakers, and plodded into the creek. Mary did the same.

Rachel tromped around, going from one side of the creek to the other, kicking water in all directions. "This is so much fun! The chilly *wasser* [water] feels good on my legs!"

"It felt good at first, but now I'm getting cold." Mary shivered, stepped onto the grass, and sank to her knees. "Brr. . ."

Playing in the creek alone wasn't nearly as much fun as it had been with Mary, so Rachel waded out of the water and took a seat on the grass.

Just then, she spotted Cuddles and Snowball leaping through the tall grass, batting at grasshoppers.

"There's my silly *katze* [cats]!" Rachel laughed and pointed at the cats. "Looks like they're having a good time!"

Mary jumped to her feet. "Let's see if we can catch 'em!"

Rachel joined the chase. "Here, kitty, kitty!" she called, clapping her hands.

Cuddles and Snowball acted as if they didn't want

to be caught, for they scampered up the nearest tree and climbed all the way to the top.

Rachel groaned. "At this rate we'll never get to play with my cats."

"Let's go back to the house and see if Hannah's awake," Mary suggested.

Rachel shook her head. "It's too hot to be inside. Besides, the boppli usually sleeps most of the morning. I don't think she'll be awake yet."

Mary frowned. "Guess we'll have to find something else to do."

"Would you like to blow some bubbles?" Rachel asked.

Mary shook her head.

"Why don't we jump on the trampoline? That's always fun!"

"It's too hot."

"We could sit on the fence by the pasture and watch the horses."

"I don't think so."

Rachel sighed. "What would you like to do?"

Mary shrugged.

"We could go up to the house and sit on the porch swing," Rachel suggested.

"I guess that would be all right," Mary said.

The girls picked up their sneakers and started for the house. They were halfway there when the dinner bell rang. *Ding! Ding! Ding!*

"It must be time for lunch," Rachel said.

"I wonder why your mamm didn't call us to help her fix it," Mary said.

"She probably thought we wanted to play." Rachel sighed. "I know I did."

Mary hurried toward the house.

"Tell Mom I'll be in soon," Rachel called. "I'm going to the phone shed to make a couple of calls."

Mary gave a nod and kept walking.

If Orlie and Audra can come over after lunch, maybe Mary will feel more like playing, Rachel thought as she headed to the shed. *Besides, I did promise they could see her.*

"It's good to have you visiting with us," Pap said to Mary as everyone gathered around the table. "I'm sorry I wasn't here when you arrived, but the boys and I had a lot of work to do in the fields."

Mary smiled. "That's okay; I understand."

"Maybe we can make some homemade ice cream while you're here," Pap said.

Mary smacked her lips. "That sounds real good."

"I called and left a message on Audra's and Orlie's answering machines," Rachel spoke up. "I told them. . ."

Mom put her finger to her lips and looked at Rachel over the top of her glasses. "Shh. . . It's time for prayer."

Rachel bowed her head with the others. *Dear God,* she silently prayed, *thank You for this food. Thank You for bringing Mary here to visit. Help Audra and Orlie to hear my message and come to play. Help us to have lots of fun today. Amen.*

Rachel finished her prayer and opened her eyes. She was relieved to see that everyone else's eyes were open, too. Sometimes she prayed too fast and opened her eyes before the rest of the family did. Then she had to close them again and think of something else to pray about.

"Here you go." Mom handed Rachel a bowl of pickled beets.

Rachel forked several beets onto her plate and drew in a deep breath. "Yum." She loved the smell of pickled beets. She loved the way they tasted, too.

"As I was about to say before we had prayer. . . I went out to the phone shed before I came inside, and—"

"Say, Mary, I've been wondering about something," Jacob cut in.

"What's that?" Mary asked as she reached for a piece of ham.

"Do they have lightning bugs in Indiana?"

"The correct word is *fireflies*," Henry said before Mary could answer Jacob's question.

"Fireflies. . .lightning bugs—they're both the same." Jacob turned to Mary and grinned. "Do they have any *lightning bugs* in Indiana?"

Mary nodded. "Some things are the same in Indiana as they are here, but some things are different."

"Like what?" Henry wanted to know.

"For one thing, Indiana doesn't have a lot of hills like Pennsylvania does."

Rachel nudged Mary's arm. "As I was saying before. . ."

Jacob pushed the salad bowl toward Mary. "What about stinkbugs? Do they have stinkbugs in Indiana?"

She nodded and crinkled her nose. "I don't like stinkbugs at all! They smell really bad—especially if they get squished!"

Grandpa chuckled. "I remember once when I was a boy, my brother Sam put a stinkbug in my bed." He slowly shook his head. "I rolled over on it, of course. Boy, did that critter ever smell up my bed. Phew!"

Everyone at the table laughed. Everyone but Rachel. She ground her teeth and clutched her fork so tightly that her fingers began to ache. She wished everyone would quit interrupting her and let her speak what was on her mind!

"One time, when I was a young girl, some boys at school put stinkbugs on the teacher's seat when she wasn't looking." Mom's nose twitched as she pushed her glasses back in place. "When the teacher sat down, the whole room smelled so horrible that we all had to hold our breath!"

"I think most everyone has a stinkbug story to tell," Pap said with a grin.

Rachel cleared her throat loudly. "Changing the subject. . . Before I came in for lunch, I went out to the phone shed and called—"

Jacob bumped Rachel's foot under the table. "Remember the time we were having a picnic at the pond and a stinkbug landed on your piece of chicken?"

He snorted. "I saved the day by squashing that stinky critter before you could eat it."

"I wasn't gonna eat the stinkbug!" Rachel frowned at Jacob. "And I wish you'd stop talking so I can say something!"

Mom shook her finger at Rachel. "How many times must I tell you not to use your outside voice when you're in the house?"

"Sorry, Mom," Rachel mumbled, "but I've been trying to say something ever since we sat down at the table. Every time I start to say it, someone cuts me off."

Mom patted Rachel's arm. "Just calm down, and say what's on your mind."

"I left messages for Audra and Orlie on their folks' answering machines. I invited them to come play this afternoon." Rachel turned to Mary and said, "I can't wait for you to meet Audra, and I know Orlie would like to see you again."

Mary nodded. "I'd like to see them, too."

Waaa! Waaa!

"It sounds like the boppli's awake," Mom said. "I'd better get her before she becomes too worked up."

"Would you like me to get Hannah for you, Aunt Miriam?" Mary asked eagerly. "I'd like to hold her again."

Mom smiled. "I appreciate the offer, but Hannah probably needs her windel changed. I'll also need to feed her."

Mary frowned as she stared at her plate. "Oh, all right."

"You can hold the boppli after lunch. By then she'll have been diapered and fed, so you won't have to worry about a thing," Mom said, rising from her chair.

A huge smile spread across Mary's face. "Okay!"

Rachel frowned. Once Mary got her hands on Hannah, she probably wouldn't want to play at all. She'd probably want to spend the rest of the day fussing over the baby.

After the lunch dishes were done, Mary asked Mom if she could hold Hannah.

"Of course you can." Mom smiled. "If you'd like to go into the living room and sit in the rocking chair, I'll get Hannah from her crib and bring her in to you."

Mary gave a quick nod.

"I thought we were going outside to play," Rachel called as Mary started for the living room.

"We can play later, when Hannah's taking her afternoon nap." Mary scurried out of the kitchen.

Rachel groaned and slouched in her chair.

"Now don't look so gloomy," Mom said. "You and Mary can take turns holding the boppli."

"I don't want to hold the boppli. I want to go outside and play!"

Mom squinted at Rachel. "Mary's your guest. You should be willing to do what she wants while she's here, don't you think?"

Rachel turned the palms of her hands upward.

"Guess I may as well since there's no sign of Orlie or Audra."

"Maybe they didn't get your message. They could be gone for the day, you know." Mom patted Rachel's arm. "I'm going to get Hannah. Are you coming?"

"Jah, okay," Rachel mumbled.

When Mom had given Hannah to Mary, she left to get some canning jars out of the basement.

Rachel sat on the sofa and picked at some lint on the throw pillow beside her. Sitting in the stuffy living room was just plain boring! Watching Mary fuss over the baby was enough to make her feel sick.

"It's sure hot in here. Aren't you hot, Mary?" Rachel questioned.

Mary shook her head. "I feel just fine."

"Sitting here is boring. Aren't you bored?"

Mary stroked the top of Hannah's head. "Who could be bored when they're holding such a bundle of sweetness?"

Rachel tapped her foot against the hardwood floor. *Thump! Thump! Thump!* She wished Orlie and Audra were here. She wished Mary wasn't so interested in holding the baby.

"It would sure be nice if I had a baby sister." Mary leaned over and kissed Hannah's cheek. "She's so soft and cuddly."

"My bussli is soft and cuddly, too," Rachel said.

"That may be true, but a kitten's not nearly as soft

and cuddly as a human baby."

Tap! Tap! Tap!

Rachel jumped up. "Someone's knocking on the back door. I'll be right back!" She raced out of the room. When she opened the back door, she was pleased to see Orlie.

"I got your message," he said with a crooked grin. "So I came to play." He looked past Rachel into the kitchen. "Where's your cousin?"

Rachel motioned to the living room door. "Mary's in there, holding my baby sister."

"Is she comin' out to play?"

"I don't know, but I'll ask." Rachel raced back to the living room and screeched to a stop in front of Mary's chair. "Orlie's here! He came over to play and wants us to come outside."

"You go ahead," said Mary. "I'm busy holding Hannah."

"Just take the boppli to Mom and Pap's room and put her back in the crib. She'll be fine."

Mary shook her head. "I don't want to go outside right now. I want to stay in here and hold the boppli."

Rachel frowned. "You've held her long enough. Let's go outside and play."

"I'd rather not."

"Fine then, suit yourself! I'm going outside where it's cooler!" Rachel stomped across the room and raced out the back door, banging it behind her. She found Orlie sitting on the porch step, holding Snowball.

Rachel flopped down beside him. "Where'd you find my kitten?"

"She wandered into the yard with Cuddles." Orlie stroked the kitten's head. "Cuddles took off for the barn, but Snowball ran onto the porch and leaped into my arms."

Rachel grunted. "She wouldn't come when I called her earlier. She and Cuddles ran up a tree out by the creek."

Orlie looked at Rachel and squinted his eyes. "Is something wrong? You seem kind of cranky."

"I'm not cranky. I'm just— Oh, never mind." Rachel jumped up. "Are we going to play or not?"

"Just the two of us?"

Rachel nodded. "Jacob's in the fields helping Pap and Henry, so he can't play at all today. I invited Audra over, but she must not have gotten my message yet."

"What about Mary? Isn't she coming out to play?"

Rachel shook her head. "She's still holding Hannah and doesn't want to play!"

"I guess it's just the two of us then." Orlie placed the kitten on the ground and ran into the yard. He sat on the grass and moved his arms in a rowing motion.

"What do you think you're doing?" Rachel asked. She had seen Orlie do some pretty odd things, but this seemed weirder than usual.

"I'm pretending that I'm rowing a boat. Come on,

Rachel. Sit down and pretend you're rowing a boat, too."

"I don't want to."

"Aw, come on, Rachel. It's much cooler down here, and if you pretend really hard, you'll think you're sailing across the water in a real boat."

Rachel rolled her eyes. "You're so weird, Orlie."

"Am not. I'm just good at imagining and wishing for things."

"You wish you were in a boat?"

"Jah, I sure do."

"Well, I wish Mary would come outside. And I wish the three of us were jumping on the trampoline," Rachel muttered.

Orlie stopped rowing. "Does your cousin think she's too good to play with me? Is that why she's staying in the house?"

Rachel shook her head. "I don't think Mary thinks she's too good to play with you. She just wants to—"

"Maybe Mary's turned into a snob since she moved away."

"My cousin's not a snob!" Rachel's face heated up. "I think you're jumping to conclusions!"

"People change," Orlie said. "Maybe living in Indiana has changed Mary."

Rachel shook her head so hard that the ribbons on her kapp flipped around her face. "That's *lecherich* [ridiculous]! Mary's the same girl she was when she lived here in Pennsylvania!"

Even as the words slipped off Rachel's tongue, she wondered if they were true. Ever since Mary had arrived, she'd been acting differently than she had before she moved.

Rachel flopped onto the grass. What if Mary really *had* changed? What if they weren't close friends anymore? Maybe things would never be the same between her and Mary. Maybe all the fun Rachel had thought she and Mary would have had just been wishful thinking.

Chapter 8

Nosing Around

Mary had been at Rachel's house for three whole days before Audra finally showed up after breakfast one morning.

"My family and I went to Illinois for my cousin's wedding," Audra told Rachel. "We got back last night, and when my daed checked the messages in the phone shed, he said one was from you."

Rachel nodded. "I wanted you to meet my cousin Mary. She got here three days ago."

Audra smiled. "I would like to meet her. Where is she?"

"In the kitchen, writing a letter to her mamm." Rachel opened the door wider. "Come in, and I'll introduce you."

Audra glanced at the barn. "Brian came with me. He saw Jacob when we got here, and they went out to the barn."

"That's good. Maybe they won't bother us girls while we play."

When they entered the kitchen, Rachel motioned to Mary, who sat at the table, writing a letter.

"This is my cousin Mary," Rachel said to Audra.

Mary looked up and smiled.

"And this is my friend Audra Burkholder." Rachel patted Audra's back.

"It's nice to meet you, Audra," Mary said. "Rachel's told me a lot about you in her letters."

Audra smiled shyly. "She told me about you, too."

"Audra came over to play," Rachel said. "You're gonna join us, aren't you?"

Mary nodded. "I just finished my letter, so as soon as I put it in the mailbox, I'll be ready to play."

"The mailman's already come by our place," Rachel said. "So you may as well wait until tomorrow morning to put the letter in the box."

"Okay. Let's go outside then," Mary said.

Rachel smiled. At least her cousin was willing to play today. Of course, that could be because Mom had taken Hannah to the doctor for a checkup, and they weren't back yet. Rachel figured if Hannah were here, Mary would probably be holding her right now and wouldn't want to play at all.

"What should we do first?" Audra asked as the girls headed outside.

"We could play in the barn," Mary suggested.

Rachel shook her head. "I'd rather not. Jacob's there with Brian. Knowing my teasing bruder, he'd probably find something mean to do if we went out there."

"My bruder would, too," Audra said. "I think he looks for ways to tease me."

Rachel sat on the porch step. Mary and Audra sat on either side of her.

"How's Brian's problem?" Rachel asked, looking at Audra. "Is he doing any better?"

"Not really." Audra wrinkled her nose. "He had an accident while we were at Grandma and Grandpa's."

"What kind of accident?" Mary wanted to know. "Did he fall and hurt himself?"

Audra shook her head. "Sometimes Brian wets the bed."

Mary gasped. "I thought only bopplin wet the bed!"

Rachel clenched her fingers, remembering how Mom had told her that she used to wet the bed. Rachel was glad she couldn't remember that. She hoped no one else in the family remembered it either. She decided she needed to quickly change the subject.

"Is anyone thirsty?" she asked.

Mary nodded.

Audra shrugged.

"I think I'll go inside and get us something cold to drink," Rachel said.

"That sounds good." Mary smiled. "Do you need my help?"

"Thanks, but I can manage." Rachel jumped up and scurried into the house.

When she opened the refrigerator, she found a jug of Pap's homemade root beer on the top shelf. She lifted it out, grabbed three paper cups from the pantry, and headed for the door.

Rachel was about to step onto the porch when she heard her name mentioned.

"Jah, that's right," said Mary, "Rachel is. . ."

Whoosh! Snowball leaped onto the porch and darted between Rachel's legs, nearly knocking her off her feet.

Rachel righted herself in time, but the jug of root beer slipped out of her hand and fell to the porch with a splat!

"Ach no!" Rachel cried. Cold, sticky root beer covered her dress, legs, and the porch floor.

Mary jumped up. "What happened, Rachel?"

"I was standing in the doorway, and Snowball ran between my legs." Rachel frowned. "She knocked me off balance, and I dropped the jug of root beer."

Audra pointed to Rachel's dress and laughed. "Looks like you had a root beer bath!"

"It's not funny." Rachel slowly shook her head. "Now I have to go inside and change my dress."

"While you're doing that, I'll get the mop and clean the mess off the porch," Mary said.

"Okay, thanks." Rachel scurried into the house, mumbling, "Always trouble somewhere!"

When Rachel returned to the porch wearing a clean

dress, she was pleased to see that the root beer had been cleaned off the floor and a carton of milk was on the small table near the door. Mary and Audra sat in the porch swing, talking with their heads together.

When Rachel approached the swing, they stopped talking.

She frowned and squinted at them. "Were you two saying something bad about me?"

"Of course not," Mary said, shaking her head.

"Then why did you stop talking when I came out?"

Audra shrugged.

Mary stared at the floor.

"You *were* saying something bad about me." Rachel folded her arms and frowned. "I know you were."

"You're jumping to conclusions," Mary said. "Audra and I were just talking about the painted rocks you made for us."

"That's right," Audra agreed. "We think you have lots of talent."

Rachel smiled. "Really?"

Both girls nodded.

"I wish I could paint the way you do," Mary said.

Rachel squeezed in between them on the swing. "Everyone has something they're good at. I just happen to be good at painting on rocks."

"My mamm says I'm good at sewing, and if I keep practicing, someday I'll be as good as she is." Audra looked over at Mary. "What are you good at?"

Mary thumped her chin a couple of times. "Let's see now. . ."

"You're good at baking cookies. The ones you helped Mom bake last night were *appeditlich* [delicious]."

Mary smiled. "They were pretty good. Should we have some now?"

"Maybe later." Rachel jumped up. "Let's jump on the trampoline for a while!"

Audra clapped her hands and jumped up, too. "Oh good; I love jumping on your trampoline!"

The girls ran down the steps, hurried across the yard, and climbed onto the trampoline. They'd only been jumping a few minutes when Jacob and Brian rushed out of the barn and raced over to the trampoline.

"Oh no," Rachel groaned. "Looks like we've got company."

"Should we get off?" Mary asked.

"No way!" Rachel shook her head. "We were here first, so we're staying!"

"Let's have some fun!" Jacob hollered as he and Brian climbed onto the trampoline.

Boing! Boing! Boing! Jacob jumped so high that all three girls toppled over.

Jacob laughed.

Brian laughed.

Rachel glared at Jacob.

Audra glared at Brian.

Mary climbed off the trampoline. "I think I'll watch

from here," she said.

Brian did a few jumps; then he flipped into the air. "Woo-hoo! This is so much fun!" He bounced high again, causing Rachel to flip into the air and fall onto the ground.

"Oomph!" She brushed some chunks of grass from her dress; then she scrambled to her feet and shook her finger at Brian. "You'd better be careful jumping like that or you might wet your pants!"

Brian's face turned red as a ripe tomato. He scowled at Audra. "Did you tell Rachel about my problem?"

"What problem is that?" Jacob asked before Audra could respond.

"He wets the bed," Rachel blurted out.

Jacob nudged Brian's arm. "Is that true?"

Brian hung his head, and his face turned even redder. "I'm gonna get even with you for this, Audra," he muttered. "I can't believe you'd blab something like that to Rachel."

"I–I'm sorry," Audra sputtered. "I didn't think she would tell anyone."

Tears stung Rachel's eyes. "I—I didn't meant to say what I did. My tongue just slipped."

Brian looked over at Jacob with a pathetic expression. "I don't wet the bed all the time, but when I do it's so embarrassing. Mom says I'll grow out of it someday, and I sure hope it's soon."

Jacob thumped Brian on the back a couple of times.

"It's okay. I won't tell anyone; I promise." He looked at Rachel and frowned. "You'd better keep your nose out of other people's business, and you'd better keep quiet about Brian's problem. If you don't, I'll tell everyone that you used to wet the bed."

"I—I only did it until I was five." A tear slipped out of Rachel's eye and rolled down her cheek. "You can ask Mom if you don't believe me."

"Even so, if you tell anyone else about Brian's problem, then I'll tell them about yours," Jacob said.

"I won't say a word," Rachel promised. Even though her bed-wetting days were in the past, she didn't want anyone else to know.

"I think we should change the subject," Mary said.

"You're right." Audra climbed off the trampoline. "I think we girls should go up to Rachel's room and play with her dolls."

Rachel didn't play with dolls anymore. She felt too grown-up for that. Still, it would be better than staying out here with the boys.

"All right," she said with a nod. "The boys can have the trampoline all to themselves!"

Later that day, when Mom got home, Mary asked if she could hold Hannah again.

"Jah, sure," Mom said. "You can hold her until I'm ready to start lunch." She looked at Rachel and smiled. "Did you and Mary have a good morning?"

Rachel nodded. "Audra and Brian came over to play, but they went home awhile ago." She hoped Mary wouldn't mention what had been said about Brian wetting the bed. Rachel didn't want a lecture from Mom for blabbing something she shouldn't have blabbed.

"I'm glad Mary was able to meet Audra." Mom smiled at Mary. "Did you enjoy spending time with Rachel's new friend?"

Mary nodded. "We jumped on the trampoline for a while, and then we played with Rachel's dolls." She sat in the living room rocker. "I'm ready to hold Hannah now."

Mom placed the baby in Mary's lap. "I'm going to the kitchen to get lunch started. I'll call you when it's time to set the table," she said, looking at Rachel.

Rachel nodded.

When Mom left the room, Rachel sighed with relief. She was thankful Mary hadn't said anything about Brian wetting the bed.

"Since you're busy holding Hannah, I think I'll go out to the barn and see if Cuddles or Snowball is there," Rachel said to Mary.

"Sure, go ahead." Mary hummed as she rocked the baby.

Rachel rolled her eyes and hurried from the room. She didn't know why Mary thought she had to hold Hannah so much.

As soon as Rachel opened the barn door, she heard voices. It sounded like Pap and Henry were in one of the horse's stalls.

"When are Grandpa and Grandma Yoder leaving?" she heard Henry ask.

"Within the next week or so," Pap said.

Rachel held her breath and leaned against the wall as she continued to listen to their conversation.

Henry said something else, but Rachel couldn't make out the words. She inched a bit closer to the horses' stalls.

"Wisconsin's a nice place. I think they'll. . ." Pap's voice trailed off.

Rats! Rachel thought. *I wish I knew what else he said. Are Grandpa and Grandma Yoder moving to Wisconsin? Oh, I sure hope not!*

She moved a bit closer to the stall, and—*ploop!*— stepped right in a bucket.

"Oh no!" Rachel groaned as she lifted her bare foot out of the bucket. It was covered with white paint!

"Rachel, is that you?" Pap stuck his head around the corner of the stall. He looked at Rachel, and his mouth dropped open. "What are you doing with your foot in that bucket of paint?"

"I—I didn't do it on purpose," Rachel stammered. "I was trying to hear what you and Henry were saying, and—"

"You were listening in on our conversation?"

She nodded. "I heard you say something about

Grandpa and Grandpa Yoder moving to Wisconsin, and—"

"Grandpa and Grandma aren't moving anywhere," Henry said, stepping out of the stall. "They're going to Wisconsin on a trip, that's all."

Rachel's face heated up. "Oh. I—I guess I must have jumped to conclusions."

"Well, you'd better jump out of that paint bucket and wash off your foot," Pap said. "And no more listening to other people's conversations!"

Rachel hopped on one foot out the barn door and over to the hose. Then she turned on the water and washed the paint off her foot. "Trouble, trouble, trouble," she mumbled and grumbled.

When Rachel was sure she had all the paint washed off, she hurried back to the house, no longer in the mood to play with the cats.

She found Mom in the kitchen, making ham and cheese sandwiches. "Your timing is perfect, Rachel," she said. "I was just about to call you."

"Do you want me to set the table?" Rachel asked.

"Jah, and then I'd like you to go down to the greenhouse and tell your *grossdaadi* [grandfather] that lunch is about ready."

"Okay."

Rachel hurried and set the table; then she raced out the back door and headed for Grandpa's greenhouse. She was halfway there when she spotted Grandpa coming out of the greenhouse with Abe Byler, a member of the school board. The two men stood with their backs to Rachel.

I wonder what they're talking about, Rachel thought. *If I move closer, I might be able to hear what they're saying.* She ducked under the branches of the maple tree near the greenhouse and leaned against the trunk of the tree.

"Jah, that's right," Abe said to Grandpa. "Why, it's my understanding that the whole school system seems to be falling to ruins."

"That's too bad." Grandpa slowly shook his head. "It's a real shame."

"And that teacher is so lazy. I think she ought to be fired from her job." Abe grunted. "Do you know that. . ."

Bzzz. . .bzzz. . .bzzz. . .

Rachel swatted at a bee buzzing around her head. She had to hear the rest of what Abe had to say. This was all so shocking! She'd never thought her teacher, Elizabeth, was lazy!

Maybe I should say something, she thought. *Abe and Grandpa need to know that Elizabeth's not lazy. She's a wonderful teacher. Oh, I hope she won't lose her job!*

Rachel was about to move away from the tree, when—*Bzzz. . .bzzz.* That pesky old bee stung her right on the nose!

"Yeow!" Rachel waved her hands and jumped up and down.

Grandpa whirled around. "What's the matter with

you, Rachel? Why are you carrying on like that?"

"A big old *iem* [bee] stung me right here." Rachel
pointed to her nose and tried not to cry.

"I'm sorry that happened. Where were you standing
when the iem got you?" Grandpa asked. "There might
be a nest someplace that needs to be removed."

Rachel motioned to the tree. "I was right there."

"Just what were you doing under the tree?"
Grandpa's eyes narrowed. "Were you listening to Abe's
and my conversation?"

Rachel nodded slowly as tears clouded her vision.
She reached under her glasses and wiped them away.
"I—I heard Abe say that our whole school is in ruins,
and that—" *Sniff! Sniff!* "That Elizabeth is lazy and
should be fired."

Deep wrinkles formed across Abe's forehead. "I
never said that."

"Jah you did. I heard you say it." Rachel sniffed a
couple more times. "Elizabeth's not lazy. She works real
hard. She's the best teacher anyone could ever want."

Abe looked at Grandpa then back at Rachel. "For
your information, I was talking about another school
district—the one where my brother lives. It's his granddaughter's schoolteacher who's gotten lazy, not yours."

"Oh, I'm so glad." Rachel covered her mouth with
the palm of her hand. "I—I didn't mean that I'm glad
your granddaughter's schoolteacher is lazy. I just meant
to say—"

"I know what you meant." Abe looked back at Grandpa. "Guess this is my fault for spreading a bit of gossip. I really shouldn't have said anything about this at all. I hope you won't repeat anything I told you."

Grandpa shook his head. "Of course not."

Abe turned toward his buggy. "I should be on my way now." He gave Rachel a sympathetic look. "I hope that the iem *schteche* [sting] doesn't hurt too much."

She forced a smile and shook her head. "Guess I deserve it for nosing around."

Grandpa and Abe both nodded their heads.

Abe climbed into his buggy and drove away. Rachel stepped up to Grandpa and said, "Mom sent me to tell you that lunch is about ready."

"All right, but let me look at that *naas* [nose] of yours first. Then we'll head up to the house." Grandpa bent down and studied Rachel's nose. "I can see where that pesky iem got you all right. Your naas is a bit swollen."

Rachel touched her nose and winced. "It stings like crazy, too."

"It'll feel better once your mamm makes a paste with a little water and some baking soda. She'll slather that on your naas, and it should draw the stinger right out."

"I—I hope so."

As they walked toward the house, Grandpa rested his hand on Rachel's shoulder. "Proverbs 11:13 tells us: 'A gossip betrays a confidence, but a trustworthy man keeps a secret.' You've become a bit of a *schnuppich* [snoopy] gossip lately. I hope you've learned a lesson today about the problem that could come from listening in on someone's conversation."

Rachel nodded. "No more nosing around for me!"

Chapter 9

Babysitting

Rachel, Mary, and Mom were in the kitchen getting things ready for the bonfire they'd be having later. Tonight was Mary's last night with Rachel and her family, so Pap had said they could do something special. Rachel had asked for the bonfire, and Mary said she wanted to roast hot dogs and marshmallows. Rachel's sister, Esther, and her husband, Rudy, would be joining them, too.

Rachel had just removed a jar of mustard from the refrigerator when she heard buggy wheels rumble up the driveway. "That must be Esther and Rudy," she said to Mary, who stood near the sink, cutting dill pickles into thick slices.

"It's Aunt Karen, Uncle Amos, and Gerald," Mom said, peering out the kitchen window. "Grandpa and Grandma Yoder are with them, too."

"Do they know Mary's leaving tomorrow?" Rachel asked.

"Jah, I'm sure they do."

"Did they come to say good-bye to Mary?"

"I'm sure they'll say good-bye. They've also come to drop off Gerald, because they'll be leaving early in the morning."

Rachel's forehead wrinkled. "Leaving for where?"

"Gerald's mamm and daed are going to Wisconsin with Grandpa and Grandma Yoder to attend Aunt Karen's sister's wedding." Mom started for the door. "I'm sure you knew that, Rachel."

"Guess I must have forgotten," Rachel mumbled.

"Why aren't they taking Gerald to the wedding?" Mary wanted to know.

Mom glanced over her shoulder and smiled. "Gerald gets fussy when he rides in a car. Aunt Karen and Uncle Amos think Gerald will be happier staying here with us."

"Oh great!" Rachel sank into a chair at the table. Gerald could be a real handful at times. He always pestered Rachel with a bunch of questions and expected her to give him horsey rides. "How long does Gerald have to stay with us?" she asked.

"Just for a week." Mom opened the back door and stepped onto the porch. Rachel and Mary followed.

When Grandpa and Grandma Yoder came up the walk, Mary ran out to greet them.

"We hear you're leaving tomorrow," Grandpa said, patting Mary's head.

Mary nodded slowly. Rachel wondered if her cousin

might be on the verge of tears.

Grandma bent down and hugged Mary. "When you get home, tell your folks we said hello and that we'll try to come to Indiana for a visit soon."

Mary smiled. "That would be real nice."

"If you make a trip to Indiana, maybe I can go with you," Rachel was quick to say.

Grandpa Yoder nodded, and Grandma Yoder gently squeezed Rachel's shoulder.

"Can you all stay and have supper with us?" Mom asked Uncle Amos, since he'd been the one driving the horse and buggy.

He shook his head. "I'm afraid not. Our driver will pick us up early tomorrow morning. We really need to go home, finish packing our suitcases, and get to bed early." He set Gerald's small suitcase on the porch and scooped the little boy into his arms. "Be good for Uncle Levi and Aunt Miriam," he said.

Tears welled in Gerald's eyes, and his chin quivered like a leaf on a windy day. Pretty soon the tears started to flow, and then Gerald's nose began to run.

Aunt Karen wiped Gerald's nose with a tissue; then she patted his back. "You'll have a good time here with Rachel. The two of you can do many fun things together."

Rachel cringed. Did Aunt Karen think she wanted Gerald hanging around her the whole time he was here? She hoped Gerald didn't think that, because she had better things to do than babysit her gabby little cousin for a whole week!

Mom nudged Rachel's arm and motioned to Gerald's suitcase. "Would you please take that up to Jacob's room? That's where Gerald will sleep while he's here."

"Jah, okay." Rachel picked up Gerald's suitcase and went into the house. At least Gerald would sleep in Jacob's room and not hers. That meant Rachel would have a few hours to herself, even if it was only when she was asleep.

When Rachel came back downstairs, she spotted Gerald sitting tearfully in the middle of the living room floor, with Mary kneeling by his side.

"His folks just left, and he's feeling sad," Mary said, looking up at Rachel.

"Let's take him out to the barn to play with my kitten," Rachel suggested. "That should help take his mind off his troubles."

"That's a good idea." Mary took Gerald's hand and helped him to his feet. "*Kumme* [Come], let's go play with the bussli."

"Bussli," Gerald said, slightly smiling. Rachel hoped that meant he would not cry any more today.

"We'd better check with my mamm first," Rachel said. "Just in case she needs us for something."

The three of them hurried to the kitchen. They found Mom making a pitcher of lemonade.

"Do we have time to take Gerald to the barn to play

with Snowball?" Rachel asked.

Mom nodded and smiled. "Esther and Rudy won't be here for another hour or so. Since everything is almost ready for our bonfire, I think there's enough time for you to play in the barn."

"Okay. Ring the dinner bell when Esther and Rudy arrive, please," Rachel said as she, Mary, and Gerald headed out the door.

When they entered the barn, they found Snowball sleeping on a bale of hay, but they saw no sign of Cuddles. Rachel figured it was for the best. Cuddles had seemed irritable lately—probably because Snowball pestered her all the time. She might not take too kindly to a rowdy little boy bothering her, too.

"Bussli! Bussli!" Gerald squealed as he lunged for the kitten.

Yeow! Snowball leaped into the air, darted across the barn floor, and scurried up the ladder to the hayloft. She obviously didn't care for rowdy little boys, either.

Gerald scrunched up his nose, and his face turned crimson as he stomped his feet. "Kumme, bussli. Kumme!"

"I don't think the kitten wants to play right now," Rachel said. "Maybe we should find something else to do."

"Waaa! Waaa!" Tears streamed down Gerald's face as he shook his head. "Bussli!"

Rachel covered her ears. *"Ich kann sell net geh* [I cannot tolerate that]*!* You can't play with the bussli right now, so you need to stop crying!"

Waaa! Waaa!

"You don't have to yell at him, Rachel," Mary said. "It's only making things worse."

Rachel shrugged. "Have you got any idea how to make him stop crying?"

"Why don't we blow some bubbles?" Mary suggested. She leaned over and put her face close to Gerald's. "Would you like to blow some bubbles, Gerald?"

Gerald stopped crying as quickly as he'd started. "Jah," he said, nodding his head. *"Blos* [Bubble]*!"*

Rachel pointed to a plastic jug across the room. "I think there's a batch of bubble solution on the shelf over there." She hurried off and returned with a jar of bubble solution and three metal wands.

Mary made a couple of double bubbles. Rachel made a caterpillar by blowing several bubbles, the way Grandpa had shown her some time ago. Gerald made a few little bubbles, but mostly he just giggled and chased the bubbles Rachel and Mary made. At least he wasn't crying anymore. He hadn't asked for a horsey ride either.

Ding! Ding! Ding!

Rachel jumped off the bale of hay she'd been sitting on. "There's the dinner bell! Esther and Rudy must be here, so we'd better go." She grabbed the bottle of bubble solution and put it back on the shelf.

"Blos! Blos!" Gerald hollered.

"We can make more bubbles another day," Rachel said. "Right now it's time to roast hot dogs and marshmallows!"

Gerald looked up at her and tipped his head. "Marshmallows?"

"That's right; now we'd better go!"

Gerald raced out of the barn, giggling all the way.

Rachel turned to Mary and rolled her eyes. "One minute he's crying; the next minute he's laughing. I just can't figure that little boy out."

Mary snickered. "I guess you're gonna have to learn how to figure him out, since he'll be with you for a whole week."

Rachel nodded and reached for Mary's hand. "I wish you could stay and help me babysit him. You do better with little ones than I do."

Mary shrugged as she skipped out the door. "I'm sure you and Gerald will get along just fine."

As Rachel sat around the bonfire with her family that evening, her eyes darted from the glow of the burning embers to the glittering fireflies rising from the grass. It was a peaceful evening, and if she hadn't felt so sad about Mary leaving in the morning, she'd have been perfectly content.

Rachel thought back to the night before Mary moved to Indiana, and how Mary had come to spend the night with her. She'd been sad that night, too.

Saying good-bye to Mary the next day had nearly broken Rachel's heart. It had taken Rachel several weeks to adjust to Mary being gone.

Of course, Rachel thought, *it will be a little easier saying good-bye to Mary tomorrow, because I've made some new friends since she moved away. I have Audra and Sherry as friends now, and Mary's made some new friends in Indiana.*

As Rachel listened to her family sing a song about the joy of having friends, she thought about the miracle of friendship. Rachel and Mary had both changed some since Mary had moved away. Mary's visit hadn't gone exactly the way Rachel had hoped it would.

Even so, Rachel still enjoyed being with Mary, and she hoped that she and her cousin would always be good friends. She looked forward to the day she could go to Indiana to see Mary's new home.

Rachel jumped when she felt a tug on her hand.

Gerald, who sat between Rachel and Mary, pointed to the sky and said, *"Schtann* [Stars]."

Rachel smiled. "Jah, Gerald. See how the night sparkles because of the stars?"

Gerald pointed upward again. *"Munn* [Moon]. Papa made the munn."

"No, Gerald," Rachel said with a shake of her head. "God made the munn. God made everything."

"That's right," Mary agreed. "The Bible says that God made the sun, moon, stars, and every living thing."

Gerald's forehead wrinkled, and he puckered his lips. "Everything?"

Mary and Rachel nodded at the same time.

Gerald pointed to himself. "God made me?"

"That's right," said Rachel's sister Esther who sat in a chair on the other side of Rachel. She placed both hands against her bulging stomach and smiled. "He also knows my little one before it's even born."

"I wish I could be here when your boppli comes," Mary said with a sad expression. "I love bopplin. . .and little kinner, too." She looked over at Rachel and sighed. "You're lucky to be able to babysit Gerald for a whole week. I wish his folks would have brought him sooner so I could have helped entertain him."

Rachel grunted. "I'll send him home with you, if you like."

"I would like that," Mary said, "but I don't think Gerald's mamm and daed would be too happy if they came home from Wisconsin and discovered that he had gone home with me."

"No, I guess not." Rachel leaned closer to Mary and whispered, "I need to know something before you go."

"What's that?" Mary asked.

"Do you wish you hadn't come here for a visit?"

"No, of course not," Mary said with a shake of her head. "Why would you even ask me a question like that?"

Rachel moistened her lips with the tip of her tongue. "Sometimes it seemed like you'd rather be with Hannah than me."

"I'm sorry if it seemed that way. I really did enjoy being with you, but holding baby Hannah has been special for me, too." Mary reached for Rachel's hand and gently squeezed it. "You'll always be my good friend, and I'm really glad I came."

Rachel smiled and tilted her head back to look at the starry sky again. *Thank You, God, for making such a beautiful world.* She looked down at Gerald, who'd climbed into Grandpa's lap and fallen asleep; then she closed her eyes and finished her prayer. *Thank You, God, for everyone in my family. . .even Gerald.*

Chapter 10

Another Good-bye

As Rachel ran water into the sink to wash the breakfast dishes, she heard Mom and Pap talking in the hall. Her ears perked up when Pap mentioned her name. She knew she wasn't supposed to eavesdrop, but how could she not listen when they were talking about her?

She reached into the cupboard for the dishwashing soap while she strained to hear what Pap was saying.

"That's right, Miriam. I think Rachel needs to. . ." Pap's voice trailed off.

Rachel squirted the dishwashing liquid into the sink full of warm water. She heard the back door shut and figured Mom and Pap must have gone outside to finish their conversation. She was tempted to leave the dishes and follow them. She knew if she did, though, Mom would ask if she had finished washing the dishes.

Rachel dropped the sponge into the dishwater and frowned. There were no bubbles. Not even one. "Now that's sure strange."

She grabbed the bottle of dishwashing liquid, squirted it into the water again, and swished the sponge around in the water. Still no bubbles!

"What in all the world?" Rachel stared at the bottle. It wasn't dishwashing liquid at all! It was window cleaner! "Guess I should have read the label first," she muttered.

She pulled the plug on the drain to let the water out. Then she filled the sink with fresh water.

She set the bottle of window cleaner back in the cupboard and reached for another bottle. This time she carefully read the label to make sure it was dishwashing liquid. She squirted some of the liquid into the warm water and sloshed the sponge around. Several bubbles drifted to the ceiling.

"I wish I didn't have dishes to do," Rachel grumbled. "I wish I were upstairs helping Mary pack."

She swallowed around the lump in her throat. *I hope I'll get to visit Mary in Indiana sometime. It would be fun to see what life is like there. If school wasn't starting next week, I'd ask if I could go home with Mary now.*

Whoosh! The kitchen door flew open, and Gerald barreled in. "Blos!" he shouted, pointing to the colorful bubbles rising to the ceiling.

"Jah, Gerald, the bubbles are coming from my dishwater," Rachel said.

Gerald waved his hand in the air. "Blow blos?"

Rachel shook her head. "There's no time to blow bubbles right now. I need to finish washing the dishes."

Gerald's chin quivered, and his eyes filled with tears.

Rachel sighed. "Don't start crying," she said. "I have no patience for that this morning."

Just then Mary stepped into the room, carrying her suitcase. "I'm all packed and ready to go. I just have to wait for Carolyn to pick me up."

Rachel glanced at the clock on the opposite wall. "She should be here soon, I expect."

Mary nodded. "I'm anxious to see my family again, but I wish I could stay with you awhile longer. Our visit seemed awfully short."

"Short!" Gerald hollered as he pointed to himself.

Rachel giggled. "I've heard Gerald's daed call him short, so Gerald must be mimicking him," she said to Mary.

Mary nodded. "Some little kinner like to do that."

Rachel heard the rumble of a vehicle in the driveway outside, followed by *Beep! Beep!*

"That must be Carolyn," Mary said. "I think it's time for us to say good-bye."

Rachel hugged Mary then followed her out the door. Gerald tagged along behind her. When they stepped onto the porch, Rachel saw Mom, Dad, and Grandpa talking to Carolyn by her van.

As Rachel, Mary, and Gerald headed that way, Jacob and Henry came out of the barn. Soon everyone had gathered around Mary, hugging and saying their good-byes.

Just before Mary got into Carolyn's car, Rachel gave her one final hug. "Danki for coming," she said.

"You're welcome. See you soon, I hope." Mary climbed into the passenger's seat and shut the door.

As Carolyn's van drove away, Rachel watched until it was out of sight. Then she turned to Grandpa and said, "I need to keep busy so I don't miss Mary too much. Do you have some work you need me to do in the greenhouse this morning?"

He nodded and smiled. "Jah, sure. I'd be pleased to have your help, Rachel."

Rachel smiled as she headed for the greenhouse. During the time Mary had been visiting, she hadn't helped Grandpa at all. It would be good to water, trim, and repot some plants. It would be nice to see and smell the beauty of all those plants and flowers, too.

"Where ya goin'?"

Rachel stopped walking and turned around. Gerald looked up at her with an eager expression.

"I'm going to the greenhouse to help Grandpa."

"Okay." Gerald grabbed Rachel's hand. "Let's go!"

"No, Gerald. I'm going to the greenhouse to work." Rachel pointed to the house. "Why don't you go see if my mamm has something for you to do?"

Gerald hung tightly to Rachel's hand. "I go with you."

Rachel was tempted to argue but knew that if she said no, Gerald would cry. Rachel just couldn't stand Gerald's crying!

"Okay, Gerald," she said with a sigh, "but you have to be good in the greenhouse and stay out of my way. Is that understood?"

Gerald nodded and looked up at her with a crooked grin.

When Rachel entered the greenhouse with Gerald, she was surprised to see Grandpa in one corner, standing on his head again.

"I'll be with you in a minute," Grandpa said as he peered at Rachel from his upside-down position. "I'm not done clearing my head, and I need to do this so I'll have a good start to my day."

Gerald raced across the room, flopped on the floor, and stood on his head beside Grandpa.

Rachel snickered. "Say, Grandpa, how come you stand on your head out here instead of in your bedroom?"

"I used to do that," he responded. "But since I got the greenhouse, I decided to do it out here among all these *wunderbaar* [wonderful] plants that give off oxygen."

"I've been in the greenhouse many times, and until a few weeks ago, I never saw you stand on your head," Rachel said.

Grandpa chuckled. "I always did it before you came out. I was afraid if you saw me like this you might laugh."

"I probably would have," Rachel admitted, "but I'm getting used to it now."

Ding! Ding! The bell on the greenhouse door rang, letting Rachel know a customer had come in.

Grandpa quickly dropped his feet to the floor.

Gerald did the same.

Rachel was surprised to see the man who had bought strawberries from her earlier this summer step into the greenhouse. After she'd put the basket of berries on the front seat of his car, she didn't think she would ever see him again.

"You know those strawberries I sat on earlier this summer?" he said, looking at Rachel.

She nodded slowly, wondering if he was going to scold her about that mishap again.

He smacked his lips and grinned. "My wife made strawberry jam from the smashed berries, and it turned out real good."

Rachel sighed with relief. "I'm glad to hear it. Was your wife able to get the berry juice out of your pants?"

"Oh yes. She soaked them in cold water and then sprayed them with something that's good for stains." The man looked over at Grandpa, who'd taken a seat on a stool by the workbench where he repotted plants. "Today's my wife's birthday, so I came here to buy her a nice indoor plant."

Grandpa nodded at Rachel and said, "Would you like to show the man some plants?"

"Okay." Rachel led the way to the part of the greenhouse where the houseplants were kept. The man followed. So did Gerald.

Gerald reached up and touched the leaf of an ivy plant.

"No, Gerald," Rachel said. "Don't start fooling with things."

She moved down the row until she came to a shelf full of African violets. "Here's one with pretty pink blooms."

"That's a nice one. I really like it," the man said. "I think I'll take it."

Rachel started to reach for the plant when Gerald bumped her arm. The pot tipped over, spilling dirt all over the man's shirt!

Rachel shook her finger at Gerald. "I told you to stay out of the way! Now look what's happened!"

Tears welled in Gerald's eyes, and he tipped his head back and wailed. *Waaa! Waaa!*

Grandpa stepped up to Rachel and frowned. "You shouldn't have yelled at the boy like that. He didn't bump your arm on purpose. It was an accident."

The man nodded and looked at Rachel. "As you well know, accidents do happen." He reached into his pocket and pulled out a lollipop, which he handed to Gerald.

Gerald quit crying, took a seat in one corner of the room, and stuck the lollipop in his mouth.

"If you'll come with me," Grandpa said to the man, "we'll find just the right plant for your wife. I was planning to put some plants on sale for 50 percent off next week, but if you'd like one now, I'll give it to you for the sale price since the one you really wanted is ruined."

"Thank you. I appreciate that," the man said.

The man must think it's my fault, because he didn't offer me a lollipop, Rachel thought as she cleaned up the dirt that had spilled on the floor. *I wish Gerald hadn't come to stay with us. He's nothing but trouble!*

A short time later, the man stepped up to Rachel and handed her a dollar.

"What's this for?" she asked.

"I had only one lollipop, or I would have given you one, too." He patted Rachel's shoulder. "Your grandfather's lucky to have you working here. I can see that you're a real good worker."

Rachel smiled up at him. It felt nice to be appreciated.

As Rachel and Gerald walked up to the house, Rachel thought about the dollar the man had given her. *Should I put it in my piggy bank and save it toward something I really want, or should I buy some candy the next time we go to town? I think I'll save it for now,* she finally decided.

"Should I set the table for lunch?" Rachel asked Mom when she and Gerald stepped into the kitchen.

Mom tapped her foot. Her eyebrows scrunched together above her thin nose as she frowned. "You forgot to make your bed this morning, Rachel."

"I was planning to make it after Mary left, but when

Grandpa asked me to help in the greenhouse, I forgot all about making my bed," Rachel explained.

Mom tapped her foot a couple more times. "No excuses, Rachel. I want you to go upstairs and make it right now. When you're done, you can set the table for lunch."

"Okay." Rachel trudged up the stairs. *Thump. Thump. Thump.* She was almost at the top when she heard another set of footsteps, a little softer than hers. *Thump. Thump. Thump.*

She turned and saw Gerald behind her. "Oh great!" She was beginning to think the little boy had become her shadow.

"I'm busy, Gerald. Go back downstairs!" Rachel rushed into her room and slammed the door. Her stomach rumbled, so she hurried to make the bed.

Tap! Tap! Tap!

"Who is it?" Rachel called.

Tap! Tap! Tap!

Rachel groaned and opened the door.

"Whatcha doin'?" Gerald asked as he darted into the room.

Rachel pointed to the bed. "I just finished making my bed."

Gerald shook his head. "God made the bed!"

"No, *I* made my bed."

Gerald folded his arms and stared at Rachel as if she were stupid. "God made everything!"

Rachel thought about what she'd told Gerald the night before, when they'd been looking at the moon in the sky. "That's right, Gerald. God made everything. He made the trees that were turned into wood to make my bed."

Gerald pointed to Rachel and shook his head. "Rachel didn't make the bed."

Rachel sighed. How could she make Gerald understand what she'd meant about making her bed?

Suddenly, an idea popped into her head. She pulled back the covers, messed up the bed, and made it all over again. "*I* made the bed," she said with a nod.

Gerald shook his head. "God made the bed."

Rachel pulled the covers back and made the bed again. This time she said, "I pulled the covers over my bed."

Gerald nodded and said, "God made the bed! Rachel covered the bed."

Rachel smiled and took Gerald's hand. "Now that we've got that settled, let's go downstairs and have some lunch."

Chapter 11

The Worst Possible News

Wearing a backpack over her shoulders and carrying her lunch pail in one hand and a jump rope in the other hand, Rachel hurried up the path leading to the schoolhouse.

"Slow down!" Jacob hollered. "You can't be that anxious to get to school!"

Rachel turned to face him. "Today's the first day of school, and I don't want to be late. Besides, going to school is better than dealing with Gerald at home." She sighed. "I'll be glad when his folks get back and he goes home where he belongs."

Jacob shook his finger at Rachel the way Mom sometimes did. "You shouldn't talk about Gerald like that. He's our cousin, and he's a nice little boy."

"That's easy for you to say." Rachel wrinkled her nose. "Ever since Gerald came to stay with us, all he's done is hang around me and ask a bunch of silly questions."

Jacob shrugged. "I guess that means he likes you more than anyone else in the family."

"I doubt it." Rachel started walking fast again.

"Slow down!"

"I want to get to school early so I can use the new jump rope I bought the other day."

Jacob grunted as he caught up to her. "That was a dumm thing to buy with the money you saved."

"It was not a dumm thing to buy!" Rachel raced ahead of Jacob. He thought everything she did was dumb!

When Rachel entered the school yard, she set her backpack and lunch pail on the ground near a tree. Then she found a level spot on the grass, opened her jump rope, and started to jump. *One. . .two. . .three. . .* She never missed a beat. *Four. . .five. . .six. . . .* Her arms swung up and over in perfect rhythm with her feet.

"Did you know. . .what Rachel did. . .the other day. . . ?"

Rachel's ears perked up when she heard her name mentioned. She glanced to the left. Audra stood beside Orlie, whispering something in his ear.

Rachel gripped the handles of the jump rope a little tighter. *I wonder what Audra said to Orlie about me.*

Seven. . .eight. . . She'd better not have said anything bad about me. Nine. . .ten. . . Maybe I should go over there and ask.

Ding! Ding! Ding! The school bell rang, calling everyone inside. Rachel stopped jumping. She'd have to wait until later to learn what Audra had said to Orlie.

Racing across the school yard, the scholars burst into the schoolhouse.

"My, my," exclaimed Teacher Elizabeth as Rachel stepped inside, "it looks like everyone's happy to be back in school!"

Rachel forced a smile. She had been happy until she'd heard Audra whispering something to Orlie about her.

She put her lunch pail and jump rope on the shelf over on the girls' side of the coatroom; then she shuffled to her seat. After she sat down, she glanced across the aisle where Audra sat.

Audra looked at Rachel and smiled. "It's good to be back in school, isn't it?"

Rachel shrugged her shoulders then turned her attention to the front of the room when Elizabeth rang the little bell on her desk. "Good morning, boys and girls."

"Good morning," the scholars all said.

Everyone stood to recite the Lord's Prayer and sing songs.

Then Elizabeth went to the blackboard. She'd just put the arithmetic assignment on the board when Rachel heard a familiar *bzzz. . .bzzz. . .bzzz. . .*

She looked up and saw a bee buzz in front of her face. She ducked. It zipped across the aisle and circled Audra's head.

Audra squealed, jumped out of her seat, and raced to

the back of the room.

Audra's reaction came as no surprise to Rachel, for she knew Audra was afraid of bugs. And after Rachel's encounter with the bee that had stung her nose, she was a little nervous about a bee buzzing around her, too.

The bee continued to buzz and circle everyone in the room. Soon all the girls, including Rachel, joined Audra at the back of the room.

The boys jumped out of their seats and chased after the bee.

"I'll get that pesky iem!" Orlie shouted.

"Children, children, please take your seats." Elizabeth clapped her hands. "It's just a little bee; there's no need to panic." She looked at Jacob and said, "Would you please open the window? Maybe the bee will fly out."

Jacob hurried to do as Elizabeth had asked, but the bee kept buzzing and didn't go anywhere near the window.

Jacob grabbed his notebook and swatted at the bee. *Whoosh!*

The bee stopped buzzing and dropped to the floor.

"Is it dead?" Orlie called.

Jacob shook his head. "Its wings are still moving, so I think it's just stunned." He tore a piece of paper from his notebook, bent down, and scooped up the bee. Then he marched across the room and tossed it out the window.

Sighs of relief sounded around the room as Jacob shut the window.

"You may all take your seats now," Elizabeth said to the scholars.

Rachel followed behind Audra. She wished there was time to ask her what she'd said to Orlie when they were outside before school started. But she knew that would have to wait until recess.

When recess finally came, Rachel hurried out the door, tripped on the porch step, and—*floop!*—went down on her knees!

"Always trouble somewhere," she mumbled as she picked herself up.

"Are you okay?" Teacher Elizabeth asked, rushing to Rachel.

"I—I think so." Tears stung the backs of Rachel's eyes as she struggled not to cry. Her knee hurt, but she didn't want anyone to think she was acting like a baby.

"Let's go inside so I can look at your knees," Elizabeth said. "They might be bleeding."

Rachel nodded and limped into the schoolhouse. After she'd taken a seat at her desk, she lifted one corner of her dress. Sure enough, both knees had been scraped and were bleeding.

"I'll get some bandages and antiseptic." Elizabeth quickly went to her desk and opened a drawer. She returned with two bandages and a bottle of antiseptic, which she put over the scrapes on Rachel's knees. "There now, that should feel better," she said after she'd put the bandages in place.

"Danki." Rachel winced as she stood.

"If your knees hurt, maybe you should stay inside for recess today."

Rachel shook her head. If she stayed inside, she wouldn't get to talk to Audra. "I'm okay. My knees don't hurt real bad."

Elizabeth patted Rachel's shoulder. "Okay. Just be careful not to fall again."

"I'll be careful."

When Rachel stepped outside, she spotted Audra on one of the swings. Phoebe Byler sat on the other swing.

Rachel frowned. At this rate, she'd never get to talk to Audra!

Maybe I should talk to Orlie instead, Rachel thought. *I can ask him what Audra said.*

She limped her way over to the fence, where Orlie sat with Jacob and Brian.

"What do you want?" Brian asked, glaring at Rachel. She wondered if he was afraid she might say something about his bed-wetting problem.

"I need to talk to Orlie for a minute."

"About what?" Orlie asked.

"I just want to know—"

"Go play with the girls and quit bothering us," Brian said.

Rachel clenched her fingers, tempted to nibble on the end of a fingernail.

"You heard what Brian said." Jacob flapped his hand at Rachel. "Go away now—shoo, little bensel!"

Rachel flapped her hand right back at him. "I'm not a silly child!"

"Jah you are."

"No I'm not. You're a silly child!"

Before Jacob could respond, Rachel raced over to the swings. "Can you stop swinging now?" she called to Audra.

"How come?"

"I need to talk to you."

"About what?"

"If you'll get off the swing and come over here, I'll tell you."

Audra shook her head. "I'm having too much fun. You can talk to me from where I am."

"What were you telling Orlie about me before school started?" Rachel shouted.

Whoosh! Audra's swing went so high that the ties on her kapp blew out behind her. "What was that?"

"What were you telling Orlie about me before school started?"

"I wasn't telling him anything about you!"

"Jah you were. I heard you mention my name."

Audra halted her swing, tipped her head, and looked at Rachel as if she'd lost her mind. "I don't know what you're talking about."

407

"I heard you say, 'Did you know what Rachel did the other day?' "

Audra shook her head. "I never said that."

"Jah you did."

"No I didn't. What I said was, 'Did you know that Rachel's cousin lives on a dairy farm?' "

"But you said something about what Rachel did the other day," Rachel insisted. "What were you telling Orlie that I did the other day?"

"You're jumping to conclusions," Audra said. "I wasn't talking about you at all. After I mentioned that your cousin lives on a dairy farm, I said that the other day my daed decided to buy some goats because he likes goat's milk better than cow's milk."

"So you weren't saying anything bad about me to Orlie?"

"Of course not. You're my good friend. I'd never talk bad about you."

Rachel sighed with relief. "You're my good friend, too, Audra."

When Rachel and Jacob arrived home from school that afternoon, Mom had a snack waiting for them on the kitchen table. Beside two glasses of chocolate milk was a plate of chocolate cupcakes. Mom placed one glass in front of Rachel and one in front of Jacob; then she gave each of them a cupcake. "I'm going upstairs to check on Gerald," she said. "He should be awake from his nap by now."

When Mom left the room, Rachel studied the snacks on the table.

"Your glass of milk's fuller than mine, and your cupcake's bigger, too," she said, frowning at Jacob. "I think Mom favors you over me."

"Don't be lecherich, Rachel. Mom doesn't favor any of her kinner. She loves us all the same."

"I'm not being ridiculous." Rachel took a drink of milk and wiped her lips with a napkin. "Since you got the most chocolate milk, I think you should give me the bigger cupcake."

"No way! Mom gave me this cupcake, and I'm eating it right now!" Jacob quickly peeled back the paper and popped the whole cupcake into his mouth. "Umm. . .this is sure good!"

Rachel wrinkled her nose. "That's disgusting, Jacob! Don't you know you're not supposed to talk with your mouth full?"

"I can do whatever I want; you're not my boss." Jacob grabbed his glass of milk and took a big drink. Some of the milk ran out of his mouth and trickled down his chin.

Rachel looked away. She wished Mom would have come back into the room and seen Jacob acting so rude. He'd be in big trouble, and if Mom had been favoring Jacob by giving him the fullest glass of milk and the biggest cupcake, she'd probably never do it again.

"Well, guess I'd better get out to the fields and see

about helping Pap and Henry," Jacob said, pushing his chair away from the table.

"That won't be necessary," Mom said as she and a sleepy-eyed Gerald entered the kitchen.

"Why not?" Jacob asked, wiping his mouth with his hand.

"Your daed and Henry went to town to run some errands." Mom motioned to the plate of cupcakes. "So if you'd like to have more to eat, go right ahead."

"Since I don't have to work this afternoon, I think I'll go fishing in the creek." Jacob grabbed a cupcake. "I'll take this along!"

"Can I go fishing, too?" Rachel called as Jacob headed for the door.

"Suit yourself!" Jacob opened the door and rushed outside.

Rachel jumped up and followed. She'd just stepped onto the porch when she spotted Aunt Karen's buggy pulling into the yard. "Aunt Karen's here," she called to Mom over her shoulder. "She must have come to get Gerald."

Mom joined Rachel on the porch. "Would you mind keeping an eye on Gerald while Aunt Karen and I visit awhile?" she asked.

Rachel groaned. "Do I have to, Mom? I wanted to go fishing with Jacob."

"You can join him later—after Aunt Karen and Gerald go home."

Rachel sighed. "Okay, Mom. I'll take Gerald to the living room and read a story to him."

"I'd rather you get him a cupcake and go outside," Mom said. "Hannah's taking a nap in the living room."

"Oh, all right," Rachel said. "I'll take Gerald outside on the porch, and we can blow some bubbles after he's had his snack."

A short time later, Rachel and Gerald were seated on the back porch steps, blowing bubbles.

"Blos!" Gerald shouted as he raced into the yard and chased the bubbles Rachel had made.

Rachel laughed and made several more bubbles. She waved them in the air so they floated into the yard.

"I'm glad you told me this. It's important that we pray for him."

Rachel heard Aunt Karen talking through the open kitchen window, and her ears perked up. She became especially interested when she heard Mom mention Jacob's name.

"Blow more blos!" Gerald hollered as he jumped up and down.

"Okay, okay." Rachel blew several more bubbles, and Gerald chased after them, giggling and leaping into the air like a wild goat.

"I feel so bad that Jacob's sick and might not make it," Aunt Karen said through the open window.

Rachel gasped. *Jacob's sick and might not make it?*

Might not make what? Rachel wondered. Then she realized that's what people said sometimes when someone was dying—that they may not make it!

No, no, it just couldn't be! Even though she and Jacob had their share of misunderstandings, and even though he teased her, Rachel didn't want him to die.

"It's always hard when we have to say good-bye to a loved one." Mom's voice sounded very sad, and Rachel wondered if she'd been crying. She couldn't blame her if she had. Hearing that Jacob was sick and would probably die made Rachel feel like crying, too.

No wonder Mom gave Jacob the biggest cupcake and fullest glass of milk, Rachel thought. *Mom wanted to be sure that Jacob's happy.*

Rachel's hands shook so badly she dropped the bubble wand. *I've got to do something to make Jacob's last days as happy as they can be. Even though Jacob teases me a lot and makes me mad sometimes, he needs to know how much I love him.*

Rachel rested her elbows on her knees and closed her eyes. She couldn't tell anyone what she'd heard. If she did, she'd be in trouble for eavesdropping again. And if she told anyone that Jacob was sick and might not make it, that would be gossiping.

Dear God, Rachel silently prayed, *please show me what I can do for Jacob.*

That night after supper, Mom asked Jacob and Rachel

to do the dishes while she fed and diapered the baby.

"Jacob doesn't have to help," Rachel was quick to say. "I can do the dishes by myself."

Mom's forehead wrinkled as she stared at Rachel over the top of her glasses. "Are you sure?"

Rachel nodded. "I'm very sure. Jacob's free to do whatever he pleases."

Jacob grinned and thumped Rachel's back. "Danki, little sister."

At least he hadn't called her a little bensel this time. Even if he had, Rachel wouldn't have said anything about it. From now on, she was determined to be nice to Jacob.

"Have you fed Buddy yet?" she asked when Jacob started to leave the room.

"Not yet. I'm going out to do that right now," he called over his shoulder.

"I'll do it," Rachel offered. "Why don't you find a comfortable chair and rest?"

Jacob turned to face her. "If you're expecting me to pay you for feeding Buddy, you can forget it."

She shook her head. "I don't want any money."

"Do you want me to do one of your chores in exchange for feeding my hund?"

She shook her head.

Jacob's eyes narrowed into tiny slits. "What's up, Rachel? You hate feeding Buddy. You always complain because he jumps up and licks your face."

Rachel blushed. There was no way she could tell Jacob that she knew he was sick. If Mom hadn't told Aunt Karen about it, Rachel wouldn't have known the truth either. She felt sure that Mom hadn't told Jacob he was dying. If he knew, he wouldn't be acting so cheerful.

Rachel touched Jacob's arm. "I—I just want to help you, because I—" She swallowed around the lump in her throat, hoping she wouldn't cry. "Be–because I love you."

Jacob stared at Rachel for a long time. Then his face broke into a wide smile. "If you really want to feed Buddy, then it's fine with me. I'll go to my room and read a book." He patted Rachel on the shoulder a couple of times. "I love you, too, little bensel."

Chapter 12

A Big Surprise

I'm thirsty. Would you get me a glass of water?" Jacob asked Rachel when he entered the kitchen the following morning.

Normally, Rachel would have said, "Get it yourself." However, since Jacob was on the brink of death, she figured she should do what he asked. Rachel smiled and said, "Jah, sure, Jacob. I'd be happy to get you a glass of water."

"Danki." Jacob pulled out a chair at the table and sat down. "I sure feel tired this morning. Wish I didn't have to go to school," he said with a yawn.

"Actually, you won't be going to school this morning," Mom said. "You have an appointment with Dr. Adams, remember?"

Jacob stretched his arms over his head and yawned again. "Oh, that's right; I forgot."

"If you're not feeling well enough to go to school after your appointment, you'll come home with me," Mom said.

Jacob nodded. "By then, I'll probably be more tired than I already am."

Rachel's heart went out to Jacob. She couldn't imagine what he must be going through or how bad he felt.

Waaa! Waaa!

"It sounds like your little sister is awake and needs to be fed." Mom patted Rachel's shoulder. "Since Jacob won't be walking to school with you this morning, I'll ask Grandpa to hitch his buggy and take you there." She hurried from the room before Rachel could respond.

I wish Mom would stop treating me like a boppli, Rachel thought. *She let me walk to school by myself a couple of times, so why not today?*

She hung her head. *I guess I shouldn't be thinking such thoughts. Mom's worried about Jacob. She's probably worried about me, too.*

"Where's my glass of water?" Jacob asked impatiently. "I'm really thirsty."

Rachel hurried to the sink and filled a glass with cold water. When she handed it to Jacob, she noticed how tired he looked. Maybe he was doing too much and needed to rest more. Maybe when Jacob saw the doctor today, he'd be told to take it easy. And maybe, if Rachel kept doing all of Jacob's chores, he would live a little longer.

As Rachel traveled to school in Grandpa's buggy, all she could think about was Jacob. She couldn't imagine how things would be without him. She'd have to go to school every day by herself. She would miss playing in the creek with Jacob on hot summer days. She would miss jumping on the trampoline with him, too. She might even miss Jacob's teasing and calling her "little bensel."

Rachel swallowed hard, trying to push down the lump she felt in her throat. She wouldn't be the only one who'd miss Jacob if he died. Mom, Dad, Henry, Esther, Rudy, Grandpa Schrock, Grandpa and Grandma Yoder, Jacob's friends at school—even Buddy would miss Jacob. How sad that baby Hannah would grow up never knowing her brother Jacob.

Clip-clop. Clip-clop. The horse whinnied and plodded slowly up the road.

Grandpa clicked his tongue and shook the reins. "Get up there, boy! If you don't get moving, you'll make Rachel late for school!"

"I won't be late. Riding in the buggy is much faster than walking." Rachel glanced over at Grandpa. Did he know about Jacob's condition? Should she say something about what she'd heard Mom say to Aunt Karen the other day? Maybe it would be best to keep quiet. If she said anything to Grandpa, he might accuse her of eavesdropping and gossiping.

Maybe I should mention Jacob's name, Rachel thought. *If Grandpa already knows that Jacob is sick, he might say something about it to me.*

Rachel leaned closer to Grandpa and said, "Have

you noticed anything different about Jacob lately?"

"Nothing special." Grandpa shrugged. "Although he does seem to have grown a few inches over the summer."

"Uh-huh." Rachel sat quietly for several minutes. She decided to ask another question. "Does it seem to you like he doesn't have much energy these days?"

Grandpa gave the reins another good shake. "You mean my lazy *gaul* [horse]?"

"No, I mean Jacob."

"Can't really say for sure. Guess you'd have to ask your daed that question, since Jacob worked in the fields with him and Henry all summer." Grandpa tugged his beard. "Jah, your daed's the one to ask about Jacob all right."

Rachel leaned back in her seat and closed her eyes. *This conversation is getting me nowhere. Either Grandpa doesn't know anything about Jacob being sick, or he doesn't want to talk about it. I need to talk to someone about this, but who can I trust not to say anything?*

"Whoa!" The buggy lurched, and Rachel's eyes snapped open.

"I hate to wake you from your nap, but we're here," Grandpa said with a wide grin.

"I wasn't sleeping, Grandpa. I was thinking."

He chuckled and patted Rachel's arm. "You're a daydreamer, same as your mamm used to be when she was a maedel."

Rachel couldn't argue with that. She did like to daydream. It was fun to imagine herself going places and doing things she hadn't done before.

She reached down and grabbed her backpack and lunch pail from the floor of the buggy. "Danki for the ride. See you after school, Grandpa."

He nodded and smiled. "If your mamm and Jacob don't get home from Jacob's appointment before school lets out, I'll be back to pick you up this afternoon."

"Okay." Rachel hopped out of the buggy. *If Grandpa knows Jacob went to see the doctor today, then he must know that Jacob is sick,* she thought. *I think maybe he doesn't want to talk about it because he doesn't want me to know. Everyone else in the family probably knows. They haven't told me because they think I'm too young to understand. I'd hoped after Hannah was born that they'd realize I'm growing up, but, no, they think I'm still a boppli.*

As Rachel headed for the school yard, she spotted Audra standing by the swings. *Maybe I should talk to her about Jacob,* she decided. *I can't keep the horrible news I've learned about him to myself any longer.*

Rachel dashed over to Audra. "I—I need to talk to you," she said, clasping Audra's arm.

"What's wrong?" Audra asked. "You look *umgerennt* [upset]."

"I am upset." Tears welled in Rachel's eyes. "Jacob's sick and might not make it. He's not here today because Mom took him to see the doctor."

Audra's eyes widened, and her mouth formed an O. "Ach, that's baremlich!"

"I know it's terrible." Rachel sniffed and swiped at the tears trickling down her cheeks. "Sometimes I get upset with Jacob when he teases me, but I still love him. I—I don't want my bruder to die."

"No, of course you don't." Audra gave Rachel a hug. "I wouldn't want my bruder to die, either."

"Please promise you won't—"

Ding! Ding! Ding!

"There's the school bell. We'd better get inside." Audra gave Rachel's arm a pat and hurried away before Rachel could finish her sentence.

I hope Audra doesn't tell anyone what I told her about Jacob, Rachel thought as she blew her nose and trudged up the schoolhouse stairs.

"Good morning boys and girls," Elizabeth said after the scholars had taken seats behind their desks.

"Good morning, Elizabeth," everyone said.

Audra's hand went up.

"What is it, Audra?" Elizabeth asked.

"Jacob Yoder's not here this morning because he went to see the doctor." Audra looked over at Rachel and said, "Tell Elizabeth what you told me about Jacob."

Rachel's heart pounded as she shook her head. She hoped Audra wouldn't repeat what she'd said.

"What's this all about?" Elizabeth asked, moving

closer to Audra's desk.

"Jacob's sick and might not make it," Audra blurted.

Elizabeth's forehead wrinkled, and she looked over at Rachel. "Is that true?"

Rachel nodded slowly as a lump formed in her throat. Now the whole class knew. They were all looking at her with sympathy on their faces.

"I had no idea Jacob was sick," Elizabeth said. "What's wrong with him, Rachel?"

Rachel shrugged. "I–I'm not sure. I just know that he's sick and might not make it."

"I'm real sorry to hear this." Elizabeth's eyes looked watery. Rachel wondered if her teacher might break down and cry in front of the whole class. Rachel hoped not, because if Elizabeth started to cry, then she'd end up crying, too.

Elizabeth moved over to Rachel's desk. "As soon as we're done with the morning songs and have said the Lord's Prayer, I'll have everyone in class make Jacob a get-well card."

A get-well card? Oh no, Rachel thought. *Now Mom will know I was listening to her conversation with Aunt Karen.*

When Rachel arrived home from school that day, her stomach felt as if it were tied in knots. Jacob hadn't come to school at all today, which made her think he'd probably gotten sicker. To make matters worse, Teacher

Elizabeth was planning to come over this afternoon with the get-well cards the scholars had made. Once that happened, Mom would guess that Rachel was the one who'd told. Then Rachel would be in trouble for eavesdropping and gossiping.

"You can go up to the house to change your clothes and have a snack while I unhitch the horse and get him put away," Grandpa said. "Then after you get your homework done, I could use your help in the greenhouse."

Rachel nodded. Maybe she'd be working in the greenhouse when Elizabeth came over with the get-well cards. That would keep her out of trouble with Mom for a little while.

Rachel hurried into the house and slipped quietly upstairs to her room. When she'd changed out of her school dress, she took her homework out of her backpack and flopped onto the bed.

She'd just opened her spelling book when she heard, *Tap! Tap! Tap!*

"Rachel, are you in there?" Mom called through the closed door.

"Jah, Mom. I'm getting ready to do my homework."

"Come down to the kitchen to do it," Mom said. "I've got some fresh fruit cups and milk waiting for you."

"Okay, I'm coming." Rachel stayed on the bed a few minutes longer, thinking things over; then she finally gathered up her spelling book and left the room.

Downstairs, she found Mom and Jacob sitting at the kitchen table. Mom had a cup of tea, and Jacob had a glass of milk. The left side of Jacob's face looked kind of puffy. His eyelids looked heavy, too, and his shoulders were slumped. He didn't look well at all!

Rachel touched Jacob's shoulder. "I—uh—want you to know something."

"What's that?" he asked.

"I'm sorry for anything I've ever said or done to upset you."

Jacob leaned back in his chair and looked at Rachel with an odd expression. It made her want to cry and beg him not to die. "What's wrong with you, Rachel?" he asked, tapping her arm. "Are you *grank* [sick]?"

"No, of course not. I'm just real sorry that you—"

"Oh look," Mom said as she peered out the kitchen window, "your schoolteacher's here." She looked at Rachel and frowned. "You didn't do anything wrong at school today, did you?"

Rachel gulped. She had done something wrong. She'd blabbed to Audra about Jacob being sick, and then Audra had told their teacher. Now Elizabeth was here, probably with the get-well cards the scholars had made for Jacob.

Rachel figured she'd better explain things before Elizabeth came inside, but before she could open her mouth, Mom rushed out the door.

"I need to tell you something," Rachel said as she

stepped onto the porch behind Mom.

"Later, Rachel. I need to see what your teacher wants." Mom hurried down the steps and out to Elizabeth's buggy.

Rachel quickly followed.

"Hello, Rachel," Elizabeth said as she stepped out of the buggy. "Did you tell your mamm that I'd be coming by this afternoon?"

"Uh, no. Not yet," Rachel stammered.

Mom looked down at Rachel. "You knew Elizabeth was coming by and you never mentioned it?"

Rachel's face grew hot. "Well, I—"

"I brought some cards that the scholars made for Jacob." Elizabeth reached into her buggy and pulled out a paper sack. "If he's feeling up to company I'd like to come inside and give them to him."

Mom gave Elizabeth a peculiar look over the top of her glasses, but then she shrugged and said, "Jah, sure. You're welcome to come inside."

Elizabeth handed the sack of cards to Rachel, and then she tied her horse to the hitching rail.

Rachel wished she could take the sack out to the fire pit and burn it, but she knew she'd be in trouble for that. There was no getting around it: Mom was about to find out that Rachel had been eavesdropping and gossiping again. That didn't bother her nearly as much as knowing that Jacob's health was getting worse every day, and that he might not be with them much longer.

With a heavy heart, Rachel followed Mom and Elizabeth into the house. When they entered the kitchen, Elizabeth placed the paper sack on the table in front of Jacob, put one hand on his shoulder, and said, "I have a surprise for you, Jacob. The scholars made you these get-well cards." Tears welled in her eyes. "We're all very sorry to hear how sick you are."

Jacob's eyebrows shot up. "Huh?"

"Rachel told us about it. She said you weren't in school today because you'd gone to the doctor's."

Jacob opened the sack and pulled out one of the cards. There was a picture of a big, shaggy red dog on the front. The inside of the card read:

> *I'm sorry to hear that you're sick and might not make it. Buddy will miss you when you're gone, and so will I.*
> *Your friend, Orlie Troyer.*

Jacob scratched the side of his head and gave Mom a questioning look. "Am I sick and don't know it?"

Mom shook her head. "Ach no, Jacob! I don't know why the scholars think you're sick, unless—" She looked over at Rachel and frowned. "Did you make up some story about Jacob being gone from school today because he's sick?"

Rachel shifted from one leg to the other. "I—uh—didn't make up the story. I—I was just repeating what I heard you say to Aunt Karen the other day."

Deep wrinkles formed in Mom's forehead as she rubbed the bridge of her nose. "What exactly did you hear me say to her?"

"You said Jacob was very sick and that he might not make it."

"That's what Rachel told me at school today," Elizabeth said.

Mom gasped.

Jacob groaned and dropped his head to the table.

"Karen and I weren't talking about *our* Jacob," Mom said. "We were talking about my cousin, whose name is also Jacob. Cousin Jacob lives in Kentucky, and he's very sick." She pushed her glasses onto the bridge of her nose and squinted at Rachel. "For your information, Jacob went to see the dentist today, not the doctor."

Jacob lifted his head from the table.

Rachel covered her mouth with her hand. She was sorry to hear about Mom's cousin but relieved to know that Jacob wasn't sick.

Mom shook her finger at Rachel. "See the trouble you've caused by eavesdropping and then running off to school and gossiping about what you *thought* you'd heard? That's how misunderstandings get started, you know."

Rachel stared at the floor as she slowly nodded. "I–I'm sorry. It was just a big mistake."

"You should have asked me about what you'd heard

instead of jumping to conclusions," Mom said.

Tears coursed down Rachel's cheeks. "I know that, and I promise I'll never do it again."

Rachel leaned over and hugged Jacob. "I'm glad you're not sick." *Sniff! Sniff!* "I hope you'll stick around for a very long time."

He nodded and grinned. "I've gotta stick around, or else who would be here to tease you, little bensel?"

Rachel poked Jacob's arm. "I'm happy you're sticking around, but if you're going to keep teasing me, then I think you should know that I'll tease you right back."

Jacob took a drink of milk and wiped his mouth with the back of his hand. "That's not such a big surprise, but I can deal with it."

Rachel took a seat at the table and pushed the paper sack closer to Jacob. "You may as well look at the rest of your get-well cards, don't you think?"

Jacob nodded and rubbed the side of his face. "I may not be sick, but my mouth's kind of sore from being open so long at the dentist's. Maybe the get-well cards will make me feel better."

Mom handed Rachel a glass of milk, and Rachel took a big drink. From now on she would never intentionally listen in on anyone's conversation. If she accidentally heard someone say something she didn't understand, she would ask questions, not jump to conclusions!

Recipe for Rachel's
Homemade Bubble Solution

¼ cup liquid dishwashing detergent
¾ cup cold water
5 drops of glycerin (available at most pharmacies)
A few drops of food coloring (if you want colorful
   bubbles)

Measure out the detergent, water, and glycerin into a
container with a cover and stir gently. Note: The longer
you let the mixture set, the larger the bubbles will be
and the longer they seem to last.

Growing Up

Dedication and Acknowledgments

To my six special grandchildren: Jinell, Ric, Madolynne, Rebekah, Philip, and Richelle. Though in different ways, you've each been an inspiration for the books in this series.

A special thanks goes to Richelle Brunstetter, Elvera Kienbaum, Richard Brunstetter Sr., Jean Brunstetter, Lorine VanCorbach, Leeann Curtis, and Jake Smucker for sharing some of their interesting stories with me. Thanks also to my editor, Kelly McIntosh, for allowing me to write this enjoyable children's series.

Glossary

absatz—stop
ach—oh
aldi—girlfriend
appenditlich—delicious
baremlich—terrible
bensel—silly child
bett—bed
Biewel—Bible
bletsching—spanking
boppli—baby
brieder—brothers
bruder—brother
buch—book
bussli—kitten
buwe—boy
daed—dad
danki—thanks
dumm—dumb
dummkopp—dunce

fraa—wife
gut—good
hinkel—chickens
hund—dog
hungerich—hungry
jah—yes
kapp—cap
katz—cat
koppweh—headache
kumme—come
mamm—mom
naas—nose
nodel—needle
sau—pig
schliffer—splinter
schnell—quickly
schpell—pin
umgerennt—upset
windel—diaper

Alli mudder muss sariye fer ihre familyle.
Every mother has to take care of her family.

Die Rachel is die ganz zeit am grummle.
Rachel is grumbling all the time.

Er hot mich verschwetzt.
He talked me into it.

Es fenschder muss mer nass mache fer es sauwer mache.
One has to wet the window in order to clean it.

Ferwas bischt allfat so schtarkeppich?
Why are you always so stubborn?

Guder mariye.	Good morning.
Gut nacht.	Good night.
Hoscht du schunn geese?	Have you already eaten?
Was in der welt?	What in all the world?
Wie geht's?	How are you?
Windel wesche gleich ich net.	I don't like to wash out diapers.

Chapter 1

Sidetracked

Ha! Ha! I beat you home!" Rachel Yoder shouted as she raced into the yard ahead of her brother Jacob.

"Grow up, Rachel," Jacob said when he caught up to her. "It doesn't matter who got to the house first."

"*Jah* [Yes] it does!" Rachel bounded up the porch steps. She didn't tell Jacob, but she figured if she got to the kitchen before he did, she'd get first pick of whatever snack Mom had waiting for them. If Jacob got there before she did, he'd probably eat more than his share and leave her with just a few crumbs.

Rachel jerked open the back door and rushed inside. She dropped her backpack in the utility room and raced into the kitchen. Her brows puckered when she saw that no snack was on the table. She glanced around. No food was waiting on the kitchen counter either.

Rachel scratched the side of her head. "Now that's sure strange."

"What's strange?" Jacob asked, stepping into the room.

"Mom's not in the kitchen, and no snack is here for us."

"Maybe she's in her room with the *boppli* [baby]." Jacob took off his straw hat and hung it on a wall peg near the door. "We're not helpless, Rachel. We can get our own snacks, you know."

Rachel shook her head. "What if we eat something Mom doesn't want us to eat? What if we eat something she's planning to serve for supper? We'd be in trouble if we did that, and you know it."

Jacob grabbed an apple from the fruit bowl sitting on the counter. "I'm sure Mom won't care if we have a piece of fruit."

"No, I suppose not." Rachel took a banana and headed for the back door.

"Where are you going?" Jacob asked.

"Out to the greenhouse to help Grandpa!" Rachel called over her shoulder.

"Don't you think you'd better do your homework and get your chores done first?"

Rachel shook her head and kept walking. She could do those things later on.

Rachel found Grandpa in the greenhouse, snipping the leaves of a large, leafy plant. "*Wie geht's* [How are you]?" she asked.

"I'm good. How was school?"

"It was okay, but I'm glad to be home. I was anxious

to get here and work with you. It's a lot more fun than being in school."

"I'm always glad to have your help in our little greenhouse," Grandpa said.

Rachel smiled. She felt good to hear Grandpa refer to the greenhouse as *ours* and not *his*. "Have you had many customers today?" she asked.

He nodded. "This morning I was so busy I could hardly keep up. The business has slowed down a little this afternoon though."

"I'll be glad when I've graduated from school and can be here all day to help you," Rachel said.

He nodded. "That will be nice, but in the meantime, you need to study hard and learn all you can while you are in school."

"I know." Rachel glanced around. "What do you need my help with today?"

"I was planning to fertilize some plants but haven't gotten around to it yet." Grandpa motioned to a shelf full of geraniums across the room. "You can do that now if you like."

"Sure, Grandpa." Rachel had fertilized plants before, so she knew just what to do. She hurried to the back room and took out the bottle of liquid fertilizer. She squeezed several drops into a jug of warm water, carried it into the other room, and began the process of fertilizing the plants. She'd only gotten a few of them done when the bell above the greenhouse door jingled and Mom stepped in. Her forehead was wrinkled, and she didn't look one bit happy.

"Jacob said you didn't do your homework or any of your chores before you came out here," she said, peering at Rachel over the top of her metal-framed glasses.

Rachel swallowed hard. "I—uh—was planning to do them later—after I finished helping Grandpa in the greenhouse."

Mom slowly shook her head. "You know you're not supposed to come out here until your homework and chores are done. When are you going to grow up and start acting more responsible, Rachel?"

Rachel's cheeks felt as if they were on fire as she stared at the floor and struggled not to cry. She didn't like it when Mom scolded her. It made her feel like a baby. "I—I just like being here so much, and I—"

"I know you like being here." Mom's voice softened a bit. She touched Rachel's chin, raising it so Rachel could look at her face. "However, schoolwork and chores come first. After those things are done, you can work in the greenhouse. Is that clear?"

"Jah," Rachel mumbled.

"What was that?"

"I said, 'Jah,' Mom."

Grandpa stepped forward. "Rachel was in the middle of fertilizing some plants for me, Miriam. Is it all right if she finishes them and then goes up to the house?"

Mom nodded. Then she turned to Rachel and said, "Oh, by the way, I was changing your little sister's *windel* [diaper] when you and Jacob got home from school, so that's why there was no snack waiting for you. You can have some cookies and milk while you do your homework."

Rachel shook her head as she poured fertilizer onto another plant. "I ate a banana while I was walking out to the greenhouse, so I'm not really hungry."

Mom turned toward the door. "All right then. I'll expect to see you at the house in a few minutes." She stepped out of the greenhouse, and the bell above the door jingled when the door closed behind her.

"I guess I should have asked if you'd done your homework and chores before I put you to work out here," Grandpa said to Rachel. "Next time, I will ask."

Tears burned the backs of Rachel's eyes. Grandpa didn't trust her anymore. He probably thought she was a baby, too. "I like working for you in the greenhouse more than doing chores or homework," she said.

Grandpa touched Rachel's shoulder. "I'm sure you do, but there's one thing you should always remember."

"What's that?"

"The Bible teaches us to do whatever we do as if we are doing it for the Lord," Grandpa said.

"Really?"

Grandpa nodded. "If you remember that, you will find it easier to do the things you don't enjoy so much."

Rachel smiled, wondering if she'd ever be as smart as Grandpa.

When Rachel returned to the house, she found Mom peeling potatoes at the kitchen sink.

"Is it time to start supper already?" Rachel asked.

Mom shook her head. "Not quite, but your little sister might wake up from her nap soon, and then I'll be busy feeding her. So I thought it would be a good idea if I started preparing supper early." She glanced at Rachel over her shoulder. "It's always good to stay ahead of things."

Rachel nodded. "Should I do my homework first or start on my chores?"

"You'd better do your chores first. Now that summer's over, it gets dark earlier than before."

"Okay. What chores do you want me to do?" Rachel asked.

"Let's see now. . . . Jacob is cleaning the chicken coop, which I was going to ask you to do before you went out to the greenhouse."

Rachel wrinkled her nose. Cleaning the smelly chicken coop was not her favorite thing to do. She was glad Jacob had been asked to do it this time.

Mom held the potato peeler out to Rachel. "If you'd rather do an inside chore, you can finish peeling the potatoes while I take the dry clothes off the line."

Rachel frowned. The last time she'd peeled potatoes

she had nicked her finger. "I'd rather get the clothes," she mumbled.

Mom nodded. "The laundry basket's sitting on the back porch."

Rachel scurried out the door, picked up the basket, and hurried out to the clothesline. Several big fluffy towels flapped in the breeze, along with some of the men's trousers and a few dresses. There were also lots of baby diapers and some little outfits that her three-month-old sister, Hannah, wore.

Rachel set the basket on the wagon she often used to haul laundry to and from the house. Then she stood on her tiptoes, yanked the clothespins free, and dropped the towels into the basket. She was about to remove one of the clothespins from a pair of Grandpa's trousers when Cuddles leaped into the basket. *Meow!*

Rachel giggled and bent down to rub her cat's head. "You silly *katz* [cat]. What do you think you're doing?"

Purr. . .purr. . .purr. Cuddles nuzzled Rachel's fingers with her warm pink nose.

Rachel took a seat on the ground and put the cat in her lap. Cuddles purred louder as Rachel stroked behind the cat's ears.

Just then Cuddles's kitten, Snowball, zipped across the yard, leaped into the air, and landed on Cuddles's head.

Yeow! Cuddles jumped up as if she had springs on her legs and then tore across the yard, hissing and meowing as she raced to the barn.

Snowball burrowed into Rachel's lap and began to purr.

"Shame on you for chasing your *mamm* [mom] away." Rachel shook her finger at Snowball.

The cat only purred louder and licked Rachel's hand with a sandpapery tongue.

Rachel smiled. Snowball was spoiled, no doubt about it, and she liked lots of attention.

Neigh! Neigh! Rachel looked over her shoulder and saw Tom, their old retired buggy horse, with his head hanging over the fence. *Neigh! Neigh!* Tom bobbed his head up and down and opened his mouth very wide.

Rachel chuckled. "I'll bet you'd like an apple, wouldn't you, Tom?"

Neigh! Neigh!

"Oh, all right. I'll go inside and get you one." Rachel set Snowball on the ground and sprinted for the house.

Mom wasn't in the kitchen, and Rachel figured she must be in her room with the baby. She hurried to the fruit bowl and grabbed a big red apple; then she rushed back outside.

Old Tom stuck his head out even farther as Rachel approached the fence. As soon as she opened the gate and stepped into the pasture, Tom plodded over and nudged her arm with his nose.

Rachel snickered. "Okay, okay. Don't be in such a hurry." She placed the apple in the palm of her hand

and held it out to him.

Old Tom lowered his head. *Crunch! Crunch! Slurp! Slurp!* He took his time eating the apple and drooled a lot. When he was done, he nudged Rachel's arm with his nose again.

"Sorry, Tom, but I only brought one apple for you." Rachel patted Tom's flank. "You're such a good horse. I'm glad Pap put you out to pasture when you got too old to pull the buggy. I would have been sad if Pap had sold you to the glue factory, like Jacob said he might do."

Tom wandered over to a tree, dropped to his knees, and rolled onto his side. Then he reached down and out with his mouth, as though he was yawning, and let out a strange-sounding sigh. Just seeing him there made Rachel feel tired.

She leaned against the fence and closed her eyes, letting her mind wander. She thought about the letter she'd received from her cousin Mary a few weeks ago. Mary had let Rachel know that she'd made it safely home. Rachel had fun when Mary had come for a visit. She couldn't wait to visit Mary in Indiana someday.

Rachel thought about the bonfire Pap said he might build Saturday evening. They'd probably roast hot dogs and marshmallows and enjoy plenty of freshly squeezed apple cider. Rachel's sister Esther and her husband, Rudy, would be invited, too.

"Rachel! Where are you?"

Rachel turned and saw Mom standing on the porch.

"I'm coming," she called.

Rachel hurried out of the pasture and ran all the way to the house. "I'm here," she said breathlessly as she stepped onto the porch.

Mom gave Rachel a curious look over the top of her glasses. "Where's the basket of clothes?"

"Huh?"

"The clothes, Rachel." Mom pursed her lips. "I sent you to get the clothes off the line some time ago, remember?"

Rachel reached under her stiff white *kapp* [cap] and scratched her head. "Oh yeah, that's right. Guess I lost track of what I was doing."

"What *have* you been doing all this time?" Mom asked, giving Rachel a stern look.

Rachel shifted from one foot to the other, feeling like a fly trapped in a spider's web. "Well, I—uh—"

"Did you take any of the clothes off the line?"

"Jah. Well, part of them anyway."

Tap! Tap! Tap! Mom's foot beat on the porch, and she folded her arms. "If you only got part of the clothes, then what were you doing the rest of the time? And where are the clothes you took off the line?"

"Uh—some are still on the line. The others are in the basket."

Tap! Tap! Tap! "Why didn't you take all the clothes off the line, Rachel?"

"I—uh—got distracted."

"Distracted by what?"

Rachel held up one finger. "First Cuddles landed in the basket of clothes." A second finger came up. "Then Snowball came along and jumped on Cuddles's head." Rachel lifted a third finger. "Then Old Tom came over begging for an apple, so I—"

Mom held up her hand. "You became sidetracked?"

Rachel nodded. "I just wanted to have a little fun, and—"

"No excuses, Rachel. When a person's asked to do a job, he or she should do it." Mom pointed to the clothesline. "I want you to finish the job I asked you to do, right now."

"Okay, Mom." Rachel trudged to the clothesline. One by one she quickly removed the wooden pins holding the men's trousers. She put the trousers in the basket. Then she took down the dresses, diapers, and baby clothes.

Chirp-or-ee! Chirp-or-ee! A bird called from a nearby tree.

Rachel was tempted to sit on the grass and watch the bird, but knew she'd be in trouble if she did. With a heavy sigh, she grabbed the wagon handle and pulled it to the house. She wished she didn't have any chores to do!

As Rachel helped Mom fold clothes at the foot of Mom's bed, she thought about Grandpa's greenhouse.

I'd rather be out there! she thought. It was a lot more fun to water, repot, and prune plants than it was to fold Hannah's diapers.

She glanced at her baby sister, lying in the crib on the other side of Mom and Pap's room, and wondered when Esther's baby would be born. Would it be a boy or a girl? Would it have blond hair or brown? What color would the baby's eyes be?

Mom nudged Rachel's arm. "Watch what you're doing, Rachel. You're folding that *windel* the wrong way."

Rachel looked down at the pile of diapers still on the bed and frowned. "I don't like doing this. It's boring."

"Why don't you make a game out of your chores, the way Grandpa taught you to do several months ago?" Mom's glasses had slipped to the end of her nose, and she paused to push them back in place. "I'm sure you can think of something to pretend while you're helping me fold clothes."

Rachel nibbled on her lower lip as she tried to think of something fun about folding diapers. She couldn't think of a thing!

Moo! Moo! Stomp! Stomp! Stomp!

"Now what's going on outside?" Mom hurried to the window and peered out. "*Ach* [Oh] no! The cows are out of the pasture! They're running all over our yard!"

She rushed out of the room, calling over her shoulder, "*Kumme* [Come], Rachel, *schnell* [quickly]. Help me get the cows back in the pasture!"

Rachel followed Mom down the hall and out the back door. When they stepped into the yard, Mom raised her hands and shouted, "Just look at my garden! They've trampled everything to the ground!"

Rachel dashed into the yard and shooed a cow toward the pasture. Soon the other cows followed.

"Look there," said Mom, pointing her finger. "The pasture gate's wide open!" She turned and looked at Rachel sternly. "Did you open that gate, Rachel?"

Rachel quickly closed the gate behind the last cow. She turned to Mom and said, "I opened it when I went to give Old Tom an apple. Guess I must have gotten sidetracked and forgot to close it when I left."

Mom shook her head. "You've gotten sidetracked way too much this afternoon, Rachel. Now you'll have double chores to do for the next few days."

Rachel frowned. "Can't I just help you replant the garden?"

"It's too late in the season for that. Maybe a few extra chores will help you remember not to get sidetracked the next time you're asked to do something." Mom turned and went back into the house.

Rachel swallowed around the lump in her throat. She couldn't believe she'd already forgotten what Grandpa had said about doing her chores as if she was doing them for the Lord. Wouldn't she ever grow up?

Chapter 2

Too Many Chores

For the last half hour, Rachel had been sitting at the kitchen table with her notepaper, a pencil, and a stack of books. She was supposed to do her homework, but it was a lot more fun to look at the book about a cat that she had borrowed from the book mobile. The book mobile was like a traveling library that frequently came to the Amish community. Rachel had done some of her homework but not all of it. She planned to finish it sometime before going to bed.

"Rachel, are you done with your homework?" Mom asked as she ran water into the kitchen sink.

Rachel glanced at her schoolbooks then at the cat book. "Uh—jah, I'm just about done."

"That's good, because it's time for you to do the supper dishes," Mom said.

Rachel groaned. "Already?"

Mom nodded. "I want you to wash and dry them all, and then I have some mending for you to do."

Rachel frowned. "What about Jacob? Isn't he helping with the dishes?"

Mom shook her head. "Part of your punishment for leaving the pasture gate open is doing extra chores, remember?"

Rachel nodded slowly as a lump formed in her throat. She didn't think it was fair that Jacob didn't have to help with the dishes just because she had extra chores. Why should he have the evening free to do as he pleased?

"The sink's ready for you now, Rachel. Are you coming?" Mom peered at Rachel over the top of her glasses.

"I'll be there in a minute."

Waaa! Waaa! Waaa!

"I'm going to check on Hannah. Now you get busy on those dishes," Mom said as she scurried out of the room.

"I wish I didn't have to work all the time," Rachel mumbled. "I wish I was a katz. They don't have any chores to do. They get to lie around and sleep all day or scamper everywhere, having all sorts of fun. Jah, I wish I was a katz."

"Why do you wish you were a cat?" asked Rachel's oldest brother, Henry, when he entered the kitchen.

"Cats have life so easy," Rachel explained.

"You think so, huh?" Henry tapped Rachel lightly on the head. "Think about it, little sister. Your cats get

447

chased by Jacob's dog, and they have to look for warm spots to sleep on cold days. They can also get worms from eating too many birds and mice, and they often get hair balls." He tapped her head one more time. "And another thing—cats can't read books! Now do you think those furry critters have it so well?"

She shrugged. "At least they don't have to do dishes."

Henry chuckled, poured himself a cup of coffee, and left the room.

Rachel banged her book shut and jumped out of the chair. "I may as well get this over with!"

Rachel grabbed the sponge and dropped it into the soapy water. Then she picked up a dish and sloshed the sponge over it. Next, she rinsed the dish and placed it in the dish drainer.

The dishwater was beginning to cool, so Rachel turned on the hot water. She turned on a little more cold water so she wouldn't burn her hands. While the sink was filling, she stared out the window and daydreamed about how much fun she'd have if she ever visited Mary in Indiana and went to the Fun Spot Amusement Park.

"Rachel, are you almost done with the dishes?" Mom called from the other room. "And don't forget, you still have to mend some things before you go to bed."

"I'll be done soon," Rachel hollered. She grabbed another plate to wash and realized that she'd filled the sink too full. Water had begun running onto the floor.

"Oh no," she mumbled as she turned off the water. She grabbed a towel, dropped to her knees, and mopped up the spot where the water had puddled.

I need to concentrate on what I'm doing, she told herself as she began washing dishes again.

Whoosh!—a bubble flew up and popped on Rachel's chin. It made her wish this was a warm summer day and that she could be outside blowing bubbles with her bubble wand. But no, she was stuck in here, doing dirty dishes in a hot, stuffy kitchen!

By the time Rachel had finished washing the dishes, she was tired, bored, and not in the mood to dry the dishes. However, she knew if she left them in the dish drainer, she'd be in more trouble with Mom. Besides, she remembered she was supposed to be doing her chores for the Lord.

Rachel picked up a glass and dried it with a clean towel. She was about to set it on the counter when— *bam!*—the back door hit the wall as it swung open.

Rachel was so startled when Jacob entered the room that the glass slipped from her hands and fell to the floor. *Crash!* Her hand shook as she pointed to the broken glass. "Look what you made me do!" she shouted at Jacob.

He shook his head and raised his hands. "Don't blame me. You did that yourself."

"If you hadn't slammed the door and scared me, I wouldn't have dropped the glass."

"Grow up, little *bensel* [silly child], and quit blaming others for things you've caused yourself."

Rachel shook her finger at Jacob. "Stop calling me a silly child!"

"I will when you stop acting like one." He grabbed an apple from the fruit bowl on the counter and sauntered out of the room.

Rachel's chin quivered, and her eyes filled with tears as she squatted to pick up the broken glass. "Jacob Yoder, you're a mean boy," she muttered under her breath.

By the time Rachel had cleaned up the broken glass and finished drying the dishes, she'd forgotten that Mom had asked her to do mending. She grabbed her cat book and headed up the stairs.

"Where are you going, Rachel?" Mom called from the living room.

Rachel halted on the steps and turned around. She knew right then what she'd forgotten. "I'll be there in a few minutes," she called to Mom. "I'm taking my book upstairs to my room."

When Rachel entered the living room a few minutes later, she found Grandpa sitting in the rocking chair in front of the fireplace, holding Hannah. Pap and Henry sat at a small table on the other side of the room, playing a game of checkers. Jacob stood behind Henry, watching over his shoulder. Mom sat on the sofa with a basket of mending in her lap.

"Kumme," Mom said, motioning Rachel over to the sofa. "One of your dresses needs the hem let down."

Rachel grunted as she flopped down beside Mom. "You know I'm not good at sewing."

Mom handed Rachel the small metal seam ripper. "The more you do, the better you'll get."

"That's right," Grandpa spoke up. "Practice makes perfect."

Rachel wrinkled her nose. "I don't think I'll ever be perfect at sewing, no matter how much practicing I do."

Mom reached over and patted Rachel's arm. "Just do your best."

Rachel squinted as she picked at the threads in the hem of her dress. "This is what I get for growing so much this summer," she mumbled.

"What was that?" Mom asked.

"Oh nothing."

"King me!" Pap hollered from across the room, where he and Henry were playing checkers.

"I sure didn't see that coming," Henry said with a groan.

Jacob nudged Henry's shoulder. "Then you oughta pay closer attention to the game."

Henry scowled at Jacob. "Why don't you find something else to do and quit bothering me? I can't concentrate with you hovering around."

"I'm not hovering. I'm keeping my eye on the game, because I'll get to play whoever wins."

Rachel smiled. As much as she didn't like sewing, she'd rather be doing that than playing checkers with Jacob. He didn't play fair and always tried to distract her so he would win. She sometimes got frustrated and quit before the game was over, but the last time they'd played checkers, she'd let Jacob win just so he'd quit bothering her.

"I'm done ripping out the hem," Rachel said, handing the dress to Mom.

"Now you need to make a new hem." Mom handed Rachel a container of pins, a needle, and some dark green thread.

"How am I supposed to know how big I should make the hem?" Rachel questioned.

"Let's see now. . . ." Mom gave her chin a couple of taps. "You grew two inches over the summer, and you'll need to allow for more growth that might occur during this school year." She handed Rachel a measuring tape. "I would suggest that you make the hem on your dress three inches longer than it used to be."

Rachel frowned. This would take a lot longer than she'd expected.

Mom looked at Rachel again. "Once you've got the hem turned up, you'll need to thread your needle and sew it in place. Oh, and be sure you make tiny stitches so the thread doesn't show too much."

This isn't fair, Rachel thought. *At this rate, I'll be here all night!*

"Another king for me!" Pap shouted as he clapped his hands.

Rachel jumped and stuck herself with a pin. "Ouch!"

"What's wrong?" Mom asked with a look of concern.

"When I heard Pap holler, I jammed a *schpell* [pin] into my finger." Rachel stuck her finger in her mouth and sucked on it. The metallic taste of blood made her lips pucker as she scrunched up her nose. "I'm bleeding, Mom. I don't think I can finish this dress tonight."

"Let me see."

Rachel held her hand out to Mom. "It really stings."

"It always stings whenever I prick my finger," Mom said, "but it never lasts long. Just blow on it a few seconds, and then continue pinning the hem."

Rachel frowned. She didn't want to pin the hem in her dress. She wanted to go upstairs and finish reading her book. But she knew from the serious look on Mom's face that she'd better not mention it. She blew on her finger, but it didn't help much.

By the time Rachel finished pinning the hem, her finger felt a little better, but now she was bored. "Can't I finish this tomorrow?" she asked Mom.

Mom shook her head. "You're almost done, Rachel. You just need to sew the hem in place."

Rachel threaded the needle and tied a knot. She was glad she wore glasses now and could see to do it. If she had tried threading a needle before she'd gotten glasses, she wouldn't have been able to see the tiny eye of the needle at all.

In and out. In and out. Rachel yawned as she made the tiniest stitches she could possibly make. This was so boring!

"Hannah's asleep now, Miriam," Grandpa said as he stopped rocking. "It's time for me to go to bed, too."

"Here, I'll go put her in her crib," Mom said. She rose from the sofa and took Hannah from Grandpa. "I'll be back in a few minutes, so keep sewing," she said to Rachel before she left the room.

Grandpa stood and yawned noisily. "*Gut nacht* [Good night], everyone."

"Why are you going to bed so early?" Rachel asked.

"I was busier than usual in my greenhouse today," he replied. "I'd counted on your help this afternoon, but since you had other things to do, I had to do everything on my own."

Rachel felt guilty for letting Grandpa down. She wished she'd been able to help him all afternoon instead of doing a bunch of chores she didn't enjoy. "I'm sorry I couldn't help you, Grandpa. Maybe tomorrow I'll have more time."

Grandpa moved over to the sofa and squeezed Rachel's shoulder. "We'll have to see how it goes."

When Grandpa left the room, Rachel resumed her sewing. In and out. In and out. She wished she didn't have to make such little stitches. At this rate she'd be up all night trying to get the dress hemmed!

"That's it! The game's over, and I won!" Pap hollered.

Henry grunted and pushed back his chair. "It's your turn now, little *bruder* [brother]," he said, thumping Jacob's arm. "I hope you have better luck than I did. Pap's one tricky checkers player!"

"I can be pretty tricky, too." With a smug smile, Jacob dropped into Henry's chair. "Now we'll see who's the champion checkers player in this family!"

Pap rubbed his hands briskly together. "Jah, we'll see indeed!"

Rachel rolled her eyes. Jacob was such a braggart, and bragging was being prideful, which the bishop of their church had said wasn't a good thing. It would serve Jacob right to lose this game of checkers!

In and out. In and out. *Tick-tock. Tick-tock.* The clock on the mantel kept time with Rachel's stitches.

"King me, Pap!" Jacob shouted. "And then king me again!"

"Ach," Pap said with a grunt. "You outsmarted me with that sneaky move, boy!"

Jacob chuckled. "I told you I was good at this game!"

Rachel rolled her eyes again and cut the end of her thread. Finally, she'd finished hemming her dress. She stuck the needle in the arm of the sofa, made a knot in the thread, and clipped it with the scissors. Then she wandered across the room to watch the checkers game. Pap had three kings, but Jacob had seven. Unless Pap improved, Jacob would probably win the game.

Rachel was tempted to offer Pap some suggestions but figured he wouldn't be too happy about that. Jacob didn't deserve to win—not when he thought he was so great at checkers.

Tick-tock. Tick-tock. Several minutes passed. Jacob managed to get two more kings. *Click! Click! Click!* He jumped Pap's last few checkers.

"I won!" Jacob pushed his chair back and waved his arms. "I'm the checkers champion in this house; that's for certain sure!"

Pap winked at Rachel. He probably thought Jacob was a big braggart, too.

"Whew, that game about wore me out!" Jacob shuffled across the room and flopped onto the sofa. "Yeow!" He leaped up and waved his hand in the air. "There's a giant *nodel* [needle] stuck in my hand!"

"Well, what's the matter with you, boy? Take the nodel out," Pap said.

Jacob hopped from one foot to the other. "I can't! It'll hurt!"

"Oh, don't be such a boppli. The nodel's not that big." Rachel hurried to Jacob and grabbed his hand. "If you hold real still, this won't hurt a bit." She grabbed the end of the needle and yanked. "There you go! Your hand's as good as new!"

Jacob's eyebrows furrowed as he scowled at Rachel. "You put that nodel in the sofa, didn't you?"

She nodded slowly. "I was going to take it out, but I forgot."

He shook his finger in her face. "I'll get even with you for this!" Before Rachel could respond, Jacob darted out of the room.

Rachel sank to the edge of the sofa and groaned.

Chapter 3

Getting Even

Rachel sat up with a start. She looked at the clock on the nightstand by her bed and realized she'd almost overslept. She scrambled out of bed and raced to her closet. Then she took off her nightgown, grabbed a dress from its hanger, and slipped it on. She picked up her sneakers and rushed to the dresser.

In a hurry to finish getting dressed, she jerked the bottom drawer of her dresser all the way out. *Crash!* It fell on the floor, spilling all her underclothes. She flopped down beside them and fumbled around until she found a pair of black stockings. In her hurry, she put both stockings on the same foot.

"Always trouble somewhere," she grumbled as she pulled the stockings off and started over again. This time she carefully put only one stocking on each foot.

Rachel stood and smoothed the wrinkles from her dress. Then she raced out of her room and down the stairs.

Rachel's stomach rumbled when she stepped into the kitchen and smelled bacon frying. "Mmm. . .I'm *hungerich* [hungry]," she said, rubbing her stomach. "How soon until breakfast is ready?"

"As soon as you go to the chicken coop and get more eggs." Mom motioned to the carton of eggs on the counter. "I only have four. That's not enough eggs for the six people living in this house."

"What about Jacob?" Rachel asked. "Can't he go to the chicken coop and check for eggs?'

Mom shook her head. "Jacob's helping Henry and Pap milk the cows and do outdoor chores."

Rachel frowned. She guessed she had no other choice than to do as Mom asked. She grabbed her jacket from the wall peg near the door and headed outside.

When she stepped onto the porch, a blustery breeze whipped through the trees and under the porch eaves. She shivered. "*Brr. . .*" Autumn had crept in while summer faded away. Soon winter would be here, and then she'd really be cold.

Rachel hurried to the chicken coop, opened the door, and stepped inside.

Crack! Crack! Crunch! Crunch!

Rachel looked down. Six eggs were lined up just inside the door, and she'd stepped on four of them! She clenched her fists until her fingers ached. "Jacob Yoder, you'll be sorry for this!"

She grabbed the two eggs that hadn't been broken

and checked each of the hens' nests. No more eggs. With a groan, she scurried out the door and raced back to the house.

Mom smiled when Rachel entered the kitchen. "Did you get some eggs?"

Rachel held out the two eggs. "Just these. The others were broken."

Mom frowned. "How'd they get broken?"

Rachel's face heated. "I—uh—stepped on them." She debated about telling Mom that she thought Jacob had put the eggs there on purpose, but decided against it. Mom might accuse her of being a tattletale. Or she might think Rachel had made up the story just to get Jacob in trouble.

"Well," Mom said with a sigh, "I guess we'll have to make do with the eggs we have this morning. We'll just have one apiece instead of two."

Rachel sighed in relief. At least Mom hadn't yelled at her for stepping on the eggs.

"Wash your hands and set the table, Rachel," Mom said, motioning to the silverware drawer.

Rachel glanced at the clock and hurried to do as she was told.

She'd just finished setting the table when Pap, Henry, Jacob, and Grandpa entered the kitchen.

"Mmm. . .bacon and eggs." Grandpa smacked his lips. "I could smell 'em as soon as I stepped out of my room."

"There's only one egg for each of us," Mom said, "but I've made plenty of bacon and toast, so I don't think anyone will go hungry."

Jacob gave Rachel a smug smile as he sat at the table, but then he quickly looked away.

Rachel ground her teeth together. *I just know he put those eggs by the chicken coop door!* she fumed. She remembered him saying last night that he would get even with her.

Rachel ate her toast and drank her juice, but nothing tasted right. She decided she'd get even with Jacob for getting even with her.

After breakfast, Jacob, Henry, and Pap went outside to do more chores, and Grandpa headed to his greenhouse.

"I need to feed the boppli now," Mom said, looking at Rachel and pushing her chair away from the table. "It may take me awhile, and I don't want you and Jacob to be late for school, so I'd like you to make yours and Jacob's lunches." Without waiting for Rachel to reply, Mom hurried from the room.

Rachel stomped to the refrigerator. She didn't mind making her own lunch, but she didn't see why she had to make Jacob's lunch, too. It wasn't fair! After what he'd done in the chicken coop, he should make her lunch this morning!

Rachel grabbed the handle of the refrigerator and yanked the door open. As she reached inside, she spotted a jar of peanut butter. Her hand stopped in midair when she spied a jar of brown mustard. *Hmm. . .I wonder. . .*

Rachel snatched the jar of mustard along with the jar of peanut butter and some of Mom's homemade strawberry jelly; then she shut the refrigerator door. She tromped back across the room and grabbed a loaf of bread from the pantry. Quickly, she made two sandwiches—one with peanut butter and jelly. But for the other sandwich, she mixed a hefty serving of brown mustard in the peanut butter. She put the normal peanut butter and jelly sandwich in her lunch pail and the other in Jacob's lunch pail.

"That should teach my bruder a good lesson," Rachel muttered. "He deserves it after making me step on those eggs!"

As Rachel walked along the path toward school, she glanced at Jacob and thought about the sandwich she'd made for his lunch. He'd sure be surprised when he bit into it at noon and discovered it was full of brown mustard with the peanut butter!

Swallowing back the feelings of guilt creeping into her heart, Rachel tried to concentrate on something else. She looked at the sun, which was trying to peek between the gray clouds. A flock of geese glided through the sky, and the trees lining the road swayed in the breeze. If Rachel didn't have so many troubling thoughts on her mind, she might have enjoyed this walk to school. Maybe she'd made a mistake in making Jacob that mustard sandwich.

When they entered the school yard, several children were playing in a pile of leaves. Rachel was tempted to join them, but the crisp autumn air made her shiver, so she hurried inside.

All morning Rachel had a hard time concentrating on her studies. She kept thinking about the sandwich waiting for Jacob in his lunch pail.

Maybe I could sneak it out of there before it's time for lunch, Rachel thought. *But then when Jacob goes to eat his lunch, he'll wonder why he has no sandwich.*

Rachel nibbled the tip of her fingernail as she continued to mull things over. By the time Teacher Elizabeth dismissed the class to get their lunches, Rachel had bitten almost every one of her nails.

I need to quit worrying about this, she finally decided. *Jacob deserves that mustard sandwich. Jah, he surely does!*

"Say, Rachel, what happened to all of your fingernails? They look really short," Orlie said as he opened his lunch pail and sat on the back porch.

"They're in her stomach," Jacob said before Rachel could reply. "She's supposed to quit that bad habit of chewing on her nails, but she's still a little boppli, so she probably won't."

Rachel's face heated. "You're a mean bruder, Jacob," she mumbled. He really did deserve that mustard sandwich!

Jacob snickered and plopped down beside Orlie. "I'm not mean, but I'm sure hungerich!"

He opened his lunch pail and removed his sandwich. Then he unwrapped it and took a big bite. His eyes widened, his lips puckered, and he coughed as he spit the piece of sandwich out onto the porch. "Ugh! What's wrong with my peanut butter and jelly sandwich?"

Rachel clamped her lips shut and looked away.

Jacob took a drink of milk from his thermos. Then he pushed Rachel's arm. "You made my sandwich with mustard, didn't you?"

She nodded slowly and turned to face him. "I did it to get even with you for setting those eggs in front of the chicken coop door so I'd step on them."

Jacob scowled. "What you did to me was ten times worse than what I did to you! You should have tasted that sandwich, Rachel. It was *baremlich* [terrible]!" He nudged Rachel's arm again. "Mom's not gonna like it when I tell her what you did."

Rachel glared at him. "You do and I'll tell her about the eggs."

Ping! Ping! Ping! Rain started splattering on the roof and blew under the eaves of the porch. All the scholars who'd been sitting there grabbed their lunch pails and ran into the schoolhouse.

Rachel hopped up, but Jacob just sat there, staring at his sandwich.

"Aren't you coming inside?" Rachel asked.

He glared up at her. "Give me your sandwich!"

"What?"

"I said, 'Give me your sandwich!'"

She shook her head. "Why should I?"

"Because you ruined mine!"

"You ruined all the eggs we should have had for breakfast."

"Did not." Jacob tossed the rest of his sandwich into his lunch pail. "You ruined the eggs when you stepped on them."

"I wouldn't have stepped on them if you hadn't put them on the floor by the door."

Jacob folded his arms and glared at her.

"Well, I don't know about you, but I'm not going to stay out here and get wet." Rachel hurried into the schoolhouse and shut the door.

As Jacob and Rachel walked home from school that afternoon, Rachel walked slower than she normally would have. The rain had stopped, but mud puddles filled the path by the road. She tried to dodge them, but one was so big she stepped right in, soaking her sneakers and splattering the hem of her dress. Her wet shoes made a squeaking sound as she continued to walk, and when she came to the next puddle, she jumped right over it.

Rachel usually liked coming home from school, but not today. Besides the extra chores she knew would be waiting, she was afraid Jacob would tell Mom about the mustard she'd put on his sandwich. Then she'd be in big trouble with Mom. Well, if he did tell, then she'd tell on him, too!

As Rachel turned into their driveway, Jacob ran past her and made a beeline for the house. Rachel ran as fast as she could, but Jacob leaped onto the porch ahead of her. Rachel's face was hot, and she was out of breath when she entered the house.

"Please don't tell Mom about the sandwich," she whispered, tapping Jacob on the shoulder.

"What was that?"

"I said, 'Please don't tell Mom about the sandwich,'" she said a little louder.

"Huh?"

She poked his arm. "You should get your hearing tested!"

"You don't have to yell. I'm standing right beside you, little bensel."

"Don't call me that!"

Jacob snickered.

When they entered the kitchen, Rachel saw a note on the table from Mom. Mom had gone to Esther's to see how she was doing.

Rachel plopped down on the floor and removed her wet sneakers. After being out in the chilly, damp weather, Rachel thought the kitchen felt warm and cozy. The longer she sat there waiting for Mom to get home, the more nervous she became.

I sure wish I hadn't made that mustard sandwich. I sure hope Jacob keeps quiet about it, she thought.

When Mom stepped into the kitchen a short time later, Jacob rushed to her and said, "You know that sandwich Rachel made for me this morning?"

Mom nodded. "What about the sandwich?"

"She put brown mustard on it!" Jacob wrinkled his nose and made a horrible face. "It tasted baremlich, Mom!"

Mom turned to Rachel and frowned. "What in all the world possessed you to do something so mean?"

"I—I did it to get even with Jacob for putting eggs on the floor of the chicken coop this morning so I'd step on them," Rachel said.

Mom peered at Jacob over the top of her glasses. "Is that true, son?"

He nodded and hung his head.

"You two should be ashamed of yourselves. Don't you remember what the Bible says about doing unto others as you would like them to do to you? We're supposed to love everyone, even our enemies. We're not supposed to do mean things or try to get even with anyone." Mom pointed to Jacob. "For the next week it will be your job to clean the chicken coop and gather eggs every day." She pointed to Rachel. "It will be your job to make Jacob's lunch every day, and you have to fix him something he likes."

Jacob grunted. Rachel gasped. So this was what she got for trying to get even!

Chapter 4

Daydreaming

I shouldn't have to do this," Rachel complained to Jacob as she began making his lunch the following morning.

"Then you shouldn't have fixed that mustard sandwich for me yesterday." Jacob peered over Rachel's shoulder. "You'd better put all the things I like in my lunch pail today. Mom said you have to."

"Stop hovering!" Rachel shooed him away with her hand. "And for your information, Mom didn't say I had to fix *everything* that you like. She said I have to fix *something* you like."

Jacob put his fingers around his throat and made a gagging sound. "Well, I don't like mustard sandwiches, so you'd better not make that again!"

"Don't worry, I won't." Rachel frowned at him. "And you'd better not put eggs on the chicken coop floor ever again!"

He grunted. "Why would I, when I'm the one going to the chicken coop to fetch eggs every morning? I wouldn't

468

want to step on any of those eggs; that's for sure."

Rachel slathered a bunch of tuna on Jacob's sandwich and held her nose. Tuna was one of his favorite sandwiches, but she didn't like the strong smell. It wasn't something she cared to eat either.

"What are you putting in my lunch for dessert?" Jacob asked, leaning on the counter with both arms.

"I thought I'd put in an orange."

Jacob wrinkled his nose. "I don't want an orange. I want something else."

"How about an apple or a banana?" Rachel asked.

He shook his head.

"What do you want?"

"I'd like two powdered sugar doughnuts." Jacob held up three fingers. "On second thought, make it three— no, I think four."

Rachel rolled her eyes. "You're such a *sau* [pig]. *Oink! Oink!*"

"I'm not a pig. I just know I'll be hungry by lunchtime." Jacob smacked his lips and patted his stomach. "Some powdered sugar doughnuts sound real good to me."

"Is a tuna sandwich and four powdered sugar doughnuts all that you want?" Rachel asked as she reached for the container of doughnuts.

Jacob tapped his chin a couple of times. "Let's see now. . . . How about a thermos full of chocolate milk? Oh, and I'd also like some potato chips and a piece of leftover chicken."

"*Oink! Oink! Oink!*"

Jacob poked Rachel's arm. "Stop saying that. I'm not a sau!"

"Jah, you are. Only a pig eats that much at one time."

Jacob stood straight and tall. "I eat a lot because, in case you hadn't noticed, I'm growing into a man."

"*Puh!*" Rachel flapped her hand at him. "You're not a man. You're an *oink-oink* sau!"

"Am not!"

"Are so!"

"Am not!"

"What's all the yelling about?" Grandpa asked when he stepped into the room. "I could hear you two clear down the hall."

"She's calling me names."

"He's acting like a sau."

Grandpa motioned to Rachel. "Would you please explain to me what's going on?"

She pointed to Jacob's lunch pail. "Just because I'm supposed to make his lunch, he expects me to fix a whole bunch of food that he doesn't even need. So I called him a sau."

Grandpa frowned. "Jacob's wrong if he expects you to fix more food than he needs, but that doesn't give you an excuse to call him names." He put his thumb under Rachel's chin. "I think you should apologize to your bruder, don't you?"

Rachel stared at the floor. "I don't see why I have to

apologize. He's the one who started it by asking for so much food."

"Well, if she hadn't been grumbling about having to fix my lunch, I wouldn't have asked for more food." Jacob glared at Rachel. "*Die Rachel is die ganz zeit am grummle* [Rachel is grumbling all the time]."

"I am not!" Rachel shouted.

"Are too!"

"Am—"

Grandpa held up both hands. "That's enough! I want you both to apologize for the things you've said to each other, and you'd better be quick about it."

"Sorry," Jacob and Rachel mumbled at the same time.

Grandpa motioned to Jacob's lunch pail. "Now finish the lunches, Rachel, or you'll both be late for school."

"I'm almost done with Jacob's lunch," Rachel said. "And then I'll need to fix my own."

Grandpa nodded at Jacob. "Why don't you wait outside for Rachel? She'll be along in a few minutes."

"Okay." Jacob slipped into his jacket, plunked his hat on his head, and hurried out the door, letting it slam shut with a bang.

Rachel sighed. "He makes me so angry! Sometimes I wish I didn't have any *brieder* [brothers]."

Grandpa patted Rachel's arm. "I'm sure all sisters feel that way at times. Brothers sometimes wish they didn't have any sisters, too. I know I felt that way when I was a *buwe* [boy]." He gently squeezed Rachel's arm.

"Remember that even though Jacob sometimes gives you a hard time, he's still a member of this family, and I'm sure he loves you. Just try to be nice to him, Rachel."

Rachel nodded slowly. "I love him, too. I just wish he'd be nice to me all of the time."

"Maybe someday he will—when you're both grown up."

Rachel grunted. "Jah, if that ever happens."

As Rachel and Jacob walked to school, Rachel kicked at the stones along the path while she watched the falling leaves drift on the wind. It was easier than talking to Jacob, and a lot more fun.

"What are you looking at, Rachel?" Jacob asked, poking her in the back.

"I'm looking at the autumn leaves and thinking how much fun it would be if I could fly through the air like a leaf or a bird."

Jacob grunted. "What a daydreamer you are. Won't you ever grow up?"

"Grown-ups sometimes daydream," Rachel said. "Grandpa does it whenever he stands on his head. He told me so once."

Jacob shook his head. "That's not why Grandpa stands on his head, and you know it. He stands on his head so he can think better."

Rachel kicked another pebble with the toe of her sneaker. "A lot you know, Jacob Yoder."

"I know more than you think, and I don't daydream or grumble all the time."

As they entered the school yard, Jacob ran off. He bounded up to Orlie Troyer and shouted, "Guess what, Orlie? My little sister's a daydreamer!"

Orlie snickered and looked at Rachel.

Rachel gritted her teeth. If she hadn't been trying so hard to do as Grandpa suggested, she'd have said something mean to Jacob.

Rachel glanced around the school yard, hoping to find her friend Audra, but she wasn't anywhere in sight. A few minutes later, the school bell rang, and Rachel followed the other scholars inside. She was disappointed to see that Audra wasn't at her desk. She wondered if Audra might be sick.

Ding! Ding! Teacher Elizabeth rang the bell on her desk. Just then, Audra and her brother Brian raced into the room with red faces and breathing heavily.

"Sorry we're late," Audra said, looking at Elizabeth. "Our mamm's sick in bed with the flu, so we had extra chores to do this morning."

"It's all right; you're not that late," Elizabeth said. "Just take your seats."

A few minutes later, the scholars rose to their feet and recited the Lord's Prayer. As the children sang a few songs, Rachel gazed out the window at some birds sitting on the branch of a maple tree. She wished she could be outside to hear the birds sing.

"Singing's over, and it's time to take your seat," Audra whispered in Rachel's ear.

Rachel's face warmed, and she hurried to her desk.

As Elizabeth handed out the arithmetic assignment, Rachel's mind began to wander. *I wonder what Grandpa's doing right now. I wish I could be there helping in the greenhouse. It would be a lot more fun than being cooped up in the schoolhouse all day.*

"Rachel, are you working on your arithmetic assignment?"

Rachel jerked up straight when she heard her teacher's voice. "Uh—yes, I'm almost done." She looked down at her paper and realized that she'd only done two of the twelve problems.

Tap! Tap! Tap! Rachel tapped the edge of her pencil on the side of her desk. *I wonder what Mary's doing right now. Is she doing arithmetic at her school in Indiana? Does Mary like school this year, or does she wish she could be at home, too?*

Rachel glanced out the window again. She wished it was open so she could hear the birds singing and smell the fresh fall air. She wished she could gather some fallen leaves and compare their sizes, shapes, and colors.

"All right, class. Your time is up," Elizabeth said. "Please pass your papers to the front of the room."

Rachel gulped. Her paper wasn't done. She couldn't turn it in with only two problems solved. She'd get a bad grade for sure.

Orlie, who sat in front of Rachel, turned around.

"Where's your paper, Rachel? You're supposed to turn it in now."

Rachel moistened her lips with the tip of her tongue. "I—uh—"

"You'd better give it to me, Rachel," Orlie said.

With a sigh, Rachel handed her paper over to Orlie, along with the ones from the children behind her. Orlie stood and walked up to Elizabeth's desk; then he handed her the papers.

When he returned to his desk, he glanced at Rachel. "Have you been daydreaming again?" he whispered.

She just looked away.

When it was time for morning recess, Rachel jumped out of her chair and raced for the back door. She could hardly wait to get outside!

"Rachel Yoder, can I see you a minute, please?"

Rachel whirled around. "What is it?" she asked her teacher.

Elizabeth motioned for Rachel to come to her desk. Then she held up Rachel's arithmetic paper. "Why isn't this done, Rachel? You had plenty of time to do the assignment, and it wasn't that difficult."

Rachel shifted from one foot to the other. "Well, I—uh—got distracted when I was looking out the window, and—"

"You were daydreaming instead of doing your school-work?" Elizabeth leaned across the desk and stared hard at Rachel.

Rachel nodded slowly as her face grew warm.

Elizabeth handed Rachel's unfinished paper to her. "I want you to sit at your desk and finish this assignment right now."

"But—but what about recess?"

Elizabeth shook her head. "No recess for you this morning. You must learn to be more responsible and to do your assignment like the other scholars did." She squinted her eyes at Rachel. "There's a time and a place for daydreaming, but it's not here at school. Do you understand?"

Rachel nodded and swallowed around the lump in her throat. She didn't like missing recess, and she didn't like being scolded by her teacher!

When it was time for lunch, Rachel grabbed her lunch pail and hurried outside to eat on the porch with several other scholars, including Jacob.

Rachel ate her peanut butter and jelly sandwich first; then she took out the doughnut she'd put in her lunch pail. When she bit into the doughnut, powdered sugar poofed out, sprinkling the front of her dress. She laughed and popped the last piece into her mouth. Then she licked her fingers.

"Grow up, Rachel," Jacob said. "Only a boppli licks her fingers."

"That's not true," Rachel said. "I've seen you lick your fingers when Mom serves fried chicken. I think everyone in our family does."

Jacob shrugged. "Maybe so, but you lick yours more than anyone else. Besides that, you're a *boppli* who likes to daydream and grumble all the time." Jacob gulped down the last of his doughnuts, took a drink of chocolate milk, and wiped his mouth with the back of his hand.

"I do not daydream or grumble all the time! You're just a—" The scripture verse Grandpa had mentioned the other day popped into Rachel's head. She clamped her mouth shut.

"I'm a what?" Jacob asked, nudging Rachel's arm.

"Nothing," she mumbled.

"So I'm a nothing, huh?"

"I didn't mean that. I just meant—oh, never mind!" Rachel grabbed her lunch pail and scooted to the other end of the porch. She decided it was best not to talk to Jacob at all.

When Rachel arrived home from school that afternoon, she smelled the spicy aroma of hot apple cider as soon as she entered the kitchen. *Yum!* She licked her lips in anticipation.

Mom stood at the stove, stirring the cider in a big kettle. She turned and smiled at Rachel. "Did you have a *gut* [good] day?"

"It was okay." Rachel chose not to mention that she'd missed morning recess to finish her arithmetic assignment. She also didn't mention the trouble she'd had with Jacob when she'd made his lunch.

"Where's Jacob?" Mom asked.

"He went to the chicken coop. Said he wanted to clean it first thing so he'd have some free time to do something fun." Rachel's stomach rumbled. "I'm hungerich," she said, sitting at the table. "Are there any more of those powdered sugar doughnuts?"

Mom shook her head. "I gave the last two to Henry and your *daed* [dad] after lunch." Her forehead wrinkled. "I thought there were a lot more when I put them away last night. Did you put some in your lunch pails this morning?"

Rachel nodded. "Jacob insisted on having four, and I had one."

"Oh, I see," Mom said.

"So is there anything for me to eat?" Rachel asked.

Mom motioned to the refrigerator. "You can have some cheese if you like."

"Just cheese?"

"How about some crackers to go with it?"

"Jah, okay." Rachel figured cheese and crackers would be better than nothing, so she headed to the pantry to get the box of crackers.

By the time Rachel had fixed a plate of cheese and crackers, the apple cider was heated.

"Here you go," Mom said, placing a mug in front of Rachel.

A curl of steam drifted up from the cider, and Rachel sniffed deeply. "Mmm. . .this smells *appenditlich* [delicious]. *Danki* [Thanks], Mom."

"You're welcome." Mom poured herself a cup of cider and was about to sit down when—*Waaa! Waaa!*—Hannah's shrill cry floated into the room.

"Guess I'd better tend to your baby sister." Mom set her cup on the counter and hurried from the room.

Rachel ate her cheese and crackers and had just finished her cider when Mom called from the other room, "Rachel, your daed and Henry are in the barn grooming the horses. Would you please run out there and ask if they'd like some cider?"

"Okay, Mom." Rachel set her dishes in the sink and scurried out the door.

She'd just stepped off the porch when she spotted Snowball playing with a ball of string.

"Here, kitty, kitty!" Rachel called, clapping her hands.

Snowball's ears twitched, and she took off for the barn. Rachel raced after her.

When Rachel entered the barn, she didn't see any sign of Snowball. Cuddles wasn't anywhere in sight, either.

Rachel flopped onto a bale of hay, leaned her head against the wall, and closed her eyes. Soon she was daydreaming about going on a wild amusement park ride, like the one she'd gone on when she went to Hershey Park with Sherry and Dave this summer.

Rachel felt something tickle her nose, and her

eyelids fluttered open. Jacob stood over her with a goose feather in his hand.

"*Absatz* [Stop]!" Rachel pushed his hand away. "Leave me alone!"

"What's the matter, little bensel? Are you upset because I woke you, or were you daydreaming again?"

"Stop saying that to me!" she shouted so loudly that Snowball ran out from behind a bale of hay with her ears straight back. She hissed loudly as she raced out of the barn.

"Now look what you've done!" Jacob tickled Rachel under the chin with the feather. "You scared that poor cat of yours right out of her fur!"

"Did not!"

"Did so!"

Rachel put her hand over her mouth to keep from screaming. She was trying to be nice to Jacob, but he was sure making it hard.

"Daydreamer, daydreamer," Jacob taunted as he continued to tickle her with the feather.

Rachel jumped up and shook her finger in his face. "Absatz, right now!"

"What's all the ruckus about in here?" Pap asked, stepping out of one of the horse's stalls.

Rachel pointed to Jacob. "Ask him; he started it."

Pap turned to face Jacob. "What's the problem?"

"There's no problem, Pap." Jacob gave Rachel an innocent-looking grin. "I was just tickling her with a goose feather, and she got upset."

"He was doing more than that," Rachel said. "He was picking on me because I like to daydream."

Pap shook Jacob's shoulder. "Stop picking on your sister and find something else to do with your time."

Jacob scuffed the toe of his boot against the concrete floor. "Guess I'll go to the house and see if Mom made me a snack."

Just then Rachel remembered the reason Mom had sent her to the barn. "I almost forgot," she said to Pap. "Mom wanted me to ask if you and Henry would like some hot apple cider."

Pap nodded. "That sounds good. Run back to the house and tell her we'll be in as soon as we finish grooming the horses." He squeezed Rachel's arm. "And no daydreaming along the way."

As Rachel left the barn, she said to herself, "What's wrong with a little daydreaming now and then? I'm just doing a bit of wishful thinking."

Chapter 5

Borrowing Brings Sorrowing

For the next several days, Rachel tried not to daydream so much. She wanted people to think she was growing up. So instead of daydreaming, she kept busy doing her homework and chores and helping Grandpa in the greenhouse.

On Saturday morning, Rachel headed for the greenhouse, hoping she could spend most of the day there.

"Where are you, Grandpa?" she called when she stepped inside and didn't see him working with any of the flowers.

"I'm back here in my office." Grandpa's voice sounded muffled, like he was talking underwater.

I'll bet Grandpa's standing on his head again, Rachel thought.

She hurried to his office, and sure enough, Grandpa was in one corner of the room with his feet in the air and his hands resting on the floor.

"Are you trying to clear your head?" Rachel asked,

bending down so she could see Grandpa's face.

He gave her an upside-down smile. "Jah, that's what I'm doing all right."

"Should I wait until you're done, or is there something I could be doing in the greenhouse right now?" Rachel asked.

"Once my head's clear enough, we'll prune some of the plants," Grandpa said. "In the meantime, why don't you check the Christmas cacti I recently got in and see if they need any water?"

"Sure, I can do that." Rachel skipped out of the room and over to the shelf where Grandpa had put the plants. She was about to put her finger in the dirt to see if the first one was dry when she remembered that Grandpa had recently bought a little gauge that showed whether or not the plant needed water.

She found the gauge in the drawer under one of the workbenches and stuck it in the dirt of the first cactus. When she saw the moisture reading, she smiled. The plant still had plenty of water. Down the row she went, testing each cactus with the gauge. Only one plant needed water, and she took care of that right away.

When Rachel put the gauge away, she spotted a book about wildflowers on the shelf. It looked interesting, so she picked it up, took a seat on a wooden stool, and opened the book to the table of contents. The first section included a description of several kinds of wildflowers. The next section told some places where wildflowers might grow. There was even a section about pressing wildflowers and putting them in an album, or using them to make bookmarks, postcards, and stationery.

Rachel hummed as she studied a page showing hooded cluster plants, such as jack-in-the-pulpit, sweet flag, and yellow skunk cabbage.

"What are you reading?" Grandpa asked when he entered the room.

Rachel held up the book. "It's called *Wildflowers*, and it looks like an interesting book. I've never seen it here before. Is it new, Grandpa?"

He nodded. "I thought it might be fun to grow some wildflowers in the garden next spring. What do you think of that idea?"

"I think it's a very good idea." Rachel smiled and pointed to the page she had opened. "I'd like to study this book some more and learn about pressing flowers so I can make some pretty cards and things. Can I borrow the book for a few days?"

Grandpa tugged his beard and frowned in thought as his bushy gray eyebrows pulled together so they almost met above the bridge of his nose. "Well, let's see now. . . ." He gave his beard one more quick pull. "I guess it would be all right, but I want you to remember one thing."

"What's that, Grandpa?" Rachel sat up straighter and listened with both ears. She remembered the things that were really important to her—at least most of the time.

"I'd be happy to loan you the book, but I need to know that you'll take good care of it, and I'd like to have it back by the end of next week."

"I promise I'll take care of the book, and I'll be sure to return it to you next week," Rachel said with a nod.

After lunch that afternoon, Grandpa said he wouldn't need Rachel's help in the greenhouse for the rest of the day. Rachel decided it would be a good time to read some more from the wildflower book.

She carried the book outside to the porch, sat on the porch swing, and opened the book to the section that told about pressing flowers. She'd only read a few pages when Mom stepped outside and said, "Jacob's having an ice cream cone. Would you like one, Rachel?"

Rachel nodded eagerly. She loved ice cream, especially strawberry-flavored ice cream, which Pap had made last night after supper.

"Would you like to come into the kitchen, or would you rather eat your cone out here?" Mom asked.

"I'd rather eat it out here."

"Okay, I'll bring the cone right out." Mom went into the house and returned to the porch a few minutes later with a sugar cone heaped high with strawberry ice cream.

"You'd better set that book aside while you're eating this," Mom said, handing Rachel the cone. "Grandpa wouldn't like it if you got ice cream on any of the pages."

"Okay, Mom." Rachel set the book on the small table nearby. "Oh, by the way, I was wondering what time Esther and Rudy will be coming over for the bonfire tonight."

Mom shook her head. "When I checked the answering machine in the phone shed earlier, there was a message from Rudy. He said they wouldn't be coming because Esther isn't feeling up to it."

"That's too bad. Will Pap build a bonfire anyway?"

"I don't think so, Rachel. I believe we'll have to do it some other time."

Rachel was disappointed, but before she could say so, Mom went back in the house.

Rachel sighed and stared at her ice cream cone, wondering which side to lick first. She was glad it was a warm, sunny day. Before long it would be too cold to eat ice cream outside. She was also glad that Jacob had chosen to stay inside. She didn't need him out here pestering her. Knowing Jacob, he'd probably eat his cone really fast, and then he'd expect her to give him a couple of licks from hers.

She crinkled her nose. No way would she let Jacob get any of his germs on her ice cream cone!

Slurp! Slurp! Rachel licked one side and then the other. "Yum! This is appenditlich," she said, smacking her lips. When she'd eaten half the cone, she reached for the wildflower book.

She placed the book in her lap and opened it to the

page that showed how to make a bookmark using dried flowers and leaves. It would be fun to create a pretty bookmark and send it to Mary in her next letter. Maybe Rachel would even make some stationery using dried flowers.

Rachel lifted her ice cream cone to take another bite, when—*floop!*—Snowball leaped from the porch railing and bumped Rachel's arm, knocking the cone out of her hand.

Rachel gasped when a blob of ice cream landed on the book, right in the middle of a picture of a hollyhock plant!

"Ach, Snowball, look what you've done to Grandpa's *buch* [book]!" Rachel pushed the kitten away and jumped up. She had to do something quickly or the book might be ruined.

She raced into the house, grabbed a sponge from the kitchen sink, turned on the water, and soaked the sponge. Then she squeezed the excess water from the sponge and raced back outside.

"No, no, no!" she hollered when she spotted Snowball sitting on the swing, licking the ice cream that had fallen onto the book. "Get away from there, you silly *bussli* [kitten]!" She pushed Snowball aside and picked up the book. There wasn't much ice cream left on the page, but now there was a big ugly-looking pink stain where the ice cream had been.

Rachel's heart pounded, and her head began to

throb. "I can't give the book back to Grandpa like this," she whimpered. "If I do, he'll say I didn't take good care of it."

She sat on the edge of the swing feeling sorry for herself. Why did she always have so much trouble? She hated feeling helpless like this.

After several minutes, an idea popped into Rachel's head. *I'll hide the book. Maybe Grandpa will forget he loaned it to me and I won't have to tell him what happened.*

Rachel jumped off the swing and raced for the barn. She would hide the book in the hayloft where no one would see.

The next several days went by, but Grandpa didn't mention the book. With each day, Rachel felt guiltier and guiltier for not telling Grandpa what she'd done with his book. Finally, when she could stand it no more, she decided to go to the hayloft and get the book.

Rachel entered the barn and looked around to be sure no one was watching. Then she climbed the ladder to the hayloft and hurried to the mound of hay where she'd hidden the book. She reached inside and felt all around. The book was gone!

"No! No! No!" Rachel hollered. "This can't be happening!"

Rachel remembered the time she'd put her glasses inside a box and hidden it in the hayloft. Jacob had found them and hidden them in his room to teach

Rachel a lesson. He'd obviously done it to her again.

Rachel sprinted down the ladder and ran all the way to the house. She found Jacob in his room, sprawled on his bed, reading a book.

"Give it to me!" she demanded.

"Give what to you?" Jacob mumbled without looking at her.

"The wildflower book."

Jacob set his book aside and sat up. "I have no idea what you're talking about. This book is about a dog."

Rachel gritted her teeth. "Don't act so innocent. You went into the hayloft and took the book I hid there."

Jacob's raised his eyebrows. "You hid a book there?"

She nodded slowly. "Please give it back."

Jacob lifted the book he held. "This is the only book I know anything about, and it has nothing to do with wildflowers."

"I know you took that book!" Rachel shouted. "*Ferwas bischt allfat so schtarkeppich* [Why are you always so stubborn]?"

"I'm not being stubborn. I'm telling you the truth."

Rachel moved closer to his bed and peered at the book. It was about a dog. "So you never saw the book about wildflowers?"

"Nope."

She scratched her head. "Then what could have happened to it?"

Jacob shrugged his shoulders. "Beats me." He

motioned to the door. "Now go away and leave me in peace to read my book."

Rachel shuffled out the door, feeling hopeless and sad. What if she never found Grandpa's book? How could she explain that to him?

Rachel could hardly eat supper that night, and when she went to bed, she couldn't sleep. She could only think about the missing book and how she wished she'd never borrowed it in the first place.

When she got up the next morning, she knew she needed to tell Grandpa the truth.

Rachel waited until after breakfast. Since it was Saturday and there was no school, she knew Grandpa would expect her to help him in the greenhouse.

She'd just started for the greenhouse when she spotted Grandma Yoder's horse and buggy coming up their driveway.

"*Guder mariye* [Good morning], Rachel," Grandma said after she'd stopped the buggy. "I've come to do some baking with your mamm. Are you going to join us?"

Rachel shook her head. "I'm going to the greenhouse to help Grandpa." She kicked at a pebble with the toe of her sneaker and stared at the ground.

"You seem to be *umgerennt* [upset]. Is something wrong?" Grandma asked.

Rachel nodded and lifted her gaze to meet Grandma's. "I—I've lost something important and can't find it." She sniffed a couple of times. "I think my name should be Trouble, because trouble seems to find me wherever I go." *Borrowing brings sorrowing,* she thought. *At least it has for me.*

Grandma smiled at Rachel. "Remember now, no matter how much trouble you have, it too will pass."

"I'll try to remember," Rachel mumbled. As she headed for the greenhouse, a sudden breeze rattled the leaves on the trees. She shivered and pulled the collar of her jacket tighter around her neck.

When Rachel entered the greenhouse a few minutes later, she found Grandpa in his office, sitting at his desk.

"I—I have something I need to tell you," she said tearfully.

"What is it, Rachel?" Grandpa asked.

"I spilled ice cream on the wildflower book I borrowed from you, and—and then I hid it, but now it's missing."

"Ah, I see." Grandpa reached into his desk drawer and pulled out a book. It was the wildflower book. "Is this what you've been looking for?"

Rachel was so surprised she could hardly talk.

"I found this book in the hayloft when I went there looking for a box." Grandpa frowned. "What do you have to say about this, Rachel?"

Rachel hung her head, unable to meet Grandpa's gaze. "I–I'm sorry. I shouldn't have been looking at the book while I was eating ice cream." *Sniff. Sniff.* "And I shouldn't have hid the book in the hayloft to keep you from finding out what I'd done." Tears streamed down her cheeks. "I'll save up my money and buy you a new book."

Grandpa shook his head. "That's not necessary. The book isn't ruined; just one page has a stain on it." He leaned forward with his elbows on the desk. "I do want you to learn a lesson from this, however."

Rachel's heart hammered in her chest as she waited to hear what her punishment would be. Would Grandpa tell Mom and Pap? Would they give her a *bletsching* [spanking] or make her do a bunch more chores? "I'm really sorry, and I know I deserve to be punished," she said, nearly choking on a sob.

Grandpa pulled Rachel into his arms. "It's good that you've apologized to me, but you need to tell God you're sorry, too." He patted her back. "A sign that a person is growing up is when that person is willing to admit to doing something wrong, and to make it right with the person involved and also with God."

Rachel nodded and bowed her head. She'd make things right with God right now. And the next time she asked to borrow anything, she would try extra hard to make sure accidents didn't happen!

Chapter 6

Mistakes

"Rachel, don't forget to put your sheets and clothes in the laundry basket before you leave for school," Mom called up the stairs on Monday morning. "And hurry; we're ready to eat breakfast!"

Rachel cupped her hands around her mouth and hollered, "Okay, Mom!"

She dashed across the room, opened her closet door, and stepped inside to get her dirty clothes. She looked around and noticed her jump rope lying on the shelf. She scooped it up.

I'll take this to school today and play with it at recess, she decided.

"Rachel, are you coming?" Mom called again.

"Jah, I'll be there soon."

Rachel noticed the stack of newspapers she'd placed on top of the flowers Grandpa had given her to press several days ago.

"I'd better check and see how they're doing," Rachel

said, kneeling. She lifted the newspapers and the cardboard covering the flowers. They looked pretty good. Soon they'd be ready to use in a bookmark or a card. Rachel could hardly wait! She sat several minutes, thinking about all the different designs she could make.

Rachel's stomach rumbled, and she remembered that she was hungry. So she left the closet, hurried out of her room, and skipped down the stairs.

When Rachel entered the kitchen, she found Mom clearing dishes off the table. Grandpa sat by the fireplace reading a newspaper, but Rachel saw no sign of Jacob, Henry, or Pap.

"Hoscht du schunn geese [Have you already eaten]?" Rachel asked, stepping up to Mom.

Mom nodded and placed the bowls and cups into the sink.

Rachel's mouth dropped open like a broken window hinge. "You ate breakfast without me?"

"That's right," said Mom. "I called you several times, but you didn't come, so we ate without you."

Rachel's stomach rumbled as she stared at the table. "Can I have some breakfast now?"

Mom shook her head and motioned to the clock on the wall. "I'm afraid there's no time for that, Rachel. You still have to feed the chickens and check for eggs. Then you'll need to head to school." Mom's forehead wrinkled. "You should have come when I called you for breakfast."

Rachel stood frozen, unable to say a word. She could hardly believe Mom would send her to school without any breakfast. She bit her bottom lip to keep from crying, and then she looked at Grandpa, hoping he'd come to her rescue.

"Rachel, you've developed a bad habit of fooling around and not doing what you're told," he said. "Bad habits are like a comfortable bed: They're easy to get into but hard to get out of."

Rachel swallowed around the lump in her throat as she gave a quick nod. Then she grabbed her jacket from the wall peg and rushed out the back door. Maybe if she fed the chickens quickly, Mom would let her have some breakfast.

The shrill cry of a crow drew Rachel's gaze upward, but she had no time to dawdle. She dashed across the yard to the chicken coop and jerked open the door.

Quickly, she scooped out the chicken feed and poured some into the feeders. The chickens appeared to have plenty of water, so she decided not to add any more. She glanced in each of the nesting boxes but didn't see any eggs.

"The hurrier I go, the behinder I get," Rachel said as she raced out the door.

"I'm done feeding the chickens," Rachel said when she returned to the kitchen. "Can I have some breakfast now?"

Mom handed Rachel an apple. "There's no time for

that. Jacob's already left for school, and even if you leave right now, you'll probably be late."

Rachel's forehead wrinkled. "Jacob left without me?"

Mom nodded. "I didn't think it would be fair to make him wait for you and then have both of you late for school. I told him to go on without you."

Rachel looked at Grandpa. "Will you give me a ride to school so I won't be late?"

He shook his head. "Sorry, Rachel. Not this time. I have a customer coming to pick up some plants in a few minutes. I need to get out to my greenhouse right now."

Rachel looked at Mom. "Can't Pap or Henry take me to school?"

"No," Mom said. "They left to run some errands in town right after breakfast."

"Could you take me, then?"

"Sorry, Rachel, but I have washing to do and can't leave the baby." Mom handed Rachel her backpack and lunch pail. "Hurry to school now."

"B—but you always say I shouldn't walk to school alone," Rachel stammered.

"I think you're old enough now. Besides, you have no other choice." Mom shooed Rachel toward the door. "Schnell!"

Rachel headed up the path toward school. The leaves on the ground curled up on the edges as the breeze whistled them along. Rachel's feet dragged with each step she took. Besides knowing she was going to be late, she was tired from staying up past her bedtime last night. She decided she might as well take her time getting to school.

"Guess that's what I get for reading when I should have been sleeping, and for not paying attention when Mom called me to breakfast," she mumbled, feeling sorry for herself. "It's not fair that everyone ate breakfast without me. Someone should have come upstairs and told me it was time to eat."

By the time Rachel got to school, she felt even worse. When Rachel entered the schoolhouse, Elizabeth stood at the blackboard, writing the arithmetic assignment, so Rachel knew she'd missed the morning prayer and the songs they always sang.

As Rachel stepped down the aisle toward her desk, Elizabeth turned and frowned at her. "You're late, Rachel."

Rachel nodded. "Jah, I know. I woke up late, and then I—"

Elizabeth motioned to Rachel's desk. "Please take your seat and get out your arithmetic book. We can talk about your reason for being late during recess."

Rachel swallowed hard as her throat started to burn. She knew she probably wouldn't be allowed to go outside and play during recess. Elizabeth would probably have some work for Rachel to do during recess. She might even have to stay after school because of her tardiness.

Rachel sank into the seat at her desk. *It seems like I'm always in trouble. Why do I make so many mistakes?*

As Rachel headed home from school that afternoon, she fretted and fumed. She'd not only had to stay in from recess today, but Elizabeth had made her stay after school to clean the blackboards and sweep the floor.

Jacob hadn't waited for her either. He'd said he had better things to do.

"That's fine with me," Rachel muttered. "At least I don't have to listen to him scolding me for being late to school and calling me a little bensel."

When Rachel entered her yard, she saw clothes on the line, flapping in the breeze. Mom stood on the back porch, tapping her foot and staring at the porch floor.

"What's wrong, Mom?" Rachel asked as she climbed the porch steps. "You look umgerrent."

"I am upset." *Tap! Tap! Tap!* Mom tapped her foot some more and pointed to the floor. "See this mess the *hinkel* [chickens] made with their droppings?"

Rachel nodded.

"Well, they made that mess because someone left the door to the chicken coop open this morning." Mom peered at Rachel over the top of her glasses. "What do you have to say for yourself, Rachel?"

Rachel gulped. "Well, I—uh—was in a hurry when I left the coop, so I—uh—guess I must have forgotten to shut the door."

"How many times have I told you to close the door to the coop?" Mom asked.

"Lots of times."

Tap! Tap! Tap! "I shouldn't have to keep reminding you, Rachel." *Tap! Tap! Tap!* "You want to be grown up, yet you act like a bensel."

Tears stung Rachel's eyes. It was bad enough that Jacob called her a little bensel. Did Mom have to call her that, too?

"And another thing happened because you left the door open," Mom said. "Some of the chickens ate the cat's food." She pointed to the porch. "I want you to clean up the mess and then get busy on your homework."

Rachel shuffled into the house to get the mop and a bucket of water. This really had not been a good day!

When Rachel climbed into bed that night, she expected to find clean, sweet-smelling sheets since Mom had done laundry. But she discovered her sheets were the same ones as the night before—they looked dirty and wrinkled. They didn't smell fresh and clean either.

That's strange, she thought. *I saw clothes on the line, so I know Mom did the laundry today. Why didn't she wash my sheets?*

Rachel hurried across the room and opened her closet door. She reached for a clean dress to have all ready for school the next day. But all her dresses were on the floor in a heap.

"Ach, now I remember! This morning Mom asked me to put my dirty clothes in the laundry basket." Rachel frowned. She knew that part of her problem was not listening carefully to Mom. The other part of the problem was that she got sidetracked easily and forgot important things.

"Now I'll have to sleep in dirty, smelly sheets," she grumbled. "Worse yet, tomorrow I'll have to wear a dirty, wrinkled dress to school."

After school the next day, Rachel headed to the greenhouse to see if Grandpa needed any help.

"Have you done your homework yet?" Grandpa asked, his bushy eyebrows pulling together.

Rachel nodded. "I only had a little bit, and I did it right after I ate a snack."

"All right. I'd be happy to have your help."

"What would you like me to do?" Rachel asked.

Grandpa motioned to the broom leaning against the wall. "I spilled some potting soil a few minutes ago. Would you please sweep that up for me?"

"Jah, sure." Rachel grabbed the broom. *Swish! Swish! Swish!* She swept up the dirt in no time at all.

When she put the broom away, she noticed the book about wildflowers lying on a shelf, so she asked Grandpa if she could look at it.

Grandpa nodded. "But only while you're here in the

greenhouse. I don't want you to take it outside or even up to the house."

"Okay."

Ding! Ding! The bell above the greenhouse door jingled, and an elderly English couple stepped in. While Grandpa waited on them, Rachel decided to try making a bookmark, following the directions in the wildflower book.

She opened it and frowned as she stared at the page. *I'll need some flowers in order to make this bookmark, and the ones I'm pressing in my room aren't ready yet. I wonder. . .*

Rachel glanced at Grandpa, but he was still busy with his customers. She moved to the shelf where some African violets were and plucked off a few purple blossoms. *I'm sure Grandpa won't mind if I thin a couple of these plants,* she decided as she picked a few more blossoms.

Rachel set to work making her bookmark, gluing each flower petal on an index card she'd cut in half. Then she covered it with clear contact paper, only it didn't look right. It looked kind of lumpy. "Hmm. . . . I wonder if I made a mistake."

She read the directions again. "Cut the index card in half lengthwise. Arrange the pressed flowers in whatever design you like." Rachel slapped the side of her head. "I needed pressed flowers, not fresh ones. I made a big mistake!"

"What mistake is that?" Grandpa asked, stepping up to Rachel.

She pointed to the bulky bookmark. "I tried making this with fresh flower petals instead of dried ones, and it turned out wrong."

Grandpa tugged his beard. "And just where did you get these fresh flowers?"

"I took them from a couple of African violet plants over there." Rachel pointed to the other side of the room.

Grandpa frowned. "You should have asked first, Rachel. If you'd asked, I would have told you which plants you could pick flowers from."

He glanced at the bookmark. "This would have looked better if you'd used pressed flowers, because the moisture needs to be taken out of a flower blossom for it to lie flat."

"I figured that out after it was too late," Rachel said.

"This is what happens when you do things without asking."

Rachel sniffed. "I'm sorry, Grandpa."

Grandpa gave Rachel a hug. "Just try to do the right thing, okay?"

Rachel nodded. "I don't like making mistakes, and I promise I'll try to do better."

Chapter 7

Aunt Rachel

On the first Saturday morning in October, Pap came into the house with a huge smile on his face.

"I checked our answering machine in the phone shed. There was a message from Rudy," Pap said. He hung his straw hat on a wall peg near the door and sat at the kitchen table.

Mom sipped her cup of tea. "What'd the message say?"

Pap's smile stretched even wider. "Esther had her boppli last night, and it's a buwe! Rudy said Esther and the boppli will come home from the hospital this morning."

Mom set her cup down and jumped up from the table. "*Alli mudder muss sariye fer ihre famiyle* [Every mother has to take care of her family]*!* I need to get over there right away, because I'm sure she'll need my help."

Mom looked at Rachel, who was sitting at the table writing a letter to Mary. "Do you know what this means?" Mom asked.

Rachel smiled and nodded. "It means I'm an aunt."

Rachel figured being an aunt would make her seem grown up in her family's eyes. Jacob might even stop calling her a little bensel.

Mom patted the top of Rachel's head. "Jah, that, too, but it also means if I go to help Esther today, I'll need your help here."

Rachel's smile turned upside down. "Can't I go over to Esther's with you?"

Mom shook her head. "You need to stay here and take care of Hannah."

"Can't she go with us to Esther's?"

"It'll be easier for me to help Esther if I don't have Hannah to care for, too," Mom said.

Rachel frowned. "Do you expect me to take care of Hannah all by myself?"

Mom nodded. "There are several bottles of milk in the refrigerator and a fresh supply of clean diapers on the dresser in my room. I'm sure you'll do just fine." She patted Rachel's head again. "If you want to be grown up, this will give you a chance to prove it."

Rachel's heart sank all the way to her toes. She did want her family to think she was growing up, but she'd planned to do other things today. Watching Hannah wasn't one of them!

"I shouldn't be gone more than a few hours," Mom said. "But if you need anything, just ask one of the menfolk, because I think they'll be around most of the day." Mom grabbed her jacket and black outer bonnet and started for the door. Then she halted. "I'd better check on Hannah before I go."

Rachel let her head fall forward onto the table and groaned. She wondered if she'd ever get to go over to Esther's to see her new nephew.

I may as well finish this letter to Mary, Rachel decided. *If I don't do it now, I'll probably be so busy watching Hannah that I won't get it done at all.*

Pap pushed his chair away from the table and stood. "I'm going outside to hitch your mamm's horse to one of our buggies. When I'm done with that, I'll be in the fields working with the boys." He smiled at Rachel. "Ring the dinner bell when it's time for lunch, and if you should need anything, you can ring the bell for that, too. Oh, and if Esther feels up to company, we'll all go over there tomorrow after church to see the new boppli."

"Okay," Rachel said as Pap stepped out the door.

A few minutes later, Mom rushed back into the room. "The baby carriage is in the yard," she told Rachel. "The sun's shining, so I'd like you to take Hannah for a ride around the yard so she can get some fresh air."

"I'll do it as soon as I finish this letter," Rachel said as she concentrated on what she wanted to say to Mary. Now she really had some good news to share—she'd become an aunt!

"Okay, and do the best that you can today," Mom said as the door clicked shut behind her.

Rachel hurried to finish Mary's letter; then she left the kitchen and went into Mom and Pap's room to get Hannah.

"Okay, little sister; we're going outside for some fresh air," she said as she walked to the crib.

She halted, and her heart pounded. Hannah wasn't there!

Think, Rachel, think, Rachel told herself. *Let's see now. . . . Mom said I should take Hannah for a ride in her carriage, so maybe Mom put Hannah in the carriage before she left.*

Rachel raced out of the room, grabbed a jacket, and ran out the back door. Sure enough, Hannah's baby carriage sat in the yard. What a relief!

Rachel grabbed the handle and started pushing the carriage around the yard. She pushed and pushed and pushed some more, until she got tired and was completely bored.

"It's time to go back in the house now, Hannah." Rachel bent over the carriage, pulled the blanket aside, and gasped. Hannah wasn't there! Rachel felt so foolish when she realized that she'd been pushing around an empty carriage! *Could someone have come into the yard while I was still in the house and taken Hannah?* she wondered.

Rachel's heart pounded so hard she could hear it

echo in her head. She was getting ready to head to the greenhouse to tell Grandpa what had happened when she heard a faint cry. She tilted her head and listened. The cry sounded like it was coming from inside the house.

Rachel ran up the porch steps two at a time, jerked the door open, and rushed into the house.

Waaa! Waaa! The closer Rachel got to the living room, the louder the crying became. She spotted Hannah's cradle across the room and raced to it. There lay Hannah, with a red face from kicking and screaming.

"It's okay, Hannah," Rachel said as she sat in the chair next to the cradle. She rocked the cradle with her foot, hoping to keep the baby from fussing. She was glad none of her family had been there to see the foolish mistake she'd made. *I should have listened better to Mom*, Rachel thought. *She must have told me that Hannah was in her cradle and that the baby carriage was outside.*

Waaa! Waaa!

Rachel picked up the baby, sat in the rocking chair, and put Hannah in her lap. Rachel patted Hannah's back until she stopped crying. Rachel smiled as she began to rock and hum.

Hannah's eyelids fluttered, and soon she was fast asleep.

Rachel carried Hannah to Mom and Pap's room,

where she put her to bed in her crib.

Now maybe I can do something fun. I think I'll paint a few animals on some of my rocks, Rachel thought as she tiptoed out of the room. *When I'm done with those, I might make some bookmarks with the flowers I've pressed.*

Rachel went to the kitchen and had just placed her paints and some newspaper on the table when Hannah started to howl.

Waaa! Waaa! Waaa!

Rachel looked at the clock. Only five minutes had passed since she'd put Hannah in her crib, and already she was crying. *Maybe if I ignore her, she'll go back to sleep,* Rachel thought as she picked up her paintbrush.

Waaa! Waaa! Hannah's crying got louder.

Rachel's chair scraped against the floor as she pushed away from the table with a groan. "Always trouble somewhere!"

When Rachel entered Mom and Pap's room, she first checked Hannah's diaper. Sure enough, it was sopping wet. She looked for the diaper pail but didn't see it. Then she remembered that Mom sometimes rinsed the baby's diapers in the toilet, so she carried the diaper into the bathroom and dropped it into the toilet bowl.

"*Windel wesche gleich ich net* [I don't like to wash out diapers]," Rachel said as she bounced the diaper up and down.

Waaa! Waaa! Hannah screamed even louder. Her cries seemed to bounce off the walls. Rachel dropped the diaper into the toilet and gritted her teeth, trying not to cry herself. She hoped she could get Hannah settled down soon so she could paint those rocks.

She hurried back to the bedroom and quickly put a clean diaper on the baby. "There, that's better isn't it, Hannah?"

Waaa! Waaa!

Maybe she's hungry, Rachel thought. She stroked the baby's flushed cheeks. "I'll go to the kitchen and get you a bottle of milk. I'll be right back."

Rachel raced into the kitchen. Then she opened the refrigerator and took out one of the baby bottles Mom had filled with milk. She placed the bottle into a kettle of water and turned on the stove. Every few seconds she tipped the bottle upside down and let some milk drip onto her wrist to test it. When it felt lukewarm, she knew it was ready for Hannah.

When Rachel returned to the bedroom, Hannah was still crying and kicking her feet. Rachel set the bottle on the nightstand by Mom's side of the bed. Then she picked Hannah up, sat in the rocking chair, and put the bottle in Hannah's mouth.

Hannah quit crying, and her little lips went in and out as she sucked on the milk.

When the bottle was empty, Rachel lifted Hannah to her shoulder and patted her back. After several pats, Hannah let out a loud burp!

Rachel was relieved that Hannah had burped so

quickly. Usually it didn't happen so fast.

Rachel rose from her chair and was heading down the hall with Hannah when Henry came into the house.

"Did you need something?" Rachel asked her brother.

"Just using the bathroom." Henry smiled at Rachel. "Then I'll refill my thermos with coffee and take it out to the fields. Everything going okay?"

"Jah. I'm going to put Hannah in her cradle, and then I'll be in the kitchen painting rocks," Rachel said as she started for the living room.

Rachel had just gotten Hannah settled in her cradle when Henry hollered, "Who left a windel in the toilet?"

"Oh no." Rachel's palms grew sweaty as she raced from the room. "I hope you didn't flush that diaper down the toilet!"

When Henry stepped out of the bathroom, his face was bright red. "Did you put that windel in the toilet?" he asked Rachel.

She nodded. "I put it there so I could rinse it out. I've seen Mom do it."

"Well, she doesn't walk away and leave it there." A little vein on the side of Henry's head stuck out. "If I'd have flushed the toilet, that windel could've gotten stuck and clogged the drain. You really ought to grow up and learn to be more responsible!" He frowned at Rachel and slowly shook his head.

"I was going to get the diaper, but Hannah started

fussing, and I sort of forgot it was there." Rachel swallowed a couple of times. She felt as if she'd swallowed a glob of sticky peanut butter that wouldn't go down.

"You seem to have a short attention span lately," Henry said.

Rachel stared at the floor as she struggled not to cry. "I do not; I just have a lot on my mind. Besides, it's perfectly normal for people to forget sometimes."

"Well, get your head out of the clouds and start paying better attention!"

Rachel's shoulders started to shake. She dropped her head into her hands as she gave in to her tears.

"Oh, now, don't start crying on me." Henry patted Rachel's trembling shoulder. "I'm sorry for yelling, but if you're going to take care of the boppli, you need to pay close attention to what you're doing."

Sniff! Sniff! Rachel swiped at the tears rolling down her cheeks. "I'm trying to be grown up, but it seems like no matter how hard I try, I always mess up."

Henry gave Rachel's shoulder another pat. "I'm sure you'll grow up someday. But in the meantime, go get that windel out of the toilet."

Chapter 8

Gone Fishing

"It's cold out there this morning. I think it might snow," Rachel said as she dashed into the kitchen the next morning. She'd just finished feeding the chickens.

Jacob, who'd followed Rachel into the house, grunted and rolled his eyes. "It's not going to snow, little bensel. It's too early for that."

Mom turned from the stove and frowned. "Stop calling your sister a silly child, Jacob."

Meow! Hiss! Hiss! Meow!

Rachel jumped when her cats raced into the house, bumped into her leg, and slid across the kitchen floor.

"Ach! Who let those cats in?" Mom asked with a frown.

"Jacob did!"

"Rachel did!"

Rachel and Jacob had spoken at the same time.

"Look, the door's open!" Rachel pointed to the back door; then she pointed to Jacob. "You were the last one in, so you must not have shut it."

Jacob glared at Rachel. "It's your fault because you started talking about the cold weather and said it might snow."

Rachel frowned as she shook her head. "What's that have to do with anything? You left the door open; that's all there is to it!"

"Oh, grow up, Rachel, and quit trying to put the blame on me."

"I'll grow up when I'm good and ready!"

Mom stepped between them. "It doesn't matter who left the door open. You need to capture those two crazy critters running around my kitchen!"

"I'll get Cuddles!" Jacob shouted as he dashed across the room after the cat.

"I'll get Snowball!" Rachel hollered.

Hiss! Hiss! Yeow! Cuddles darted across the floor and swooped under Grandpa's legs when he entered the kitchen.

Grandpa teetered unsteadily and grabbed the back of a chair. "Wh–what's going on in here?"

"Rachel's cats are loose and we're trying to catch 'em," Jacob yelled as he ran down the hall after Cuddles.

Snowball raced into the living room, and Rachel followed.

Meow! The kitten leaped into Hannah's cradle.

Waaa! Waaa! Hannah wailed.

"Snowball, no!" Rachel grabbed the kitten by the

scruff of its neck and raced out of the room. She was almost to the back door when Jacob came running down the hall holding Cuddles in his arms.

"We'd better get them outside before there's any more trouble," Rachel panted.

Jacob nodded, and they both hurried out the door.

When they returned to the kitchen, Mom was back at the stove, and Grandpa was sitting at the table holding Hannah.

"That bussli of yours scared our Hannah," Grandpa said to Rachel.

She nodded. "She's okay, isn't she? I don't think Snowball scratched her or anything."

Grandpa kissed the top of Hannah's head. "She seems fine to me."

Just then, Pap and Henry came in from doing their chores.

Whoosh! Cuddles streaked into the room with Snowball right behind her.

"Levi, you forgot to shut the door!" Mom shook her finger at Pap like he was a little boy. "We've already dealt with those crazy cats once this morning. Must we do it again?"

Pap's face turned red. "Sorry, Miriam. I didn't realize I'd left the door open."

Meow! Hiss! Meow! The cats raced around the room as if their tails were on fire.

"I'll get Cuddles!" Jacob shouted.

"I'll get Snowball," Rachel said.

They both took off after the cats, hollering and waving their arms.

By the time they got the cats outside again, Rachel was exhausted. She was glad it wasn't her fault that they'd gotten in the house this time. It was nice to know she wasn't the only one who got in trouble with Mom.

Rachel chuckled. She could hardly believe it, but even Pap had been scolded by Mom this morning.

"Could you get me a carton of eggs?" Mom asked Rachel. "I need a few more, because your daed likes to have three."

"Okay, Mom." Rachel scooted to the refrigerator, removed the carton of eggs, and handed it to Mom.

"Just set it on the counter." Mom took out the eggs she'd been frying and placed them on a plate. Then she reached for an egg from the carton. The oil in the pan sizzled, and Mom wasn't watching what she was doing as she cracked the egg and dropped it in the pan. A horrible smell rose from the pan and made the whole room stink.

"Eww. . .that was a rotten egg!" Mom turned to Rachel and frowned. "Apparently you haven't been checking for eggs very well."

Rachel frowned. She knew she was supposed to check the chicken coop carefully. Sometimes if an egg was hidden for days, it would be rotten when it was found.

Mom grabbed the frying pan with a pot holder and

hauled it to the garbage can. Then she dumped the egg in the can and handed it to Rachel. "Please take this outside and dump it in the trash can. And from now on, when you're asked to check for eggs, be sure you look in every nesting box and anywhere else in the coop that the chickens might lay their eggs."

Rachel held her breath as she lugged the garbage outside. From now on she'd try to do better about checking for eggs.

After church that afternoon, Rachel's family headed down the road in their buggy. They were on their way to Esther and Rudy's to see the new baby. Even Grandpa and Grandma Yoder went along, only they rode with Uncle Amos, Aunt Karen, and their little boy, Gerald.

When the Yoders arrived, Rachel was the first one to jump out of the buggy. "I'll meet you at the house," she called to Mom as she raced across the lawn.

When she entered Esther's house, she found Esther and Rudy sitting on the sofa in the living room. Esther held a baby in her arms.

"Well, Aunt Rachel," Esther said with a wide smile, "what do you think of your new nephew, Ben?"

Rachel looked at the baby. His face was bright pink and kind of wrinkly. Unlike Hannah, who was born with pretty blond hair, little Ben had no hair at all!

Rachel wasn't sure what to say. She didn't think

"cute" quite fit this baby, but she wanted to say something nice. "He—uh—is sure little."

"Jah, he's that all right," Rudy said with a nod. "But I'm sure he'll grow up fast."

Ben opened his blue-gray eyes and worked his tiny mouth, making a strange snuffling noise.

Soon the rest of Rachel's family entered the room. Everyone started talking at once, making silly sounds and wanting to hold the new baby.

Rachel moved over to stand near the fireplace. She'd finally realized that all babies got a lot of attention when they were young. But when they got older, folks didn't fuss over them so much. Rachel figured in a few years, neither Hannah nor little Ben would be the center of attention. They'd both have a bunch of chores to do and be told to keep quiet if they made too much noise.

"Kumme! Kumme!" Gerald said, tugging on Rachel's hand. "Horsey ride!"

"No." Rachel shook her head so hard the ties on her kapp flipped in her face. "The last time I gave you a horsey ride, you poked me in the eye."

Gerald's lower lip jutted out, and his eyes filled with tears. "Horsey ride!"

"Why don't you and Gerald work on a puzzle together?" Esther suggested. "There's one in the bottom drawer of Rudy's desk, and it's fairly easy."

Rachel wasn't in the mood to put a puzzle together, but she figured it would be better than turning herself into a horse so Gerald could kick her in the side. "Jah, okay," she said, taking Gerald's hand and leading him to Rudy's desk.

When she found the puzzle, she dumped the pieces on the floor and told Gerald to sit down.

While they worked on the puzzle, Rachel listened to the grown-ups talk.

"Now, Esther," Mom said, "don't try to do too much too soon. The boppli will keep you up at night for several weeks, so rest as much as you can whenever you have the chance. I'll come over tomorrow afternoon to fix supper for you and Rudy."

Mom turned to Rachel and said, "Be sure you come straight home from school tomorrow, because I'll need you to watch Hannah while I come over here."

Rachel nodded and reached for a puzzle piece.

The next morning, Rachel headed to the coop to gather eggs before breakfast. She was in a hurry and didn't want to be late for school, so she hurried to feed and water the chickens and decided not to check all the nesting the boxes.

I can check them after school, she decided. *Mom said we're just having cold cereal this morning, and she doesn't need any eggs for that.*

Then she remembered the horrible smell the rotten egg had made in the kitchen, so she turned around and thoroughly checked each nesting box.

Carrying a basket full of eggs, Rachel hurried back to the house, anxious to eat breakfast and head for school.

As Rachel and her family sat around the table, Mom turned to Rachel and said, "Now don't forget, Rachel, I need you to come straight home from school this afternoon."

"Why?" Rachel asked.

"Because I want you to watch Hannah while I go over to help at Esther and Rudy's. I mentioned this to you yesterday, remember?"

"Oh yeah; I guess so," Rachel mumbled around a spoonful of cereal.

After school, Jacob went to see Orlie, and Rachel, excited to see if Grandpa needed any help today, headed straight for the greenhouse. She was surprised to find the door locked, and even more surprised when she discovered a note tacked on the door that read "Gone fishing."

Rachel frowned. She'd been looking forward to smelling the greenhouse scents, watering some plants, and helping Grandpa with whatever he needed.

Maybe I should go fishing, too, she decided. *Mom said something about her taking Hannah and going over to Esther's place, so she shouldn't need me for anything. Even so, I guess I should leave a note.*

Rachel set her backpack on the ground, took out a pencil, and wrote on Grandpa's note: "Rachel went fishing, too." Then she ran to the shed where everyone's fishing gear was kept and took out her pole. After that, she dug several worms, put them in a can, and headed across the field toward their neighbor's pond.

When Rachel arrived at the pond, she expected to see Grandpa, but there was no sign of him. *Maybe he went fishing somewhere else,* she thought as she sat on a fallen log.

Rachel baited her hook, threw her line into the water, leaned her head back, and stared at the puffy clouds overhead. Today was a warm fall day—nothing like the cold weather they'd had lately.

She closed her eyes and let the sun warm her face as she imagined a nice big fish tugging on the end of her line.

Woof! Woof!

Rachel's eyes snapped open. She turned just in time to see Buddy running across the field toward her.

"Oh no," she moaned. "That overgrown mutt's gonna scare away all the fish!"

Woof! Woof! Whomp! Buddy bounded up to Rachel so hard that he knocked her off the log, and—*splash!*—she landed right in the water!

She came up sputtering and hollering, "You stupid mutt! I'll get you for this!"

Buddy took off like a flash, heading in the direction of home.

Rachel's teeth chattered as she clambered out of the chilly water. So much for an afternoon of fishing!

She gathered her things and started for the house. She'd only made it halfway there when she met Grandpa. "Where have you been, Rachel, and why are your clothes sopping wet?"

"I—I saw the n–note you left on the greenhouse d–door and decided to j–join you for some f–fishing." By now Rachel was shivering so badly that she could hardly talk.

"We need to get you back home and into some dry clothes," Grandpa said.

"O–okay." Rachel hurried along. "Where were you, Grandpa? I th–thought you were going f–fishing."

"I was. I went over to the Burkholders' place and fished in that big pond behind their pasture." Grandpa lifted a bucket full of fish. "I've got plenty of fish for us to have for supper tonight."

He stopped walking and looked at Rachel with a strange expression. "Say, if you're here with me, then who's up at the house watching Hannah?"

"W–what?" Rachel's lips were so cold she could barely move them.

"Your mamm was going over to Esther and Rudy's to help them and fix their supper. She wanted you to babysit Hannah, remember?"

"Oh no," Rachel groaned. "I th–thought that—" She clamped her mouth shut and started to run. "I'm gonna be in b–big trouble for this!"

When Rachel entered the house, she was greeted by

Mom, who didn't look happy. "Where have you been, Rachel, and why—" She stopped talking in midsentence and stared at Rachel's dress. "Is it raining outside?"

Rachel shook her head. "I—uh—fell in the p–pond when Buddy knocked me into the w–water."

Mom's mouth formed an O. "What were you doing at the pond when you were supposed to be here watching Hannah?"

"I forgot about w–watching Hannah, and I w–went fishing instead." Rachel hung her head, unable to look Mom in the eye. She'd messed up again, big-time!

"When are you going to grow up and stop being so forgetful?" Mom asked as she led Rachel into the kitchen.

"I—I don't know. I want to be g–grown up, but—" *Ah-choo! Ah-choo!* Rachel grabbed a napkin from the basket on the kitchen table and blew her nose. "I th–think I might be getting a cold."

"Let's get you out of those wet clothes and into a warm bath," Mom said, guiding Rachel down the hall toward the bathroom. "I need to get to Esther's right now, but I'll get some hot water going on the stove before I go. You can make yourself a cup of tea after your bath."

"Wh–what about Hannah? Who's g–going to watch her?" Rachel wanted to know.

"I'll watch Hannah," Grandpa said as he joined them in the hall. "I can keep an eye on her while I clean my fish."

"Danki, Dad," Mom said, giving Grandpa a quick hug. Then she turned to Rachel and said, "Into the bathroom with you now. We can talk about your poor memory after I get home."

When Rachel headed down the hall, she thought to herself, *I wish I'd never gone fishing!*

Chapter 9

Total Chaos

Rachel pressed her nose to the window and watched as Mom got into the buggy. Dad handed Hannah to her. Then he went around to the driver's side and got in, too.

It's not fair, Rachel thought as she watched the horse and buggy move down the driveway toward the road. *They should have let me go to town with them.*

She sniffed a couple of times. *They shouldn't make me stay home and clean house all day just because I forgot about watching Hannah the other day.*

"Es fenschder muss mer nass mache fer es sauwer mache [One has to wet the window in order to clean it]," Grandpa said when he entered the living room. "Looks to me like you're putting more smudges on the window with the end of your *naas* [nose]."

Rachel pulled back and stared at the window. Sure enough, there was a smudge where her nose had been. "I was just watching Pap's buggy head down the road and wishing I could have gone with them," she said with a sigh.

"You know why you can't go," Grandpa said.

She nodded and swallowed.

Grandpa put his hand on Rachel's shoulder. "It's never fun to be punished, but that's how we learn from our mistakes." He gave her shoulder a gentle squeeze. "Besides, a little hard work never hurt anyone."

"That's right," Henry said as he entered the room. "Those who work hard eat hearty!"

Rachel frowned. "I never said anything about eating."

Henry shrugged and headed for the door. "I'm going over to see my *aldi* [girlfriend], Nancy," he said, turning to look at Grandpa. "If Mom and Pap get back before I do, tell Mom I won't be home for supper."

"I'll be sure to tell her," Grandpa said with a nod.

Just then, Jacob entered the room with a wide smile.

"Why are you so happy?" Rachel asked as she squirted some liquid cleaner on the window.

"Orlie got a new scooter the other day, and I'm going over to ride on it."

"Well, have fun," Rachel mumbled under her breath. "I sure won't have any fun here."

"What was that?" Jacob asked as he moved toward the door.

"Oh nothing." Rachel wiped the window with the clean cloth and stood back to take a look. She was glad when Jacob went out the door without saying anything else to her.

"You missed a spot," Grandpa said, pointing to the left side of the window.

Psshheew! Psshheew! Rachel shot some more cleaner on the window and wiped the cloth over it again. Cleaning the house was boring. No fun at all on a Saturday morning!

Rachel moved away from the window and picked up the dust cloth she'd laid on the coffee table. "Work, work, work!" she grumbled as she wiped the cloth carelessly over the table. "That's all I'm good for anymore. I never get to do anything fun at all!"

"You're never too young or too old to be God's helper," Grandpa said as he lowered himself into his rocking chair.

"I'm not helping God, Grandpa," Rachel said. "I'm helping Mom."

Grandpa reached for his Bible on the small table by his chair. He opened it to a place that had been marked with a long white ribbon. "I mentioned this verse from the *Biewel* [Bible] to you several weeks ago, but I want to read it to you now, so please have a seat," he said, motioning to the sofa.

Rachel sat down with a weary sigh.

Grandpa picked up his reading glasses from the table and slipped them on. Then he began to read: " 'Whatever you do, work at it with all your heart, as working for the Lord, not for men.' " He smiled. "That's in Colossians 3:23."

Rachel sat still for several seconds, staring at the floor and letting the words Grandpa had read sink into her brain. Finally, she looked up at Grandpa and said, "I guess if the work I'm doing is for the Lord, then I'd better get busy."

Deciding this was a good chance to show that she was grown up, Rachel rose to her feet. Then she bent down and picked up the braided throw rug in front of Pap's favorite chair and hauled it outside to the porch.

Honk! Honk! Honk!

Rachel dropped the rug onto the porch and stepped into the yard to watch a flock of geese fly over the house in a perfect V formation. She wished she could fly away, too—at least for today.

When the geese disappeared, Rachel stepped back onto the porch, picked up the rug, and shook it well. She would do the best that she could so she would please the Lord.

When the rug was as clean as she could get it, Rachel went back in the house. She left the rug in the hallway then went to the utility room to get a broom.

When Rachel returned to the living room, she started sweeping hard. *Swish! Swish! Swish!* Bits of dust flew up and tickled her nose.

They must have tickled Grandpa's nose, too, for he soon began to sneeze. *Ah-choo! Ah-choo! Ah-choo!* Rachel kept count. Grandpa sneezed eight times in all.

She giggled and giggled and giggled some more.

Grandpa's sneezes sounded so funny, she couldn't help but giggle.

When Grandpa finally quit sneezing, he started laughing, too. "All that dust you were sweeping must have gotten to me, Rachel."

Rachel's smile faded. "I'm sorry about that, Grandpa. I didn't mean to make you sneeze."

"It's okay. The floor needed to be cleaned." Grandpa smiled. "Now I'm going to give you an object lesson."

"What's that?" Rachel asked.

He motioned to one corner of the room. "Look over there. Do you see any dust in the air?"

"No," Rachel said with a shake of her head.

Grandpa pointed toward the window. "Now look at the sunlight coming through the window glass. What do you see there?"

"I see a lot of dust particles where the sun's shining through."

Grandpa nodded. "It's just like God's Word."

Rachel tipped her head. "What do you mean?"

"When the light of His Word shines on us, it reveals the sin in our lives."

"Hmm. . ." Rachel stared at the dust particles as she thought about this.

"When we have sin in our lives, we have to sweep it away by asking God to forgive us."

Rachel nodded and a lump formed in her throat. She knew it was a sin whenever she disobeyed her parents or teacher. She bowed her head and closed her eyes. *Dear God, forgive my sins and help me to do better from now on.*

When she opened her eyes, she smiled at Grandpa and said, "I think I'll clean the kitchen and bathroom next. Then I'll head upstairs and clean my bedroom."

Grandpa smiled. "That's a good idea, Rachel. I'm pleased to see you working so hard today, and I'm sure that God is, too."

Rachel grabbed the broom and skipped out of the room.

By noon, Rachel was hot, tired, and hungry. She'd just finished scrubbing the bathroom floor, and her back had begun to ache. She straightened up and rubbed at the kinks in her back. She was so tired of cleaning. She just wanted to go upstairs, lie down on her bed, and read a good book.

Her stomach rumbled noisily, reminding her that she needed to prepare lunch for Grandpa and herself. Grandpa was probably feeling hungry, too.

"I'm going into the kitchen to fix us something to eat," she called as she passed the living room on her way to the kitchen.

No response.

Rachel poked her head into the living room. Grandpa's head leaned against the back of the rocking chair. His eyes were closed, and his mouth hung slightly open. Several loud snores escaped his lips.

Rachel figured he would probably sleep for a while, so she headed upstairs to rest a few minutes before starting lunch. After she ate, she would clean her room.

When she entered her bedroom, she froze. Jacob's big shaggy mutt was on her bed, sitting in the middle of her rumpled sheets. She'd forgotten to make her bed this morning.

"I have no idea how you got in here," she said, shaking her finger at Buddy, "but you're not taking a nap on my *bett* [bed]!"

She waved her hands, but Buddy didn't budge. He just sat staring at Rachel as if to say, *I'm staying here, and you can't make me move.*

Rachel gritted her teeth. "Get off my bett, you hairy beast!" She hoped if she let him know she meant business, he might obey her for a change.

Woof! Woof! Buddy lunged for Rachel and licked her arm with his big wet tongue. Then he slid off the bed, knocking the quilt on the floor and pulling the sheets, which had somehow gotten wrapped around his body.

Rachel screamed and grabbed one end of the sheet as Buddy tore out of the room. She hung on for dear life as the troublesome mutt ran down the stairs, dragging her and the sheet behind him.

"Absatz! Stop, right now!" Rachel hollered. "You're making it hard for me to act grown up!"

Thump! Thump! Thump! Rachel thumped and

bumped her way down the stairs, still clinging to the sheet.

When Buddy reached the bottom of the stairs, he plodded into the living room, thumping and bumping everything in sight. Then he raced into the kitchen, barking and growling all the way!

Thud! One of the chairs at the table fell over. *Thunk! Thunk!* Buddy slammed into the table, knocking the bowl of sugar over and sending the napkins sailing through the air.

"Bad dog!" Rachel hollered. "Stop where you are, right now!"

Woof! Woof! Buddy tore out of the kitchen and down the hall, pulling Rachel along on her backside.

When they got to the end of the hall, he turned and raced back again.

"Let go of my sheet, you crazy critter!" Rachel hollered.

"What's all this ruckus about?" Grandpa asked, stepping out of the living room.

Woof! Woof! Buddy whipped past Grandpa at lightning speed. Rachel hung on for all she was worth. No flea-bitten mutt was going to get the best of her! She would get that sheet back no matter what!

"*Was in der welt* [What in all the world]?" Mom asked as she entered the house. Pap was right behind her, holding Hannah.

Woof! Woof! Buddy raced out the open door, dragging Rachel behind him. *Rip!*—the sheet came loose from Buddy's body, leaving a big tear in one end.

Rachel gasped as she fell on the ground. "No! No! No! You are nothing but a big bag of trouble, Buddy!"

Buddy slunk off toward his doghouse with his tail between his legs.

"Out of sight, out of mind," Rachel mumbled as she picked herself up and brushed off her dress.

Mom rushed out of the house, stepped up to Rachel, and frowned. "Rachel Yoder, I left you home to clean the house. I sure didn't expect to come home and find you playing with Jacob's dog!"

Rachel shook her head. "I wasn't playing with Buddy. That big hairy beast got up on my bed, and then—"

"You know you're not allowed to have any pets on your bed," Mom said. "How many times have I told you that?"

Rachel's chin trembled as she struggled not to cry. "Many times, but—"

"You're never going to grow up if you don't learn to be more responsible," Pap said when he joined them on the lawn. "You need to pay closer attention to what you're doing."

Determined not to give in to her tears, Rachel quickly explained everything that had happened. "If anything's my fault, it's probably that I left the door open for too long when I was outside shaking the rug."

"She's right, Miriam," Grandpa said, stepping

outside. "Rachel worked real hard today. I'm sure she didn't let Jacob's *hund* [dog] in the house on purpose."

Rachel nodded. "No, I sure didn't. I just wanted to do a good job of cleaning the house."

Mom looked as if she might say something more on the subject. Instead, she patted Rachel's shoulder and said, "We left town earlier than we'd planned and haven't eaten yet. Why don't the two of us go into the house and see about making some lunch?"

Rachel nodded and followed Mom inside. This had not been a good day. It had been a day of total chaos! She hoped tomorrow would be better.

Chapter 10

Rachel's Pie

Two whole weeks had passed since Rachel had gone fishing when she was supposed to watch Hannah for Mom. She was glad her two weeks of not going anywhere and doing extra chores were finally over. Since today was Saturday and there was no school, Rachel looked forward to doing something fun. She'd wanted to help in the greenhouse this morning, but last night Grandpa had said he didn't have anything for her to do there right now.

Rachel put both elbows on the kitchen counter as she stared out the window.

Maybe I'll go to the barn and see if my cats are there, she thought. *Or I could write Mary a letter on the stationery I made with pressed flowers. Jah, that's what I'll do. She'd probably like to hear about my day of total chaos and how Buddy ruined the sheet on my bed.*

As Rachel continued to gaze out the window, she reached across the cupboard to grab a pen from the basket of writing supplies. *Squish!* She felt something gooey and sticky on her elbow.

"Ach no!" Rachel groaned. "Now look what I've done!" She had put her elbow in the apple pie Mom had made before she'd left for Esther's. At least this time Mom had taken Hannah with her, which meant Rachel had plenty of time to make a new pie before Mom got home.

It can't be that hard to bake another pie, she thought. *I've helped Mom bake some pies before. I'll try to remember what Mom has taught me to do, but if I get stuck, I can always find her recipe book to help me.*

Rachel went to the sink and washed her elbow. Then she scurried to the refrigerator to get more apples but discovered that there were none. *Guess I'll take this ruined pie out to Buddy and pick some more apples from the tree,* Rachel decided. She slipped into her jacket, picked up the pie, and hurried out the door.

Buddy was lying on the roof of his doghouse with his eyes closed and his big old nose stuck between his paws. As soon as Rachel stepped into his dog run, his eyes popped open and he jumped off the roof. *Woof! Woof!* Buddy headed straight for Rachel!

Quickly, she dumped the pie into Buddy's dish and dashed for the gate. Once she was safely outside the door, she stood at the fence and watched Buddy dive into the pie as if it were his last meal.

"Greedy glutton," Rachel said, shaking her head.

"All you do is eat, sleep, and cause a lot of trouble."

Slurp! Slurp! Buddy licked his dog dish clean; then he bounded over to the fence to greet Rachel. *Woof! Woof!*

"Go back to your doghouse and take a nap!" Rachel whirled around and hurried toward the apple tree on the side of the house.

When she got to the tree, she looked up and gasped. It was bare! There wasn't one single apple on any of the branches. Then she remembered that Pap had used the rest of the apples to make a batch of apple cider.

"I need to think," Rachel said out loud. "Do we have any more apple trees in our yard?"

She glanced around. She saw a maple tree, an oak tree, and a walnut tree, but no more apple trees.

Rachel wandered around back and spotted a tree in the pasture. It looked like it had a bunch of red apples growing on it, but they seemed kind of small.

Rachel opened the pasture gate and made sure to shut it. Then she hurried until she came to the tree. Looking up, she could see that it was full of apples! They were a lot smaller than most—in fact, some were barely larger than cherries—but they looked nice and red. She was sure they would work just fine for an apple pie.

Rachel was tempted to climb the tree and pick the apples, but she thought about the broken arm she'd ended up with when she'd climbed a tree to rescue Cuddles.

"I need a ladder and a bucket," she said, racing back across the pasture. She opened the gate and shut it again then headed for the barn. She found a bucket near the door and a small ladder in one corner of the barn. She put the handle of the bucket over her arm and grunted when she tried to pick up the ladder. It was too heavy to carry.

Think, Rachel. Think.

She grabbed the ladder and dragged it out of the barn, across the grass, and into the pasture. She continued to drag it until it was under the apple tree; then she stepped carefully onto the first rung and then another, keeping the bucket over her arm. She reached overhead and picked an apple. *Plunk!* She dropped it into the bucket and reached for a second apple and then a third. *Plunk! Plunk!*

Rachel kept picking until she'd picked sixteen apples. They were sure little, but she figured sixteen small apples would equal eight larger apples.

She climbed down the ladder and started back across the field. She was almost to the gate when old Tom plodded up and nudged her arm with his nose. *Neigh! Neigh!*

Rachel giggled. "I bet I know what you want, boy." She set the bucket on the ground and offered Tom one of the apples.

He took one bite, shook his head a couple of times, and dropped the apple to the ground.

"Well, aren't you the finicky one this morning?" Rachel picked up the apple and held it out to Tom.

Neigh! Neigh! The old horse shook his head and trotted away.

"Guess maybe you've eaten too much hay, and now you're not hungry." Rachel bent down, picked up the bucket, and headed back to the tree. She climbed the ladder again and picked another apple.

When she climbed down, she discovered Snowball sitting in the bucket on top of the apples. She laughed and picked up the kitten.

"You silly bussli," Rachel said, petting Snowball's furry head. "You can't stay in this bucket; I have a pie to bake." She placed Snowball on the ground and hurried out of the pasture. She would put the ladder away after she'd finished baking the pie.

As soon as Rachel entered the kitchen, she turned on the oven to 425 degrees. Then she poured the bucket of apples into the sink and washed them thoroughly. After that, she cut each apple into slices and put all the slices into a bowl with a bit of lemon juice to keep them from turning brown.

Next, she made the piecrust. After that, she took out Mom's recipe book and made the filling according to the directions. Then she mixed it with the apples she'd cut up and poured everything into the crust.

Finally, she placed the pie in the oven, shut the door, and set the timer for fifty minutes.

"Now I think I'll make some bookmarks using the pressed flowers I have in my room," Rachel said. She hurried out of the kitchen and was halfway up the stairs when she remembered that she'd forgotten to take the ladder back to the barn.

"Guess I'd better do it now," she mumbled. "If I don't, I might forget."

Rachel raced out of the house and headed straight for the pasture. The ladder seemed even heavier as she dragged it back to the barn.

By the time Rachel returned to the house, she was tired. *Guess I can make the bookmarks some other time,* she decided.

Rachel flopped into a chair and rested her head on the table. She felt so drowsy.

Ding! Ding! Ding! Rachel's eyes popped open, and she jumped out of her chair. "The pie! I've gotta check on the pie!"

She opened the oven door and stuck a knife into the pie. The apples seemed tender, so she grabbed a pot holder, removed the pie, and placed it on a cooling rack on the counter.

"It looks pretty good," Rachel said, feeling rather pleased with herself. Juice oozed through the piecrust, begging her to taste it, but she summoned her willpower. She needed to wait until it was time to serve the pie for dessert tonight, and she couldn't let on that this wasn't the pie Mom had baked.

Rachel yawned and stretched her arms over her head. Doing grown-up things sure took a lot of work.

"I smell somethin' good," Jacob said as he entered the kitchen through the back door. "What's for lunch?"

"It's an apple pie you smell, and I don't know what's for lunch yet, because I've been busy with other things," Rachel said.

"Are you going to start lunch soon?" he asked.

"I guess so."

"Well, do more than guess so. Grandpa will be in from the greenhouse soon, and he'll be hungry." Jacob marched across the room, took the cookie jar down from the cupboard, and grabbed four peanut butter cookies. Then he turned to Rachel and said, "I'll be outside with Buddy. Call me when lunch is ready."

"You could at least offer to help," Rachel mumbled when the door banged shut behind Jacob. She glanced out the window and saw him heading for Buddy's dog run. When Jacob opened the gate, Buddy ran out, jumped up, and licked Jacob's face. Jacob pushed Buddy down and held out a cookie. Buddy opened his mouth and took a bite; then Jacob popped the rest of the cookie into his own mouth.

Rachel wrinkled her nose. "Yuk! Boys can be so gross. I'd never let that bad-breathed mutt touch my cookie with his big dirty mouth!"

She turned toward the refrigerator to find something for lunch.

That evening, Esther, Rudy, and their baby came for supper. Little Ben still had no hair, but at least his face wasn't so red and wrinkly anymore. Rachel figured that after a few more weeks, he might look almost as cute as Hannah.

"Who's ready for dessert?" Mom asked after the family members had finished their chicken and dumplings.

"I'm pretty full," Rudy said, "but I might have room for a little more. What are we having?"

"I baked an apple pie this morning before I came over to your place," Mom said. She pushed back her chair and started to get up, but Rachel jumped up first.

"I can serve the pie," Rachel said. "Why don't you stay at the table and visit?"

"Are you sure?" Mom peered at Rachel over the top of her glasses. She looked as though she thought Rachel couldn't serve the pie by herself.

"I'm very sure." Rachel hurried across the room and took a knife and pie server from the drawer. Then she pulled back the dish towel covering the pie and cut the pie into eight even pieces. Next, she took eight plates down from the cupboard.

"You're certainly getting tall, Rachel," Esther commented. "You didn't have to reach very far at all to get those plates."

Rachel smiled and stretched herself so she would appear even taller. "I think I've grown almost an inch this week."

"I think you might have at that," Pap said with a chuckle and a twinkle in his eyes. "Jah, Rachel's growing like a weed."

Rachel grinned as she lifted the pieces of pie out of the pan and placed them carefully on the plates. After she'd given everyone some pie, she took a seat at the table.

"Mmm. . .this sure looks good." Rudy took a big bite, and a strange expression came over his face. He grabbed his cup of coffee and quickly swallowed some.

Jacob bit into his piece of pie. "*Agggh*. . . this pie's baremlich!" He jumped out of his chair, rushed over to the garbage, and spit out the pie. Then he grabbed a glass from the cupboard, turned on the water at the sink, and took a big drink.

Mom took a bite of pie and made a horrible face. "This can't be the same pie I made today," she said with a shake of her head. "Something is definitely wrong with this pie."

Rachel slumped in her seat as her face turned warm. She'd blown it again, and she figured she'd better confess right away.

"I baked the pie," she admitted.

Mom's mouth dropped open. "What?"

Rachel quickly explained how she'd put her elbow in Mom's pie and then went out to the pasture and picked some apples so she could make another pie.

"You picked apples from a tree in the pasture?" Pap asked.

Rachel nodded. "They were kind of small, so I had to use sixteen instead of eight."

Pap stared at the piece of pie on his plate; then he looked back at Rachel. "Those apples you picked from the pasture are crab apples, Rachel. They're sour and tart and not meant for baking pies."

"Oh no!" Rachel cried. "How could I have made such a mistake? I'm just a big *dummkopp* [dunce]."

"Now, Rachel, don't be so hard on yourself. Everyone makes mistakes sometimes." Mom patted Rachel's arm. "If you'd told me what happened to my pie as soon as I got home from Esther's, I'd have helped you bake another pie."

"But there were no more apples on the tree in our yard," Rachel said.

"We could have baked some other kind."

"Trouble, trouble, trouble!" Rachel moaned. "My life's always full of trouble!"

"Trouble's like a bubble," Grandpa said. "It soon pops and moves away. Why, I'll bet by tomorrow you'll have forgotten all about the pie you made today."

Rachel sniffed, trying to hold back her tears. "But now we have no dessert."

"I think I can take care of that." Pap rose from his chair. "I'll make a big batch of popcorn, and we'll have some warm apple cider to go with it."

"You didn't make it with crab apples, I hope," said Henry.

Pap shook his head. "Although I've heard that adding a few crab apples to a batch of cider can make the flavor a bit more interesting."

Rachel wrinkled her nose. "I think I'd prefer my cider and pie without any crab apples, thank you very much."

Everyone laughed, even Rachel. She was glad that no one in the family seemed to be mad about the pie she'd ruined.

My day might have started out on a wrong note, she thought, *but it turned out good in the end, and that's all that counts.*

Chapter 11

Bad Advice

*T*ap! *Tap! Tap!* "Rachel, are you in there?"

Rachel sighed. She'd just sat on the floor to look at some of the flowers she had pressed, and she didn't want to be disturbed.

"What do you want, Jacob?" she called through her closed door.

"I need to talk to you."

"About what?"

Tap! Tap! Tap! "Can I come in?"

Rachel sighed again. "I suppose."

The door opened, and Jacob stepped into Rachel's room. He raked his fingers through the sides of his hair. "I was wondering if you'd do me a favor."

"What favor?" she asked.

"I need a haircut."

Rachel's eyebrows shot up. "You want me to cut your hair?"

He gave a quick nod.

Rachel shook her head really hard. "I've never cut anyone's hair before. That's Mom's job."

"But Mom's not here. She's been busy helping Esther, and she never has time to cut my hair."

Rachel sat there shaking her head.

Jacob came over and took a seat beside her on the floor. "Come on, Rachel; you can do it. I know you can."

"I—I don't think so. I might mess it up."

"I'm sure you won't. You've seen Mom do it many times. Please, Rachel, it can't be that hard."

"I don't know—"

Jacob touched her arm. "It's just a simple cut. Maybe you could put a bowl on my head and cut around it."

Rachel snickered. "Jah, right, Jacob. Now that would really be *dumm* [dumb]."

He chuckled. "Maybe so, but I'm sure if you just take your time, you can cut my hair with no trouble at all."

"I have trouble with almost everything these days," Rachel said. "I think you should wait until Mom has time to cut your hair."

"She may never have the time," Jacob argued. "Between taking care of Hannah, helping Esther with Ben, and keeping things going around here, she's busier than a bird building a nest."

Rachel couldn't argue with that. Mom was busier than ever these days, and Rachel had been given a lot more chores to do since Hannah came along.

Jacob shook Rachel's arm. "Will you cut my hair or not?"

"No."

"I'll pay you a quarter."

"That's not enough."

"How about fifty cents?"

"Make it a dollar and I'll do it."

Jacob frowned. "You drive a hard bargain, Rachel. Are you sure you won't do it for less?"

She folded her arms and shook her head.

"Okay, I'll pay you one dollar for cutting my hair." Jacob jumped up. "I'll get the scissors and meet you in the kitchen," he called as he raced out the door.

Rachel groaned and rose to her feet. "I sure hope I don't mess up Jacob's hair."

When Rachel entered the kitchen a few minutes later, she found Jacob sitting in a chair in the middle of the room. A pair of scissors and a comb lay on the counter. He smiled up at her. "Ready?"

"Ready as I'll ever be, I guess." Rachel picked up the comb and ran it through the sides of Jacob's hair.

"What are you doing? You're supposed to be cutting my hair, not combing it," he grumbled.

"I know, but I need to make sure all the ends are straight before I begin." Truthfully, that was only part of the reason Rachel had combed Jacob's hair. She was really stalling for time. "I—uh—need to clean my glasses so I can see clearly what I'm doing."

"Your glasses don't look dirty to me." Jacob grunted.

"Just hurry up and get this done. I don't have all day!"

Rachel gritted her teeth and picked up the scissors. It would serve Jacob right if she cut all his hair off and he ended up bald like baby Ben. *Snip! Snip!* She cut one side, and then she moved to the other. *Snip! Snip!*

"Oops!"

"Oops, what?" Jacob's forehead wrinkled. "What'd you do to my hair, Rachel?"

"Uh—the left side looks a little shorter than the right side."

Jacob raced to the mirror hanging on the wall. "It's not so bad," he said, pulling his fingers through the left side of his hair. "All you need to do is cut a little more hair off the right side of my head and everything will be fine."

Rachel wasn't so sure about that, but she nodded and said, "Take a seat."

Jacob plunked down in his chair and turned his head so the right side was facing Rachel.

She picked up the scissors. *Snip! Snip!*

"Oh, oh."

Jacob's eyes widened. " 'Oh, oh,' what, Rachel?"

"Now the right side looks shorter."

"Then take a little more off the left side." Jacob glanced at the clock on the wall. "And hurry up. I don't want to be sitting here all day."

Rachel studied the left side of Jacob's hair; then she studied the right side. She snipped a little here and a little there. Finally, she smiled and said, "I think both sides are even now."

"What about the back? You haven't cut any of that yet," Jacob said.

Rachel moved behind Jacob and lifted the scissors. *Snip! Snip! Snip!*

"'Oh no!" she groaned.

"'Oh no,' what?" Jacob frowned. "What'd you do to my hair, Rachel?"

Rachel shifted from one foot to the other. "Well, I— uh—"

"Just say it, Rachel! Tell me what you did!"

Rachel's chin quivered, and her eyes filled with tears. "Th–there's a chunk of hair missing, and—and it looks real bad."

Jacob touched the back of his head and winced. "Can't you fix it?"

She shook her head. "Not unless you want me to glue it back on."

"Very funny, Rachel." He scowled at her. "Wait until Mom sees what you've done!"

Rachel gulped, wondering what kind of punishment Mom would dish out for this.

"This is what I get for listening to you," she said, pointing at Jacob. "You begged me to cut your hair, and you said it wouldn't be hard." She slowly shook her head. "You gave me some very bad advice!"

Jacob grunted. "You're the one who messed up my

hair, so don't blame me. You should have held the scissors steadier and paid closer attention to what you were doing."

Rachel dropped the scissors on the counter and held out her hand. "Where's my money?"

"What money?"

"The money you said you'd pay me for cutting your hair."

Jacob pulled his fingers through the back of his hair and grunted. "You expect me to pay you for messing up my hair?"

Rachel nodded. "You said you would." She figured if she got paid, it might make her feel a little better. After Mom came home and looked at Jacob's hair, Rachel knew she wouldn't feel good about anything.

Jacob marched across the room to the mirror. He turned his head from side to side; then his face got red.

"I can't see what you did to the back of my head," he said, glaring at Rachel, "but I can see what you did to the sides, and they look baremlich!" He grabbed his straw hat from the wall peg and pushed it on his head. "I'll never be able to take my hat off again!"

"Sure you will. . .as soon as your hair grows out." Rachel held out her hand. "Are you going to pay me or not?"

"No, I'm definitely not!"

"You'd better keep your promise, Jacob Yoder." By now, Rachel's patience had ended. She hadn't wanted to cut Jacob's hair in the first place, but he'd insisted. She wished she hadn't let him talk her into it. What a huge mistake.

"I won't pay you one single cent!" Jacob shouted.

"What's all the yelling about?" Mom asked as she came through the back door with Hannah. "I could hear you two hollering clear out by the buggy shed."

Mom halted, and her mouth dropped open. "Ach, Jacob! What happened to your hair?"

Jacob pointed at Rachel. "She cut it, and now it's ruined!"

Rachel gulped. How could she explain her way out of this? She couldn't fix the mistake she'd made on Jacob's hair, and she sure couldn't hide it, either. "*Er hot mich verschwetzt* [He talked me into it]," she said, pointing at Jacob.

Mom squinted at Jacob as she shifted Hannah to her other arm. "You asked Rachel to cut your hair?"

Jacob's face turned red as he nodded slowly.

"Why'd you do that, Jacob? Why didn't you ask me to cut your hair?" Mom questioned.

"I did ask, but you always said you were too busy." Jacob pointed to his hair. "I didn't think it'd be that hard to cut, so I asked Rachel to do it."

"Actually, he begged me to cut it," Rachel said. "He even promised to give me a dollar if I cut it, but now he won't pay what he owes."

Mom's eyebrows furrowed as she looked at Jacob.

"I'm not happy that you asked Rachel to cut your hair. You should have waited until I had the time."

Jacob hung his head. "I know that now."

"But since you did ask her, and since you promised to pay her for doing it, then you need to make good on that promise." Mom tipped Jacob's chin up so he was looking at her. "I should make you go around with your hair like that until it grows out."

Jacob's eyes got real huge. "Aw, Mom, please, can't you do something to make me look better?"

"I suppose I can try to even it up some." Mom handed the baby to Rachel. "Hannah has a dirty windel, so I'd like you to change it while I trim Jacob's hair."

Rachel wrinkled her nose. "Eww. . .do I have to?"

Mom nodded. "You should be glad I'm not punishing you for cutting your bruder's hair."

"Changing a dirty windel is punishment to me," Rachel mumbled as she carried Hannah out of the room.

On Saturday morning that week, Rachel was headed outside to feed her cats when a blond head appeared around the corner of the barn. It was her English friend Sherry.

"Hi, Rachel," Sherry said. "I came over to see if you could play."

Rachel smiled and lifted the sack of cat food in her hands. "As soon as I feed my cats, I'll be free for the rest of the day."

"Do you need to check with your folks first and see if they want you to do something else?" Sherry asked.

Rachel shook her head. "Mom took Hannah over to my sister Esther's house awhile ago, and she'll probably be gone for several hours. Pap, Henry, and Jacob are working in the fields, so they won't need me."

"What about your grandpa? Will he need your help in the greenhouse?"

Rachel shook her head again. "I don't think so. He hasn't had much for me to do there lately."

"That's too bad. I know how much you like working in the greenhouse," Sherry said.

"I do," Rachel agreed, "but I've been busy with schoolwork and other things."

"I know what you mean. It seems like the older I get, the more homework I have." Sherry shrugged. "Guess it's all part of growing up."

"I suppose so." Rachel started walking for the barn. After the chickens had made a mess on the back porch and had eaten the cats' food, Mom had made Rachel keep the cats' dishes in the barn. She guessed that made sense since Snowball and Cuddles liked to play and sleep in the barn.

"You can help me feed the cats if you want to," Rachel said to Sherry. "When we're done we can think of something fun to do."

"Sounds like a plan." Sherry ran ahead of Rachel and opened the barn door.

When they stepped inside, Cuddles and Snowball darted out from behind a bale of hay and ran toward Rachel.

"Are you hungry?" she asked, pouring food into their bowls.

Meow! Cuddles stuck her head in the dish and started crunching away.

Meow! Snowball did the same.

Sherry snickered. "They act like they haven't been fed in days."

"They've been fed all right." Rachel shrugged. "They always act desperate, and Snowball is a regular sau."

"What's a sau?" Sherry asked.

"It means 'pig.'" Rachel motioned to the cats' dishes. "See what I mean? They've eaten almost all the food I put in."

Sherry laughed. "My dog Bundles eats like a sau, too."

Rachel moved toward the door. "Let's leave these two alone to finish their meal while we find something fun to do."

When they stepped outside, Sherry pointed to the horse and buggy tied to the hitching rail near the barn. "Whose rig is that?" she asked.

"It belongs to my oldest brother, Henry," Rachel said. "He was planning to run to town for some supplies, but Pap asked him to go to the fields to help with something first."

"You know," said Sherry as she continued to stare

at the buggy, "I've always wondered what it'd be like to ride in one of those."

Rachel shrugged. "It's nothing special to me, but I've ridden in buggies since I was a baby."

"I'd sure like to take a ride in that buggy," Sherry said wistfully. "Do you think I can?"

Rachel shook her head. "I don't think so. When Henry gets back from helping Pap, he'll be heading for town to run his errands, and I'm sure he won't have time to give you a buggy ride."

"It's not fair," Sherry said. "You got to ride in my brother's car when we went to Hershey Park this summer. I'd really like a ride in that buggy."

"Like I said, it's not possible because—"

"You could give me a ride," Sherry said. "If your brother went to help in the fields, it might be quite awhile before he gets back."

Rachel shook her head vigorously. "No! I've never driven a buggy before."

"Never?"

"Nope."

"But I thought Amish kids learned how to drive a horse and buggy when they were young. That's what my brother, Dave, told me he heard someone say."

"Well, I did sort of drive the buggy once," Rachel said. "It was last summer, and I was sitting on my dad's lap, and he let me hold the reins. I'm not sure I could do it alone though."

"You'll never know until you try." Sherry touched Rachel's arm. "Would you do it as a favor to me?"

"I—I don't know. . . ."

"Please, Rachel. I know you can do it, and we wouldn't have to go very far. . .just to the end of your driveway and back."

Rachel thought about that. Would it be okay to do as Sherry suggested? They wouldn't go far, and she was pretty sure she could make the horse do what she wanted him to.

"Okay," Rachel said. "I'll take you for a ride down our driveway and back."

"Yeah!" Sherry clapped her hands and jumped up and down. "I can hardly wait!" She tossed her sweater into the buggy and scrambled into the passenger's side on the left.

Rachel untied the horse, backed him away from the hitching rail, and climbed into the buggy on the right side, where the driver was supposed to sit. Then she gathered the reins and clucked to the horse, the way she'd seen Pap do many times.

Clip-clop. Clip-clop. The horse plodded along the driveway. *This is easy,* Rachel thought. *It's actually kind of fun.*

"Can't you make him go faster?" Sherry asked, nudging Rachel's arm.

Rachel snapped the reins, and the horse picked up speed.

"Let's go out on the road," Sherry said.

Rachel shook her head. "No! That could be dangerous."

"It won't hurt anything, Rachel," Sherry said. "You're doing a good job driving the buggy, and we don't have to go very far."

Rachel bit her lower lip. If she could drive the buggy out on the road by herself, she would prove she was grown up.

"Okay, here we go." Rachel guided the horse onto the road and smiled when he did as she directed.

Sherry nudged Rachel's arm again and giggled. "This is sure fun, isn't it?"

Rachel nodded and tried to concentrate on what she was doing.

They'd only gone a short distance when the buggy hit a rut in the road. Sherry's sweater slid off the seat and landed on the floor by Rachel's feet. Rachel leaned to pick it up, and then—*Beep! Beep!*—a car honked its horn as it sped past.

Neigh! Neigh! The horse jerked its head and pulled the buggy straight into a ditch!

Rachel gasped. "Oh no, we're stuck!" She looked over at Sherry. "What are we going to do?"

Chapter 12

A New Opportunity

Sherry clutched Rachel's arm. "Can you get the horse to pull us out of here?"

Rachel leaned out the side opening of the buggy and groaned. "I don't think we'll be going anywhere in this buggy."

"Why not?"

"Looks like the right front wheel is broken."

"Oh great!" Sherry frowned. "Now what are we going to do?"

"We'd better get out and walk back home to get help." Rachel didn't really want to go ask for help. She knew she'd be in trouble for taking the buggy out, but she had no other choice. She wished she hadn't taken Sherry's advice and driven the buggy. She knew now that it had been a really dumb thing to do.

Rachel and Sherry climbed out of the buggy, and Rachel unhitched the horse.

"What are you doing?" Sherry asked.

"I'm taking the horse with us," Rachel said. "We can't leave him here by himself."

"Oh, okay."

As Rachel turned the horse around and started walking back toward the house, a feeling of dread filled her. She'd really blown it when she'd listened to Sherry's bad advice. She hated to think of the trouble she'd be in, but she couldn't undo what had been done.

The closer Rachel got to home, the more nervous she became. By the time the girls entered the yard, her hands were so sweaty she could barely hang on to the horse's reins.

"Where have you been, Rachel, and what are you doing with that horse?" Pap asked as he, Henry, and Jacob came running out of the barn.

With a shaky voice, Rachel explained what had happened. She ended it by saying, "I'm very sorry, Pap. I know what I did was wrong."

"You're right about that." Pap's face was red, and a muscle on the side of his neck quivered like a bowl of jelly.

"You don't even know how to drive a horse and buggy," Jacob said. "It was sure a dumm thing to do!"

Tears welled in Rachel's eyes. She didn't need her brother's reminder that what she'd done was dumb.

"It was my fault," Sherry spoke up. "I'm the one who wanted to take the buggy ride." She slipped her arm around Rachel's waist. "I talked her into driving the buggy and said I knew she could do it."

Pap looked at Sherry and slowly shook his head. "Asking Rachel to give you a ride was very bad advice." Then he turned to Rachel and said, "You shouldn't have listened to your friend, but I'm glad no one was hurt."

Rachel swallowed the lump in her throat. "I'm glad of that, too."

"The boys and I will see about getting the buggy home now. We'll talk about your punishment when we get back, Rachel." He looked at Sherry again. "You'd better head for home, because Rachel's done playing for the day."

Sherry nodded and hugged Rachel. "I'll see you some other time, Rachel."

"Good-bye, Sherry," Rachel mumbled.

As Rachel headed for the house, she determined that she'd never listen to anyone's bad advice again. From now on she'd try to remember to think things through.

Rachel had just finished making some bologna and cheese sandwiches when Pap came into the house.

"Did you fix the buggy wheel?" Rachel asked.

Pap shook his head. "Had to replace it with a new one." He plunked his hat on the counter and turned to Rachel. "I know that you realize you did wrong by taking the horse and buggy out by yourself. However, you need to be punished so you'll remember not to do such a foolish thing again."

She dropped her gaze to the floor. "Are you gonna give me a bletsching?"

"No, Rachel, but you will have to save your money and pay me back for the buggy wheel I just bought from Audra Burkholder's daed." Pap lifted her chin. "And you won't be allowed to go anywhere but church and school for the next two weeks."

Rachel nodded slowly. She wondered if she would ever grow up and quit doing things that got her into trouble. When she was old and gray, she might still be trying to stay out of trouble.

Pap rested his bearded chin on top of Rachel's head and gave her back a couple of pats. "Now finish getting lunch on the table. The boys and Grandpa will be in soon, and I'm sure they'll want to eat."

"What about Mom?" Rachel asked. "Won't she be coming home for lunch?"

"I don't think so," Pap said. "She told me before she left this morning that she planned to stay at Esther's for most of the day."

"Oh, okay." Rachel reached into the cupboard, took out five plates and five glasses, and placed them on the table. Then she opened a bag of potato chips and put it on the table, along with a jar of dill pickles. She'd just started pouring apple cider into one of the glasses when Grandpa, Jacob, and Henry came into the kitchen.

"What's to eat?" Jacob asked. "I'm hungry as a mule."

"Rachel made some sandwiches." Pap pointed to the sink. "After you wash your hands, we can sit at the table."

The menfolk took turns washing at the sink while Rachel poured the apple cider.

They'd just sat down when the back door flew open and Rudy stepped into the kitchen, holding Hannah and looking quite upset. "Levi," he said to Pap, "your *fraa* [wife] tumbled down our back porch steps, and I'm pretty sure her leg is broken."

Rachel gasped. Henry and Jacob's eyes widened. Pap and Grandpa jumped out of their seats.

"I've already called for help," Rudy said, "and an ambulance is on its way. I came to tell you what had happened so you could call someone for a ride to the hospital."

Pap grabbed his hat and started across the room. "I'll do that right away."

"I'm coming with you," Grandpa said as he followed Pap out the door.

Rudy came over to Rachel and put Hannah in her lap. "I could have left her with Esther, but I figured she's got enough on her hands looking after Ben."

Rachel nodded and stroked her baby sister's soft cheek. "I can watch Hannah. I've done it before, and I'm sure we'll get along okay."

Rudy hesitated a minute; then he rushed out the door.

Rachel looked at Jacob and Henry, hoping one of them would volunteer to help her look after Hannah. They just sat there, shaking their heads and wearing worried expressions.

"We need to ask God to be with Mom and help her to be okay," Rachel said.

Henry nodded. "That's all we can do right now, and praying for Mom's a good thing."

Rachel closed her eyes and bowed her head. *Dear God,* she silently prayed, *Please be with my mamm, and help her to be okay and not be afraid.*

It was almost time to start supper when Pap and Grandpa brought Mom home from the hospital, wearing her left leg in a cast. Mom hobbled in the door using a pair of crutches and sat on the living room sofa.

Rachel rushed over to Mom and sat down beside her. "Is your leg broken? Does it hurt very much? Will you be okay?"

Mom held up her hand and smiled. "Slow down, Rachel. I can only answer one question at a time."

"Sorry, Mom, but I've been so worried about you."

"We all have been," said Henry as he took a seat on the other side of Mom.

"I broke my leg." Mom motioned to her cast. "I'll have to wear this for six weeks, but I'll be fine." She glanced over at Hannah's empty cradle. "Where's the boppli?"

"She's in her crib taking a nap," Rachel said. She

reached over and grabbed Mom's hand. "I know you won't be able to do much for the next several weeks, but I promise to take over your chores, even if I have to stay home from school."

"That won't be necessary," Pap said from where he stood across the room. "I'll see if Grandma Yoder can come over during the day so you'll only be responsible for watching Hannah before and after school."

"And I'll watch her on the weekends," Rachel said.

Pap nodded. "Right."

Rachel smiled. She felt bad about Mom breaking her leg, but she saw this as a new opportunity to show her family that she was growing up. She hoped God would give her the wisdom to make good decisions and help her stay focused on whatever jobs she was required to do.

That evening, after supper was over and Rachel had done the dishes, she sat at the kitchen table with some heavy notebook paper, pens, glue, and several of her most colorful pressed flowers.

"What are you doing?" Grandpa asked after he'd poured himself a glass of milk and taken a seat across from Rachel.

"I'm making Mom a get-well card," Rachel said. "I'm going to take it in the living room to her as soon as I'm done."

Grandpa smiled. "I'm sure she'll appreciate the card."

Rachel yawned. "I hope I can get it done before I fall asleep. It's been a long day."

"Would you like me to finish it for you?" Grandpa asked.

She shook her head. "If I'm going to give Mom the card from me, then I need to make it."

"I guess you're right about that." Grandpa pushed his chair away from the table and stood. "I think I'll go to my room and read awhile." He yawned and stretched his arms over his head. "And then I'll be going to bed."

"Okay. See you in the morning, Grandpa."

When Grandpa left the room, Rachel picked up two of the flowers and glued them to the front of the card. Then she added one more flower inside and wrote a poem. When that was done, she covered the card with contact paper, put it in an envelope, and scurried out of the kitchen. She found Mom in the living room, stretched out on the sofa. Pap sat in his recliner, and Henry and Jacob sat on the floor in front of the fireplace, playing checkers.

Rachel knelt in front of the sofa and handed Mom the card. "This is for you."

Mom smiled and opened the envelope. "What pretty flowers," she said. "Are they some that you pressed?"

Rachel nodded. "I wrote you a poem on the inside, too."

Mom opened the card and read the poem out loud. "While your leg is broken and you're waiting to get well, remember, if you need my help, just ring the little bell."

"That's a very nice poem," Mom said, patting the top of Rachel's head. "But what little bell are you talking about?"

Rachel jumped up and ran to the desk on the other side of the room. She opened the top drawer and removed a bell. She brought it to Mom and said, "I found this in the bottom of my toy box. I used it when Mary and I played school. When you need me for something, just jingle the bell, and I'll come right away."

Mom smiled and took the bell from Rachel. "Danki, that's very thoughtful of you."

"You're welcome." Rachel yawned noisily. "If you don't need me for anything else, I think I'll go to bed."

"Your daed and brieder are here, so I'll be fine," Mom said.

Rachel bent down and hugged Mom. "Gut nacht, Mom. See you in the morning."

For the next few weeks, whenever Rachel wasn't in school, she kept busy doing the dishes, cooking meals, cleaning house, and taking care of Hannah. She worked hard and was very tired when she went to bed each night, but she was glad she could help Mom.

One Saturday morning, as Rachel started breakfast, Grandpa stepped into the kitchen and hugged her. "Growing up is hard work, isn't it?" he asked.

She nodded and wiped her sweaty forehead with

one corner of her apron. "That's for sure, but I think I'm getting there."

Grandpa smiled. "Jah, I think you are, too." He turned toward the door. "I'm going outside now to bring in some more wood for the fireplace, but I should be back before you have breakfast ready."

"Okay, Grandpa."

Rachel hummed as she took a carton of eggs out of the refrigerator. She knew they'd be good and fresh, since she'd been checking each nesting box every day. No more rotten eggs would be brought into this house. At least not as long as Rachel was collecting them.

She was about to crack the first egg into a bowl when the back door swung open and Jacob stepped into the room. "I need Mom."

"What for?" Rachel asked.

"I was helping Grandpa gather some wood, and I got a nasty *schliffer* [splinter] in my thumb." Jacob frowned as he held up his hand.

"Mom's not up yet." Rachel motioned to the closest chair. "Sit down and I'll get that old schliffer out for you."

Jacob shook his head. "No way! I'm not lettin' you dig around in my thumb and cause me all sorts of pain."

"Ach, don't be such a boppli." Rachel marched across the room and opened the cupboard where Mom kept her first-aid supplies. She took out a needle, a pair of tweezers, a bottle of antiseptic, and a bandage. "Now sit down," she said to Jacob. "I'll have that schliffer out of your thumb in no time."

Jacob looked like he didn't believe her, but he sank into the chair and held out his hand.

"Hold still now," Rachel said as she stuck the needle into Jacob's thumb.

"Yeow! That hurts like crazy!" Jacob jerked his hand, and his face turned red.

"I never said it wasn't going to hurt. I just said I could get it out, but you have to hold still." Rachel gritted her teeth as she stared at the splinter sticking halfway out. She was glad she was wearing her glasses. Without them, she'd never be able to see that tiny piece of wood.

Rachel picked up the tweezers and pulled the splinter right out. "There now, is that better?"

Jacob nodded and blew out his breath. "Danki. You did a good job with that, little ben—" He stopped speaking, gave Rachel a crooked grin, and said, "Guess I can't call you a little bensel anymore. Especially since you've been acting so grown up lately. From now on I think I'll just call you my 'little sister.' How's that sound?"

Rachel smiled. "Sounds good to me. In fact, I feel really good about it."

Henry came into the room then and flopped into the chair on the other side of the table with a groan.

"What's wrong?" Rachel asked.

"I've got a *koppweh* [headache]," he mumbled as he put his head in his hands.

"No problem; I'll get you some aspirin." Rachel jumped up, scooted over to the first-aid cupboard, and took out a bottle of aspirin. "Here you go," she said, handing it to Henry. "This should take away that koppweh."

Henry looked up at her and smiled. "Danki. You're sure growing up, Rachel. You've been a big help around here lately."

"I hope so," she replied.

The teakettle whistled, and steam rose from the spout. Rachel hurried over to the stove. "I'm making a pot of tea this morning because we're almost out of coffee," she said just as Mom and Pap entered the kitchen. "Will that be okay?"

"It'll be fine," said Mom as she hobbled across the room with her crutches.

Pap pulled out a chair for her. "I wish I didn't have to wear this cumbersome cast," Mom said with a frown. "I feel so helpless, and I'm not much use to anyone right now."

"You only have a few more weeks to wear your cast," Pap said. "Then you can have your old jobs back." He grinned at Rachel. "I'll bet you'll be glad when that happens, huh?"

Rachel shrugged. "I haven't minded helping."

Pap patted Rachel's back while he looked at Mom. "Our Rachel's sure growing up; don't you agree?"

Mom nodded. "She's been a big help to me around

here since I broke my leg. She does most of the chores without even being asked, and I appreciate it." She smiled at Rachel and winked. "Why, it won't be long until you're a young woman, ready to make a home of your own."

Pap gave Rachel's shoulder a gentle squeeze. "Even when you do become a woman, you'll always be my little girl."

Rachel grinned and went back to her job of cracking eggs. The thought of always being Pap's little girl didn't bother her at all. In fact, she kind of liked that idea.

Waaa! Waaa!

"It sounds like Hannah's awake," Mom said. "Would someone please get her for me?"

"If someone will take over cracking the eggs, I'll get Hannah," Rachel said.

"Hand me the bowl, and I'll crack the eggs," Mom said. "That's one job I can easily do from a sitting position."

Rachel set the carton of eggs and the bowl on the table in front of Mom; then she hurried from the room.

When she entered Mom and Pap's bedroom, Hannah was in her crib, kicking her feet and hollering like crazy.

Rachel stepped up to the crib, and to her surprise, Hannah stopped crying, reached her chubby arms out to Rachel, and giggled.

She's growing up, Rachel thought. *Just like me.*

Directions for Making Rachel's Pressed Flowers

Things you will need:

Flowers
Newspapers (black and white sections only)
Scissors
Heavy books
Colored pens or pencils
Corrugated cardboard

1. Place flowers between 10 sheets of newspaper. (Note: Put down 5 sheets of newspaper with no flowers on them; then put flowers on 5 separate pieces of newspaper and add more pieces of blank newspaper to the top. The blank newspapers act as blotting paper to take the moisture out of the flowers.) You can put several flowers on one layer, but make sure the flowers don't touch.

2. Place a piece of corrugated cardboard over the newspaper. For each set of flowers you want to press, add layers of newspaper and cardboard.

3. Place several books on top of the stack of cardboard and newspaper.

4. Write down the date you begin pressing the flowers and keep them in a warm, dry room for about 3 weeks. Remove the books and gently separate the flowers from the newspaper. If the flowers feel stiff and dry, they're ready to use. It's a good idea to keep your flowers inside the newspapers with cardboard between them until you're ready to use them. Pressed flowers can be used to decorate bookmarks, postcards, stationery, or scrapbooks. Be creative and have fun!

About the Author

WANDA E. BRUNSTETTER is a bestselling author who enjoys writing historical, as well as Amish-themed novels. Descended from Anabaptists herself, Wanda became fascinated with the Plain People when she married her husband, Richard, who grew up in a Mennonite church in Pennsylvania. Wanda and her husband live in Washington State, where he is a minister. They have two grown children and six grandchildren. Wanda and Richard often travel the country, visiting their many Amish friends and gathering further information about the Amish way of life. In her spare time, Wanda enjoys photography, ventriloquism, gardening, reading, stamping, and having fun with her family. Visit Wanda's Website at www.wandabrunstetter.com and feel free to e-mail her at wanda@wandabrunstetter.com.

Other books by
Wanda E. Brunstetter

ADULT FICTION
Lydia's Charm
White Christmas Pie

INDIANA COUSINS SERIES
A Cousin's Promise
A Cousin's Prayer
A Cousin's Challenge

SISTERS OF HOLMES COUNTY SERIES
A Sister's Secret
A Sister's Test
A Sister's Hope

BRIDESS OF WEBSTER COUNTY SERIES
Going Home
Dear to Me
On Her Own
Allison's Journey

DAUGHTERS OF LANCASTER COUNTY SERIES
The Storekeeper's Daughter
The Quilter's Daughter
The Bishop's Daughter

BRIDES OF LANCASTER COUNTY SERIES
A Merry Heart
Looking for a Miracle
Plain and Fancy
The Hope Chest

CHILDREN'S FICTION
Rachel Yoder—Always Trouble Somewhere Series

The Wisdom of Solomon

NONFICTION
Wanda E. Brunstetter's Amish Friends Cookbook
Wanda E. Brunstetter's Amish Friends Cookbook Volume 2
The Simple Life
A Celebration of the Simple Life

Follow Rachel in All Her Adventures!